HAMILTON

THE CAÑON SERIES BOOK #3

GIGI MEIER

GiGi Meier

Cover Design by Just write. Creations

Editing By Robyne Hunt

Author Photograph by Tara L. Grundemeier

ISBN: 979-8-9877336-4-6 (e)

ISBN: 979-8-9877336-5-3 (pb)

GiGi Meier Media LLC

DEDICATION

To those in law enforcement who embody unwavering courage, selflessly serving, protecting innocent strangers, and inspiring us through their relentless commitment to upholding justice and ensuring our collective safety.

HAMILTON

1

"Dispatch to all units. We have a report of a robbery in progress at the 24-hour convenience store on 5th and Main. The suspects are armed and dangerous, requesting immediate back-up."

The radio crackles to life, jolting me from my thoughts on this cold and clear night. My heart rate spikes as I reach for the radio, pressing the button on the side for my transmission.

"This is Unit Three. I'm en route to the location. ETA five minutes."

"Copy that," the female dispatcher confirms.

I drop the radio into its holder before reaching for my seat-belt. Once it's fastened, I throw the car in drive, hit the siren and lights, and take off full speed down the highway, weaving past a few eighteen-wheelers.

Adrenaline pumps through my veins while I grip the steering wheel. Calls fly over the radio as other units race across the vast territory to get to the scene. Matt's unit took the initial call. Requesting backup is both a precaution and a precursor, the former I hope when dispatch tries Matt's radio and there is no response. No one on the force wants to hear the dreaded 10-999.

Racing off the exit ramp, I slam on my brakes and narrowly avoid a car changing lanes. Swerving into the right lane, I hook the corner and speed up. The engine revs under my foot, and the buildings whiz by on both sides as I barrel down the steep road.

Glimpsing his squad car in the distance, I radio my arrival to dispatch. My blood runs cold when I see him crouched behind his open car door, taking on heavy fire. I angle my unit diagonal to his and duck for cover as the bullets tear into my car.

Matt is returning fire, giving me seconds to grab my weapon and open my door to join him in the melee. Peering over the window frame, there are two assailants inside the convenience store. One man is waving a gun and shouting at the cashier. The other is firing at Matt, who continues taking cover and shouting into his shoulder mic.

The noise is deafening, the wailing from customers trapped inside the store mixes with the sirens and gunfire. Sweat pours down my back as I survey the parking lot lights, how bright the inside of the store is, and the advantage we have. While Matt reloads I return fire, drawing the assailant's gunfire toward me.

Shattering glass rains over me as he shoots out the driver's side window and I duck down behind the door, waiting for a chance to fire again. Blood surges into my head, my heart's beating outside my chest and my body is overdosing on adrenaline.

When the second assailant fires on us, I press my back into the car and aim for the parking lot light directly above me. Carefully squeezing the trigger, I shoot directly into the light-bulb, sending orange sparks through the night sky and drowning me in darkness.

I do the same to the light above Matt and hear him curse and then scream, "I'm hit. I'm hit. I'm hit."

"Fuck!" I grab my mic, hit the button, and yell that dreaded 10-999. "Hang on, Matt."

With us shrouded in darkness and the store lit up like a stage, I creep to the back of my unit. Rounding the trunk, I keep my gun ready as I sprint to Matt's side. He's rolling around on the ground, blood pooling from the top of his chest.

"Shit! I need an ambulance! Now!" I yell into my mic and tug on the top of his vest to pull him out of the line of fire. "Stay with me, man."

I kneel over him, checking the side of his neck and, thank fuck, his pulse is strong. I feel around for the top of his chest, searching in the dark for the wound when his blood squirts through my fingers.

"I got-got a . . ." Matt gurgles on his blood and this is fucking bad.

"I know, man. They are coming."

The hole is warm. The bullet is lodged at the top of his chest and the edge of his vest. I flatten my palm across the wound, applying as much pressure as he can take and feeling his fucking breath against my fingers.

"You're doing good, Matt."

He moans. His body wiggles and his legs flail back and forth. All good signs. I straighten as much as I can while keeping the same pressure on his chest to return fire until my gun clicks. Out of bullets.

"Fuck!"

More sirens scream into the night air as another unit speeds into the parking lot, followed by an ambulance. I holster my gun, reaching for Matt's weapon laying a few inches away when Rico flanks my hip, dumping his medic bag on the ground behind him.

"Where's he hit?" Rico asks, his voice tense.

"Upper clavicle."

He hovers over Matt's legs, searching up his vest to find my hand. When he grips my wrist and follows it down to the wound, we change positions.

"Matt, it's Rico. We're going to get you out of here," he yells, straddling Matt's waist and applying far more pressure than I was. Knowing that Matt's in good hands, I army crawl past them and keep my frame low as I get to the front of Matt's car.

Peering over the edge of the hood, one suspect is using the cashier as a body shield, yelling at the other officers who just arrived on the scene. The other fires through the broken window, taking cover between the aisles.

"Police! Drop your weapon!" the Police Chief yells over the bullhorn, his voice echoing through the bullet-riddled store.

The man holding the cashier startles, pointing the gun at the woman's head instead of at the police outside. For a moment, it seems like he is going to fire but must have thought better of it, realizing he is outnumbered.

"Hell no. You guys are gonna shoot me," he hollers, wrestling with the crying woman as she struggles against him.

I keep my eye on the other assailant nervously striding up and down the aisles without the same body protection as his friend. This guy knows he's trapped and is looking for a way out.

"Put your weapon on the counter and let her go," the Chief continues, his voice booming over the horn.

The first assailant hesitates, his gaze shuffling between his partner yelling at him and the officers' guns trained on him. Panic covers his face as he debates what to do. The Chief continues pressing him over the horn. His friend gets edgier, and I ease forward, crouching against the brick wall of the convenience store.

The first assailant slowly raises his hands, the gun clattering to the floor as the cashier runs to my colleague, waving her toward him. The suspect drops to his knees, his hands on his head while his friend yells a string of expletives and dashes toward the back of the store.

I advance on him, jumping through the shot-out window and over snacks strewn across the floor to glimpse him barreling through the back door. His hoodie and ball cap block his face, but I make out a large snake tattoo on the top of his hand as his arms pump faster to get away from me.

"In pursuit of the assailant heading West on Main behind the shopping center," I shout into my mic, the radio crackling with shouted commands.

My hot breath comes out in white puffs, visible in the night sky while the cold air rips the sweat from my forehead. The assailant is fast for his size, putting more distance between us with each echoing step through the dark alley behind the center. My gun belt rattles as I run full tilt after him, the moon shining a path as he darts into the adjoining neighborhood, hoping to lose me.

The assailant's footsteps pound against the pavement, growing fainter and fainter as he runs away. I refuse to give up, willing myself to sprint faster and forcing my legs to burn with exertion. This isn't enough.

I lose him on the deserted streets, jogging to a stop and surveying the row of houses to my right and the open clearing to my left. As I reach for my mic to call it in, a dog barks in the distance, garbage cans crash, and running footsteps signal his location. I take off again, rounding a corner, and the assailant disappears into the shadows.

"Stop! Police!" I yell.

He doesn't stop, breaking into a full sprint to scramble over a fence and disappear on the other side. As fast as I am running, I'm halfway up the wood planks and throwing myself over it to catch up to him. We hit the pavement with a hard thud, knocking the gun out of my hand to skid several feet away and sending a spray of dirt into the air.

"Get off me, pig."

The man reeks of weed. If he's high, it might account for his actions back at the convenience store. He twists, kicks, and wrestles in my hold, delivering blow after blow— fighting being subdued. The junk he's on gives him more strength than it should.

"You're under arrest," I start on his Miranda rights, knowing I'll repeat them when he's cuffed. I use my weight advantage on him as we fight over the gun in his hand. He stretches it out of my reach, long enough for him to sink his teeth into my forearm and latch on.

"Fuck," I groan, punching the side of his head and trying to dislodge his jaw from my flesh. My legs clench over his in a wrestling maneuver I learned in high school. Neither of us is willing to give up.

"You have the right to remain silent."

He locks his jaw and I grunt, landing an even harder punch to his ears, eliciting a shriek and his teeth loosen from my flesh.

"I can't fucking hear," he screams into my ear, and I almost can't hear. I turn him over, grabbing for his gun when a glint of silver catches the dim streetlight before his blade sinks into the side where my vest twisted.

"Shit."

I grind my teeth, the blade lodging in between my ribs and sending a radiating pain over my torso. My breath is harsh as I bear down, gripping the end of the knife and pulling it out. My head falls back as I shout obscenities at the star-lit sky and ram his face into the pavement.

"Anything you can say." I pant through my clenched jaws, putting him in a chokehold while I try to get his hand tucked underneath us. "Will be used against you in a court of law."

He throttles his head back, connecting with my jaw and

rattling my teeth as my blood seeps under my vest and drenches my clothes. My temporary lapse causes a gap in my hold as he tries to break free.

He thrusts his back into my chest, forcing me onto my back long enough for that arm I am trying to get to brandish his gun. His eyes are crazy. Wide and wild as he spits on my face.

"You're gonna die, pig."

He fires the gun, the click loud in my ear as I roll us forward, changing the trajectory of the bullet. It tears into my leg.

"Fuck!"

I collapse, my hold loosening enough for him to slip away. Searing pain separates the flesh of my upper thigh. The gunshot is on the same side of my body where he stabbed me. The assailant aims his gun at me but then takes off, hearing footsteps pounding on the concrete near to us.

I hold my breath, bearing down as I roll to my stomach and use my forearms to drag myself toward my gun.

"Freeze!" Rico yells, his gun drawn, running past me and ducking for cover as he exchanges gunfire with the suspect. Bullets speed by as I cover my head. Rico ducks behind a car, firing back and then weaving up the street to get closer.

The suspect is quick, but Rico is quicker. After getting a couple of hits in, the suspect goes down, cries out, and hits the pavement with a thump. His weapon discharges one last time as Rico and another officer approach, their guns trained on him.

I ease onto my arms, my gun still a foot away and the assailant isn't moving. Fuck. Rico's rushing to my side, shouting for an ambulance when my head falls to the concrete.

"It's going to be okay," Rico says, shoving a hand against my side that has me surging back to life. The pain is indescribable as the pressure threatens to tear into my internal organs. "Just hang in there. Help is on the way."

"Matt?" It's all I can muster past his fucking hand digging into my wound, trying to see how bad it is. My breath is labored as he applies pressure to my wounds in an attempt to stem the bleeding.

"Transported."

That can mean a lot of things.

I grit my teeth, my heart pounding in my chest and the adrenaline is wearing off as exhaustion and pain take over. As the minutes tick by, I feel my strength vacating my body. I pant, white puffs exiting my chest to dissipate in the cold air. A chill seeps into my bones, and I tremble on the pavement. My body is going into shock.

As I stare at the twinkling stars in the dark night sky, I think about one star. Not part of the constellation above, but in a world all her own. I never knew if she made it. I stopped looking long ago when her number was disconnected and I had no other way of contacting her.

Another ambulance races through the streets, the sirens wailing loudly as it draws closer. As the haze of excruciating pain and confusion takes over, I fight to stay conscious to enjoy the fantasy of her bending over me with concern instead of Rico.

As the paramedics rush toward me, falling to their knees on either side to administer help, I slip into unconsciousness, hearing a voice in my head that sounds like her.

"You're a hero, Alex. Never forget that."

2

Antiseptic stings my nose, drawing me into the conscious world. Pain rockets across my body when I shift, going in two different directions and intersecting across my lower half. I hear the commotion before I see it.

Mom's crying in my right ear, and Pops's mumbling is a fraction above that. Someone grabs my arm, holds my hand, and applies pressure.

My eyelids are heavy, and my eyelashes are stuck together. It takes a couple of attempts to peel open my eyes. My legs feel anchored to concrete blocks, and when I raise my left arm, it's tangled in cords.

"Alan, he's awake," Mom gushes, releasing my hand to clasp the bed railing and hover over me. Pops is directly behind her. His hand rests reassuringly on her shoulder as she pulls on the edges of her favorite sweater with the embroidered flowers around the collar. Both look weary.

Not for lack of trying on their part, but I am an only child. A miracle child, Mom always said, after a few miscarriages and a conclusion from her doctors that children weren't in the cards for them. Shitty thing to tell a patient, but old-school doctors are like that. Then I came along. When they had stopped trying and were facing a childless life together, surprise. It was an understatement to say they were ecstatic, more so with Mom than Pops. She still has to convince me sometimes that he loves me with his hard exterior and gruff demeanor.

"You had us scared, son," Pops says in a tense voice.

It's surprising to hear that my old man, who has been in law enforcement for forty-five years, including the last twenty as sheriff, has been scared. Being the reason for it makes it worse. Mixed with Mom's tears, I feel like absolute shit.

Mom never wanted me in law enforcement, and Pops always did. She's terrified of losing her only child in the line of duty. I think if it were to happen, it would kill her. This is almost her worst nightmare coming true.

A sob catches in her throat. Flashes from last night flood my mind. The call came in on an otherwise quiet night, erupting into gunfire, hostages, the foot chase, getting shot and stabbed, and Matt.

The hit he took didn't look good. The smoke plumes emanating from the bullet's entry point, the sight of blood spurting past my fingers, and feeling the force of his breath against my hand terrified me. I never want to feel that again.

I clear my throat. "Matt?"

Mom's hand trembles as she finds mine. Her tears flow faster while Pops runs a hand over his mouth. His whiskers scrap against his fingers, looking wrecked, and I close my eyes, already knowing the answer.

Matt Tenner. The lanky rookie with a young wife and a newborn baby. Gone. Fuck. He shouldn't have been on duty last night. It was his only night off.

Losing a guy to the Denver Police Department and another to Florida to care for his ailing parent is only part of the problem. Mandatory overtime has left the department thinly staffed and running ragged for the past two months.

It should have been two units out there last night. Two of us responding to the first call, not just the rookie. If I had been closer and had taken the call, it would have been me and not him. It would have devastated Mom and Pops. But at least the rookie would be safe at home with his wife and kid.

"Fuck," I mutter and open my eyes, dragging my hand away from Mom's to shift in the bed. I know she hates cussing, but this time it's warranted.

Pain shoots across my abdomen, stealing my breath as my heart rate spikes and the blood pressure cuff tightens. My left leg is useless, immobilized in a tight casing that burns whenever my muscle clenches.

"You did everything you could, Alexander." Mom's voice trembles as she dabs her eyes with Pops's handkerchief.

I don't want to hear it. If I had done more, he'd be here. Protecting and serving is what we sign up for. Dying in the line of duty is honorable, even if it's the ultimate sacrifice no officer wants his brother or sister to make.

Pops knows by the look on my face what I think. That's something being in law enforcement does. It trains us to read people, register their facial expressions and watch their body language—something Mom doesn't understand.

"Margaret, can you give us a moment?" Mom looks even more upset that he's asking her to leave, and she sobs into the white cloth adorned with the initials Pops and I share. "Maybe find a doctor to tell us the plan now that he's awake."

She hesitates. Her faded green eyes linger on mine as I lick my lips and grimace while hauling my body further up the bed. She waves the cloth at her heated face before looking at Pops.

"Of course. If I can't find him, I'll grab us a couple of coffees. It's been a long night."

Her eyes never leave mine until she turns to go. I glance at the closed blinds. Sunlight slips in through the sides, leaving me to wonder how long I've been out.

Pops steps up to the spot Mom occupied and pats my shoulder. Not one to dole out affection, this is probably the first time he's touched me in years, whereas Mom hugs and kisses me every chance she gets.

"I lost a deputy some years back. Good kid. His dad was a cop, both on the force simultaneously. The dad was called out to a domestic dispute while his son worked traffic," Pops starts, removing his hand from my shoulder and glancing at the numbers on the machine after the cuff releases my arm. "Routine stop. The kid did everything right. Standard procedure, exactly by the book."

More than several years back. Pops entered the den, removed his boots, and stared vacantly at Mom. I remember that night. I was seven or eight at the time. I had waited up for Pops after he missed my little league game. When I heard his squad car pull into the driveway and saw his headlights shine across my bedroom wall, I snuck down the staircase, sat on a step, and listened to their conversation.

"His name was Washington, right?"

Pops's eyes meet mine, the memory ghosting across the etched lines of his aging face.

"Yeah. Deputy Washington. There was a scuffle. The guy he was arresting was on something and got ahold of a needle and jabbed it into the deputy's arm. It didn't faze Washington. He wrestled until the suspect got his service piece and shot him repeatedly."

He shakes his head, glancing at one of the hospital machines as if recalling the night the call came in. The look on his face now resembles the one he had that night. When he fixes those hard eyes on me again, I brace myself.

"These things happen, son. I don't know why the Lord called him home, and I never will."

This is what I was expecting. Faith and religion have always been Pops's explanations for things that made little sense. It's his way of explaining all the awful shit he's seen over the decades. It's where we differ.

I need order and rational thought, questions asked and answered. Leaving this up to a higher power doesn't sit right with me. I once asked him if he genuinely believed the stories of the Bible and the fallen third. He looked straight at me and said, "Evil walks amongst us."

It sent a chill down my spine. After almost six years on the force, I know exactly what he's talking about.

"It's not your fault what happened last night. It was just his time." With that, he looks at my hospital gown loosely draped around my shoulders and the thin blankets pooled at my waist. "I'm going to see about your mother. She's been beside herself about you, and with her heart, it's the last thing she needs."

Leave it to Pops to console and cast blame at the same time.

"I'll be right here," I say, my sarcasm garnering a hard stare as his mouth sets into a flat line.

He says nothing else, nor do I expect him to. He's a man of few words, and even those are tightly held as if he judges their worth before releasing them into the world.

Once he's out of the room, I groan and hit the call button for a nurse to fetch me something to drink, even though they have me connected to an intravenous line. I lick my lips again. The chapped flesh is uncomfortable from the dryness, and my throat is parched.

I'm in a private room. There is a halo of machines around my head and a few clustered on my left. The repetitive sounds and racket make it impossible to close my eyes and nod off.

A bedside toilet is against the wall, and a small blue loveseat is tucked under the window. A television is mounted on the wall directly in front of me, and a whiteboard with the names of my care team hangs beside it.

I drag the covers down and my gown up to see a large bandage taped from my stomach around my side to my back. The muscles underneath are tight as fuck, making it difficult to move. It will be weeks before I'm back in the gym and that causes me to sigh.

The gym is my respite. It's where I go to escape work pressures, and I enjoy pushing myself to see what my body is capable of. I assume rehab will be in the cards before I can return to patrol. Fuck. How long will I be off?

Stitches. It's not my first time having them. I got my first set when I was sixteen. Mary Ann Higginbotham stole a four-wheeler from old man Miller's farm and picked me up at my house to ride with her. We made it to the park in the middle of the town square before she gunned it, sending me tumbling off the back and into a shaved-off traffic pole sticking out of the ground. It narrowly missed my kidney and I was bleeding profusely.

She had stood there, hovering over me on the cold concrete curb. Her long, bouncy curls had framed the sides of her worried face. As the distant sound of sirens grew louder, she gently touched my chest, her chestnut eyes expressing her gratitude and concern. And then, without a word, she vanished into the night.

Pops's furious voice reverberated through the sterile hallways, capturing the attention of the bewildered hospital staff. Amidst the chaos, the truth came crashing down—I learned she stole it after telling me she hadn't.

Though her betrayal initially weighed heavily upon me, the depth of my affection for her overshadowed it all. At that moment, I realized that my love for Mary Ann surpassed any desire for personal vindication. I took the blame, bore the consequences, and shielded her from harm.

Her laughter at my fate, once puzzling, now makes me

smile with fondness. I close my eyes, reflecting on that nostalgic time.

3

Time has no meaning in a place like this. The next time I awaken, it's crowded with my parents murmuring on one side of the room, with Rico and the police chief on the other. I'm not anti-social, but having this many people watching me sleep is a little uncomfortable. I tug on the covers to ensure my dick is covered since there are only a couple of sheets separating it from everyone in the room.

"Hamilton, good to see you're awake," Chief Reynolds bellows.

He's a large man, trained to command a room from all his years of service, and the only replacement suitable to fill my old man's shoes when he retired.

Chief Reynolds and I have a tumultuous relationship. One where he tries to prove I'm not good enough, not like my old man, and me not wanting to be like my old man. If he'd get past his boastful ways long enough, he would notice that I don't want to be the police chief. Growing up in the limelight of my father was a sufficient reason for me to flee from it.

"Sir."

It is the only thing I get out when everyone clusters around the bed. Not one for attention—this is overkill.

"You did a good job out there," the Chief continues, pushing past Rico to stand on my left side and pats my arm. It's all for show, and when his eyes meet Pops's on the other side of the bed, I want to roll mine. "Apprehended both assailants. One is a dangerous felon that had eluted the law for quite some time. The one you shot." He nods at Rico, but Rico doesn't react.

"And Matt," I say. I want to hear it from him, even though I already know.

He sighs, bothered, and at least I can count on him being decent enough to recognize Matt's sacrifice.

"Yes. Officer Tenner paid the ultimate price for his service. His sacrifice won't go unrecognized. I've spoken to his widow, and plans are being made. I'll see that you are discharged in time to attend his funeral."

I appreciate what he's saying even though he doesn't control the hospital or staff. They'll release me when they release me, not when the Chief says so.

"Thank you, sir."

I learned long ago that the fewer words I spoke to him, the better. Rico keeps a blank expression, but the fierceness in his eyes lets me know he hates the guy, too. I release a ragged breath when the Chief removes his hand from my skin. It's surreal.

Mom's eyes dart from everyone's faces before looking over her shoulder at Pops. His jaw sets. The steely look I grew up avoiding almost penetrates the Chief, something I don't mind.

"And my son. Surely, he will receive the Purple Heart, Merit Award, and—" Pops starts, pressing into Mom enough for her to grip the bed railing.

"Pops, it's unnecessary. I'm gl—"

"Alexander, this is standard protocol. Not up for debate.

The Chief knows it, and it will allow for extra benefit pay while you're out on leave," Pops continues, ready to cite the section of the code or article that governs this.

My old man is fair to a fault. An eye for an eye is his mantra, and he holds everyone to that standard, whether they like it or not. Now is not the time to debate with Pops. He'll get his way, regardless. He always does.

"Of course, Alan." Chief nods, but the way he stares across the bed says he's not entirely in agreement. I don't need awards for doing my job. If awards brought back the rookie, I'd easily trade them in to get him back. "Susan, back at the station, is already working on it."

I bet a nickel that Susan isn't already working on it.

"How long am I out for? Anyone talk to the doctor yet?" I ask, cutting the tension between the former Chief and the acting Chief. "I assume Internal Affairs will interview me?"

That is protocol when an officer discharges his weapon. I'm surprised that the Chief didn't mention that. He's not a man for red tape, so he might hope it goes away. With Rico killing the assailant, Matt dying in the line of duty, and my injury, Chief has more red tape than he knows what to do with.

"I caught the doctor in the hallway. He wants to keep you another day or two, and then you'll be heading home with us," Mom interjects, and my eyebrows pop up at the news. "I can care for you while your father takes you to rehab."

"Mom, I can handle myself at home. I don't need to burden you and Pops." I take the diplomatic approach, trying not to hurt her feelings.

"Alexander, you are not a burden. Never. We are more than happy to take care of you while you heal. Aren't we, Alan?"

All eyes turn to the old man, casting a curious glance between us. "Of course. If you fall in the shower, who will help you up?"

Blunt and to the point. Pops plucking my naked ass off the

shower floor if I slip reminds me only to take sponge baths. He's practical in his reasoning, making it hard to argue. Rico's blank face cracks with a smirk, but no one else notices. A few awkward seconds pass when Pops clears his throat.

"Then it's all settled. Alexander comes home with us. You'll see that he has full benefits, and the award ceremony will be held after he's recovered. I assume desk duty when he's able to return."

Chief Reynolds dislikes not being in charge but defers to the more senior and decorated Chief out of respect.

"Yes, Alan. We'll see to all of it," he says before turning to me. "Get well, Hamilton, and call Susan if you need anything."

"Sir," I mumble, wincing when I shift away from his foul breath in my face. He glances at my blanketed body, his eyes narrowing as if trying to determine if I'm faking it. I don't care. I just want him to leave. I say nothing as I return his stare so he gets the idea.

"Margaret, always good to see you. I'm sorry it had to be under these circumstances. Retirement suits you, Alan," the Chief says, not waiting for a reply when he turns to Rico. "I expect you to return to the station in a few hours."

"Of course," Rico says for the first time since I opened my eyes.

He's usually a jokester, but even he knows the Chief is never on the receiving end. He doesn't want to be fired, and Chief is just unpredictable enough to do it. Although he can't now, even if he wanted to with the active investigation starting. It seems everyone is waiting for the Chief to leave and the seconds tick by until he does. When he's out the door, the conversation picks up again.

"Honey, I'm going to prepare your room, so you'll be nice and comfortable when you come home. And I'll make your favorite chicken pot pie with gravy on the side. Ricardo, you must join us as well."

Yep. Mom is beaming that I got shot, and she gets to take care of me.

"And do you remember Joyce from three houses down? She's going to bring over a banana pudding for dessert. We can play cards and listen to your father's records. It will be just like old times."

She claps her hands. This will not be like old times. It's not a social gathering. It's my recovery. If Mom plans to turn it into that, I'll work as hard as possible in rehab to get better and go home.

"Now Margaret, the boy needs to recover first," Pops warns as if he's reading my mind. If Mom had her way, I'd never go home.

"I know, Alan. But he needs good food to build his strength back. And good company never hurt a soul." She swats at his hand when he tries to guide her toward the door. "I'll check in with you later to see how you feel. Otherwise, I need to get to the store to pick up a few things," she says to Pops even though she's looking at me.

"I appreciate it, Mom and Pops. I'll be out of your hair in no time," I say, much to Mom's dislike by the sudden downturn of the corners of her mouth as she pats Rico on the arm. Pops gives me a curt nod before shuffling Mom out the door. Rico lets out a hearty chuckle, then rounds the bed to collapse in the chair to my right.

"Glad I didn't get to miss all the fun," Rico says, propping his black boots on the edge of my bed. Chief is put out, Pops is his usual indifference, and Mom is ecstatic. Yeah, a barrel of laughs.

"Tell me what happened with Matt."

I tighten my muscles, bearing down against the pain to get off my back. Laying down for so long makes me achy, and I need to sit up to see Rico better.

"He was gone, Alex. You must have known that when you

took off after the other guy." The humor slides from his face, the blank expression back. "It was too late for the kid."

My chin drops as I look down at the bedding covering my legs. Did I know? Last night is a haze. Glimpses and flashes of events are all I can piece together.

"I felt his breathing on my hand. His pulse was in my palm."

Rico drags his legs from the bed, a pained expression when he leans forward to look me square in the eye.

"Are you sure about that? When I removed your hand, there was nothing. His chest wasn't moving, Alex."

I study Rico, then look away, recalling his life in my hand so prominently that I was talking to him, telling him to hold on and that it would be okay. Was I telling myself that? No, he was there. I'm convinced.

"He was talking to me. Gurgling on his blood."

I remember that. Rico shakes his head—no indication of whether he believes me.

"They'll do a full autopsy and investigation. You don't have to tell me what happened. I was there. Just save it for the investigators."

I look at him, honestly believing I'm right. Rico's tone creates doubt, and a sliver of guilt slides through my consciousness that I could have contributed to the rookie's death. I let the conversation die. The quietness in the room hits me now that almost everyone is gone except him.

He's like a brother to me. Raised in the same Catholic church by a single working mother. We would acolyte together on Sunday mornings. Growing up, he'd come over after school instead of going home to an empty house. His mom worked long hours to keep a roof over his head, and my mom always wanted a house full of children. It was perfect.

Mom learned to cook authentic Puerto Rican food to make him feel at home until he assured her he liked her midwestern cooking. From then on, they would chat about food and recipes, ingredients, and what she saw on the cooking channel. She'd ask Rico to make new recipes with her, something Pops and I weren't ever interested in doing.

Rico stands and walks over to the window, opening the blinds and bathing the room in warm, gold light. I blink against the intrusion as Rico gazes past the metal slits to something beyond.

"Hey man, I've been meaning to ask you something."

"Yeah?"

He walks to my bedside. The badge hangs around his neck, catching my attention, as it already has a black band around it in honor of Matt's death. His Henley shirt is half tucked into his jeans. He must have grabbed a quick shower and changed before heading here. It's been a long night for everyone.

"What did you want to ask?"

His eyes narrow, studying me before saying, "Last night. What were you saying?" My confusion is obvious. "When you were laying on the ground, waiting for the paramedics. You were mumbling about stars or something. I couldn't make it out."

Not stars.

Just one star.

One who wanted to be a star to many people, even though she was already a star to me. I grunt, my lips pulling in as I think about her.

"You will not believe this. But I thought of Mary Ann," I reply, waiting for the recognition to appear on his face. He knew I was over the moon for her. Something he helped me hide from my parents when they banned me from spending time with her after Pops suspected her of being behind the four-wheeler stunt.

"Higginbotham?" Rico's dark eyes leave mine as his hand runs through his wavy black hair. As his mouth opens to respond, a slow smile spreads across his full lips as his eyes flash to the hallway.

"Who the hell is Mary Ann? And why the fuck did I have to see your ass on the news to find out you've been shot?" Dani shouts from the doorway.

I'm fucked.

4

Those cerulean blue eyes flash daggers at me and then size up Rico before dismissing him entirely. She misses how his chest inflates when he thinks he stands a chance with her. She's as tied up in Takahashi as he was with her when I pulled him over coming out of that bar.

He was speeding down the dark road and blew past me. When I inquired why he was in Canon City despite living in Denver, he replied he was seeing about a girl. He looked rather upset about it, so I let him off. Little did I know our paths would cross again.

Life has a way of weaving people together, whether we like it or not. Although I definitely like this one. She's as tough as they come. Tougher than most men I know and a really good friend to Isla, Eli, Ronnie, and myself.

"If you're done ogling my tits, you can introduce yourself," Dani calls out Rico for doing just that.

I can't blame the guy. She has them pushed to the ceiling in that tiny bra thing she always wears. I had difficulty keeping my eyes off them until she came out in an even smaller pair of underwear in front of her boyfriend, back at the garage once.

How he doesn't make her change is beyond me. I couldn't have my girl running around town like that, but he's the better man for allowing it.

"My name is Ricardo Rodriguez, but everyone calls me Rico."

I smother my amusement when his voice lowers, trying again to entice her. If he thinks he has a chance with her, I need to teach him observation skills because this girl doesn't have eyes for anyone except Takahashi.

"Danielle Louise Winters, to what do I owe the pleasure of this visit?" I interject as she ignores Rico's outstretched hand hovering over the bed.

Her finger is in my face before I can finish my question.

"Why didn't you have someone call me? Like Luke Alvez over here. Or this Mary Ann chick?" She tosses a thumb at Rico, but those dagger-filled eyes never leave mine.

Holding in my laughter, I groan as my arm comes across my midsection to the bandage on my left side. Her finger falls, as does her gaze when she watches my hand, still covered in dried blood. Mine or Matt's, I don't know.

"I'm not exactly sure where my phone is, so I couldn't have called you," I say, leaving Mary Ann out of this conversation.

As far as Dani calling Rico a television cop, well, I might have to use that later on him. She can be clever when she wants to be. She steps back. Her eyes roam over the hospital equipment, taking it all in and then wrinkling her nose.

"Tell me what happened."

Having realized he lost his shot, Rico moves back to the chair, again unnoticed by her.

"Long story, but I was shot in the upper thigh. They did surgery last night or today. I'm unsure and have a stab wound under my ribs."

I don't tell her about Matt. The news would have already reported it.

"And the crooks that did all this?" She plants her hands on her hips.

"Rico killed one."

I toss my head toward Rico. She sets her gaze on him, but he remains silent. Surprisingly, not adding to my explanation.

"Good. And your officer friend?" The question hangs in the air as her eyes bounce between him and me. "The news didn't say. They just had both of your pictures up about an officer-involved shooting. You gave me a fucking heart attack, Hamilton. I'd have been up here last night if Tomlin hadn't hidden my keys and made me promise not to get an Uber. He was worried about me creating a scene. As if."

She huffs and tosses her purse on the counter by the array of machines, forgetting that she asked about Matt and didn't wait for the answer. That's okay. I do not want to talk about that loss just yet.

"You cause a scene? I'd never guess."

Having her up here changes the mood instantly. Her fiery energy brings a normalcy I welcome. One that isn't the tension of overbearing parents or the scowling of a blistering police chief.

"Yeah, well. I've turned over a new leaf and shit, so I can't keep breaking noses anymore. Gotta grow up sometime, Hamilton." She waves a dismissive hand in the air and starts pacing at the side of the bed. I glance at Rico, who's admiring her chest as it bounces. "All right, that's it."

I expect her to chew Rico out for staring at her assets again, but she turns to me and says, "You stink, and you're covered in blood. I can't take it anymore. Who's your nurse?"

She points to the board mounted on the wall at the foot of my bed before coming over and mashing the call button on my bed frame several times.

"Do I? I can't smell anything beyond the antiseptic stuff they used. And I'm all bandaged up."

I pull the side of the gown over to show her the one on my side. Then tug on the blankets to uncover my leg while covering my privates. Not that she would care if they flopped out, as she treats me like a brother.

"I didn't say to get your ass in the shower, but damn, at least clean you up and stuff. Whose blood is that?" I clench my teeth, and she understands entirely. "Exactly."

She looks at the time on her watch before raising a challenging eyebrow at Rico. I know he loves lively women, but even she's too much for him. She rings the call button about five more times, and when no one answers, she mutters, "I fucking hate hospitals. I'll be right back."

She tosses her long blond hair over her shoulder and spins on her tennis shoes, loudly squealing as she charges out of the room.

"I think I'm in love," Rico says finally, and it is as I expected. "Why were you holding out on me? She's hot as fuck, and those tits, I could get a handful of—"

"Don't even think about it. She'll cut your balls off and wear them like earrings in front of you," I cut him off because I don't need any more problems than I already have. "And she's already got a guy that can handle her far better than you ever could."

Rico stands as if I insulted his manhood. "That tiny thing couldn't hurt a fly."

"She's the one I told you about. From the truck stop."

Dani isn't wrong. I get a whiff of myself and I smell. Getting up, going to the bathroom, and cleaning up would be nice. It'd also be nice to have something to eat. Maybe she can get me something from the vending machine while I'm in the bathroom.

His eyes widen slightly, and he presses his lips together while nodding. "Respect for her then. I'd still do her. Hold on to that hair and—"

"Finish that sentence, and the badge won't be the only thing hanging around your neck," Dani yells, walking in the door with a nurse trailing behind her. His mouth falls open at her threat, and I suppress a chuckle when he looks at me.

"She's going to help you. Fall risk or something like that," she directs at me but points her finger at him. "And you. Don't you have crimes to solve or paperwork to do? Ya know, the shit us taxpayers are paying you to do?"

His eyebrows roll into his hair, and he looks more intrigued the mouthier she gets. Either way, he's never going to get her. It's entertaining to watch and takes my mind off the pain. She'll rip his ego to shreds and laugh while doing it.

"Since when do you worry about taxpayer money?" I quiz her, feeling bad for Rico, who's moving closer to the door. That annoyed stare moves from my best friend to me.

"Since I'm a business owner and now have to pay extra for that bond fund that just passed." As if proud of herself, she adds, "Look at me being a law-abiding citizen, President Alexander Hamilton. Who would've thought that was possible?"

Rico stops and looks at me, but I merely shake my head.

"Hey man, I'm going to do as the little lady has instructed and go back to work," Rico agrees, and I know it's more of a show to get in her pants.

She doesn't buy it either when she rolls her eyes and picks up the hospital menu from the bedside table. His gaze lingers on her, and when she doesn't return it, he tosses his head up to say goodbye before leaving. The nurse is busy checking my intravenous line and looking at the remaining liquid in the bag.

"Your friend is annoying," she mutters, not looking up from the trifold. It's ironic that she calls him annoying. She can be pretty irritating herself when she wants something. "I called Eli. He was sobbing and couldn't be here because he had to get Isla off to school and then open the store. He'll be by here later tonight. Do you want something from here, or I can get you some fast food?"

"You can't bring in outside food," the nurse says in a low tone. "Now, Officer Hamilton, I'll need to help you out of the bed and into the bathroom. No showering now, and I'll be right outside the door if you need help."

This petite nurse is going to help me? This should be interesting.

"Can you grab the walker for me?" she asks Dani, pointing at a walker tucked against the wall behind Rico's abandoned chair. Dani immediately drops the menu on the table and goes to retrieve it—a hard line cuts across her face as if recalling something unpleasant.

"What is it?" I ask, and she looks at me before picking it up and placing it on the side of the bed while the nurse puts the railing down.

"Thank you," she says to Dani while watching me. "I stopped the IV for now. We're going to do this in stages. I will move the bed up to make it easier to move your legs over the edge, and once you're in position, I'll help you stand. We'll make sure you are stable on your feet before we walk to the bathroom."

"Okay."

"Let the bed do the work, and we can stop anytime you need a break."

The nurse hits the button on the bed, and the mattress under my upper body slowly glides up. It's okay for a second or two, but when my body hunches forward, it pulls on my stitches, and a burning sensation shoots across my midsection, taking my breath away.

Dani moves to the end of the bed, her jaw tight as she takes it all in. Dani's a fighter, building her muscles with each car she works on. She must know how this feels, or at least be closer to understanding how it feels other than getting shot.

29

"Is this payback?" I pant, trying to catch my breath while the corners of Dani's mouth turn down.

"How so?" she asks, her fingers curling tightly over the hospital bed footboard.

"When you were hurt, I debated arresting you rather than helping you."

I never told her this, but I felt guilty for not doing more for her that day. I assumed she was part of the problem at the truck stop. Little did I know she has a heart of gold buried under that crusty personality.

"You hit your head last night? You're dumb as hell if you think you didn't help me back then." Her assurance falls short of absolving my guilt. "Did you look at my rack one too many times? Yeah. Did you give me a hard time about not letting me go and causing my truck to get impounded? Sure. Could you not have ogled my ass in my boy shorts when you entered my apartment? Probably. But you and I are good."

Busted on all counts makes me smile against the throbbing at my waist.

"In fact, could I be kinder to you? Yeah. Could I be a better friend from here on out? Sure. Could I work on not riding your ass so much about Isla's case? Probably." She pauses, a line forming between her eyebrows as her gaze zeros in on my injuries. "If you need me, I'm here. I'll help you, Hamilton."

The change in her voice dropping into a lower register with a hint of worry lets me know she will.

"That's kind of you, but I got it covered."

I don't want to be a burden to her too. I'll already be a burden to Mom and Pops, mainly Pops, which will be enough to deal with. I can't add Dani's volatile temper to the mix.

"Don't blow me off like that. It's not like I go around offering to help just anyone. You know that." That temper flairs, and the nurse looks at her watch impatiently, which doesn't go unnoticed by either of us. "Fine, I'll back off for now."

She raises her hands and tilts her head. I believe her momentarily and then remember how much she rides my ass about Isla's case, which is coming up. She'd back off for about a day or so, but then she'll be right back in my life, bossing me around or bitching me out.

"Thank you," I say to Dani before nodding at the nurse.

5

I'm not peeing or shitting again until I get out of here. The entire process is embarrassing enough with how laid up I am, but having a male nurse in there to help me the entire time . . . let's say my pride and privacy took a double hit.

Not that being around dudes bothers me. I've played enough sports to be around plenty of naked guys in the locker room, but needing their help and cleaning up in front of them is entirely different.

By the time I'm back in bed with clean skin and a fresh gown, I'm wiped out and ready for some aspirin. I get how easy it is to get hooked on painkillers with how much pain I'm in. Regardless, I won't take it, even if this is the worst pain I've been in my whole life. Even after all the idiot stuff I did in my youth.

My room is empty again. Dani must have left to go to work. Not that I needed her to say goodbye, but I'm surprised that she didn't. It's not like her. As I close my eyes to nap, the door opens to her carrying bags of fast food and juggling two large drinks.

"I don't care what they said. I looked at the menu, and it's all shit."

She deposits the drinks on the rolling cart and dumps the bags next to it before throwing her purse in Rico's chair.

"Why is this way over here?" she mutters, moving the table near me and lowering it over my lap to make it easier for me to eat. I didn't think I was hungry, but the smell of burgers and french fries makes my stomach growl.

"I didn't know what to get you, so I ordered a loaded burger and a chicken sandwich. Have one or both, but you at least need to have something. And no vomiting it back up, 'cuz I'm not the type to hold your hair back and shit."

She doesn't have to tell me that she's not nurturing. It's pretty clear and something I respect. I'll get enough smothering when I go home to Mom.

"I appreciate it, Dani."

She stops digging in the bag for a second to stare at me. Her eyes narrow when she does it. I know this look. It's the one that comes before she bitches me out or says nothing. With her, I never know what to expect. She's a loose cannon, and it's usually too much, even if her heart's in the right place.

"Yeah, well. I didn't know what you liked, so I guessed. Hope you still appreciate it if it sucks."

Not what I expected her to say, but when she resumes taking stuff out of the bag and making a tray out of the wrapper, I figure it's her way of saying she cares.

"I'm sure it's fine," I assure her, even though I don't think she cares if I like it.

She'd probably make me eat it regardless and spout off something about being wasteful. One thing I've learned about her is that her poverty has made her very resourceful, and she lets nothing go to waste. She doesn't respond, too busy setting everything up to make it easy for me.

"Are you a lefty or a righty?"

"Left."

"Okay."

She switches the drinks to the left side of the table and opens the ketchup packets for me to dunk my fries in. She arranges everything how she likes it and then moves the tray closer before stepping back.

"We're good?"

I smile when her hands plant on her hips as if this is the extent of her help.

"Yeah. You know you don't have to do all this."

"Shut up and eat your food."

I chuckle. Praise and kudos aren't her thing, but spending the day up here is still very caring of her. She drags the chair closer to the bed, fishes out the television remote from the wall, and plants her sneakers on the edge of the bed. If people didn't know any better, they'd probably assume we were brother and sister with our light coloring, although my hair is darker than hers.

She clicks on the television and flips around before asking me what I want to watch. I don't care. I'm content to have the pain calmed down to a deep ache so I can eat. The food is from Burger World, a popular place around here known for its double-decker burgers and steak-cut fries. The amount of food she got will last me through dinner.

She puts on some car restoration show and dives into her food, filling the space with an easy contentment of not being alone but not engaging. I'm not used to this side of her. It's relatively new, and I suspect a byproduct of her relationship. Whatever that guy is doing is working because she seems calmer and less combative than before. I'm done with my burger and starting on my chicken sandwich when she breaks the silence.

"Who's Mary Ann? Your girlfriend?" she asks, turning those big blue eyes at me, genuinely intrigued.

"No."

Beyond Rico and my parents, no one knows her. The edge in my voice has her turning back to her food and letting the rest of the inquiry die. A long while passes with both of us content to eat and watch her show. After we finish, she tidies everything up and throws the bags into the trash. When that line returns between her eyebrows, I know something's up.

"Let's try this again. Who's Mary Ann?" She twists in her chair, curling her legs under her as if intending to stay longer. My injured leg seizes with a cramp that steels my breath again. "Do you need some pain meds?"

"I don't take them. Don't want to get addicted," I mutter through clenched teeth.

"That's dumb if they will help, and I'm pretty sure you can't get addicted just taking them in here."

She's wrong on that account, but I won't tell her.

"Then consider me dumb."

"I already do. Now spill your guts about this mystery woman," she presses, plopping her elbow on the arm of the chair and setting her chin on her hand to stare at me.

Mary Ann is a distant memory from the corner of my mind. So far in the past that she feels like a made-up person. A dream of what I thought she was versus what she was. How do I explain that without sounding like an idiot? And I'm not exactly sure why she came to mind last night as the cold concrete penetrated my body.

I hadn't thought of her in years, and then she was there. Her laughing face hovering above me as I gazed upon the stars. Her brunette waves careened down the sides of her thin face as those chestnut eyes held laughter and love in them. She has so many expressions, and I memorized them all to where it bordered on obsession. And then she was gone.

"Just a girl I used to know."

"That look doesn't say 'just a girl I used to know.' So, what gives?"

Dani picks at a hangnail, her eyes moving from me to it and back. I clench my jaw, not ready to have this conversation with her or anyone. I barely woke up from surgery, and it's been a parade of people ever since. I haven't thought about this, and it doesn't seem fitting to do so now.

"Nothing gives."

I'm on the defense, and I'm unsure why. She stops messing with her nail to stare at me. Really stop and stare as if deciding what to say to get me to spill my guts, as she always says.

"The fact that you're getting all bent out of shape at such an innocent question means that you're either guilty of something or trying to hide something or both. Either way, it's not like you to lie to me. You always give me the real deal, even when I wish you wouldn't. So, I'm trying to figure out why you're lying to me now. Especially after all the shit we've been through."

I lick my chapped lips and take a long drink of water, worrying that I'll regret telling her.

"She's a girl I grew up with."

Dani's piercing clicks against her teeth as she looks away, processing the brief sentence I gave her, hoping it would be enough to disinterest her. When those blue eyes return to mine, I prepare for more.

"Your first love?"

She says the words that used to haunt my mind for years. I agonized over those words, that girl, and how I used to feel so many times. It made me angry and rather proficient at sports. I used that anger, channeling it and taking it out on my opponents, which took us to states my senior year when she told me she was moving to California after we graduated.

"I don't know. I used to think so, but then maybe it was just puppy love or an infatuation," I admit, cringing as I say the words out loud and voice the doubts I've had for years.

"How long ago?" Dani nibbles on her bottom lip, deep in thought and putting together the puzzle pieces I'm reluctant to give her. "Like, when was the last time you saw her?"

I clear my throat, my gaze drifting away from her and flickering to the television that's lost all interest to her now that she's moved on to my past.

"A decade. She skipped our high school graduation ceremony to become an actress in Hollywood." I don't know why I'm telling her all this. Bringing it up opens the deep aching chasm in my heart that's always there when I dwell on Mary Ann.

"What's her last name?" she asks, drawing my gaze back.

"Higginbotham. Why?"

"Mary Ann Higginbotham, I've never heard of her. Not that I follow Hollywood actresses, but with that kind of name, you'd think you would have seen her on a show, in a movie, or at least on social media. Something."

Dani says all the things I've wondered myself. When she first left, I used to scour the Internet, looking for any sign of her. But as the months passed, her number disconnected, and her socials deleted, I lost hope. I eventually stopped looking, only entertaining her in my thoughts and memories.

"I don't know, Dani. I never heard from her again."

The room is silent again as her stare bores into me with such an intensity that I raise my eyebrow, wondering what in the world she's thinking.

"What? Why are you looking at me like that?" I finally ask after a few long seconds.

She stops nibbling on her lip, turns in her chair, and drapes her legs over the arm, so we're face to face.

"I'm sorry, Hamilton." Her voice drops to a whisper as if waiting to share a secret. "I know what it's like to look for people that don't want to be found. They're selfish and walk away without a backward glance, taking your heart with them. It's fucking brutal."

It's the most profound thing I've ever heard her say, which surprises me. I knew her dad passed away several years back, and I heard her talk about a half-brother she recently discovered. Beyond that, I do not know who she's talking about, but it's obvious the pain cuts deep in her as it does in me. An unexpected thing that we have in common.

"I'm sorry for you too. If you ever want to talk about it, I'm here," I say the words she told me a few hours ago. Not that I'd ever expect her to take me up on it. She guards herself more than anyone I know.

"Yeah, well."

She turns in her chair to resume watching her restoration show. Although I don't think she's watching it at all. The comfortable silence between us has me closing my eyes and thinking about that wild girl I once knew.

6

When I wake up, Dani is gone with a note scribbled across the nurse's board that she had to go to the garage. It was nice of her to stay as long as she did and to bring me food. But that little nap costs me big time, with the pain surging through my body.

I groan and shift in the bed, wincing as my muscles protest. The pain is like a constant throbbing that refuses to go away. Every movement reminds me of the bullet that tore through my leg, leaving behind a trail of destruction.

I press the call button, hoping the lovely nurse from earlier can bring me another round of pain medication. Every minute feels like an eternity as I wait for relief. She enters, looking at me sympathetically.

"How are you doing?" she asks, checking my vitals.

"I'm in a lot of pain," I reply, clenching my teeth as I shift, trying to escape the hot burning in my side.

"I'll see what I can do about getting you something for that," she says before leaving the room.

I try to distract myself by looking around the room. The sterile white walls and the monotony of the medical equipment offer no solace. My mind races with thoughts of the unknown future and what lies ahead. The challenges and obstacles that I might encounter during my recovery process. The fear of being unable to regain my strength and be fully mobile to return to work creeps into my mind. Eventually, the nurse returns with a small cup of pills and a glass of water.

"Here you go," she says, handing them to me. "This should help with the pain. It will be another four hours before you can have your next round."

I take the pills gratefully and swallow them down, feeling a sense of relief wash over me as I wait for them to take effect. I lean back against the pillows, trying to relax my aching body. A few minutes later, the door opens and a doctor walks in, looking at my chart.

"Good evening, I'm Dr. Williams. How are you feeling?"

"I'm in a lot of pain," I reply, my voice hoarse.

Dr. Williams nods, his expression empathetic. "I can see that. It's understandable, considering what you've been through."

I can't help but feel grateful for his compassion. It's a slight comfort amid this whole situation.

"So, what's the prognosis? When can I go home?"

Dr. Williams looks at me thoughtfully.

"Well, it's still early, but I'm cautiously optimistic so long as the swelling goes down and you don't spike a fever. The bullet didn't hit any major organs or arteries, so the damage is relatively minor, albeit muscle damage is the issue we solved last night. We worry about infection in the stab wound, which fever will show. You're on a heavy course of antibiotics and steroids. However, we will continue to monitor you closely to ensure no complications."

It's good news, but I know I still have a long road ahead.

"How long do you think I'll need to stay here?" Pops said a couple of days, which I'm sure is what the doctor will say.

"It's hard to say," he admits. "It depends on how quickly you heal and how well you respond to treatment. But I would estimate at least a couple more days if all goes well. If not, then possibly longer."

My heart sinks at the thought of being stuck in the hospital for longer than forty-eight hours. The constant beeping of machines and the smell of disinfectant is already wearing on me. I'm also not overjoyed to return to my old room, with Pops helping me bathe.

"I'll do whatever it takes to get better."

Dr. Williams smiles at me. "That's the spirit. And speaking of getting better, once you're feeling up to it, we'll start you on physical therapy to help you regain strength and mobility."

"I tried to go to the bathroom on my own today but couldn't. The burning pain from the two wounds was too much."

The idea of enduring even more pain to get back to par is something I'm not looking forward to, but my pride won't let me continue needing help to shit and shower.

"You won't be doing anything unassisted, I can assure you of that. It's a standard protocol for injuries like yours," Dr. Williams continues, sensing my apprehension. "Physical therapy and walking the halls will help you regain your full range of motion and prevent long-term complications. Don't worry. We have a great team of therapists here who will work with you to ensure you return to your old self in no time."

I nod, feeling relief and apprehension as I want to recover fully and return to my life.

"Thanks for letting me know," I say before settling back against the pillows.

I focus on the positive as Dr. Williams leaves the room. As I lay in the hospital bed with my eyes closed, my situation sinks in. The pain medication takes the edge off, but the constant ache remains. The low hum of the television that Dani was watching drowns out the occasional pump of the blood pressure machine on my left. Otherwise, I'm alone with my thoughts when flashes of last night's scene hit me.

Matt's blood pumping through my fingers, and his breath against my palm. He wasn't dead when I got to him. Dying, now that I can admit it, but still talking to me. I don't know why Rico said I knew he was already gone when I ran off. He's putting things together that don't belong together, and I don't know why that is.

"Oh my, Alexander."

I flip open my eyes to Eli, cupping a hand over his mouth. His eyes are red and puffy from crying, and his voice chokes with emotion.

"I can't believe this happened to you. We were distraught when we heard."

The sounds of last night's physical altercation fade from my mind as Eli races to my bedside to lay his trembling hand on my arm.

Taking a deep breath before speaking and then wincing when I forget about my sutures, I swallow my profanity to say, "Thanks. I appreciate you coming. I know you're all busy with work and school. How is Isla?"

Eli squeezes my arm before releasing it, seeming to calm down now that he's here and can see how I'm doing.

"I closed earlier and got Isla as soon as school let out. Understandably, she's distraught. I wanted Ronald home with her before I came here."

He sniffs, tears threatening his lower lids as he walks over to pluck the tissue box off the counter. He pulls a few out and dabs his eyes and cheeks.

"Now tell me what happened. Don't leave a single thing out because the news said very little," Eli insists after collecting himself and moving to the chair that everyone has occupied today while gripping the tissue box tightly.

As I recount the events to Eli, I feel a lump in my throat.

42

The memories of last night race forward, and the adrenaline and fear are still raw. He listens intently, gasping and clutching his chest as I tell him about Matt. The sympathy on his face is evident, and I can tell how deeply this tragedy has affected him.

"He was a great guy," I say, my voice catching. "I'm going to miss him."

"I'm so very sorry, Alexander. I can't imagine how hard this is for you." Eli expression is solemn as he wipes the tears streaming down his cheeks. "Is there anything I can do for his family? Anything at all?"

His question brings unexpected tears to my eyes. Strangers rarely offer to help in times of crisis, and the selflessness in his voice is overwhelming.

"I'm not sure yet, but I'll let you know. Thank you, Eli. It means a lot." I choke out a few words of gratitude before the lump in my throat becomes too much.

He gives me a sympathetic smile. "Of course."

His compassionate demeanor comforts me, and I feel grateful to call him my friend. I think back to Father Michael's sermons about the importance of serving others, and I can see that lesson embodied in Eli. He is a shining example of what it means to care for those around you, even in the darkest times. As we sit in silence for a moment, exhaustion sinks in. Not only the physical toll but the emotional toll as well.

"Tell me about your injuries," Eli asks gently. "What did the doctors say about your recovery?"

"I'm going to need therapy and rehabbing before I can return to work."

"But you can do it. You're a fighter, Hamilton. And we'll be there every step of the way to support you. Once you are up for it, you can run with me. That's great therapy, both physical and respiratory. I get in about eight to ten miles most days and longer on the weekends. If all goes well, maybe we can train for a half marathon. It's been some years since I did one."

His voice lightens, sparking a cheerfulness about his new idea. I've never been much of a runner. Too much bulk on my frame that causes my knees to hurt. It will be interesting to see what the rehab program will be, as I assume it would include some cardio, probably an elliptical or stationary bike to start. Something low impact while my leg heals.

"I appreciate the vote of confidence, Eli. However, we may have to put off booking a half marathon since I've never been a runner and didn't plan on becoming one at almost thirty."

Eli lets out a small chuckle and stands to place the tissue box back on the counter while throwing away his used tissues in the trash can.

"Of course, I wouldn't book you until we're fully ready. Plus, we must pick the destination and where we'd want to run and train for that specific climate." He chuckles again, schooling me on all the intricate details of booking a race. "Do you go to a rehab facility once they release you from here?"

When I think about returning to Mom, and Pops's house, a different dread settles into my gut. And it must have been clear on my face when Eli digs for more.

"What's with that face?" he asks, stepping closer to the bed to touch the railing.

"Long story short, I'm returning to my parents' house, where they will care for me for a few days. It's not ideal, but I need help physically getting up and down with my size and weight. Pops is the only one that can help me," I explain, the thought souring my mood.

"Well, that should motivate you to take your rehab seriously so you can get back to your house."

Eli's usual perceptive self shines right through in reading the situation with the small amount of information I disclosed. Sometimes I think he missed his calling by not going into law enforcement. He's the most intuitive and insightful person I know.

"If I had my way, I just go home and figure it out. But the hospital won't release me on my own reconnaissance, so I get to go back to sleeping in my childhood bedroom with my mom fawning all over me."

"Sounds terrible. You'll have my sympathies, Alexander." He chuckles. "I'll leave you to your peace before you have none at your mom and dad's house. I'll check on you again. And don't hesitate to call me if you need something. It's no trouble at all."

I nod, feeling grateful for his friendship. "Thanks, Eli. I appreciate everything you've done for me."

"Of course, Alexander. That's what friends are for. Take care of yourself."

As he walks out, I can't help but feel a sense of comfort in his presence. He's always been there for me, both on and off the job, just like with Isla. And even now, as I lay in this hospital bed, I know he means every word he says.

7

As the days pass, I slowly start to feel better. The pain is still there, but it's becoming more manageable thanks to the medication and physical therapy. The therapists are kind and patient. They push me hard, making me work through the discomfort to regain my strength and mobility.

Dr. Williams checks on me regularly, always encouraging me and answering any questions I have about my recovery. He tells me that my progress is looking good and to take it easy going home.

Rico drops by when he can to bust my chops, ask about Dani and keep me updated on the investigation into the shooting. Mom and Pops are here bright and early every morning. Mom updates me on everything that is going on with her life. I'm all caught up on her church volunteer work, the gossip at her bridge game, and how many people are praying for me and waiting for me to come home so they can pay me a social visit.

Flowers, balloons, and all sorts of well wishes flood my room. I redirect them to the children's ward after Mom reads me the card and saves them. She's been taking them home and writing thank you cards on my behalf.

Pops reads the newspaper, occasionally commenting or contributing to the conversation from behind the pages. Apart from chauffeuring Mom to her various events and the grocery store, as she's been cooking and freezing meals for me to have when I return home, he's content to focus on riding the Chief's ass regarding my pay, the awards, and the investigation. Between what Rico tells me and what Pops finds out, I'm well-informed and prepared for my interview when it happens later this week.

On the day of my discharge, I feel a mix of emotions. I'm excited to leave the hospital and finally go home, but also anxious about managing this with my parents. The nurses give me a bag of medications and instructions on taking them, and the therapists give me some exercises to continue doing at home between appointments. Dr. Williams comes in to see me one last time before I leave.

"I'm proud of you for how far you've come. But remember, your recovery is still ongoing. Take your medication as prescribed, follow the exercises, and come back for your follow-up appointments."

"I will."

I'm grateful for his care and guidance as the nurse pushes the wheelchair toward the front door, where Pops's waiting with the car door open.

Mom twists a tissue in her hands, dabbing the tears as the hospital staff makes a line on both sides to cheer and clap at my exit. It's standard protocol to do this when hurt in the line of duty, and it's a gracious gesture, even if it makes me very uncomfortable. I didn't tell Dani or Eli about my discharge as I didn't want them to be a part of this fanfare, although Rico's smirking face by the sliding glass doors says it all.

He takes over for the nurse when I reach him, pushing my wheelchair as she carries my crutches to the car. Pops grabs and stows them in the back before helping Mom into the passenger seat.

"A hero's farewell," Rico jokes, and if I could twist around and grab his collar, I'd pull a Dani and deck him. The badge dangling from his neck hits me in the head when he leans forward to whisper in my ear.

"Wait till you get to Alan and Margaret's house. They have quite a little reception arranged."

"Fuck," I groan. The last thing I want is to entertain their friends and hear more accolades for doing my job. Easing into bed and resting sounds much better.

"Your mom asked me to stop by this morning to help your dad move some furniture to make it easier for you to get around. It looks like a regular birthday party in there. I even helped hang the welcome home banner."

The amusement in his voice is unmistakable. He's already gloating at my misery.

"I knew this would be a mistake," I mutter, wiping a hand down my face and catching it on the scruff of my fast-growing beard since standing and shaving were impossible in the hospital.

"Remember when we were ten, and your mom had that huge blowout party?"

"The Star Wars one?"

Mom didn't understand that franchise's appeal, thinking Darth Vader was a terrible influence on an impressionable young boy. After talking to Father Michael at the church and him educating her about the correlation between God and the Devil and Star Wars, she relented. I still had to go to church three times that week to make sure I got all the influence out of me.

She made me clean the fellowship hall that day while they decorated the house. I thought I was in trouble and doing a penance on my birthday. It turned out they needed me out of the house to decorate. Rico even helped them while Father Michael gave me extra bible lessons. They picked me up, and I was angry, only to walk into a huge surprise party with all my friends and their parents. It turned out to be one of the best birthdays I ever had.

"Yes, it reminds me of that. Surprise included, so don't ruin it now that you know," he finishes, straightening up and pushing me toward the car. "Alrighty, Mama, here's your boy."

Rico's loud and unnecessary announcement has her twisting in her seat, Pops glaring at him, and the nurse hovering on my right, ready to help me out of the wheelchair.

"Alan, get out and help him," Mom says, her hands waving feverishly as if I'm going to fall out of the wheelchair with Rico and the nurse right here. Pops frowns but goes to unbuckle his seatbelt when I stop him.

"That's unnecessary. I got it," I say, gripping the armrests tightly and clenching my teeth, bracing myself as I prepare to transfer from the wheelchair to the car.

The sooner I do things for myself, the faster I can get home to my own house. I'm not ungrateful for Mom and Pops taking me in, but the thought of being a burden through this process adds to my worry about my overall recovery.

Rico locks the wheelchair parallel to the car, allowing me enough room to maneuver out. The nurse tries catching me under my arm, but she's tiny and more of a hindrance than a help. If I lost my balance, I'd crush her. That's the last thing I need. Slowly and deliberately, I shift my weight to the edge of the wheelchair, enduring the fierce throbbing in my thigh and the sharp jolt shooting through my ribs.

Once transferred into the car, I wipe the sweat from my

upper lip and run a hand across my forehead. Rico's expression is weary and concerned, something I've seen more times this week than ever. Same with Mom, Pops, Dani, and Eli. All looks I want to stop receiving.

"Thanks, man. I appreciate it." I clasp Rico's hand as he stoops to look in the car. "I'll see you later."

"What are you talking about? Mama invited me back to their place to hang with you."

Rico smirks now that he shared their secret. I'm reasonably certain he doesn't care so much about the party but more about my reaction to it. That and all the food Mom probably prepared for this.

"Of course, I have a slice of lemon Meringue pie with your name on it," she says over her shoulder, cementing their pack of lies and attempting to fool me into thinking nothing awaits at their house.

"We need to get going."

Pops's curt tone cuts through their well wishes, signaling he's had enough.

"Yes, sir," Rico says, nodding as Pops's gaze cuts through the rearview mirror at me, the same way he did when I was growing up. Some things never change.

Rico smiles before closing my door and tapping the top of the roof. Pops wastes no time pulling away from the curb while Mom chats me up about how great it is to have me out of the hospital, how worried they have been, and how the church has been praying for me. I sigh, half listening to her, while Pops and I occasionally lock eyes in the rearview mirror before I resume staring out my window.

The therapist warned me of depressive thoughts after sharing that I was returning to my childhood home. She was extremely sympathetic and gave me physical exercises to do at home and mental tactics to help deal with the trauma and emotions that would eventually arise. Luckily, I hadn't had any of that so far, but she assured me it was coming and, when it did, to get help from the hospital's counselors. All are paid for by taxpayer dollars. That made me uneasy. I'm not a charity case. I can afford a psychiatrist if I need one.

The town bustles around us as Pops drives the familiar roads home. It's an odd feeling as the shopping center and fast-food restaurants blur past. The rhythmic hum of the engine and the muffled traffic sounds seem distant, unable to penetrate the heavy fog of my thoughts.

Life continues as if untouched by tragedy. How can it be so? The world seems to ignore Matt's sacrifice in keeping this place safe. It feels wrong, unsettling, and it gnaws at my soul.

"Officer Tenner's funeral is in a couple of days."

It's as if Pops can read my thoughts and the fury brewing within them. I lock eyes with him, the only acknowledgment of what he says.

"It will be held at St. Cecilia's."

I nod, letting silence fill the car, heavy with unspoken words.

"If it's too much for you to handle, dear, we can always—" Mom says, letting me off the hook in the way mothers do to protect their children.

"I'll be there," I say, knowing she mistook my silence for something other than my survivor's guilt. I'm here with them instead of a young cop with a family.

The rims of Pops's eyes narrow when I answer. The difference between fathers and mothers. He understands fully and would never have offered to bail me out.

He glides the car to a stop in front of our house. The banner hanging between the columns on the wraparound porch is bright and colorful, welcoming me home. I take a deep breath, steeling myself for what lies ahead as Mom twists in her seat, her face radiating joy.

"I hope you don't mind, honey, but we set up a little

welcoming party for you. It's just that when we first got the news ..."

Her voice trails off for a different reason when emotions clog her throat and tears appear in her eyes. Pops leans over to drag a handkerchief from his pocket to hand to her, which she uses to dab her cheeks.

"The boy understands, Margaret."

Being called a boy again takes me back to every childhood memory when Pops sided with me while not wanting to upset my mother. It was always a delicate balance between these two. Hard as nails, father and empathetic mother.

"Don't you, Alex?"

"It's very nice, Mom."

I eliminate any inflection of sarcasm and infuse it with gratitude. Entertaining people is Mom's way of dealing with grief. She's the first person to bake cookies and make a casserole when there is bad news or a grieving family.

She's legendary at church for her compassionate heart, dragging Pops and me along as support to make awkward conversations with people we barely know. We often missed watching college football games to sit at a churchgoer's house with the family and hear tales of those they had lost.

"Well, let's get you out of the car. Might take a few tries," Pops announces when I don't add more to my statement to Mom. Sometimes I think she should've had a girl—someone like her rather than two crusty law enforcement men.

"I'll run inside and make sure the walkways are clear of any clutter to make it easier," she says as a believable excuse. She always kept a clean and tidy house. When I was younger, she used to call it 'model home ready' so that she wouldn't feel embarrassed if anyone dropped in unannounced. She'd be horrified with how messy I keep my house, but luckily, nobody drops in unannounced.

She bustles out of the car and up the curved sidewalk, stopping once to straighten her patriotic yard sign and inspecting a blooming flower before searching for her house keys. Pops shuts off the engine and slips out his door before throwing open mine and pausing.

"Your mother has a few people inside to see you. It's probably not how you wanted to start your recovery, but she's been at the church daily, lighting candles for you. You're included in the church's prayer chain, and even though you refused Father Michael's request to visit at the hospital, he's here now."

My parents are certainly Catholics in good standing. My mom could apply and be granted sainthood based on her good works. Me, well, I'm neither of those. My relationship with God is complicated, and with the Church, non-existent. Thus, having Father Michael at my bedside didn't sit right. Although I'd never be rude or disrespectful to him, I don't need to be proselytized because I was saved when another, more deserving man wasn't.

"Yes, sir," I clip, hearing the implied warning in his voice. The rule in our house has always been if you give Mom trouble, Pops will return it.

"I assume you'd prefer to rest, but put in the time as best you can before you beg off the rest of the gathering," he finishes, grabbing the crutches from me as I pluck them off the seat and opening the car door wider.

Summoning my resolve, I move the right leg out until it's planted on the ground, then bear down as I twist the rest of my body to follow. A wave of heat washes over me as I clutch underneath my thigh and move my leg to prevent the strain on my thigh muscles.

"Slowly," Pops mutters, his hand in front of him as if waiting to receive the blessing from Father Michael. I grasp the edges of the car frame and, with painstaking effort, I shift my weight forward to gingerly stand on my right leg. The pain is overwhelming, and I falter. Pops catches my right hip and left shoulder, steadying me.

"We'll have to work on this to prevent atrophy."

Something the therapist already said. My old man is not one to shy away from hard work. If I know him, he'll be exercising right along with me before this is over.

"Yes, sir."

My jaw clenches. Sweat collects at my underarms and the back of my neck as the bright winter sun beats down on us. I adjust the crutch on my left and release the door frame to take the right crutch from Pops's hand. Once I am steady on both, he steps back and keeps both hands in front to catch me if I falter again.

I exhale deeply and nod my head that I'm ready to start. Every step is a test of endurance, and my breathing becomes labored as I struggle to maintain my composure. My breaths come in ragged gasps, the strain etched across my features when I look at the long glass pane on the side of the front door. Before Pops reaches for the handle, I swipe my arm across my forehead to collect the sweat and look somewhat presentable.

Pops swings open the front door, revealing a living room adorned with decorations and filled with Mom, her friends, and members of our church. Their eager faces light up with delight as they collectively yell, "Surprise!"

Mom rushes forward with the ladies from her bridge group, each asking nearly the same question in different ways. There's barely enough room for Pops to come through the door behind me and close it.

I shuffle further into the living room and fall into an armchair with a heavy groan. Little do I know, my ass is planted there for the next several hours recanting details of what happened, discussing Matt and his upcoming funeral, how long I'll be staying with my parents, and how long rehab will take before I'm back on duty.

Through all the small talk, Mom remains by my side, bringing me food, dessert, and drinks until I'm stuffed, slightly nauseated from the small talk, and sporting a pounding headache from hours of stiffly sitting there. Only when I whisper I need to go to the bathroom does she get Pops, and I get a reprieve from her party.

8

"You did good, son," Pops mumbles, loud enough for my ears only. "Longer than I expected."

His hand braces under my elbow as I maneuver the crutches down the tight hallway leading to the back of the house, which opens to a larger, less formal den with my old bedroom off to the left and my parents off the kitchen to the right. The upstairs houses the guest bedrooms and game room. No one goes up there anymore, but when we were younger, my friends and I practically lived up there.

"I'd like to lie down after this. Can you bring me a couple of pain relievers when I'm done?" I clench my teeth against the throbbing from three places in my body. My head, my side, and my leg. All are begging for relief.

"Sure, I'll let your mother know you're done for. She'll probably be entertaining for a few more hours, which should give you some time."

I find relief in his words. Pops understands that men who live independently aren't enthused about moving back home, even if they are healing from a gunshot.

"I appreciate it, Pops. The sooner I get home, the better, though."

His eyes catch mine so close that I can see the hazel flecks in them. "I understand. Albeit, don't let your mother hear that. It will hurt her feelings."

His warning is unnecessary and already known. Again, another reason they should have adopted kids after I came along. Mom needs someone to dote on, and Pops isn't enough.

"Understood. I'll manage from here," I say, letting my independent streak fly now that we're not within earshot of anyone. He grunts, his only acknowledgment of having heard me when he releases my elbow to open the bathroom door.

As his heavy footsteps fall on the hundred-year-old wood floor, I gaze around the bathroom that has remained unchanged since childhood. The walls are adorned with intricately patterned black and white wallpaper featuring delicate floral motifs above glossy black and white checkered tiles, meticulously laid out in a diagonal pattern that further enhances the nostalgia of this place.

Positioned along the far wall, the clawfoot tub was rimmed with clay from the baseball field too many times to count, nearly ruining the porcelain-coated exterior. I used to complain to Mom that I wanted a man's bathroom, and she would look around the room, gaze at the chandelier that hung in the middle of the room, and politely say no. After too many times, I stopped asking and accepted that I had a vintage bathroom with antique finishes.

It takes some maneuvering, and I'm glad this bathroom is oversized to handle the wide splay of the crutches as I work to get my pants lowered. After a grueling ten minutes to do my business, get off the toilet, and wash my hands, I'm huffing and puffing down the hallway to my bedroom, where I gingerly slip onto the bed to lie down.

The room's emptiness echoes the emptiness in my heart,

amplifying the raw emotions that swirl within me. My gaze roams the familiar surroundings. The room that once held so many cherished memories now feels like solitary confinement, stifling and boring.

My eyes trace over the sports trophies on the shelves and the baseballs displayed in shadow boxes, artifacts of my past victories. They serve as a stark reminder of the person I used to be, the athlete, the popular kid, the do-gooder, all things that should make me proud but don't, as they don't mean a damn thing now after what happened.

A knock on the door interrupts the heaviness that ruminates in my mind. I look at the doorway to find Rico with a concerned expression.

"Can I come in?" he asks, his voice full of worry.

My gaze leaves him to look down the hallway, ensuring he's alone before waving him in.

"Yeah, and please close the door."

Rico steps into the room, his eyes scanning me and the room we used to hang out in when we didn't crash upstairs in the game room.

"How are you feeling?" he asks, closing the door and leaning against it.

I let out a deep sigh.

"Like shit," I mutter, hollow and weary. "It's like I'm living in a fog. Going through the motions, but they aren't mine. As if this is not my life, these are not my injuries, and . . . every breath feels stolen as if I'm undeserving of the air to breathe since Matt isn't here. I keep going back to that night. If I hadn't left him . . ."

Never have I doubted Rico's ability on the job or his EMS training, but it sounds like I am doubting him now. Rico frowns, his expression empathetic. He moves off the door to sit in the desk chair across the room.

"I know it's hard. Recall distorts our perception, making us question everything we thought happened versus what really happened. But you can't blame yourself. You did nothing wrong. I told you I had him. You trusted me. Going after the assailant was what you were supposed to do. You saved lives that night. What about all the people in the store? They matter too."

I turn my head slightly, meeting Rico's gaze with lingering doubt.

"It's hard not to wonder. What if I had stayed? What if I had done something differently? What if I hadn't blown out the lights? Did that give the shooter an advantage? Maybe things would have turned out differently."

"Those 'what ifs' will eat you alive, man." His expression is one of sorrowful understanding. "But you can't change what happened. You can sit here and stew, but nothing will bring Matt back. I know it's harsh, but you must make peace with it and find a way to move forward."

A sense of frustration wells up within me, the weight of my doubts and regrets threatening to choke me.

"How do I make peace with it, Rico?" I ask in desperation. "How do I live knowing my choices may have cost Matt his life? The guilt consumes me, relentlessly haunting my thoughts. What if it had been me? What if I had taken his place? He has a wife and baby, Rico. I have nothing. It should have been me."

My eyes well with tears, the depths of despair sagging my body forward as Rico approaches the side of the bed to glare at me.

"Don't you fucking say that. It shouldn't have been you. It shouldn't have been Matt, either. It shouldn't be any of us. Ever. Matt knew the risks, the same as you and I do. We hope and pray to God that it never happens, but when it does, you don't get to decide who's just and worthy to go home." His voice carries a blunt edge as he doles out some harsh truths. "I get that you're drowning in guilt, Alex, but dwelling on it won't change a damn thing. You need to live with the fact that he's gone."

His words land like blows, striking deep into the raw wounds of my guilt. Rico's hand rests heavily on my shoulder, a gesture that feels more like a grip, grounding me in the harsh reality rather than comforting me.

"Survivor's guilt is a bitch," he continues. "But you've got to face it head-on. Accept what happened. It's fucked-up and unfair, but life doesn't give a damn about fairness. You have to learn to carry this burden and keep moving forward."

His brutal honest cuts through my self-pity, stirring anger within me. The tears that threatened to flow now mingle with frustration and rage.

"And don't think for a damn second that blaming yourself is productive," Rico adds, his tone unyielding. "You can't change the past. You did what you thought was right at that moment. Maybe it wasn't enough, but second-guessing won't bring him back. It'll only destroy you."

"So, what am I supposed to do? Am I just supposed to accept it?" I retort with bitterness. "To live with the guilt, knowing I may have cost Matt his life? How the hell am I supposed to move on from that? Tell me, Rico!"

Rico's gaze hardens, his eyes locking onto mine with an unwavering intensity.

"There's no magical answer," he replies, his voice unyielding. "You face it. You accept the pain, the guilt, and the regret. You let it fuel you to be better to honor Matt's memory. And you fucking fight to make something worthwhile out of this mess."

His words pierce through my despair, fueling a flicker of determination. There's a certain truth in his words.

"And you lean on me when it gets too much. He squeezes my shoulder as the inflection of his words sinks in. "You're not alone in this. You got me, your parents, and that hot little *chica* . . . how is she, by the way? Has she asked about me?"

The somber seriousness disappears in a flash. Leave it to him to make it about Dani. It makes me smile that he's no longer letting me dwell on this.

"I told you to forget about her."

As the words leave my lips, he smiles. "How can I forget about those curves?"

"Those curves belong to someone else."

He grunts. The arrogance that is classically Rico doesn't believe me. I don't think he's ever been turned down, and that perfect record makes for a dangerously big ego.

"I'll tell you what. That little firecracker wouldn't stand for your wallowing bullshit. Maybe we need to get her hot little ass over here."

That's true. Dani has been texting me daily to hear about my progress, although she hasn't returned to the hospital since the first day. She said something about a problem at the shop, and she's been following up, demanding to know everything I know. And like Isla's case, she lets me know when she hears something she doesn't like or disagrees with.

"No, Dani would probably have a military-style boot camp in the backyard doing two-a-days as my rehab."

"You need to find yourself a strong woman like that."

I had a strong woman once. It was like harnessing a hurricane. The adrenaline rush, her unpredictable nature, and never knowing what came next made me a storm chaser to the powerful Mary Ann. Yet when it was over, she just left me in the wake of her wreckage.

Rico's watch chimes the time, and I cast an eye to the dust sky. The day has flown by with getting out of the hospital and the welcome home party. My body is tired, but I can't stop thinking about our conversation. I want to get out of here as the walls of my sports-themed room are closing in on me.

"Can we get out of here? With everything that's happened, I

need some air and something that doesn't involve my parents, rehab, or any of my problems."

Ignoring the pounding in my head, I groan as I maneuver to the edge of the bed. He hesitates, his eyes glancing at the closed door.

"How are we supposed to do that with them right down the hall? Those crutches are loud as hell, and you're not small like those girls you used to sneak in here."

Rico has no clue because I never snuck girls in here. I only ever snuck one girl into this place. She was the sole reason I would risk getting into trouble with Pops.

"You had the entire apartment to yourself growing up when your mom was at work. That was way better than this room." I smirk, knowing he used it frequently. He shakes his head in disbelief and strides to the door, opening it with a sudden gust of bravado.

"Fine, let's go, but you're dealing with your parents, not me."

With Rico's strong presence, a flicker of resilience stirs within me. Family, friends, and brotherhood surround me, all lifelines to get my life back on track.

I flash him a grateful smile. "I don't have the words."

"Get your sappy ass out this door before I change my mind."

9

Leaving the house with all Mom's friends and Father Michael lingering around to talk to me took some convincing. With Rico oozing compliments to all the older ladies and Pops's humming his understanding, I'm sitting in the front seat of his truck with the crisp air drying the sweat on my face. He casually throws the crutches into the rear of his cab before adjusting the air vents to make his jet-black hair sweep backward with the gust of air.

"Well, that was a feat getting out of there. I think an old lady pinched my ass," Rico says, his grip squeaking against the leather-wrapped steering wheel as he exits the driveway. I chuckle, knowing no one grabbed his ass. "Where are we escaping to? That wing place? I'm stuffed from Mama's spread, but I could go for a few beers and a nice pair of tits."

Rico being a regular at Twin Peaks is not a surprise. Women, sports, beer, and food are all he needs in life.

"I'd like to go out to the truck stop."

His face sets into a deep frown as he turns the corner leading out of the neighborhood.

"Not this again." The annoyance in his voice is unmistakable. "I thought you gave it up when the other agency got involved? Or is that what you lead me to believe?"

His eyes narrow when he looks at me. Rico loves to push the limits at work but will never cross over into other investigations or agencies' work. He draws an odd line, but he says it's keeping his nose clean with the Chief.

"No," I say, failing to expand on it.

He groans before cutting the wheel toward the highway that leads to the truck stop.

"Why are you pursuing this? The kid's trial? Is it coming up? If it is, you can't investigate it when you're called as the prosecutor's witness. You know that." Nothing he says is new. It's the same argument we've been having for months.

"No one is investigating that place. Aside from her case, they rarely patrol, and prostitution runs rampant. No one seems interested in investigating at all. It's not just a random occurrence. They're running a full-fledged trafficking ring. They bring in young girls like Isla and ship them out before anyone catches on."

"Fuck. Did you tell the Chief yet?"

"I don't have enough evidence. Now with this, everything is on hold."

I gesture to my leg, knowing it's impossible to remain undetected, hobbling on crutches. Dust particles float in the fading sunlight of the cab as he glints at me.

"Then why are we going out there?" he questions, punching the accelerator and throwing me back in my seat as if irritated by my request.

"I think the manager is in on it. It's too coordinated of an effort to run the women through at the pace they are and not get caught when they do a random patrol. I've seen the place suddenly clear out as if tipped off beforehand, and I can only think that tip comes from someone inside who knows and alerts the store."

His eyebrows rise, intrigued.

"How do they alert the pimps or the lot lizards, then? I've passed through there a few times, and it's packed with drivers and johns."

Ah, this is good. Rico being interested gets me help—something he can investigate while I'm at my parents' house.

"I noticed a blue light at the end of the center. It's mounted to the edge of the building and is rarely ever on. The first time the place cleared out was a total fluke. I was there at the right time on the right day. It happened in about fifteen minutes when the place was crazy busy inside, and customers flooded out the back. I heard the idling rigs take off and went to watch the commotion by the sliding doors."

"You were in uniform?"

Unlike Rico, who always wears his badge, I don't. I prefer to keep it in my pocket, and this night I was glad about that. I looked like a civilian stopping in for a fountain drink and snacks when I got caught up in what was happening.

"No."

"Good," he says stiffly. "Go on."

"The second time, I went inside to get a coffee and a donut and then returned to my truck in the back lot. Nothing unusual inside, and for almost an hour, nothing outside either. However, a dim blue light on the wooded side of the property turned on, and I wondered what that meant. That's when I noticed a swarm of activity both in and out."

"What activity, exactly?"

"Cabs stop rocking, ladies escaping out of the side door, truckers jogging back to their rigs, and most pulling out even though some had just arrived. It seems too orchestrated to be anything else. I've racked my mind for any other reason and can't. Can you?"

He gives me a knowing glance, realizing the gravity of the situation and the responsibility our oath holds us under to uphold the law and arrest those that violate it.

"You're saying they have their own blue light special?" He smiles at his terrible joke, knowing the blue light special store went out of business long ago.

"Anyway, it's been a week since I've been out there. I try to break up the days and times to see if I can put together a pattern."

"And?"

"Nothing, so far." His hands tighten on the wheel when changing lanes to speed up, weaving in and out of traffic to get there. "And I need something to distract myself, considering . . ."

I let the rest die as the loss hits me again. Rico says nothing. He already knows I'm struggling. Rico nods, his expression resolute.

"Enough said. Let's see what we see."

He floors it, causing me to grab the handle to hold on. He frequently breaks traffic laws and doesn't care when doing it. He's been pulled over and flashed his badge to get out of it more than once. Everyone knows he has a lead foot. It's a few minutes later that he's exiting the highway and blazing through a yellow light to fishtail it into the front of the truck stop.

"Where do you normally park?" His jaw sets, ready for our makeshift stakeout.

"I normally set up on the north corner of the building. The light is on the southwest corner." As he creeps around the back, he stops for a couple of truckers to pass when I point it out. "There's the light. I park over by the dumpsters."

Rico skillfully maneuvers his black 4x4 truck into a spot several spaces away from the row of rigs. The lift kit and flashy rims make his vehicle stand out, but the illegally tinted windows give us the advantage of remaining concealed.

"This should give us a good angle of the light." His wrist drapes over the top of the steering wheel before retrieving the badge hanging around his neck and stowing it in the console. "Can't risk anyone seeing this."

The soft glow of the dashboard illuminates his face, casting a shadowy ambiance in the cabin. We sit in silence, our eyes fixed on the building's entrance in the distance.

"Probably best to kill the engine," I murmur, watching a couple of truckers appear from the shadows of the trucks. Rico cracks the window, sending a surge of cold air into the cab before he cuts the headlights and engine.

I adjust my position, trying to find a comfortable spot amidst the pounding headache I never got aspirin for. Rico's eyes narrow, scanning the surroundings.

We settle into a routine, taking turns monitoring the area and scanning for signs of prostitution. The honk of a rig entering the truck stop or the ping of a notification from our phones occasionally interrupts the silence in the truck.

"Can you believe that guy's outfit?" Rico chuckles, pointing toward a guy walking out of the stop, looking like Elvis. "Looks like he raided a '70s disco."

I stifle a laugh, my eyes briefly darting toward the flamboyantly dressed individual. "Yeah, fashion choices aside, I wonder what he's up to. Probably doesn't know we're watching him."

"Watching everyone."

As the night deepens, the building's exterior lights flicker to life, casting a yellowish glow over the back lot.

"Look over there."

His gaze follows my finger to a group of individuals clustered between trucks. Some lean against their rigs, taking cigarette puffs, while others engage in lively conversations. Among them, a couple of women move around, their attire and provocative mannerisms hinting at their profession.

"Lot lizards," he murmurs, leaning on the console again. "Looks like they're working the crowd tonight."

I nod, never taking my eyes off the group. "Exactly. However, I don't recognize those two ladies. They must be new or rotated in."

As we continue observing, one trucker pulls the taller woman to him, wrapping his arm around her back and bunching her coat up to see her bare ass peeking out.

"You see that?" Rico murmurs, his eyes widening when we exchange a glance. "Look, there's more. Is it just me, or do they seem fine with this? Almost happy?"

His shoulder brushes mine as he points two rigs over where one woman is climbing into the open driver's door of the rig while two others giggle below her. Rico is more surprised than I thought he'd be. Maybe it's because I'm used to staking out the place, and, honestly, this is not much activity compared to a weekend night.

The astonishment in his voice matches my initial thoughts when I first started coming here until I noticed the pinch of a nose or tap of the arm—all signs of drug use. It makes sense if that's what it takes to visit as many truckers as they do in a night. One night, I tallied the same woman getting into ten different trucks. Unbelievable. It made me worry for her safety and if I'd never seen her again.

"I used to think so myself, but most are on drugs. It's a numbers game for their pimps. I suspect they'd have to be on something to survive this harsh life."

I glance at Rico. His expression is hard and concerned. No one wants this for their sister, daughter, cousin, or loved one. It's a terrible life for them, and with the right resources, they could get off the street, into somewhere safe, and start their life over.

"Shit." Rico nods, watching the scene unfolding before us. The parking lot is quiet once the group dissipates, with the women going with different men. "Should we be taking pictures or something?"

He scratches his head and reaches for his phone, trying to figure out what to do since it is not our agency handling this case.

"Not tonight. I have a bunch of stuff already. I wanted to see if they were the same as a week ago, but they were not. I haven't figured out exactly the rotation, but there is one."

"I hate not doing anything," he admits, and I agree.

It's a worthless feeling but necessary so that he can help me with this. Especially if I'm stuck at my parents' house, Pops would probably call Father Michael to join us and try to convert everyone in this parking lot.

The rig with the three ladies jostles back and forth as an exiting semi-truck slowly pulls through the parking lot and blocks it from our view. When it's gone, I notice one woman slipping from the truck cab. A shockwave ripples through me. It's her.

Her long brunette hair cascades down her back, flowing like silk in the faint glow of the parking lot light. With a flick of her hand, she tosses it over her shoulder, a familiar gesture sending a pang of nostalgia through my heart. My breath catches in my throat as she raises a cigarette to her lips. Her actions are so effortless, so reminiscent of the past.

Time stands still as she takes a drag from her cigarette, her face momentarily illuminated by the flickering light. In that fleeting moment, I see her features, etched with time but still undeniably her. The shape of her eyes, the curve of her smile— it's her, without a doubt.

Disbelief washes over me, mingling with a surge of conflicting emotions. My mind races, reconciling my childhood memories with the reality before me. How did she end up here in this dark underbelly of society?

Fueled by shock, concern, and a desperate need to understand, I instinctively reach for the door handle. My thigh protests with the sudden movement, but I push through the pain, urgency driving me forward as I reach for my crutches.

"What are you doing?" Rico glances at me, his brows furrowed. "Alex, what's wrong?"

I swallow hard, my voice barely above a whisper. "It's her."

10

Confusion flashes across Rico's face as I open the door and exit. I hobble toward the figure, crutches tapping against the pavement with each determined step. As I draw closer, my eyes widen with surprise. It is her. The girl who captured my heart years ago as my childhood friend and first love. And here she is, gazing at the stars and oblivious to my presence.

The weight of the past hangs heavy in the air as I make my way toward her. Rico follows close behind, his presence offering support in this unexpected encounter. Mary Ann glances in our direction, a flicker of surprise passing over her face. She stares at me momentarily, then quickly shifts her gaze to a guarded look.

"Mary Ann?"

Before I can comprehend the flood of questions raging within me, she takes a step back, a hint of defiance in her stance.

"Not interested in a threesome," she says without missing a beat. "And you don't look like you could do it, anyway."

The casual way she turns me down as if I am a potential

customer is shocking. She is a lot lizard, to use Rico's phrase, and I'm so taken aback, I don't know what to say.

She flickers her ashes onto the cold concrete and side eyes Rico.

"Now he could do the trick."

The rasp in her voice is unfamiliar. Gone is the assertive, booming tone of her previous self. Instead, this voice bears the marks of excessive alcohol, cigarettes, and a life filled with hardships, evident in the carved lines on her drawn face.

"Give me fifteen minutes, and then I'll be ready."

Rico's face contorts with disgust, and he quickly averts his gaze, his body language expressing his blatant rejection of the proposition. He steps back, distancing himself from her and her offer as if the mere suggestion taints the surrounding air.

Unbothered, she blows a long string of smoke into the night sky, dancing in the cold air until it dissipates.

I recover enough to try again. "Are you Mary Ann Higginbotham?"

Her eyes cut to mine, a renewed hardness in them. "You a cop?"

Rico and I trade glances until he blows a frustrated sigh, saying, "I'll wait in the truck."

She takes another long drag, giving me a chance to study her. Black eyeliner circles her eyes with colored rhinestones stuck to her temples. Her fake scarlet nails match the smeared lipstick staining her puckered lips. Her multicolored rabbit fur coat keeps the chill out, but her bare legs and high heels turn inward to conserve heat, signaling she's cold.

"It's me, Alex. Alexander Hamilton. We dated."

She nonchalantly lifts her chin with indifference, releasing another stream of smoke into the atmosphere above her. It pains me that she doesn't remember who I am and what we shared.

"We went to school together. My dad was the police chief back when you stole that four-wheeler."

I see the recognition flicker in her wide eyes when she grounds the cigarette under the toe of her high heel. She takes a step back, her eyes widening in disbelief.

"Alexander Hamilton. I'll be damned. You never left?" she asks, her voice tinged with surprise and curiosity.

In that instant, I realize the profound impact our divergent paths have had on our lives. She doesn't know the pain, the anger, the betrayal I felt all those years ago. And I don't know the struggles, the choices, and the circumstances that led her to this moment. This culmination led her to become a sex worker and not a famous Hollywood actress.

After endless years of pondering whether she succeeded, yearning for a glimpse of her name shining brightly, a fraction of me remained perpetually curious about her fate. Engaging in prostitution is the ultimate shocker—a role I'd never fathom for her. It's the last thing I'd want for the girl who once held my heart.

"I didn't." Emotions swirl within me, and I struggle to find my words. "Mary Ann—"

"It's Molli now. Molli with an I. Molli Sitara is my full name. Mary Ann Higginbotham is dead."

Her voice carries a frigid undertone that speaks to her past. The period following our parting of ways must have been when things were their roughest, judging by her reaction to being addressed by her given name.

"Molli with an I," I echo to myself.

Despite the similarities in her appearance, the passage of time has transformed her into someone entirely different from the girl I once adored. That carefree spirit, the girl who used to laugh with abandonment, has vanished, replaced by a weathered and guarded woman entangled in illicit activities.

Why did this happen? What events transpired to lead her

down this path? To erase the girl's name that I whispered a few nights ago. My mind races inundated with a torrent of questions demanding answers. Answers I know she won't give me under these circumstances.

"Sitara is Persian. Its means luminescent star."

A distant, dreamy expression overtakes her face while her hands gracefully sweep across the expanse above her head as if trying to connect with the stars hidden behind the low cloud coverage.

As her hands fall to her sides, I'm struck with the familiarity of that action. So many times, when she spoke of Hollywood and her name up in lights, she swept them across the sky. It makes my heart unexpectantly twist.

"That's nice, Mary—Molli."

She smiles. Her once flawlessly straight, pearly white teeth bear tobacco stains, while her upper gum appears to have been bleeding. It saddens me to witness how that once radiant smile has dulled into the shadows, mirroring the darkness that consumes her life.

"Thanks," she clips, letting the smile fade away and tugging at the sudden sadness consuming me.

"What about you, Hamilton?"

She always did call me by my last name. Only when we made love did she utter my first name in the sexiest way possible.

Her head tilts as her arms cross to keep the seeping chill out. I know I'm selfish in keeping her here, but I must know more. I must know what happened and warn her about this place's dangers. Why I'm here, and what could happen to her?

"I'm . . . I'm a police officer."

"You're a police officer?" Her sarcasm deepens. "That's expected, considering your dad is the chief. He was pretty tough on you if I remember."

I'm slow to respond. Her remembering that, but not remembering us is another punch in the gut.

"Pops is retired now."

I don't bother responding to the rest. It's unimportant, as I shake my head at how fate brought me here on this night to find her again while escaping them.

"Good."

The tension between us builds as the familiarity of old lovers fades away in my mind, replaced with a long awkward silence while I adjust my crutches.

"I need to head on." She motions to the row of trucks behind me, and my stomach turns.

"Mary—Molli, you don't have to do this." I edge closer, leaning heavily on my uninjured leg to convince her. "There are resources available, agencies that can assist women like you. Women in your situation. I can connect you with them, help you find a way out."

Her eyes flash, and her voice bristles with defiance as she challenges my words.

"Women like me? You mean hookers, prostitutes, and whores. What do you call us, Hamilton?"

I pause, realizing the weight of my words and the potential judgment they may carry. I take a deep breath, choosing the following words carefully.

"No, that's not what I meant," I reply empathetically. "I meant women who deserve support, understanding, and opportunities to create a better life. Women who have faced challenges, just like you. Women who are strong and deserve more than this life."

A sarcastic laugh escapes her lips, laden with bitter skepticism.

"Are you trying to save me?" Resentment and a hard edge line her words. "Where were you for the past decade? What gives you the right to think that you can swoop in and save me now?"

I falter momentarily, realizing the truth in her words.

"I didn't know what happened to you. Your phone was disconnected. I searched social media for your accounts, but you deleted them. You were gone. You left before graduation. But it doesn't mean I don't care." I stand straighter, letting the top of the crutch lean against the side of my body. "Come on, Molli. Surely, you can't want this for yourself."

A flicker of regret crosses her face, only to be swallowed up by hardness and life. Her gaze intensifies, and the walls around her heart reinforce with every passing second.

"Save your speeches," she retorts dismissively. "I've made my choices and live with the consequences. Don't think for a second that you can show up out of nowhere and make judgments about me. You don't know me at all, not anymore."

Truer words couldn't be spoken. I don't know her anymore. This is not the girl I used to know and love. It pains me to the core, yet I'm undeterred. I'm not ready to give up entirely.

"I'm not judging you. I understand you've been through stuff I don't know about. But you're not alone. If you change your mind, need help, or ever need someone to talk to, remember I'm here." I shuffle around on my crutches to reach my wallet and pull out my business card. "That's every way to get a hold of me."

My hand floats between us, a lifeline to a connection long since broken. Her gaze shifts between mine and the card before she reluctantly unravels an arm from her waist to accept it. The intensity of her chestnut eyes lingers on the card longer than expected, scrutinizing its presence. Eventually, they return to meet mine with a slow shake of her head.

"You have to know I won't call you."

Her body language is about self-preservation, pushing away anyone willing to help, including me. I've seen this before.

Years of disappointment and feeling abandoned by others have molded her into this person.

"I understand, but that won't stop me from being here if you need help. Take care of yourself, Molli."

She flicks the card between her fingers before stuffing it into her coat pocket.

"You too," she says, her tone devoid of emotion.

Before I say anything else, a door slams beside us as a sex worker climbs out of the cab and races over to Molli.

"Molli, we gotta get the hell outta here, now!" Her voice pierces through the night air with fear and desperation.

Without hesitation, she glances over her shoulder, the blue light on, and her eyes widen. I watch Molli and the other prostitute swiftly retreat, their footsteps echoing the urgency of their escape.

In that fleeting moment, I witnessed Molli's hardened resolve, her refusal to rely on anyone but herself. As they disappear into the shadow of the trucks, I sink into my crutches, utterly defeated.

I'm left with a mixture of emotions—sadness for the life's choice that is determined to keep her trapped, sorrow for the girl I used to know now is completely gone, and despair for hoping I offered her enough without completely scaring her off. I climb into the truck and Rico shifts in the driver's seat.

"What the hell just happened back there?" His tone is tinged with the same concern and confusion I feel.

I release a heavy sigh. My gaze fixes on the spot where we conversed, even though she's long gone. Running into the night with the other worker when they caught sight of the shining blue light.

"I don't even know, man."

My brain is scattered with images of her now compared to then. I keep wondering what happened in the last ten years to make her embrace this life over the helping hand I'm offering her.

"She goes by Molli now. Molli with an I, she said." Her mannerisms when she said it was the same girl I knew, even if everything else was entirely different. "She's not the same person."

Rico's grip on the steering wheel tightens, his knuckles turning white.

"Molli, huh? Never in a million years would I have thought I'd see her like that. She used to be so full of life, so vibrant. She talked so much about going to LA that I thought if anyone could make it, it would be her. She's almost unrecognizable and so damn skinny."

Skinny. I hadn't even acknowledged that. Too busy looking for any remnants of her in that shell of her former self. Her face is drawn. Dark shadows hang under her eyeliner-crusted eyes, accentuating the hollows of her cheekbones and the lines etched across her forehead. Once vibrant and youthful, her complexion carries a pallor that hints at drug use.

Her once athletic legs are thin, almost skeletal, forcing the contours of her knees to push out unnaturally. Clusters of purple veins on her pale skin interrupt some faded bruising on both thighs, signaling physical abuse.

"Fuck." Why did she have to be so damn stubborn when I offered my help? "She didn't trust me. It's like that was Mary Ann standing there, but it wasn't. She's given up. Given up on any chance of finding a way out."

Rico collapses in his seat, his eyes fixed straight ahead, looking out the windshield.

"We've seen this before. This darkness. It's no different for her. This world has swallowed her whole. It's consumed her."

"She looks like she's on drugs," I voice another worry.

"I agree."

A heavy silence fills the cab. Through all my years on the

force and encountering enough to know addicts only get help when they want it. However, I've never had someone I care about be an addict. I've seen how addiction tears apart families. Good families want the best for their loved ones, while the addicts are looking for their next fix. The very nature of addiction is destructive. My head falls against the seat as Rico makes eye contact with me.

"Why wouldn't she let me help her? Why can't she see I'm still a friend? Do you know she didn't even acknowledge what we were? I saw recognition on her face only when I mentioned the four-wheeler."

That fucking hurt. My first love doesn't even remember me in that way. It's like she shot me in the heart when her vacant gaze met mine.

"Sometimes, people get so lost they forget what hope looks like. They become suspicious of it to where they stop believing in the good of humanity. It's tragic, but it's their reality."

I shake my head, unwilling to believe she'll become another addict prostitute statistic.

"I know you don't want to think she's in that category, but from what I saw, she is," he continues with a grim expression.

"I can't stand by and do nothing," I retort, my voice filled with a hint of determination. "There has to be something I can do. Someone I can reach out to talk to her or convince her somehow. Do you remember what happened to her parents? The mom and stepdad?"

"Whoa, hold on." Rico's hand grips the console. "I know you want to help her. But you can't just charge after her and demand she change all this. I know it's fucked up, and I completely agree, but you can't force someone that's not ready or willing. And getting her family involved will surely cause her to run away. You know that house must have been fucked up if she was always running the streets. You were with her. Did you ever go to her house?"

"No."

"Exactly. Hell, if I know where they are at. I can drive by their old house tomorrow, but I don't think they're here anymore. I thought they moved away some years back."

"I don't know. All I remember is asking her stepdad at graduation where she was, and he glared at me before saying she's gone and good riddance."

I used to drive by their house in the following weeks, looking for any sign that she had returned when her number stopped working and she deleted her socials. I eventually stopped doing it to preserve my heart and repair my damaged ego.

"I just can't help but feel like I failed. Like I should have done more."

Rico places a hand on my forearm, a small act of comfort.

"You did what you could tonight. She took your card when she could have tossed it on the ground. It's a start. And we'll keep coming out here. Try to keep an eye on her. It's all we can do at this point."

I nod, acknowledging Rico's words, yet a part of me still yearns for a different outcome. As Rico starts the truck, the engine roaring to life, I can't help but stare at that damn blue light flashing like a beacon to the truckers pulling out of here in record concession. Uncertain whether he notices it since he says nothing about the bustle of activity as we pull out of the parking lot ourselves. The whole reason we came tonight is tossed out the window at the discovery of Molli reentering my life.

Maybe that was a premonition the other night. A calling to me to save another, as I needed saving myself that night. Perhaps I will meet with Father Michael and talk about redemption.

11

"You came in late last night," Pops's voice cuts through the silence in the truck as I settle into the worn passenger seat, the familiar scent of aged leather mingling with Armor All.

His mouth is set in a line. More disapproval because Mom waited up for me, worrying like she did when I was younger. Mom's habit of waiting up for me caused Pops to do the same, disrupting the entire house.

"As I told you last night, we went to Twin Peaks in Colorado Springs. It takes time to get back."

He knows this, having grumbled about us 'boys wanting to see half-naked women' while making my mom worry.

"Is that the only place you were?"

It's always a balancing act with Pops. Say too little, and he digs for more. Say too much, and you get the lecture. I'm not in the mood for either. I was already terrible company with Rico last night. He said as much over wings. He knew I was rattled by seeing Mary—Molli again, after all these years, giving me a pass and holding most of the conversation on his own.

"What's this about, Pops?" I erase the frustration from my tone, even as it surges through my body.

His eyes cut to mind briefly as his weathered hands cut the steering wheel to the right, heading to my physical therapy appointment.

"You boys running the streets isn't wise, considering you have tomorrow's investigation interview. Best not to run them again tonight. Need a sharp head to recall the events from that night."

His disapproval drowns every word. This is Police Chief Alan Hamilton talking now. His modus operandi is to blend chief dad and regular dad, so it's part scolding and part concerning.

"I hardly consider getting a couple of beers, running the streets," I mutter, gazing out the window at the buildings dotting this part of the medical campus. "Besides, Rico's on duty tonight, so you're stuck with me."

A monotone hum escapes his chest. An acknowledgment that he heard me but doesn't weigh in on it being good or bad, that he's stuck with me. My joke falls flat.

The bench seat of the old truck bounces with each divot in the road, causing my body to take unexpected hits. Why he drove me in this beat-up old farm truck with blown shocks is beyond me. Maybe Dani could look at it and fix it up for a more comfortable ride if he continues to take me to therapy in it.

"Your mother's making a roast and cobbler. Since you can't help in the kitchen, maybe you can spend time with her watching one of her shows," he volunteers, moving his arm to drape against the back glass of the cab.

By shows, he means her soap operas or her romance movies. Both warrant a bullet to my head, but it's the least I can do while they're taking care of me. Pops usually uses this time to work on his ship in a bottle, a recent hobby he has taken up in retirement.

Now I'm the one humming at him. More silence ensues until I realize he might know more about Molli leaving town than I do. Maybe she was trying to escape the law, which would explain her sudden departure.

"Pops, do you remember when I took old man Miller's four-wheeler into town and crashed it into the fountain?"

Once the sutures healed, I had to do countless hours of community service to fix the fountain. Pops suggested to the town mayor that the stone could be resurfaced. He wanted to make an example out of me. Even the police chief's kid gets a stiff punishment to discourage other teenagers from acting out.

"I do. It's a shame they took it down and replaced it with a statue. All that hard work of yours is gone," he says, his voice both firm and empathetic.

Once I fixed and restored the fountain, Pops would brag to everyone he could about the workmanship. Little did they know, he supervised the entire process and wouldn't let me cut corners, no matter how hard I tried.

"I also remember you lied."

Taking a deep breath, I wrestle with telling him the truth now or seeing how this plays out. I go with the latter.

"Lied? Why would you think that?" I keep my voice neutral with a hint of surprise not to overplay my hand.

He doesn't answer immediately. Instead, he turns into the parking lot and hunts for a spot to pull into before putting the truck in gear. Once parked, he turns to me, those hazel flakes dancing in the morning light streaming in the window.

"Son, anyone could see you were over the moon for that girl. You worked several summers at Mr. Miller's farm. The last thing you'd do is steal a piece of his equipment. I knew it was her, but then you got your chest all puffed out like a peacock at the hospital, saying you did it and were by yourself. The evidence didn't match."

I hold Pops's gaze, my surprise genuine yet carefully

restrained. I had indeed proclaimed my guilt in that hospital room, a desperate attempt to shield Molli from the consequences of her actions, but I hadn't considered Pops doubting my confession. That's what being young, dumb, and in love does.

"Why didn't you ever say anything?" I gaze upon his weathered face, searching for answers, when an easy smile appears.

"When you raise a kid, watch him grow, make mistakes and see his character take shape, you know it's not just about the evidence. It's about the kid. Something didn't add up, but you were insistent, so I made your punishment much harder. Hoping you'd break and confess. You never did."

I take in his words, letting them sink in. Pops had seen through my façade and recognized the contradiction between my actions and the person he knew me to be. It makes me both grateful for his perceptiveness and regretful that I lied and continue to lie to his face.

"I'm sorry, Pops," I finally apologize over a decade later. "I didn't want her to suffer the consequences. I thought I was doing the right thing by protecting her."

The hand that drapes along the back of the seat clutches my shoulder, silently expressing his acknowledgment and acceptance of my apology.

"It's all right, Alex. I understood your intentions back then," he says, imparting his paternal wisdom. "But sometimes, the greatest way we can help others is by allowing them to face the consequences of their actions. It's a hard lesson, one I reckon you've learned yourself."

That statement right there sums up my life with Pops. I didn't always understand his ways, but now I do. Harsh, firm, or unyielding, it was done out of love. All the times I grumbled about him being too hard on me, preaching about taking the high road, leading by example, actions speak louder than words, you reap what you sow, or being the fisherman of men, all dovetail into how he expresses love. Not openly and sometimes smothering like Mom, but imparting quiet wisdom and strategic consequences. It's as if he opened the good book and transferred all the lessons to me in his way.

I sit dumbfounded, my gaze moving away from his to stare out the windshield as the medical personnel pass by. Not a man of many words but is very well-versed in the complexities of human relationships and the importance of accountability. Pops's grip on my shoulder tightens momentarily, a silent affirmation of his support before it slides off to reach for the engine keys.

"What about redemption?" I ask something that has been bothering me since I saw her last night. Something I was going to ask Father Michael, but I prefer Pops's take on it instead. "Where does it fit into all this? Can someone truly find redemption after causing so much harm?"

Pops leans back in his seat. His gaze fixes on me. The weight of my question hangs in the air, chasing away old memories and the new understanding of them.

"Redemption," he begins, his expression hardening. "It isn't a destination that you arrive at. It's a journey. A path marked by remorse, forgiveness, and a commitment to change."

I listen intently, even though doubts fill my thoughts. She was not inclined to accept the help I offered her last night. She was skeptical and wary of my help, causing her to abruptly end our conversation and hurry off with the other woman beckoning her.

"We've all got darkness inside us," Pops continues. "It's what we choose to do with that darkness that defines us. Redemption isn't about erasing the past or pretending it didn't happen. It's about accepting the weight of our actions, seeking forgiveness, and striving to make amends."

I nod my mind in overdrive, trying to absorb everything before I sort through it and apply it to her. Or at least absorb enough to become a supportive friend for Molli, to be here and help her find her path toward redemption.

"And you . . . have you had to do this?" I ask from both a place of curiosity and yearning.

Pops's gaze is unwavering, boring into me. "I still am doing it, and it's not quick or easy. It takes time and effort to reckon with the past, face your mistakes, and make things right. I don't believe anyone is beyond hope or too far gone to be saved. It boils down to how hard they want it or not. That's what you have got to ask yourself. It will also carry you through when times get tough, and you want to quit. Life isn't roses blooming all year, but if you're lucky, they'll bloom once a season."

The path to redemption is complex. It requires introspection, perseverance, and a willingness to confront the darkest corners of our souls. Would Molli be willing to do this? Leave the darkness that is her world behind to start new again, start over in her hometown? If only I knew why she left.

"Hope is a powerful thing, son. It can light the way even in the darkest of times. Remember, you're not alone on this journey. We all stumble and fall, but it's in getting back up and continuing forward that we find strength." Pops nods, and I forgot he thinks we're talking about me.

"Thank you, Pops. I needed to hear that. I needed to know there's hope, even when things seem impossible."

Even though I'm not seeking redemption for myself, my words are still valid. Saving Molli seems like an impossible task. How do I save someone that doesn't want to be saved?

12

The days blur into an endless cycle of Mom and Pops's daily lives, continuing as usual, with me orbiting on the fringes. Mom's schedule is busier than ever with her bridge group, church service twice a week, organ and choir practice, gardening, baking, and making more food than we can eat. She's steadily filling the garage fridge with a plethora of dishes shrouded in Tupperware and marked with labels on what it is and how to reheat it for when I go home.

Pops continues his shipbuilding, walking with his neighbors in the morning and sometimes stopping for coffee and a donut before heading home. When he's not putzing out in the garage or his workshop, he's driving me to rehab and my doctor's appointments in that bumpy old truck. He flatly refuses to have Dani look at it. It's an ego thing.

"I've worked on cars since before you were born. I don't need to waste my money on someone else doing my work," he blusters when I suggest it.

Beyond that, I spend my time doing the same four things. Eating far too much, going to rehab, watching Mom's soap operas with her, and thinking about Molli. When Pops asked me to do it the night she made the roast and cobbler, I felt obligated because of 'running the streets' with Rico. When she patted the couch the next night, I didn't have the heart to turn her down, and that's been the pattern ever since once the dishes were washed and put away.

Despite Pops's warning about running the streets again, I haven't seen Rico again. Being two officers down, coupled with the existing shortage and Matt's funeral today, has him working extra shifts. He's checked in with me, the same as Eli, Dani, Isla, and even Tomlin once. I expect that will change when I'm home after the funeral today.

"You look nice, dear."

Preoccupied with the button on my cuff, I don't hear Mom behind me. Our eyes catch in the long mirror in the Narthex of the Church. Hers well with pride, as do her rosy cheeks. This look is familiar to me, having seen it at my high school graduation, college, and the police academy.

She'd insist on smashing herself between Pops and me, as we are both our dress blues and taking a picture if the circumstances were different. For posterity's sake, she'd always say, then frame and hang it in the hallway wall with the others.

The day I've dreaded and wished for all at once is here. Guilt lives in the pit of my stomach. As much as I want to finish this day, I can't ignore the overwhelming need to pay my respects to Matt's family, whisper I'm sorry, and hope his widow can forgive me for my failures.

"You ready, son?" Pops removes his peaked hat and stows it under his arm while adjusting his white gloves.

"Yes, sir."

I copy his actions, except I hand my hat to Mom and adjust my crutches to follow behind them. Mom tucks her hand into the crook of Pops's elbow as the line shuffles toward Matt's open casket.

Mourners pay their respects to Matt as they fill the adorned church, overflowing its pews. The air is heavy with a somber ambiance, punctuated by the sorrowful melodies played by a lone violinist in the upper balcony, resonating deep within my soul and intensifying my grief and guilt.

As I navigate down the long aisle, I can't help but notice the sea of law enforcement officers present, representing various agencies that Matt had served alongside during his brief career. The sight of their stoic expressions, clenched jaws, and rigid posture further emphasizes the weight of the loss.

The officers stand shoulder to shoulder, forming a solemn guard of honor, their presence respecting the loss of Matt's life and the impact his death has on the law enforcement community. Their badges, adorned with black bands, are a visual reminder of the sacrifice made in the line of duty.

While we continue shuffling forward, my heartbeat grows louder in my ears, drowning out the hushed conversations and muffled sobs around me. The weight of guilt settles heavily upon my shoulders, each step toward my friend's casket feeling like an arduous journey through my remorse.

The air becomes hot and heavy as if the entire room judges me and silently questions if I did everything I could to save him. When I chance a glance away from the mourner's line in front of me, darted glances and sympathetic expressions meet me, intensifying my sorrow.

As we draw nearer to Matt's casket, the image becomes clearer, etching itself into my memory with painful precision. Seeing the American flag draped meticulously over the polished wood strikes a deep chord within me. It symbolizes sacrifice, duty, and the ultimate price paid to serve others. And in this moment, it represents the chasm between the man I thought I was and the reality of who I am.

Pops and Mom approach first, her hand slipping from his arm as he steps ahead, his movements deliberate and filled with a sense of duty. His posture is straight and unwavering as he snaps his gloved hand to his eye, saluting the fallen officer. It's beautifully done with grace and dignity.

Mom joins him, reaching out a trembling hand and brushing her fingers against the smooth surface of the casket, her lips moving in silent prayer. Pops stands beside her, his weathered face etched with sorrow and reverence.

When Mom finishes her prayer, she clenches my hat tighter and moves to the side with Pops, waiting for me to take my turn. A lump forms in my throat, making it difficult to breathe. The physical ache in my chest mirrors the lingering effects of my wounds, now paling compared to this loss.

I fight to maintain my composure, to hold back the torrent of grief that threatens to consume me. But the battle is futile as my vision blurs and tears stream down my face. The saltiness lingers on my lips.

The memory of that fateful gunfight flashes before my eyes. The deafening sound of gunfire, the chaos ensuing, and the desperate scramble for cover.

Matt, my colleague, and my friend, lies motionless before me, his face peaceful in eternal slumber. I bow my head and whisper, "I'm sorry, Matt. I wish it were me instead. Forgive me for failing you."

As I draw away from the casket, I straighten, lean on my good leg, and salute him as Pops did. A profound emptiness settles in my chest as I maneuver toward Mom. Pops stands aside to let me proceed down the side aisle, inching past fellow officers waiting their turn. When we reach our pew, I hobble toward our seats and settle in.

The service is long, with colleagues sharing stories and remembrances of him. The music and church choir are perfectly somber in their delivery, and the scent of lilies fills the air from the floral sprays blanketing the altar. Mom pats my knee at different times throughout the service, understanding how difficult this is because she has had to sit through these before.

Time seems suspended until the pallbearers appear from the side of the altar, awaiting their duties as the two priests close the coffin lid and adjust the flag to drape wholly across it.

In perfectly coordinated steps, the pallbearers shuffle down each side, meticulously placed and lifting in time with the music. Rico's brown eyes hold mine, an unspoken apology in them before they move on to the priest and processional, starting down the center aisle.

As the casket passes eye level, I bow my head and pray for strength, healing, and resilience for the family. Mom's hand rubs circles in the center of my back as the sounds of shuffled footsteps continue.

Sarah's quiet sobs mingle with the baby's cries she cradles when I lift my head. The weight of her sorrow is palpable and stabs my heart at the long and difficult road ahead of her. Family clusters around the two, protective and shared in the anguish marring their faces.

The scene is raw and intense, causing more of my tears to fall. The pews are empty, guided by the ushers to follow the processional as the final hymn ends. Once the parishioners spill onto the church lawn, hugs are exchanged, and words of comfort are offered while they load the casket into the hearse.

"It was a beautiful service," Mom whispers behind me, her hand sliding over my back comfortingly.

"I'll bring the car around," Pops says, striding by us with his keys already in hand.

"I'll go too," I murmur, working the crutches to catch up with him. He casts me a side glance but otherwise says nothing, which I appreciate. The service was beautiful, overwhelming, and stifling. The cold winter air brings respite against the sweat rolling down my back in the warm church and clinging to my shirt every time Mom rubs me there.

"You're awfully quiet, Alexander?" Pops finally says when we are out of earshot of everyone. "You handling everything all right?"

I'm not sure if this is a continuation of the redemption conversation we had earlier this week, but ever since, Pops has been more observant than usual. I release a long breath and stop, balancing on the crutches as I gaze past his shoulder at Matt's wife touching the flag-draped coffin before they close the hearse's back door. Her sorrow stirs a deep sadness that I can't put into words.

"I don't know."

Pops's eyes meet mine, a mixture of concern and understanding in his gaze when he places a hand on my shoulder.

"It's a hard day following a hard week."

The hardest week of my life, if I am being honest, second only to losing Mary Ann and not knowing what happened to her.

"Losing both a friend and colleague while recovering from injuries yourself. It's enough to make any man crater under the weight of their regrets." His gaze is laser focused when I look at him as if he knows exactly what I've thought since I awoke from surgery. "It takes time to sort through it all."

Time is all I have ahead of me.

"I just can't shake the feeling that I'm responsible for everything that's happened. It should be me in that box, not him," I confess, my voice laced with remorse.

His head shakes slowly with a grim expression. "It wasn't your gun that fired the bullet that took that boy's life. It was the suspect's. No matter the reason, God called him home, and not you. It wasn't your time," he says sternly as if both worried that I'd take my life and discouraging me from doing so at the same time.

"You see, son, life has a way of throwing curveballs at us. We make choices based on what we know at the time, but we can't predict or control every outcome. Matt's passing is a tragedy, but it wasn't your fault. You were a friend who cared deeply and did what you had to do to save lives, yours included."

I appreciate his compassion even if I don't feel worthy of it.

"Blaming yourself won't bring Matt back and won't help you find the peace you need to return to the job. What matters now is how you choose to move forward, honor Matt's memory, and find healing within yourself."

My crutch slips forward, distracting me from responding to him.

"Now, let's go get your mother. We've left her on the curb long enough," he finishes with a pat on my arm before switching his hat to the other hand to unlock the car.

I close the distance to the back door, having gotten good at figuring out a system for getting in without banging my healing leg. Once I'm settled, Pops pulls out and heads to the front of the church.

13

The mournful notes of Taps fill the air from the bugler playing across the gravesite. The haunting melody elicits more tears from the mourners. The crisp sound of military footsteps echoes through the cemetery, signaling the arrival of the honor guard. They stand in perfect formation, their uniforms gleaming in the sunshine, each holding a rifle—a final salute to Matt's bravery and service.

I watch as the honor guard proceeds with precision, their practiced movements a testament to their dedication. They raise their rifles, pointing them skyward in unison. The 21-gun salute is a deafening crack of gunfire pierces the air. Each shot echoes through the peaceful cemetery and sends birds scattering from the trees into the sky.

The Captain of the Guard presents the folded flag to Sarah while we stand in silence. Tears stream down her face as she accepts the flag, cradling it to her chest while her mother holds the baby.

I clear my throat and wipe my eyes while the priest makes the sign of the cross over the casket for the last time. The family stands to lay flowers on top of it and says their final goodbyes.

Sarah is the first with her flower, grief-stricken and hovering over the casket, sobbing. Her father, retired military in his crisp uniform, collects her in his arms and escorts her away.

As they draw near, I separate myself from the semi-circle formed around the tent for all those that wouldn't fit to have a moment with her. I approach her cautiously. The crutches thud the hard ground with each step. I can't imagine her pain, the void in her life, and the new struggle of raising a baby alone.

Sarah's eyes meet mine, swollen and red, filled with pain and devastation. Her father practically holds her up, her mom on the other side, snuggling her baby boy against the chilly air.

My voice quivers as I speak, struggling to find the right words. "Sarah, I . . . I'm so sorry for your loss. Matt, he was . . ."

Her expression softens momentarily, a glimmer of understanding mingling with her pain.

"Alex, thank you for being there for him," she whispers, her voice quivering." He always spoke highly of you, and I know how much he cherished your friendship."

Tears well up in her eyes again, threatening to spill over, and her hand tightens on her father's arm.

"I promise you, Sarah," I respond, my voice steady with determination. "I'll do whatever it takes to support you and the baby, just like Matt would have wanted."

A small smile appears on her grief-stricken face.

"Thank you. I appreciate your support, and I know Matt would have to. We're all here for each other." Her eyes glisten when she leans forward to give me a loose hug. "Please know that I am also praying for you and your recovery."

My grasp barely reaches around her shoulders before she withdraws and turns toward her father. A silent understanding that it's time to leave. I nod at him and then her mother as they pass, watching as they depart into a series of limousines with the rest of the family trailing behind.

"I need a beer," Rico murmurs from my left side.

The rim of his peaked hat is pulled down to shade his eyes against the sun. He's tugging off his gloves to hold in his hand, slapping them against his open palm. It's his way of releasing some of the anxiety coming off him in waves. Being a pall-bearer is challenging under ordinary circumstances, but this funeral takes it to another level, given the grandeur and cere-monial rituals associated with the burial of a fallen officer.

"Yeah, I could go for one."

"Mama Hamilton said you could escape so long as I bring you home in one piece. Your dad had to remind her that you're going home today. She wasn't happy. I think she wants you to stay longer," he says, with a tinge of humor.

"She wants me to stay forever," I mutter, touching the brim of my hat as a passing gesture to other officers leaving the gravesite.

"True, maybe I'll move in, eat home-cooked meals and sneak girls in the back," he jokes, bringing levity to the situa-tion. It's a welcome break from my cyclically depressing thoughts.

"Be my guest, but Pops will meet you in the hallway in the middle of the night to stop you."

I think back to that one night when Pops almost caught Molli as she came out of the hall bathroom and ran to my bedroom. She ducked in the closet when we heard his footsteps creak on the old floor by my closed bedroom door. I faked being asleep, but we both knew I wasn't. He never said anything. He just glared at me across the breakfast table as Mom chatted about the upcoming Harvest Festival.

"All right then, let's get out of here."

Rico strides toward the large parking lot on the other side of the cemetery while the remaining mourners disperse, scat-tering all over the lawns, crying, hugging, and exchanging last words. I'm steadily following behind him, getting pretty fast using my crutches. Being sticklers for proper etiquette, Mom and Pops attend the reception at Sarah's parents' house immediately following the burial.

When I catch up to Rico, he's already in the truck, the engine humming and the warm exhaust creating a cloud of smoke as it hits the cold air. I hand him the crutches and hoist myself into the passenger seat, settling in as I take off my hat and place it on the dashboard.

"We probably shouldn't go to any of the obvious places to drink," I say to Rico, sounding eerily like my parents. A slight pang of guilt tugs at me for escaping obligation and respect to get drunk with my buddy. "It wouldn't look good, you know."

Rico puts the truck in gear before casting me a curious look as the engine rumbles beneath us.

"That hasn't stopped you before, so why are you worrying about it now?" His tone is skeptical as his black eyebrow twists above his left eye.

"Just doesn't seem right, is all." I glance out of the window. The blue sky is bright, endless, and full of hope—opposite of the dark gloom that's settled into me.

"Okay." He navigates out of his parking spot, careful of the people flooding into it to make their way to the reception. "Any suggestions on where we should go?"

I think for a second. Nothing comes to mind until I snap my fingers. "Got it. There's this dive bar I know of. Never been, but I know someone that's a regular."

With his curiosity piqued, he asks, "In town? What's the name of it?"

I give a half-hearted shrug. "Honestly, I don't know. Something Donkey. The neon broke off in the last snowstorm and only says Donkey now."

The skepticism on his face is clear as he swipes a hand over his short haircut before pulling onto the open road.

"It's over on 115."

"By the prison?"

"Yeah, that's the one," I confirm, leaning back in the seat as we drive. The familiar sights of Cañon City pass by. Its scenic beauty contrasts the dive bar we're headed to. I can't help but feel a twinge of irony at the situation.

"You really know how to pick 'em, man. A dive bar by the prison? Sounds like the perfect place to drown your sorrows unseen by reputation people."

I chuckled dryly. "Yeah, sometimes the most unexpected places offer a little solace."

As we approach the outskirts of town, the neon glow of the bar's sign comes into view, flickering with broken letters. Sure enough, all that remains is the word 'Donkey' illuminated in the pale glow of the day. Rico parks the truck, and we exchange glances before he opens the black door.

"Alright, Donkey, something it is," he says with a smirk. "Let's hope they've got something stronger than their neon lights."

"Let's hope."

Upon pushing open the creaky door, the air is filled with the pungent scent of stale beer and cigarettes. The jukebox plays a blend of country and classic rock, providing the backdrop to the scene. Scattered around the bar, only a few patrons occupy the space, each lost in their thoughts, nursing their drinks solemnly.

Rico and I find an empty spot at the worn-out counter, the bartender giving us a nod of acknowledgment before drying some beer mugs. I lean against the bar and scan the room, searching for a temporary distraction.

The bartender approaches a gruff-looking man with a no-nonsense attitude. "What'll it be, boys?"

Rico leans in, a mischievous glint in his eyes. "Whiskey, my friend. Make it strong enough to knock the socks off a cowboy."

I chuckle and add, "I'll have a cold beer, something local if you've got it."

The bartender plops an empty bowl on the bar top before us and pours peanuts out of a canister before wandering away.

"Do you want to try my nuts?" Rico grabs a handful and pauses before throwing them into his mouth. "That didn't come out right."

I merely shake my head at his nonsense and look at the long mirror on the back wall behind the various liquor bottles.

The bartender slides our drinks across the counter, his eyes reflecting the weariness of the place. We raise our glasses in a silent toast before taking a sip, the familiar burn of the alcohol offering temporary relief.

"Damn, Hamilton, you really clean up," Dani says, catching Rico off guard and causing him to choke on his mouthful of peanuts. She slaps his back and pushes the bowl away while he's coughing and spewing fragments into his hand. "Hasn't anyone ever told you not to eat the nuts? They're full of piss, knucklehead."

He spins around on his barstool to Dani's hands, now planted on her hips, with her ample chest about to spill over her tiny shirt and her hair in ponytails on the sides of her head. It takes me back to the day I met her on the side of the road with that fake accent. She rolls her eyes as the remnants of coughing and clearing his throat ebb away.

"Choking on nuts, Rico. Don't worry, you'll get it with a little more practice," she finishes. She's always been straightforward and sharp-tongued, never one to mince words. Rico's eyes are watering as he reaches for a napkin to wipe his hand and mouth.

"What are you doing here?" I ask when her eyes move from glaring at him to staring at my crutches and then my leg, even though it appears normal under my dress blues.

"Getting food." Her tone drips with disdain, as if I'm a

knucklehead, too, for asking. "So, what's the occasion that you two losers are drinking in full uniform in the middle of the day in my bar? Hiding out or something?"

I glance at Rico, exchanging a knowing look before he replies with his hand over his heart. "You could say that. Just a couple of lost souls seeking solace in the company of good friends."

"Don't bullshit me," she huffs, turning to face me when she doesn't like his retort. "Tell me why you're here."

Her big blue eyes are a mixture of concern and annoyance —the former for me, the latter for him.

"Our buddy's funeral was today. Rico was a pallbearer," I answer, the guilt and remorse surging forward again as her eyebrows raise and she plays with her tongue piercing. Rico leans forward as if trying to get a clearer look at it.

"So, you're hiding out."

I don't reply either way. Hiding out is accurate. Hiding, avoiding, delaying, you name it, I'm doing it. Strangely, Rico doesn't comment, content enough to watch her.

"Well, you've come to the right place. Just don't expect any heartfelt conversations or life-changing revelations here. This is a dive bar, not a therapy session."

She raises a finger to the bartender at the end of the bar to flag him over. Rico leans closer, his voice low and filled with amusement.

"Oh, believe me, we wouldn't have it any other way. The last thing we need is someone getting all touchy-feely."

Dani snorts and gestures toward the sparse patrons scattered across the dimly lit bar.

"Trust me, lover boy, nobody here's getting touchy-feely with your ass unless it involves slipping drugs into their drink. So, enjoy the low standards of your prospects."

I chuckle. Once again, Dani waltzes in and changes the dynamics in an instant. It's not the classiest establishment, but it's precisely what we need right now—a place to let loose, enjoy our drinks and forget reality for a while.

"Ah, the low standards of my prospects. Truly, I couldn't ask for more," he replies, his voice dripping with sarcasm.

She forcefully wedges herself between us to place her to-go order with the bartender, clearly requesting an excessive amount of food for just one individual. The bartender, taken aback by the size of the order, raises an eyebrow but diligently takes notes.

"How is a little one like you going to eat all that?"

Rico gets brave in questioning her when the bartender walks away to ring the bell and shove the order through the pass thru at the end of the bar.

She elbows him hard, a loud "oomph" passing from his lips before she replies, "Move your ass over. Didn't no one teach you to give up your seat for a lady?"

"A lady? Where's she at?" he challenges with his hand pressed to his side. Her ponytails fly around so fast they hit her cheeks when she looks at me.

"Hamilton, you better tell Casanova over here to move, or so help me, I'll deck the ugly right off his face."

Her angry eyes glare at me while Rico smiles in the background and remains unmoved. He's developing a real hard-on for her, and I'm caught in the middle.

"Come on, man."

I wave a dismissive hand, and he acquiescence by sliding over one bar stool but wedges it against hers. Dani overlooks that part as she sits on the stool, casting dirty looks at him.

"Fucker, it's no wonder you can't get anyone with that shitty non-chivalrous attitude," she directs at him before swiping my beer and drinking half of it. Then she belches and laughs about it without saying, "Excuse me." Rico's eyes widen, not fully believing this petite woman is more a man than he and I are.

"Can you stop breathing down my neck? It's like sitting next to a horny dog."

"Speaking of horny dogs, I'm going to go handle business," Rico says, staring at Dani's chest a little too long for my comfort.

"I hope you get a skin burn from rubbing too hard."

He leaves to jerk or piss. I don't know which and don't care.

"Now that we got rid of the annoying gnat, what's happening with you? Wait." She holds up a hand, bangs on the bar stop, and hollers to bring us a couple of soft drinks. "Drinking in uniform is trashy. Do it at home. Now spill your guts."

Her tone leaves no room for negotiation as she plucks the beer from my hand and sets it by the nuts.

"Nothing's going on. I've been keeping you up to date on everything."

I look into her ocean eyes, avoiding getting into the deep stuff like my part in Matt's death, my rehab is going slower than I thought, and running into Molli after a decade of not seeing or hearing from her.

"That face doesn't say nothing. It says I'm a sad fucker sitting in a bar getting hammered when I should be at someone's house eating crappy food and watching sad people cry."

She pauses long enough for the bartender to drop our drinks and walk away. I'd much prefer my beer, but maybe she's right. Getting drunk in uniform will only add to the whispers around town if anyone sees me leave this dive bar.

"You sad about your friend? Sad about your leg? Sad about your job? Sad about that chick? What?"

She cuts through it all, spot on with all my doubts.

Before I can answer, she continues, "Look, we may not be as close as you and that man-child you insist on hanging around with, but we're friends. And given that I lost my best friend, I might be in the market for a new one."

She doesn't bother looking at me, instead bites her fingernail and spits it on the floor.

Confused by this sudden revelation, I ask, "You're not talking to Eli anymore? Why? What happened there?"

Her chin darts up, dead staring at me.

"Eli? No, we're good, better than good, in fact. He's practically family. I'm talking about . . . never mind." She makes a face, and I still don't know who she's talking about. "Long story. Whatever. But this is about you, not me. So, spill your guts."

I shake my head, my eyes drifting away from hers to categorize my thoughts and what I should talk to her about. The thing about Dani is that she can handle almost anything. She wouldn't shy away if I wanted to discuss my doubts. Her tough-as-nails attitude takes some getting used to, but she's mentally solid.

"Well? I don't have all day," she demands before taking a long gulp.

"I saw her," I mutter, unsure why I picked that topic over all the others weighing on my mind. Her eyebrows wrinkle in confusion. "The woman I mentioned in the hospital."

That lights her up, and she adjusts in her seat, throwing her ankle over her knee as she spins the stool to face me.

"Mary Ann Higginbotham?" Surprise coats her words. "Is that right?"

I slowly shake my head, still uneasy about Mary Ann wiping away the past when she changed her name and not remembering me.

"She goes by Molli Sitara now," I say with sadness in my voice. Dani picks up on it right away and kicks the leg of my stool. I look down to see if it's on accident, and she does it again.

"Stop sulking because that seems like a good thing. You can rekindle whatever you had." She pauses, the wrinkle between her brows deepening when she adds, "Unless she's married.

That's a no-go. Ya, hear me. We agree not to mess with married women."

"She not married," I say flatly. I don't know exactly if that's true, as I assumed she's not married, given her line of work.

"Okay, then, what's the deal? Why did she change her name? Did she go all Hollywood and stuff? I heard they make you change your name if your real one sucks, but Molli Si-whatever doesn't sound any better than Mary Ann Higgin-botham. Well, maybe shorter, but yeah, not better."

"I'm unsure how her name changed or why. We didn't have a chance to talk."

I look away, the faded posters on the wall behind Dani catching my attention as I think back to our sudden and brief conversation.

"If Molli—"

"You're telling her about the lot lizard?" Rico's voice booms behind Dani, causing her to jump in her seat, and she spins around to punch him in the chest, which releases a grunt from him.

"You fucking scared me, asshole," she yells before returning to me and casting a dirty look over her shoulder at him. "I swear, why is he here? If you need someone to drown your sorrows with, then call me and Lars. We'll hang out, but this guy has to go."

She huffs, tossing her ponytail behind her while he blows kisses at the back of her head. If she sees him, she'll pummel him to death.

"Lot lizard? Who's a lot lizard?" she questions, her expression fierce as the words fly with accusation at me.

"Can we stop using that term? It's offensive," I say, mainly to Rico, as he's the one that started with it the other night. Dani's face remains unchanged. Offensive, not offensive. I don't think she cares either way. She's the last person who is politically correct in this world and the last person to care to be.

"Molli's a prostitute? Is that what I'm hearing?" Her face is a mask of confusion, studying my blank face and searching for answers. When she doesn't find any, she turns on the barstool to look at Rico. "Is she?"

"It appears so. We saw her the other night, working."

Surprisingly, Rico dials down the volume when he responds, looking at me with sympathy.

Dani hunches and looks away, the questions popping up on her face as they process through her mind until she finally says, "Well, shit."

Well, shit is about right. I don't know what to make of it. I immediately hate it. I don't want it to be true, but I can't deny what we saw. I can't imagine what she's gone through to make this all right. To make her want to do it unless she's in debt with a pimp or on drugs and is selling herself to feed her habit.

"Wait, how do you know this? Where did you see her at? Downtown or—"

"The same truck stop where you saved Isla," I murmur, watching a myriad of emotions cross her face, which usually only occurs whenever Isla comes up.

"Holy shit."

Her eyes are bigger than I've ever seen when she looks at me. Her mouth opens long enough for me to see her barbell piercing until she covers it with her hand.

"Order's up," the bartender announces, setting the to-go food on the bar top in front of her while she's aghast. She continues staring at me as she pulls some money from her pocket to throw on top of the bill and waves the guy off when he mentions getting change.

"I gotta go. Lars and Tomlin are waiting for me, but don't think we're not talking about this. Are you going to go back out there? Convince her to stop or something? Hell, save her like I did with Isla. I mean, if she has a dude forcing her to do this? Man, it's rare that someone blows my mind, but damn, you sure did." Her words are fast and rushed, a stream of consciousness. "Wait, I'm sorry. Let me say that first. It's got to hurt, and that sucks. When are you going home?"

She finally looks at Rico, who has remained quiet, the seriousness of the situation keeping his usual jovial manner silenced.

"Today. Rico is dropping me off today, and his truck is already packed," I answer as her worried eyes turn back to me.

"Alone, or will he be staying with you? If you need me to stay, I could shuffle some things around . . . "

That line is back between her brows as she thinks through her options.

"I appreciate it, Dani. I do, but I'm looking forward to going home alone. Having my space and privacy back, not to mention my bed. I hope you understand."

I try to let her down gently, as I don't want to offend her, and she slowly nods.

"Yeah, I get it. I'm glad Tomlin trains in Denver. Too much togetherness is a bad thing." Her fiery independence may have waned a little with her relationship, but if anyone understands wanting to have some solitude, it's her, and I appreciate that. "Plus, he smashes himself to me at night, and it's too damn hot."

"Agree."

I drink my soda, still wishing it was the remains of my beer sitting near Rico.

"Okay, well, text me when you're home and settled. I'm not baking shit and dropping it off like Eli probably will, but I can come over and help with stuff," she offers, and I smile.

"I've got a leaky pipe I need help with," Rico leans over to whisper at her, and she slides off the bar stool so fast he nearly loses his balance jolting back.

"STDs will do that, Romeo. I'm no doctor or nothing, but they make medicines for that." Dani smirks, her words dripping with sarcasm as she picks up her large bag of food and turns to me. "Text me your address. I don't have it."

Rico's face reddens slightly, a mixture of embarrassment at being shut down so fast and amusement at her quick response. I nod, trying to suppress a smile.

"Will do, Dani. Thanks for the offer."

With a final nod at me and a disgusted look at Rico, she walks toward the bar exit. A smile tugs at his lips as he watches the sway of her naturally curvy hips.

Rico can't help but call out to her, a genuine warmth in his voice. "I'll text you my address too!"

She raises her middle finger at him without turning around before pushing out the front door, leaving Rico with a lingering smile.

"What a woman."

14

Finally home and free from the confines of my dress uniform, I sink into my mattress, my mind a scattered mess from today. No, a scattered mess from the last two weeks. The coolness of the sheets is refreshing against my skin after spending so long at Mom and Pops's warm house. I'd blame it on the age of the home if they didn't put in a new air conditioning unit two summers ago.

The silence of my house envelops me, offering solace from everyone and everything. Without a moment to myself, I haven't been able to truly relax until now. I take a deep breath, savoring the solitude that being home in my bed brings to my injured body and weary mind.

The desire to jerk off had waned after the first time I tried in the shower, and Pops walked in on me, wondering if I had fallen because I had been in there so long. After that, I stopped trying, and anytime the desire sparked, most often after a hard workout, I willed it away by spending time with my mom watching her shows. Nothing will kill your libido faster than hanging with the parents, and that twenty-four-seven togetherness turned me into a monk.

Now that I'm alone with the moon high in the sky and its' light cascading through the sides of my blinds, the pent-up fury of a good orgasm is beyond necessary. I widen my legs, finding a comfortable position that won't cause a muscle spasm to my injured thigh, and tuck my hand behind my head before closing my eyes. I'd love to watch a good porno, but with my remote across the room and my phone on the nightstand, I settle for an old memory.

Her.

The last time we were together, she asked me to jerk off in front of her. She said she wanted to get better at hand jobs. Why? I never thought to ask, but it's always lingered in my mind. My palm slides over my stomach, reminiscent of how her fingertips dipped in and out of the muscles on her way south. She tugged on my pubic hair once, complaining it was too bushy. I didn't know any better back then, but I have kept it trimmed ever since.

The memory of her flawlessly tanned skin and athletic body pressed against mine instantly makes me hard. My dick is already leaking from an overwhelming desire to push inside her soft folds and from restraining myself for countless days. This orgasm will be quick and quickly followed by another. My recovery rate has always been fast. If I could, I'd have sex every day, several times at that, if I could find a girl that could keep up.

Mary Ann ruined me that way. She had a high libido to match mine, sometimes getting me hard before I fully recovered. She could go four or five rounds before collapsing into exhaustion. It's one of many things I loved about her. She'd wanted me as much as I'd wanted her.

I grip my shaft in my hand, hard and unrelenting, giving it a tight squeeze at the base nestled near my balls, that are already tingling and ready to blow. Jerking off needs to last longer than a minute, and if I don't stave off the orgasm, it won't. Mary Ann used to edge me until it was painful, laughing at my groans and pleas to finish deep inside her. She enjoyed my misery, but it made the reward pure bliss.

With that hard squeeze, killing my pending orgasm, I spit in my hand and start lazily stroking. Sensations fill my body, building desire and the climb to evitable release. As my skin warms, I kick the sheets off, enjoying the cool draft from the ceiling fan over my skin and hardening my dick even more.

My balls constrict as I increase the stroking, settling my fist under the head of my cock where the nerves are most sensitive. Setting the perfect rhythm, I envision my hand as her hand, pumping me as her mouth covers mine. Her hand tugs relentlessly, almost painfully, with need while her tongue dives into my mouth, seeking every corner to taste and touch and leaving no trace of my breath behind.

My hips jerk into my fist, wishing and imagining it was her tight, wet pussy stretching to fit my large girth. She'd force me to go slow, asking me to wait so she could adjust, and then wind up fucking the shit out of me. I fucking loved the duality, and she knew it. Loved our size difference. I loved that I could throw her skinny ass against the wall and plunder her pussy with my cock, and hear her screams in my ear and her nails in my back.

"Fuck."

The thought of all the times I treated her roughly, like a fucking rag doll, and her loving it rockets my orgasm to the top of my cock, nearly spewing out the top. Squeezing the base again to stave it off, my dick pulses the same as my elevated heart rate, and I level out my breathing before starting again.

Edging myself isn't as fun as Mary Ann doing it, but damn if it will not result in one hell of an explosion when I finally come. She'd get me on the edge of coming and then release my dick entirely to cup and roll my balls in her hand while sucking on my neck. How she didn't give me a string of hickeys, I'll never know. She'd listen to my breath, slip her fingers down to my taint and stroke the underside of my balls.

I'd do it now if it didn't pull on my sutures, but just imagining her small hand and soft touch on my sensitive flesh makes me stroke faster and more focused. Wetness drips from the tip of my dick, and I swirl the slickness over the head, wishing it were her lips and tongue.

Those chestnut eyes would survey my junk, eyeing it like candy before looking up at me, wondering if she should continue with the hand job, give me a blowjob, or jump on. It was usually the latter, and I never complained.

Pushing into her pussy until I hit her cervix was the best feeling in the world. It was the only place I ever wanted to be, and the little sounds that escaped her throat when I was fully seated had me blowing my load.

I pump into my hand. The surge of excitement and explosion sends pleasure to the ends of my body as long streams of cum flow from my cock. My breath is harsh, panting as my pulse races into my ears. I convulse violently, the aftershocks almost stronger than coming. It feels good. Great, even, but it leaves me wanting a lot more. A lot more of her. A day in bed, fucking, teasing, making love, and enjoying each other like we once did.

As my dick softens, I loosen my fist, and a dark realization settles into the recesses of my mind. The girl from my memories and fantasies no longer exists. The spontaneous, lighthearted, and adventure-seeking girl from my youth is gone, replaced by a hardened, skeletal, cigarette-smoking sex worker named Molli with an I.

Oxygen leaves my lungs at that sad thought. I pull my fist off my dick, laying it on the covers and knowing I need to get cleaned up as cum pools on my abdomen. It's a tough realization to bear. Knowing whom I want is already gone, even though she was right in front of me a few days ago.

The way she looked at me and looked at my card, I knew I'd lost her again. I lost her before I even had her this time. It's the most fucked up situation in the world, knowing I can help and she will never let me.

"Fuck."

As I contemplate cleaning up, the shrill ring of my phone slices through the stillness of my haunting thoughts. Annoyance creeps into my tired mind as if it's Mom checking in on me for the millionth time. I appreciate their help but am ready to return to my everyday life. When I stretch to grab it from the nightstand, I do not recognize the number. It's the middle of the night. Worry chases away the pleasure of a moment ago, and I reluctantly answer it.

"Hello?"

The automated voice crackles with static, notifying me of a collect call from the local jail. Confusion clouds my thoughts as I wonder who could reach out to me from behind bars. With a mix of trepidation and curiosity, I accept the call. The line connects with a hollow click.

"Hamilton?" Her voice is heavy with remorse and desperation. "Are you there?"

My breath catches in my throat when I hear the way she says my name. Always drawing it out slowly and intentionally, making it three distinct syllables back when she was mine, and I was hers. The only thing that didn't change in the last decade.

"Mary Ann."

It comes out as a whisper, almost a painful plea to return to the girl I used to know, not the one calling me now. It hurts in my heart when I think of the last time I saw her blowing smoke into the night air and not remembering what we were.

"It's Molli."

She reminds me again, and I can't accept it even though I should. Molli is nothing like Mary Ann. They are two distinct people, and I need to get over it if I want to help her.

"Sorry, Molli. Uh, what's going on?"

I suspect they caught her in the dragnet, something I hadn't got back to staking out since that night with Rico.

"I messed up, and I need your help."

Despite my weariness, a sense of loyalty stirs within me. I sit up, the cum oozing down my stomach as I ease out of bed and hobble to my bathroom with the phone smashed to my ear.

"Tell me what happened," I respond, keeping my tone firm and neutral as I wet a washcloth and start cleaning myself.

"I got picked up for prostitution. I didn't know who else to call," she whispers into the receiver, making it hard to hear over the shouting in the background. "They are holding me at the county jail."

I'm conflicted between the duty of my profession and the lingering emotional connection we once shared. As a police officer, I am responsible for upholding the law, but I also can't ignore her reaching out to me for help. Maybe this is the chance I've been waiting for, but she'll be gone the second she's out and leaving me holding the bag.

"Isn't this your jail? Could you talk to your father about letting me go?"

Another favor. Another incident of laying my good name on the line for her. And for what? She's a huge flight risk, transient by definition under the law, and not someone I'd risk my career for anymore. Doing it at sixteen was one thing. Doing it now is stupid, and the ramifications are too great.

"I already told you, Pops retired years ago," I say, putting my phone on speaker to wash my hands. I could say more, but I don't, and neither does she. The automated voice cuts in, reminding us how much time is left on the call.

"I'm scared, Hamilton."

The fear in her voice is laced with regret, and it does something to me. The bitterness that struck me a few days ago is back, hitting harder now that she is suffering the consequences of her actions.

"I understand that you're scared," I finally respond with sympathy and frustration. "But you have to understand, it's been years since I last saw you, and things have changed. You made it quite clear the other night that you don't want nor need my help."

It pains me to turn her down, but doesn't she realize how much she hurt me all those years ago? She's only calling me now because I'm a police officer and not for any other reason.

"I was wrong. I need your help."

I hear the regret and the desperation in her voice, but I know that giving in now would only enable her destructive behavior if she's unwilling to get off the streets and into a program.

"What about your parents? Does your mom still lives off Broadmoor Street?"

The silence stretches between us, the automated voice interrupting again to remind us of the one minute left on the call.

"I don't know. I haven't seen them since I left."

I wasn't the only one she turned her back on. Her mother and stepfather received the same treatment as I did.

"Hamilton, can you get me out of here?"

"I'm sorry, Molli, but I can't just make this go away," I say with an unexpected firmness that hints at the anger I still hold for her. "Once you're arraigned, you'll be able to be released on bond, mostly likely with geographical restrictions."

"Meaning?"

"You can't leave the county. And you can't go back to, uh, work."

There's a defeated sigh on the other end of the line, a sound that echoes through the receiver and into my bathroom, where

I stand naked, arguing with myself about going to jail or going to bed.

Before she can respond, the call abruptly ends, leaving me staring at my reflection in the mirror. Conflicting emotions swirl within me, battling for dominance. I can't help but question my resolve, wondering if I made the right choice not to get her. Her desperation and our shared history gnaws at my conscience, threatening to weaken my resolve.

Part of me wants to rush to her aid, to be the knight in shining armor she desperately needs. But another part, a stronger part, reminds me of the countless times I've tried to save her before. Each time, she slipped through my fingers, leaving me with the consequences of her actions.

I take a deep breath, trying to steady my racing thoughts. The memories of our tumultuous relationship, the broken promises, and the pain still linger. I chose law enforcement to follow in the old man's footsteps, have a steady career, and eventually settle down with a good woman. A woman who wouldn't leave me and certainly wouldn't be arrested for prostitution.

But as I stand here, naked and vulnerable, the guilt weighs heavily on me. The thought of Molli sitting in a jail cell, abandoned by those she should be able to rely on, stirs a flicker of compassion within me. Maybe this time would be different. Perhaps she truly wants my help aside from needing it.

The exhaustion from the day tugs at me, tempting me to ignore the call and go back to bed. But the nagging feeling that this could be different and that I could help Molli break free from this destructive life persists.

In the end, the choice becomes obvious. I won't abandon her. With unwavering determination, I walk into the closet to get dressed and grab my crutches. Figuring out how to drive will be interesting but necessary if I want to face her and the consequences of her actions head-on. I pray I don't run into the Chief at this late hour, as he might ask about how my interview went with the investigators. That might be another problem I have to face if they ask about discharging my weapon more times than necessary.

15

My leg and side throb as I leave my house, but it pales in comparison to the whirlwind of conflicting thoughts churning within my skull. There are thoughts of duty to my job, loyalty to my first lover, and even Father Michael's sermon several Christmas's ago. It was about forgiveness for past transgressions and how they bring peace and joy to relationships. The new and old thoughts swirl around without resolution.

The drive to the county jail is slow as my left leg cramps even with the seat all the way back. Anticipation and apprehension flow through my body as I brace myself for what lies ahead, uncertain how this encounter will unfold. I won't allow Molli's troubles to take me down again, that's for sure.

I park my truck and grab my crutches, readying myself for a myriad of questions about my health and probably about Molli when my colleagues find out I'm here for her.

"No time like the present."

The cold air nips at my bare legs. Shorts in winter aren't the best idea, but they were the easiest to get on at this late hour. I step inside the county jail. The environment is familiar with the echoing sound of heavy metal doors slamming shut and the chatter of radios, phones, and people talking. As much as I'd like to avoid being here, I suck it up and head straight toward the intake desk.

"Alex, what are you doing here?" Shonda asks with wide brown eyes that look me up and down before settling on my face. "I thought you were still on medical leave."

The cadence of her voice is hard, opposite to her feminine features, which prisoners underestimate all the time. Known for enjoying MMA, she competes at an amateur level yearly to keep her skills up and usually wins. Being a mom of three also confuses people, as her caramel skin is youthful and wrinkle-free, even though she's in her forties.

"I am. I'm here for—"

"Don't tell me she called you." Rico's voice booms from behind me before his hand claps me on the back. I glance over to see he's out of his dress blues and in his regular uniform.

"You pulling a double?" I ask, concerned he's stretched too thin with all the extra shifts.

Rico lets out a tired chuckle, his weariness wearing on his face. "Double, triple, who knows anymore? So, she called."

Shonda is content to watch and listen, her gaze moving between us as she leans back in her chair.

"She did," I admit reluctantly, knowing how Rico feels about her. "I guess she thought I could help somehow."

Rico's hand comes to rest on his gun belt. His gaze fixes on me as he weighs his words carefully.

"Alex, you've done more than enough for her in the past. You can't keep bailing her out. At some point, you got to let bygones be bygones and force her to be responsible for her own actions."

His words strike a chord within me, echoing the conflict I've been wrestling with on the ride over. I appreciate Rico's concern and his reminder of the boundaries I must set for my well-being.

"I know, Rico," I reply with resignation. "Believe me, I'm well aware of the risks. But there's still a part of me that feels responsible, that can't fully let go."

His expression softens, a glimmer of understanding in his dark eyes. He knows the complexities of my past with her and the small glimmer of hope I held for her to return.

"I get it, man. But remember, she's made her choices. You can't carry the weight of her decisions on your shoulders."

His words resonate with a truth I can't deny. I know I have to let go of the sense of obligation that keeps me tethered to Molli's troubles. But I did offer her my help, and I'd be an asshole to turn my back on her when she needs it. Acknowledging Shonda's interest in our conversation, he turns to her and says, "First love."

While tossing his head in my direction. Her eyebrows raise toward her black hair while she leans forward to tap on her keyboard and squints to read the computer screen.

"Hmm, this isn't her first time in jail. The girl has got a rap sheet," she mutters before the printer comes to life, spewing page after page of her criminal record.

I sigh. I should have expected this. Molli isn't a liar per se, but she never tells the entire truth, either. Something I learned later that I grew to hate.

"Says here that she is in for assault. Beat up some guy that wouldn't pay?" she continues, leaning closer to the screen and tapping on the keyboard again. "She listed you as the nearest relative on the arrest report. Interesting."

Shonda's sudden interest makes me very uneasy. I was already uncomfortable involving Rico, but having two colleagues involved is too much. I approach the printer, balancing on my crutches to pluck the pages from it and scan them.

"Lots of offenses, but this appears to be her first assault," Shonda explains, her voice tinged with surprise. Her eyes scan the screen, reading aloud even though I'm holding them in my hand.

"There are multiple counts of drug possession, prostitution, and theft."

My jaw tightens as the reality sets in. Molli's choices have led her down a path of self-destruction and paint a bleak portrait of her life.

"And it doesn't stop there," Shonda continues, her voice trailing slightly. "There are also instances of public indecency and resisting arrest. It seems she's been caught up in quite a few altercations with the law over the years."

A heavy sigh escapes my lips, and disappointment sets in. Violence and a disregard for the very law I uphold mars her past.

"She's been leading a turbulent life," I murmur, still reading through the pages. When I look at Rico, he's shaking his head.

"I know what you want to do, but I'm telling you to walk away, Alex." His voice is as steely as his face, not his usual joking manner, but the same seriousness he uses when the Chief is around. "She's not worth it. You have a lot on your plate with rehab, the investigation, and—"

"Don't."

"Alex, I know you have a big heart, and I've seen you go above and beyond for people," Rico counters, his hands waving around in front of him. Something he does when he's passionate about a subject or arguing. "But this is different. Molli's history and choices could cast a shadow over your integrity as a cop."

My fingers curl into a fist around the papers listing all her convictions. I hold his gaze, struggling with my decision to come here. My career and the trust of my colleagues are at stake, not to mention additional scrutiny by the Chief if I got involved in her criminal case.

"I hear you, Rico. I do, but I also believe in the power of redemption and second chances. Perhaps this time will be different? I did offer my help at the truck stop the other night. Maybe I can steer her toward a better path."

"Truck stop?" Shonda interjects, turning around from her computer to look at me. "Did you know that's where they picked her up at? Did she tell you that?"

Rico's gaze moves from me to her and then back, leaving her questions unanswered when he throws up his hands in frustration.

"I can't believe you're going through with this, Alex," Rico says, taking a step back, distancing himself physically and emotionally from my decision. "I've tried to warn you, to protect you, but it seems you've already decided."

His words sting, a pang of guilt washing over me. I never want to disappoint Rico or put our friendship on the line, but I can't ignore the pull in my heart to help Molli.

"I have. I need to try one more time. And maybe I'm a fool for believing it might work, but I have to try."

Rico shakes his head with a frown of disapproval. "You're risking everything you've worked for, Alex. Your career, your reputation, and even your own well-being. Is she worth it?"

I pause. Doubt is creeping in. What if I'm making a mistake? What if the consequences cost me everything? What if she leaves regardless?

"Yes," I answer firmly, shoving the doubt and underlying fear aside.

Rico's face softens momentarily, a flicker of understanding crossing his features. But it quickly gives way to resignation because he and I have been down this road before. The first time, she was a fool for leaving me. This time, I'm a fool for believing her.

"Well, just remember, Alex, that I warned you. I'll be here if you need me, but I can't support this decision."

With that, Rico turns away, his steps loud on the concrete floors, leaving Shonda to shake her head too. I watch him go, disappointed that, for the first time in years, he doesn't have my back. I never want to lose his support, but I understand why he's walking away. He's always been there for me, a brother from another mother, and even he can't support a terrible decision when he sees it. This might be the worst one I've ever made.

With the printed records safely nestled under my arm, I take a moment to readjust my crutches. Shonda's attention returns to her computer, engrossed in her work as she switches screens. Knowing time is of the essence, I navigate down the hallway, my eyes scanning the wall until I locate the keycard reader. I slide my card, causing the door to unlatch, granting access to the hallway leading to the holding cells—the hallway that marks the onset of the ill-fated choice I'm making, driven solely by pursuing lost love.

The closer I get to the holding cells, the louder the noise is until the wall ends, and the bars appear with a disheveled Molli huddling in the corner, away from everyone else. She doesn't see me right away, too occupied with picking at her nails with her bare legs crossed for privacy in her tiny skirt and her foot wiggling with nervous energy.

Her lustrous hair is stringy, tangled, and dirty, with strands falling haphazardly around her face. The harshness and stress of her life have faded the vibrant color that used to grace her cheeks. There are dark circles under her eyes and remnants of makeup smudged on her face, with a few scratches alluding to the assault charge. Even her bottom lip is split.

She still wears that multi-colored fur coat which gaps open to reveal scraps of lingerie crisscrossing her skinny frame. Her once full breasts are gone, replaced by a protruding breastbone. I suspect her ribs would show if it weren't for her heavy coat.

It pains me to see her like this. A ghost of the beautiful girl she was when filled with hopes and dreams. Now she's succumbed to the cyclical nightmare that sex workers face.

As if feeling the weight of my stare and sorrow for her, her face lifts, and recognition wrinkles across her face. Beyond that, no expression at all. Not a frown at what I told her on the phone or a smile that I defied myself and came, anyway.

With caution, she gradually unfolds her legs, exerting considerable effort to rise onto her high heels, and I realize she's more hurt than she lets on. Her actions are slow, accompanied by painful grimaces, as she navigates toward the metal bars separating us.

"I didn't think you were coming."

The rasp in her voice still catches me by surprise, but the curiosity in those chestnut eyes is still the same.

"I didn't think I was either. Yet here I am."

I adjust the crutches to lean against the bars, and she does the same. Our faces are so close it speaks to an intimacy that hasn't existed in a long time.

"Are you hurt, Molli?" I lower my voice, wanting to keep as much of this conversation out of the listening ears of the officer to my left and her cellmates to my right.

"Nothing I haven't been through before."

I immediately hate that, but I'm not surprised. She grabs the edges of her jacket to pull tighter across her frame to hide anything I might see. It's a defensive move, rehearsed so many times I doubt she even realizes she's doing it.

"Did you receive medical attention? A doctor perhaps or—"

She laughs, harsh and bitter. A sound so vile I hate it almost as much as I hate knowing she's been hurt many times before.

"Idealistic as always. I guess that part of you didn't change after all these years."

She rests her head against the bars, closing her eyes momentarily, and the exhaustion cuts deep lines across her forehead and mouth. It pulls at my gut. When they open again, they are as vacant and dead as before.

"If you're hurt, and they didn't offer you medical assistance, that violates your civ—"

"They did, Hamilton," she interrupts in a low voice and prolonged exhalation. "They did."

"And what? You just refused or something? Help me understand why you're here if you're hurt and need a doctor?" I raise my voice, releasing my frustrations. If she wants out, this is one way to get out until she's arraigned. Doesn't she know that, given her rap sheet?

"Why are you here?"

She cuts to the chase, her voice weary and her patience wearing thin with my questioning.

"You called and said you need my help."

"You turned me down. So again, why are you here, Hamilton?"

She clutches the bar. Each finger has one or more rings on them, but it's the scrapes on her knuckles and the faint scars on her wrists that draw my attention. When she catches me looking, she adjusts the cuff of the sleeve to cover most of it but keeps clutching the bar.

The tension in the air thickens as her question hangs between us, the weight of it pressing against my conscience. Trust. She doesn't trust me. Maybe she doesn't trust herself anymore, either. Look where it's gotten her.

I meet her gaze, unable to hide the anger any longer. The sight of her visible and concealed injuries makes me want to throttle her for being so stupid, making shitty choices that landed her here, and being so damn stubborn to call for help and interrogate me when I show up here. It makes me hesitant to intervene, just like Rico's reservations.

"You said you wanted my help. Or was that a lie? What? Were you thinking I could pull a few strings, and they would let you out so you can re-offend again and again?"

Rage builds within me. Pulling from the years of pain, disappointment, and anger this girl put me through. Years of trying to understand when I didn't have all the answers and crying myself to sleep when she cut me off. It's all coming up now, and I'm hesitant to force it back down.

"I've seen your rap sheet." I hold up the fist full of papers and shake it in the air. Her eyes shift to it and then back to mine. That's the only response I get. "You're a career criminal, so why should I help you? Why should I help someone that didn't even have the decency to tell me she was leaving rather than disappearing one day and disconnecting her phone?"

Her fingers tighten on the bars while she holds my gaze. My body is trembling, holding back my fury when I only want to scream at her, demand answers, and make her pay for the hurt and anguish she put me through. I can't be her savior. Not again.

"You shouldn't."

Her head raises from the bars, and her fingers loosen, falling to her side as she straightens, her chin raised in defiance.

"Go, Hamilton. Forget I ever called you."

Her insolent posture and cold eyes tell me she has made her choice. She's resigned herself to her fate, accepting the consequences of her actions, and is expecting nothing from me. It fans the flames of my anger at how easily she is giving up and how stubborn she's being with me. If she would relent for once, say she messed up, that she's sorry, and take responsibility, then I'd dive in wholeheartedly.

I grip the bars, her rap sheet stuffed between my palm and the cold metal, as she walks away. My knuckles turn white as I struggle to contain my fury with her and the damn situation she has put herself in.

"You're better than this, and you know it." I raise my voice at her when she doesn't stop ambling back to her corner. She's done with me, walking away like she always did, and here I am chasing her down an overgrown road we've been on before. I know how our story ends and won't let it happen again.

She doesn't look at me when she resumes her position in the corner, and I exhale, feeling my heart pounding in my head with how angry I am. I release the bars, clutch the papers tighter as I grip my crutches, and head back to Shonda. She raises a curious eyebrow when I toss the crinkled rap sheet on my desk.

"She's hurt. Can you get a medic over here to look at her?"

"She denied our help already," Shonda says with an attitude since I'm interrupting her work on another case.

"Please? For me?" I acquiesce by lightning my tone. "Even if she refuses, make them check her out."

It's obvious she's in pain from the assault, and denying medical attention is idiotic. I know it's not my place to take care of her, but I'd do the same for any assailant brought in for assault. Or at least that's what I'm telling myself.

"Fine, but you owe me one of your momma's apple pies."

16

The knock on my door is expected. Eli and Ronald are bringing Isla by to visit. The shooting happened well over two weeks ago, and now I'm off my crutches, having graduated to a cane. They feel the timing is right for an in-person meeting. Due to Isla's history of violence from men and their unpredictable behavior, we all agreed that in-person meetings were a no-go until today. Not that I would ever hurt Isla. The opposite is true.

I'd hurt anyone who ever hurts her again, but others' injuries can trigger abuse victims. I wanted to ensure I had enough mobility that my injuries wouldn't trigger her. However, I'm surprised when I open the door to find Rico standing there.

"What's up, man?" I ask, having traded text messages with him but treading lightly in asking about Molli since he didn't support me seeing her.

"You've got to get her out," Rico says urgently, brushing past me as I stand still, holding the door. Confused by his sudden arrival and urgent tone, I slowly close it behind him, trying to make sense of his words.

"Rico, what do you mean? Get Molli out?" I lean on the cane, having had a particularly aggressive rehab session today.

He turns to face me, his expression grave. "Yeah. It's not safe."

My pulse spikes, and worry creeps into my thoughts, followed by guilt for leaving her there two nights ago. Something must have happened, something that poses a threat to her well-being if Rico's here.

"What happened? Why isn't she safe?" I wave him out of the foyer and into the den so that I can rest my legs. His eyes dart around the room as if he's cautious of being overheard in my house.

"She refused bail today. I overheard some guys talking before her hearing, so I followed them into the courtroom. They're after her and are trying to get her out. It was intense. She's terrified. I could see it. She told her public defender she wouldn't go with them and wanted to stay in jail. Then she started shaking when they began yelling, insisting that the court release her to them. I don't think they will stop until they get her. You need to protect her."

Rico paces before me as I sink into the chair, reclining it to rest my tired muscles.

"Who are these guys?" A surge of protectiveness shoves forward despite her refusing me the other night. Rico's expression hardens before answering.

"I don't know, but they seemed well-connected and not from around these parts. From what I overheard, they were assigned to collect her. As if she's the girlfriend of someone important, a boss, maybe?"

"She's involved with organized crime?" I ask in astonishment, and he sinks into the armchair across from mine. My mind races, trying to piece together the little information I know. It makes sense if she had a pimp, which is very common in prostitution, but those are lower level and not mob or mafia.

"I don't know. I couldn't find anything, but that's not our jurisdiction, typically."

"Could that be why they do the dragnet at the truck stop? I assume it's the State, but you're thinking federal?" I speculate, trying to connect the dots and understand the scale of the situation we find ourselves in.

Rico leans forward, resting his elbows on his knees, his gaze fixes on me.

"Yeah, I think it's possible," he agrees gravely. "Given the level of interest and the resources these guys seem to have, it wouldn't surprise me if federal agencies are involved. We might be dealing with something bigger than we anticipated."

A chill runs down my spine as I consider the situation's implications. If federal agencies are involved, it suggests a deeper complexity and danger surrounding Molli's predicament. Uneasiness settling into my gut if Molli somehow got herself wrapped up with the wrong people.

"I tried to help the other night, but she didn't want it again."

That's not entirely true. I let my pride and pain fly, wanting to hurt her as she hurt me, and it worked. Although, I'm too embarrassed to admit this to him.

"I figured as much when I saw her the next morning. She acted like she didn't remember me." He shakes his head, the corner of his mouth pulling into a smirk. "She pantsed me at vacation bible school one summer, remember? She had to sit in the corner facing the wall for four hours until her stepfather came to pick her up."

"I remember you crying and running into the men's bathroom, and Father Michael had to talk you out of there." I chuckle at the memory.

"Hey, the girl I liked saw my Batman underwear and laughed at me. It was traumatizing," he defends with a genuine smile before he exhales and returns to a serious expression.

"What do you want to do? Do we bail her out or let these guys eventually get to her?"

I know I can keep her safe here with me, but what if she flees town or goes back to work at the truck stop? Then I'm on the hook for making her bail and could face charges myself.

"It's my neck on the line if she runs."

"It is."

Rico's response is simple yet solemn. The responsibility for Molli's actions, her trust, and her fate rests upon my shoulders and fills me with trepidation. I took the fall once and lived with the consequences. The risks are far greater now with the men pursuing her, and the potential damage it could inflict on my career cannot be overlooked.

"What would you do?" For the first time, Rico looks away, his jaw tightening as he ponders my predicament. "You said I was on my own the other night. And the time before that. You keep telling me to walk away from her, and now you want me to bail her out? What changed, Rico?"

His silence lingers, stretching the tension in the room, and his gaze remains averted. I can see the internal struggle play out on his face. Eventually, he meets my eyes, and his expression is sympathetic.

"I know I've been giving you conflicting messages. I'm sorry for that," Rico begins with remorse in his voice. "I'm worried about you. She destroyed you the last time around. I don't want to see that happen again. I thought distancing yourself from her was the best course of action. But seeing her yesterday, the fear in her, and how those guys acted, maybe you're right for trying to help her. I mean, isn't that the oath we took?"

Rico's acknowledgment of our duty resonates deeply within me, reminding me of the principles that guided my decision to join law enforcement in the first place, outside of following in Pops's footsteps.

"You're right. We swore an oath to protect and serve, and that commitment extends to all those in need, including exes that destroy people," I say, even though Rico proclaims to have never been in love, and I wonder how true that is. "Despite the risks, we have a responsibility to help her and ensure her safety."

"As much as I still don't like it."

"Duly noted," I add dryly.

A knock on the door interrupts our intense conversation. The one I've been waiting for, and I grab my cane to make my way to answer it, eager to see Isla and how she's handling all this. We've become closer in the months after her case, and Eli said she cried when she first heard I was injured. Hopefully, seeing me up and around will calm her fears.

As I swing the door open, Isla's eyes widen in surprise as she looks me up and down, surveying the damage.

"Hey, Alexander!" Eli greets me with a warm smile. He's carrying a casserole dish with foil on top. Ronald stands behind him with his arms loaded with bags of food, and Isla clutches a plant with a pink blooming flower in the middle. "Look at you up and around! And here I thought we'd be playing nursemaid today."

"Showering without help is an excellent motivator to get up and around," I respond too quickly, causing Isla's eyes to dart to my face from their focus on the cane and my left leg. "Sorry, that sounded inappropriate."

Eli laughs, relieving the tension, and reassures me. "No need to worry. We've heard worse. Now, who do we have here?"

Rico joins me at the door, and I widen it further to invite them in and make introductions. Eli and Ronald introduce themselves, and Rico follows suit, but Isla hesitates. Instead of fully stepping into the room with them, she stands beside me, maintaining a cautious distance. Her wariness prevents her from getting any closer to Rico than necessary, and when he waves in her direction, she retreats behind me as I close the door.

Her reaction is quite understandable. While Rico may not be as physically imposing as me, his regular presence at the same gym and his role as my usual workout partner makes him intimidating in his own way. Having never encountered difficulties attracting women, I suppose he possesses good looks, which only adds to Isla's anxiety. She once mentioned how her mother's attractive boyfriend used his charm to evade accountability for his abusive behavior, which amplifies her apprehension.

"That's a nice plant. Is that for me?" I ask Isla, noticing the tips of her fingers are going white with how tightly she clutches it while staring at the badge hanging from Rico's neck.

"Yes," she whispers, watching her parents interact with Rico as they discuss him staying for lunch and that Eli brought enough for everyone.

"Well, thank you. Why don't you and I head into the kitchen to find a spot for it?"

She doesn't respond other than to look at me. I lead the way, taking my time with the cane on one side and her on the other, leaving the guys behind. Once we enter the other room, I notice Isla visibly relax, and I take a moment to reassure her.

"Rico is a good man, Isla. I understand he may appear intimidating, but I've known him for as long as I can remember. You have nothing to fear from him. He's a law enforcement officer, just like me."

"I want to believe you," she murmurs, hugging the plant. "It's just I've had a hard time trusting people, especially those who seem . . ."

"I understand, Isla. Trust takes time, and it's good to be cautious." Her eyes bore into mine. "But you have nothing to worry about with him, I promise. In fact, this one time when he slept over, we stayed up late watching movies and drinking sodas, and he peed the bed."

Isla's lips curl into a smile, and Eli's hearty laughter trails behind us. Rico, now beside us in the kitchen, playfully claps me on the back of my shoulder. Meanwhile, Ronald casually smiles as he places the bags on the counter to my left.

"For the thousandth time, it was sweat, not urine. Your mom keeps the house an inferno in the winter, and I was sweating my balls off," Rico defends, squeezing my shoulder and playfully giving me a gentle shake, causing Isla to instinctively step back, wary of the sudden movement.

Sensing Isla's caution, I smile reassuringly, silently communicating that there's no cause for alarm. Understanding her need for space, Rico quickly eases his exuberance, respecting her boundaries.

"Don't blame my mom for your weak ass bladder. She told you to lay off the Dr. Peppers, and you insisted you could finish the six-pack."

I elbow him in the side, laughing at his discomfort while Isla watches us intently. She remains a distance away but feels comfortable enough to put the plant on the counter near her.

"Speaking of Dr. Peppers, who's hungry? This casserole is still piping hot, and we'll be ready to eat once Ronald unpacks the salad and sides," Eli intervenes, clapping his hands together to interrupt our interaction and signaling that it's time to focus on lunch.

He steps closer to Isla, encircling her petite frame with his arms and leaning in. She tenses from being surprised by the sudden embrace but soon melts into it. Eli's affection toward her is both triggering and healing, a delicate dance they've navigated in establishing their boundaries. Observing the depth of his love for her is genuinely endearing, a testament to their bond and the care they share for one another.

"I'm starving." I glance over at Rico, who's since removed his hand from my shoulder to pull out his phone and read a text message. "You are staying, or are you going to do that thing we discussed?"

Rico's dark eyes flicker to mine, followed by a smile directed at Eli as he extends his hand.

"I appreciate the offer, but I need to head back to the station to handle a situation that arose today."

"Oh no, I hope everything is okay," Eli responds with concern, then releases Isla to touch his forehead. "I mean, that's silly of me to say. Obviously, people call you when things aren't okay. But, well, you know what I mean."

He lets out a little chuckle, his hands wringing in front of him as if eager to get this show on the road. Ronald unpacks the bags with several open containers spread across the kitchen island. The aroma fills the kitchen and makes my stomach growl.

"Don't worry. It's just some unexpected paperwork that needs attention. Alex, I'll catch up with you later. It was nice to meet all of you." He shakes hands with the guys and nods in Isla's direction.

"And you too. A friend of Alexander's is always a friend of ours," Eli says, watching Rico leave before lifting the foil off the casserole and sending steam into the air.

"Isla, why don't you tell Alex about training with Mr. Taka-hashi? I'm sure he'd loved to hear the story of how it all came together," Ronald suggests, while Eli steps away to retrieve paper plates and utensils, which make the cleanup easier for me.

"Knock me over with a feather. You're learning judo?" The astonishment in my voice reflects my genuine surprise. It's hard to believe this petite and timid individual has taken up such an assertive martial art. I couldn't be prouder. My admiration goes out to Tomlin for being her teacher. "Tell me all about it."

"Yeah, it's this youth thing he's starting, and I'm his first pupil."

A spark ignites in her eyes, and just like that, she begins enthusiastically babbling about her experiences with the training. Her excitement is contagious, and I am captivated, eagerly listening to her animated storytelling.

17

Isla's training with Tomlin was Dani's suggestion. After hitting her punching bag in the garage apartment during Eli's visit, Dani proposed the idea to Isla. Interesting. Judo is an excellent way of building her self-confidence and learning self-defense. I'll be interested to hear more about the inner city youth program he's starting when he returns from the Olympics. Perhaps I can get some of the at-risk youth living at the facility involved now that I finally got Dani to stop calling it a kid prison.

Settling deeper into my chair and reaching for the remote, my phone buzzes on the table beside me, showing a new text message.

> Company still there?

> Just left. What did you find out?

Trepidation crawls into my consciousness at what he'll tell me. My heart rate increases as I wait.

Calling you now.

It barely rings before I pick up, demanding to know what he's discovered.

"How bad is it?" I lean forward with urgency in my voice.

"Not good. She's holding up okay, but things have escalated. It turns out the guys after her are part of a dangerous criminal network. They've been involved in drug trafficking and other illicit activities. They believe Molli will turn on them for an immunity deal, so they won't stop until they get her. I've been poking my nose around, trying to get more intel, and it all checks out."

This is so much worse than an assault and solicitation charge. Turning State or Federal witness is something I've never had to deal with, but Pops did a time or two. I could talk to him about this.

Molli's fate hangs in the balance. Those guys could pay her bail and make her disappear forever. Regardless of my past with her, I can't let that happen. I wouldn't wish that on my worst enemy, and here I am sitting on my ass at home, holding out over hurt feelings from a decade ago. I must get her out now.

"I can't let them get her, Rico. I'm coming to get her tonight." Shoving my exhaustion aside, I groan, move out of my chair, and proceed into my bedroom to retrieve my wallet and keys.

"I figured you would say as much, so I'm almost at your house," he says, the lightness in his voice contradicting the graveness of the situation. "I briefly spoke to Molli about the situation. She's agreed to bail in exchange until she can pay you back."

I frown as I swipe both items off my dresser. "She doesn't need to do that. I just don't want her to flee and jeopardize my career."

"Don't worry. I already told her I'd drag her ass back by her pretty long hair if she left you high and dry this time." His words cut through the line as he blows on his truck horn. "And honestly, from what I gathered, she doesn't have many other options."

"So, I'm the last resort?"

"Sounds like it. Now get your slow ass out here so you and your cane can save the damsel in distress."

As I close the front door behind me, I hope my neighbors are understanding as Rico lies on the horn again, signaling his impatience. With one last glance at my home, I know everything is about to change with having my first roommate ever—my first love.

"Thanks for doing this," I say, getting into the passenger seat. Rico is adjusting his vents, turning down the stifling heat in the cab.

"Your dumb ass has me invested now too. And as opposed as I am, this is the right thing to do for both of you. You could use the help around the house and—don't look at me like that," he scolds before peeling out of my driveway and rocketing down the road at breakneck speeds. I grab the handle above his door while scowling at him. "Make her work off her debt."

"Rico!"

He smirks, full of guilt, and says, "Not like that. I meant by cleaning the house, cooking your meals, or, hell, shoveling the snow. Shit like that."

"We both know what you meant, and I'd never take advantage of her like that. She doesn't even interest me."

It's not a lie. When I jacked off, it wasn't to her in the parking lot. It was to the girl I used to love. They are vastly two different women now.

"Because she's a lot lizard?"

I pause for a moment, surprised by Rico's blunt question.

His raised eyebrow and serious demeanor make it clear he wants an honest answer.

"No, Rico. And stop calling her that. Molli's occupation doesn't define her worth or diminish her value as a human being. She's made some choices that led her down this terrible path, but that doesn't mean she deserves any less compassion or love from someone in this world. No one is unredeemable."

The conversation of redemption with Pops flows into my mind and through my words. I'm still wrestling with the concept myself, though. Not my redemption for her, but hers for herself.

He nods, a flicker of remorse in his expression. "Sorry, man. I shouldn't have said any of that."

"No, you shouldn't have, so lay off the lot lizard shit, and we'll be all right."

The finality in my tone lets him know we're done talking about this. I watch the night sky darken outside my window and look at the mountains, the darkest point over them, signifying it is snowing on the peaks. The same mountains we would ski and tube down.

Her smiling face appears in my mind. The cold tinging the tip of her nose red, the snowflakes collecting in her long hair, and the way her eyes danced when she would spout off a challenge and then race down the mountain, waiting for me to chase after her, only to collapse in a heap at the bottom. Always black diamond slopes with her, as if she had a death wish even back then.

"You, okay?" Rico's deep voice cuts through my memories.

"Yeah." I'm unsure if I'm okay, but I don't tell him.

"Look, I'm sorry about how this is all going down, and I was wrong for walking away the other night. This is me making it up to you."

Rico apologizing again isn't necessary. We're good like we always are. Never have we let an argument fester between us, and I'm not about to rake him over the coals for wanting to protect me.

"No need. We're good," I mumble, shifting my gaze to him. "She's not coming between us. I let that happen once, and I won't again."

If we're trading apologies, I have one of my own, about a decade too late. His mouth stretches into a line, and, with an almost indiscernible nod, he focuses on driving the rest of the way to the station. As the silence spreads between us, I make a short list of what needs to happen in my mind. Bail her out, take her to my house for tonight, and explore our options.

Doubts and uncertainties infiltrate my thoughts. Would Molli feel comfortable being confined with me?? We've become strangers as the years grew, and contact was lost between us. Though I will approach her with caution and sensitivity, I would prefer not to have this reunion take place within the confines of my home. It's far from ideal, and if she had a close relationship with her parents, I would have considered reaching out to them instead. But that consideration quickly faded when I saw her reaction.

My oath to protect the vulnerable echoes in my mind, reminding me of my responsibility. Regardless of our past, Molli is in a precarious situation, pursued by dangerous individuals. It is my duty, as well as a moral imperative, to ensure her safety and well-being. As I weigh the discomforts and uncertainties against the importance of safeguarding her, my personal reservations must take a backseat.

He's barely rolled to a stop in front of the station when I have my hand on the door handle, opening it and getting out. The chill nips at my heated skin as I walk to the front door and throw it open. The fluorescent lights glow yellowish over the otherwise musky, old building.

Rico walks briskly, his footsteps echoing ahead of me on the tiled floor.

"I'll get the paperwork started."

He doesn't wait for my reply as he peels off to the left and calls down the hall to someone he knows. Same as before, I nod my acknowledgment at Shonda before swiping my badge, hearing the beep, and opening the door to the noisiness of the cells beyond.

As I make my way toward the holding area, my pulse accelerates, and the echoing sound of my cane strikes the floor. I spot her nestled in the same corner. However, there are injuries she's suffered since my previous visit that are new, and anger surges in me.

A bruise marks her cheek, its dark hues contrasting with her drawn and pale complexion. A cut across her eyebrow has been crudely patched up, evidence of a recent altercation. Fear fills her eyes, which were once vacant and uncaring. She is jumpy, reacting to every movement around her, and when she sees me, her entire body sags with relief.

Gone is that independent indifference from a few nights ago. Her eyes dart around the cell to see who's watching as she stiffly scrambles over to me.

"Hamilton."

Exhaustion and relief cover her smoker's rasp. Tears stream down her bruised and dirt-streaked face, and her bottom lip trembles with the scab of the cut healing despite her cracked lips. She slides her arms through the bars, the sleeve catching on the metal long enough for me to see how skinny it is.

Her vulnerability and fragility are painfully clear, accentuated by the sight of her beat up face, all stirring a sadness deep within me. I hold her as best I can with the bars separating us, allowing her time to cry into my shoulder. She smells terrible, in desperate need of a long hot shower, a decent meal, and better medical care than she has received here.

The taunts from the women in the neighboring cell pierce through the air, and anger flares within me. I shoot them a stern gaze, a threat, and a promise to make them pay if they did this to her. Their jeers eventually subside, but the damage has been done. Molli doesn't need any more humiliation or degradation.

"Molli," I start, wanting to say several things simultaneously.

"I know. I'll do whatever you want."

The obligation rings in my ear as her breath caresses my neck, and I instantly hate it. I loosen my grip on her and lean away, needing to see her face when I say what must be said. She will not like it, but it will be part of the deal. The last two days have given me plenty of time to think about what I want and how I can help her.

It was an old lesson Pops taught me when we had to clean up after the Christmas pageant, and I was grumbling about wanting to go home to open gifts.

"You know, when I was a kid, Pops used to tell me that sometimes in life, we have to do things we don't want to do. Things necessary for our growth and well-being, even if they seem difficult or uncomfortable at first."

She pulls back, unwinding her arms from me, pulling them through the bars, and tucking them around her midsection. Her brow furrows, apprehension appearing on her face.

"Okay, what does that have to do with me?"

I let my gaze penetrate her. "I'll help you, but there are conditions. First and foremost, you need to be willing to make some changes. It's not just about getting you out of here. It's about giving you a chance at a better life."

She tenses up, her eyes narrowing with a hint of defiance.

"I won't be controlled."

"I don't want to control you, but I also don't know who I'm bringing into my home." As much as I hate voicing the words, they must be said and hit the target as intended. She flinches and looks away. "We need to establish boundaries that work for both of us."

"Such as?"

"For starters, no drugs. Period." A look of complete humiliation covers her face, and I already know what it means. "Which ones, Molli?"

"Um," she whispers and then stops, looking over her shoulder and scratching her face, which tells me at least one of them. Heroin. "Just coke. And a little weed. Sometimes molly."

Four. Fuck. Being in here has assured her lack of access to any of those, but the withdrawals have got to be hitting hard. If not yet, very soon.

"Alcohol?"

"Uh, yeah, of course. Everyone likes to have a drink and party," she justifies, her soft voice cutting a hard edge now that I'm putting her on the spot. I must know what I am dealing with in order to understand how to help. I doubt she sees that now, but eventually she will.

"I appreciate your honesty, and that's the only way this will work. But I need you to understand that drug and alcohol use can put us both at risk, especially in your current situation. It compromises your judgment, makes you vulnerable, and could endanger you."

She nods, having heard all this before. Maybe she didn't have help before in kicking these bad habits, and that's why it's still a problem. But I can't and won't have any of that happening in my home.

"We can talk about the rest later, but one last thing. No working," I stress, as it bothers me on so many levels that I can't get into right here. "You need something. Let me know, and I'll handle it."

"Like if you're wanting to—"

She shifts uncomfortably, defensive, and I realize how it sounds.

"No," I say too firmly, and she flinches at my rejection. "I apologize. If you need money for clothing or personal items, I'll cover it. Room and board are, of course, part of the deal."

She straightens, her gaze flickering behind me. Glancing over my shoulder, I see Rico lingering by the back wall. She doesn't acknowledge the rest. She just raises her chin to appear strong and proud despite her circumstances.

"I'll leave you with Rico while I make bail."

Her lips twitch, holding back more emotion already reaching her eyes as she tries not to cry from either humiliation or gratitude for needing me. I can't tell which.

18

The sound of the engine blends with the silence between us, creating an atmosphere heavy with unspoken words. I can sense the gravity of the situation weighing on her. It's as if she's giving up, and it's diminishing her vibrant spirit. Rico, ever the perceptive one, picks up on her subdued state.

"You doing all right, Molli?"

She nods slightly, her eyes fixed on the scenery outside the front window.

"Sure."

She continues to murmur variations of yes and no answers when he asks about the level of heat blowing from the front vents or if she wants him to pick up any fast food. Beyond that, she says nothing, allowing the silence to stretch the entire ride home. It isn't until Rico pulls into my driveway, next to my truck, that she utters her thanks to him.

I lean forward, grip his shoulder in appreciation, and say, "I'll call you in the morning."

Molli carefully unbuckles her seatbelt, her movements slow and deliberate. The click of the door opening blows in cold air as she slips from the truck and lingers by the front tire, her eyes fixed on the pathway leading to the front door of my house.

I can't imagine what she's thinking, but she offers no help as I maneuver out of the high truck and leverage my cane against the fresh snow blowing in. It's the first of the season, and it looks like there is going to be a light storm setting in over the next few days.

I shut my door and stand beside her, extending my arm for support as the flurries collect on the concrete, making it slippery in her high heels. She ignores it, her vacant eyes looking through me on her way to gaze up at the night sky.

Rico's departing truck fades into the distance, leaving us in a cocoon of silence. It's just the two of us now, surrounded by the stillness of the neighborhood. The snow continues to fall, casting a serene blanket over my lawn.

The stars are bright. The air is crisp and delicate snowflakes are lost in her hair. Her lips curve slightly upward before she sticks her tongue out to catch falling snowflakes.

My breath catches, transporting me back to so many winters of her doing this same thing. I'm nearly dizzy with nostalgia, recalling her collapsing into the snow to make snow angels before playfully throwing snowballs at me, her laughter always catching in the atmosphere between us.

It tugs at my heart. The same heart that wanted so much for us planned for our future, even back then, as I knew she was the one.

Wanting to connect to the memory one last time, I graze her hair, brushing a snowflake from it and causing her to flinch at the same time. My unexpected touch speaks to both the life she's endured and the distance between us.

"I'd never hurt you, Molli."

The uttered words pain me to say, and when those vacant eyes return to mine, there is sadness in them.

"I don't know that to be true."

Brutal honesty. I relish and despise it at the same time. She doesn't trust me as I don't trust her. This will indeed be a long road ahead.

"Let's go inside," I suggest softly, keeping my sadness to myself. "It's cold out here, and I think we both could use a hot shower. Separately, of course."

She doesn't respond to my comments. She just continues to stand and wait for me to lead the way. Wordlessly, we walk to the front door, leaving memories of the teenagers we used to be behind to be covered by the snow. Unlocking the door, I step through, my cane clacking on the tile entry as I move aside to allow her in before closing and locking it.

"Well, this is it. Here is the living room and, beyond that, the kitchen and breakfast room. And there is a den at the back of the house."

I edge forward so she can see into the dark room before taking the hallway to the right, leading to the two extra bedrooms. One is my gym. The other is an untouched guest bedroom that rarely sees a guest unless Rico is either too tired or drunk to drive home. Mom decorated it, of course. My job is to ensure it remains clean with fresh linens.

She's hesitant to follow me until I turn on the hall light and then the bedroom lights directly across from one another. The bathroom is in between, with enough light that she can see in.

"You can stay here." I scratch my head when I notice her coat and heels, the same ones from the jail and the truck stop. "I can give you some of my things to wear for tonight, and then, uh, we'll figure it out for tomorrow and the rest of the week."

"Okay," she murmurs, scratching her neck and immediately stopping when she catches me watching her.

"The bathroom is stocked with the basics, and we can make a list of things you need from the grocery or drugstore. There should be soap, shampoo, and a toothbrush with toothpaste down that, at least."

I shrug. Having never lived with a woman, I can't imagine what they use or need. Maybe Dani can help me out with all this. Although, she's like a bull in a China shop, and I don't know if Molli is ready for her. I could ask Eli, seeing as he's new to Isla and having had to go through all this. Then again, he has his hands full with her and the criminal proceedings. There is no way in hell I'm involving Mom or telling them she's here. I'll cross that bridge when I have to.

"I have a leftover casserole in the fridge if you want. I can warm you up a plate or order pizza," I offer while she hides another itch underneath her coat. I'll need to call my buddy at the hospital to see how to handle her withdrawals that seem to be coming on faster than I realized.

"It's fine."

She tugs her coat tighter around her slender frame, a physical barrier between us that indicates she is done with me. I'm also independent, and this is uncharted territory for me, making me slightly edgy.

"Uh, right." I nod, the awkwardness growing between us. "I'll be in the den if you need me. It's at the back of the house."

I realize the words leaving my lips are unnecessary when I consider that my modest home doesn't offer much space for getting lost. But in this moment of uncertainty, I feel compelled to provide some semblance of direction, if not for her but for me, so I don't accidentally invade her privacy.

Without waiting for a response, I turn and make my way toward the den. As I settle into my favorite chair, I can't shake off the lingering tension in the air. This journey with Molli is going to be interesting.

Having gotten to know the staff very well from the shooting and now the rehab center, I reach for my phone and seeking advice on how to best support Molli through her withdrawals. I wait as the phone rings, expecting to hear his voice mail message when he picks up.

"Hey Alex, what can I do for you?" His calm and reassuring voice comes through the line.

"Uh, hey, Terrance. I didn't expect you to pick up," I say, caught off guard. "I'm sorry for calling so late."

A glance at the clock shows I'm calling well past dinner time, and even though our night is just beginning, his is probably winding down.

"Not late at all. I'm just getting started. The ER is short-handed this week, so I'm taking extra shifts to relieve my colleagues." Even though he sounds calm, the background noise behind him is loud, with beeping and people's names being called over the intercom.

"I'll make this quick. I've got a situation here." I lower my voice, unsure if she can hear or not, but I need to know what I am in store for tonight and the following days. "I've got someone staying with me who I suspect is an addict. She scratches at her skin, and there is a slight tremor in her hands when they are not clutching her body. I think it's withdrawals, and I want to handle it properly. What's the protocol?"

There's a brief pause, followed by shuffling papers on his end.

"What are we dealing with, Alex? Do you know?"

I release a deep breath. "I suspect heroin. She's itching her face and neck. She admitted to cocaine, ecstasy, and weed. Not to mention alcohol."

A low hum resonates through the phone as Terrence processes the information. His years of experience in the emergency room have left him unphased by the struggles of humanity, and it's a comfort to have someone I can be brutally honest with.

"And you don't want to bring her here? We have the facilities for this kind of thing. I can get her in immediately," he offers, his voice filled with concern.

"Unfortunately, that's not an option right now. I just got her out on bail tonight, and convincing her to go to the clinic might be challenging. But I can't ignore the signs," I explain, a tinge of frustration slipping into my tone.

"I understand. We'll work with what we got. Heroin withdrawal is complicated."

He explains the physical and psychological symptoms she may experience—nausea, vomiting, diarrhea, aches, sweating, itching, cravings, anxiety, depression, and irritability. His words paint a vivid picture of what's in store for her, for us.

"Are there any medications she can take to get through this? Over the counter, of course," I ask, weary of giving her more drugs to help kick her drug habit.

He suggests providing fluids, nutritious food and encouraging light exercise to ease restlessness and improve her mood. He also suggests over-the-counter pain relievers for the worst of it. Beyond bringing her into the hospital or prescribing her something stronger under their supervision, that's about it. Taking mental notes, I absorb every word, determined to get her through this.

"Is there anything specific I should watch out for or be prepared for?"

Anxiety laces my words as I think of managing my recovery on top of hers, especially if she's unwilling to do all this. It's my plan for her, my rule to stay in my home, but will she go along with it? She argued that I was controlling already. Will the fear of those guys after her make her compliant now? I guess time will tell.

He warns of the risk of relapse and emphasizes the need for open communication and emotional support. These are already a problem since we don't trust each other.

"How long can I expect this process to take?"

I mentally tick through my schedule. Other than rehab and a follow-up appointment with my doctor, I'll be here with her round the clock.

"Withdrawal timelines can vary, Alex. Generally, the acute phase, where the most intense physical symptoms occur, can last a couple of days to around a week."

A week, fuck. That's going to be brutal for her. It's already been two days in custody, and she seems to be managing okay unless someone smuggled something in for her or she's good at masking the symptoms.

"That's only the physical symptoms. You must also consider psychological healing, which is a lengthy and gradual process. While the physical symptoms may subside within a week, she can take much longer to regain emotional balance and address the underlying issues. Recovery is a journey. It's crucial to provide her with ongoing support and therapy to help her navigate through this process. It can take months or even years for her to achieve lasting sobriety and well-being."

Fuck.

"Since she's not able to come into the hospital to meet with a drug counseling specialist, you'll need to consider other avenues to address the psychological aspects," he warns, leaving me stumped.

"Such as?"

"Do you belong to a church or have any connections within your community? Sometimes, faith-based organizations provide support groups such as AA or NA and counseling services for individuals facing addiction. It's worth exploring if they can offer assistance or connect you with resources, such as meetings or guidance, that doesn't interfere with the protection you are providing. A man of the cloth is also more likely to make house calls than a therapist. Or the Catholic Church up on Mystic has substance abuse meetings. Are you familiar with St. Martin's?"

Unfortunately, I am familiar with it. It's the church we both grew up in. Dread coils into my stomach at that thought. I don't want them to know she's here, and I feel like parading her underneath their noses at church is wrong.

"I don't know, Terrance. Bringing her to my parent's church feels . . . complicated. I'm not sure if it's the right environment for her right now." Or me, for that matter, but I refrain from telling him.

"I see your concerns, Alex. It's essential to prioritize her well-being and comfort above all else. If you believe the church environment may not suit her, we'll have to explore other options." Terrance's voice holds a note of understanding. "Are there any local community centers or counseling services that specialize in addiction recovery that you work within law enforcement?"

I ponder the question. Trying to keep her separate from my law enforcement resources seems selfish.

"There's a center across town. I can check if they offer counseling services, support groups, and meetings. Perhaps that could be a better fit for Molli."

"Sounds like we have a plan. For now, that is. If, for any reason, anything changes, please let me know, and we'll figure this out." I sigh, grateful to have made friends with him that fateful night. "In the meantime, take care of yourself. You're still recovering and need to prioritize your health as well. Call a friend if you need a break from the situation. It's paramount to both of your recoveries."

Unsure if Rico would help her more than he already has, I say, "I appreciate everything, Terrance. And I'll keep you posted. Thanks for taking my call."

A movement catches my eye in my peripheral. Molli is wrapped in a towel in the kitchen, keeping her distance. Her appearance sends a wave of concern washing over me as I take in her emaciated figure. The sharp angles of her shoulders and the protruding collarbones leave a cavernous hollow between them at the base of her throat. Her neck is so thin. I see the indentions of her windpipe, and her arms look like toothpicks hanging at her side. It's shocking and heartbreaking, a punch in the gut.

Her eyes roam the den, taking in the room and the traces of my life surrounding us. I can sense her wariness, her uncertainty about whether she belongs in this unfamiliar space. Our eyes meet, and there's a guarded curiosity in hers.

"You had offered me some clothes?" She uncomfortably shuffles, shifting her weight from one foot to the other.

"Of course. I apologize for not getting them for you." I tread lightly, her expression looking like she wants to run out of the room rather than wait for me to get her some clothes. "I'll get something with a drawstring so you can tighten them, given our size difference."

Her frown is instant, as if she takes offense to her skinny frame, even though I didn't mean it like that. Even back then, with her athletic frame, she drowned in my sweatshirts, with only her lean, tanned legs peeking out. It drove me nuts with desire. How vastly different things are now.

I clutch my cane to push out of my chair under her watchful eye and go into the bedroom to hunt for the smallest sizes I can find. Deciding it's nearly impossible, I grab my most comfortable sweats and take them out to the den.

What I don't expect is the amount of bruising on her arms and legs. Always covered by her heavy coat, the overhead kitchen lights highlight the purple and blue marks, showing deep and recent bruising.

Red ligature marks around both forearms also look like she's been forcibly tied up. Below them is a series of both healing and healed cut marks from her elbows to her wrists. Through my training, I learned cutting occurs when the victim feels powerless against the emotions inside them. The blade dragging across their skin releases a fraction of the pain locked inside while they feel empowered at being able to control something. It surprised me at first but made sense when the psychiatrist explained it.

Each bruise, cut, scar, and sore tells me a story of her pain and suffering, some at her hands, some at others. Her eyes are calculated, watching me take it all in, standing there, allowing me to judge the appearance of her body.

"Some like it rough," she whispers, tears filling her eyes and flinching as she says it.

As if recalling the exact moment that each bruise and mark was inflicted on her body. I've seen many horrible things in my life. Injustices to children and the elderly are the worst. Seeing her standing nearly naked before me and explaining why her body bears all these marks is hard to take. I meet her gaze, shaking my head as I promise this ends tonight.

"I won't let that happen to you ever again, Molli."

She looks down, her chest seems to cave in, and she bites her lip to stop bawling in front of me. I move closer to the wet bar that divides the two rooms and place the stack of clothes on the counter.

Tons of questions swirl through my mind. As much as I want answers, I haven't earned the right to ask them. Not yet, and certainly not this way. Let us get past the pending tsunami of physical withdrawal that Terrance advised me about first. Then, we can get into the invisible wounds that are apparent in every guarded look, clipped word, and cautious action.

"I was thinking about ordering a pizza." Changing the subject returns her gaze to mine and seems to be safer territory. "Maybe a supreme and some of those hot wings you used to like?"

Those chestnut eyes say way more than her mouth. It used to be one of the things I loved about her the most. Now they are a curse, reflecting fear, panic, and doubt—all things I never want her to experience again.

"You remembered?"

Her tone is hollow, flat, and one-dimensional. As if my remembering is taking her back too, and she doesn't think fondly of it as I usually do. I don't think going down memory lane with her tonight is wise. This is already a big enough change, and I don't want to push her to places she's not ready or willing to go.

"They usually take about thirty or forty minutes. Will that give you enough time?"

She nods, carefully easing toward the counter to retrieve the clothes, and I take a step back to allow her to feel comfortable.

"I said it before, but I'll say it again. You are safe here. No one will ever hurt you again, and that includes me."

She swallows hard, her eyes roaming my large physique and defined muscles as if doubting my intentions. Her voice is barely above a whisper as she clutches the clothes to her chest.

"Okay."

The tears filling her eyes drip onto her cheeks. I nod, backing away to give her more space and privacy to head to her side of the house. Once she is gone, I wait for the click of the lock on the bathroom door before going into the kitchen and grabbing all the beer in the fridge.

As I stand in the kitchen, pouring out the bottles of beer one by one, a sense of determination takes hold of me. Each splash of amber liquid hitting the sink reinforces my commitment to Molli's sobriety and the steps I need to take to ensure her success, even as Terrance's warning of relapse floats into my mind again.

"Not if I can help it."

19

She shakes the entire time she eats the first piece of pizza. I am on my third, having devoured one over the open pizza box, waiting for her to exit the bathroom. I monitor her the entire time she nibbles on her food on the couch opposite my chair. Her eyes are glued to the television, and avoiding conversation has me on edge.

With every little movement, sigh, or shift, I study her, anticipating the myriad withdrawal symptoms. Every passing second feels like an eternity waiting for them to hit. I did more research on my phone while waiting for the pizza to arrive. According to many of the sites, she should be in the throes of the symptoms by now. Maybe I am too quick to paint her as an addict.

She didn't ever say heroin, although her almost constant scratching at her face and rubbing the sweatshirt against her chest hints at it. She said a little coke and some ecstasy, which have fewer symptoms, and weed has none. I'm about to dig into another piece and offer her the wings when she bolts for the bathroom.

"Shit."

I drop the food on my plate and snap my recliner closed, scrambling to get my cane under me to hustle after her.

"Molli."

The sound of retching hits me in the kitchen before I find her huddled on the floor in front of the toilet. Her hair drapes around her face, concealing it from view. My heart clenches as I rush toward the bathroom, my cane dragging on the carpet and catching her attention.

Her vomiting intensifies into a gut-wrenching sound that echoes through the small space when I reach the bathroom. I kneel beside her, swallowing the pain from my upper thigh that stretches the tight muscle. I collect her hair, noticing its silkiness for a split second and holding it off her face and neck as she purges into the toilet. The smell is overwhelming and repugnant, causing me to stifle a gag.

"I'm here," I say, my voice full of compassion. "I got you."

Her body trembles, her fragile form racked with the start of the withdrawals. Long strings of saliva drip from her mouth, coated with foam and stomach acid. Tears stream down her face at how violently her stomach empties its content, leaving barely processed pizza chunks mixing with the watery brown liquid. I quickly flush the toilet and reach for a wad of toilet paper for her to wipe her mouth as she pants over the open bowl.

I adjust my hold on her hair when she drapes a thin arm on the toilet seat, bracing herself for another violent round of heaving. Sweat collects at the back of her neck and against her hairline, and I gently blow across it to cool her down.

"Keep spitting it out," I encourage after each round of vomit when the strings get heavy with remnants.

Her head hangs low, allowing me to wipe her mouth carefully, and gone is any fear or doubt that I will hurt her. I'm taking care of her, and she's letting me. It's the first step toward establishing the trust we'll need to continue down the path we find ourselves on. It's raw and vulnerable, her eyes more vacant and dead than before when she turns her face in my direction.

"Hamilton."

My name is infused with so much meaning as I stare at her tear-crusted cheeks. The dark purple bruise is now tinged with pink from all the heaving, and the cut on her lip is busted open and bleeding. I wait, but she doesn't say anything more as another round of vomiting consumes her.

It lasts longer than the others, turning the toilet bowl a tint of yellow as if her body is churning up stomach acid after running out of food. She pushes the sleeves up her arms, the heat getting to her as she sweats profusely and rests her forehead on the edge of the toilet seat.

"Hold your hair. I'll get you a washcloth."

After a brief pause, she finally extends her hand to replace mine. With a swift motion, she grasps the luscious strands and removes them from her head. My face contorts in disbelief. The beautiful locks she's had since her youth, and what I thought was her own, turns out to be a remarkably realistic wig. Underneath, her natural hair is rough, choppy, and short, with noticeable patches where hair is completely missing.

I take a shaky breath and clear the shock from my face to retrieve a towel from under the sink and run it under the cold faucet water. Luckily, she doesn't see my expression. However, my mind splinters in a million directions, trying to figure out if it's from drug use, abusive customers, stress, or a combination of all of it.

I squeeze out the excess water, reach for another towel and throw it in the stream of water while applying this one to the back of her neck.

"There ya go."

She doesn't respond other than panting and gazing at the floor until the next wave of vomit hits. Without her hair to hold back, I ring out the other washcloth and place it on her forehead when she vomits again. Each time brings less and less contents from her stomach until she's dry heaving.

Understandably, this is the consequence of her actions, but I feel extremely sorry for her.

"I can take you to the hospital. I have a friend—"

"No," she whispers. The rasp in her voice is even deeper and hoarser with the rawness of the acids burning her throat.

"It's no problem, Molli. He can give you stuff—"

She lifts her head. Her eyes are swollen and bloodshot. Little red dots appear on the pale skin of her cheeks, broken blood vessels from how hard she's vomiting. Her hand replaces mine on her forehead before dragging the wet towel all over her face and clutching it against her throat.

"I said no."

A fleeting flash of fear crosses her face, inches from mine, as I pull my hand from her nape, taking the washcloth with me.

"Why not? You can tell me, Molli. We're in this together now," I say, earnest in my words to convince her that I will do everything I can to protect her, including getting her through these symptoms.

Once again, she doesn't answer me. Instead, she eases onto the floor to lie with her face against the cool tile. No one ever uses this bathroom, and the floors are clean from the last time I cleaned them, but this isn't right.

"Don't do that."

I toss both washcloths in the sink to my right and then reach for her, and she flinches. I snap my hand back, internally scolding myself for acting without thinking.

"I'm sorry. I didn't mean to do that. I don't want you resting on the floor. Your bedroom is right next door, and I can help you if you need it."

Her eyes close for a long time, not responding and leaving

me to wait. Seconds tick by until, after too long, she finally says, "Tell me a story."

Caught off-guard by her comment, I watch her body curl into the fetal position, her short hair plaster to the side of her head while sticking up in the front. She's drowning in my clothes, with only her feet poking out and a distinct star tattoo on both her pinkie toes. Her head rests on her coiled arm, her tongue snakes over her blood-crusted lip, and she shifts to get comfortable.

The vulnerability in her voice urges me to comply. I groan as I move off my knee, both my side and thigh protesting as I sink to the floor, leaning my back against the cabinetry and letting my legs sprawled out before me. I can't remember the last time I sat on the floor, and as stiff and uncomfortable as I am now, I should probably add it to my rehab plan.

"A story, huh?"

Her eyes flutter open briefly, and her big toe pokes me in the leg, a playful gesture that has me giving her a small smile.

"Yes, *Officer Hamilton*. A story. I'm sure you have hundreds of them," she jests, and it feels somewhat like the old days when we would lie on my bed, and she'd tell me of her dreams to become an actress. She always was the dreamer between us, going on about her dream life, where she'd live, what she was going to do, and the movies she'd star in. I was content to follow her until she decided for both of us not to let that happen. With a shake of my head to clear away old memories, I groan as I stretch my neck and shoulders.

"Let me think."

"Tell me why you have a cane or crutches," she suggests, but I give her a stern look. That's off the table for now from her and almost everyone that asks. I'm still working through the guilt I have in losing Matt and seeing his poor widow and the baby at the funeral.

"I wanted to join the FBI," I begin, my voice filled with

nostalgia and regret. "I dreamt of becoming an agent and making a difference in the world."

Her gaze widens, urging me to continue. I've never told anyone this, not Mom or Rico. Once Pops got involved, it was game over, shutting it down before it started.

A surge of memories flood my mind as I transport myself back to that pivotal moment. Pops's voice echoes in my ears as I recall our passionate exchange as I relay the story to her.

"Alexander, the FBI is a prestigious and highly dangerous path. It's not just about fighting crime. It's entering a world of secrets, risks, and constant uncertainty. I've seen good people get swallowed up by the darkness they were trying to fight."

I remember my frustration, the burning desire to prove myself and make a tangible difference. I pushed back, determined to follow my own path.

"But Pops, I want to be on the front lines, making a difference on a larger scale," I had argued, my voice tinged with stubbornness. *"I don't want to settle for less."*

Pops had stood firm. He saw the potential in me, but he also understood the gravity of the choices I was contemplating.

"Son," Pops said, *his voice firm with paternal concern. "There are different ways to serve and protect. You don't have to dive headfirst into the most dangerous agency to make a difference. Look at what I've done as a police chief of our hometown. I've served my community, fought crime, and earned the respect of those around me."*

He had offered an alternative, a path that would allow me to channel my passion while minimizing the inherent risks and sacrifices of the FBI. It was not what I wanted. I had wanted out of there. To carve my path and not continue being 'the Chief's kid.'

"Alexander, if you want to pursue law enforcement, you can follow in my footsteps. Join the police force, learn the ropes, and one day, you can even become the police chief. You'll have the power to make positive changes within the community you love the most and

protect the lives of those you care about. What could be better than that? And have you thought about what this would do to your mother? Potentially losing her only son? Her only child?"

Pops wouldn't understand, no matter how hard I tried. Nor would he pay for my college if I did try. That was the final straw, and I shoved it away.

"And so, I listened to Pops."

I shrug and question internally why I told her that one. Probably because we both lost out on our dreams. For me, it was first losing her and then losing the FBI. After those big losses, I played it safe and conservative, hoping it would pay off one day.

"You gave up? Just like that?" She clutches her stomach, a large gurgle rising from it, and continues, "That's not the Hamilton I know."

The irony of her words. Neither of us knows each other anymore. I'm so different from what I used to be. Gone is the lovesick puppy dog at her beck and call, replaced by a proud and stubborn officer who will make her walk the line while living with me. Tonight is just the start of it.

"To be honest, Molli, we truly don't know each other. Not anymore," I say, dragging my uninjured leg up to drape my forearm over my knee. "Seems like we've both changed considerably."

She takes it as a slight. Maybe I meant it as one too. Wanting to hurt her as she hurt me until my guilt weighs in. 'Never deliver a slight for slight, be brothers and sister in Christ' runs through my mind in the same tone as the Father. He delivers it in his Sunday sermons. I'm about to apologize when an enormous belch escapes her slight frame, and she explosively vomits all over her arm and the floor, unable to reach the toilet bowl just a foot above her head.

She's clawing at the toilet seat, trying to climb to it. I scramble to hold her up, my hands feeling the bones of her ribcage as she trembles. The vomiting is so violent she has diarrhea at the same time. The smell is pungent, coming out of both ends. Her face hangs into the toilet as she kneels. The sweatpants become more soiled with the contents collecting in them.

My heart pounds with worry as I witness the violent convulsions racking her body. She's in pain, and it makes me feel fucking helpless, knowing this is what she must go through.

Maybe I fucked up by deciding not to go to the hospital, not to get professional help. I offered, but not strongly enough. I should have insisted. I could still insist she go.

"I made a mistake, Molli," I admit, my voice filled with remorse. "I should have insisted on getting you professional help. I can still call an ambulance and get you to the hospital."

The stench fills the bathroom. Distress etches her face when a break in the vomiting is prolonged enough for our gazes to meet. I can't bear to see her like this.

"No."

Before I can finish my sentence, she vehemently rejects the idea, her voice strained and desperate. Another wave of sickness engulfs her, leaving her trembling in my hands. As if her body is rebelling against the sobriety she desperately craves. Doing this cold turkey is the worst idea I've ever had.

"Molli, please. I'll be there with you every step of the way. I'll stay at the hospital. You don't have to face this alone," I plead, releasing a ragged sigh that blows against her back.

Her head shakes in defiance, revealing a patch of new hair growth on her nape. I fixate on that small sign of hope, desperately seeking reassurance amidst the chaos of the situation.

"They . . . they'll . . . find me," she manages between retches.

Torn between wanting to respect her wishes and fearing her deteriorating health, I weigh the options. The conflict rages within me.

I take a deep breath and say, "I hate seeing you suffer like this. My friend is a doctor there. He'll care for you better than I can. And he'll ensure you're safe."

"No." She hangs her head, resting it against her fist, balled on the toilet seat, and waits for the vomiting to subside. "You do it. Take care of me, *please.*"

The soft pleading in her voice twists a knife in my gut. I grapple with knowing it would be best for her to go through this medically, but I must consider her wishes.

"I'm so tired," she mumbles, closing her eyes as more small red spots dot the dark bags under her lower eyelashes. She breathes heavily, her skin soaking in sweat, and she's covered in her excrement.

"You've got to shower first," I say, my hands tightening on her waist when her knees give out, and she sags, sitting in her waste.

Her eyes remain closed as if the idea of bathing is too much for her to bear. With a deep breath, she murmurs, "I can't. Just leave me here."

"I know you're exhausted, but you can't lie in this."

There's no way I'd let her stay like this. It would be toxic to her health, not to mention inhumane. The thought is immediately vile and dismissed.

"I don't care."

"Molli, please. I'll help you. I'll . . ."

What? Help her shower? See her naked? Pops did it for me. He didn't think twice about wearing his bathing suit in the shower and holding me up when I slipped. And I'm doubting doing this for her? I hate myself for even second-guessing it.

"I'll bathe you. I'll wear my swim trunks and hold you up while you wash yourself. Will that work?"

Now it's my turn to be there for Molli. To offer her the same understanding and assistance that Pops did for me. The room falls into a heavy silence, punctuated only by the sound of her labored breathing. I hope she'll accept my offer and allow me to provide the care she desperately needs.

The silence stretches on, my heart pounding in my chest as I wait for her response. I can only imagine the thoughts racing through her mind. Finally, Molli opens her eyes, her gaze meeting mine, hesitant at first and then with a glimmer of trust.

"Okay," she whispers, her voice barely audible, and her eyes flutter open, looking past me.

It's a small word, but it carries immense significance. I assist her in lying on her side, just like when telling her about the FBI, while I struggle to stand. My body, stiff from sitting on the floor, makes it harder, and I twist at the waist to pop my back.

"I'm going to start the water warming up and will grab another set of clothes for you. I'll be right back."

Her eyes close again, and her lips part for her tongue to lick the fresh blood from her cut. She really would have me leave her here, and the thought crosses my mind that maybe she's been through this before.

I dash as fast as my cane and leg will allow me, changing out of my clothes and donning my swim trunks. Once I have a fresh set of clothes for her under my arm, I speed walk back to the bathroom to find her clawing at the air above her. Her body twists from side to side, whispering to herself.

"Molli?"

I dump the clothes on the countertop while she watches. Those chestnut eyes see me, and they don't. Hallucinations. I pause, unsure if I should bathe her, as consent runs through my mind.

"Molli?" I bend over to touch her flailing hand, and a small smile covers her face.

"Hi, Alexxx."

It's spooky the way she says it, like using a baby voice. It freaks me out enough that I wait several long seconds, and she snaps out of it. She's coming to and giving me a questionable look herself.

"Why are you wearing your bathing suit?" The baby voice vanishes, and her usual raspy voice returns. The switch is unsettling to witness, but she seems somewhat lucid.

"For the shower? You're covered in . . ." She sits up, a loud squish and a plump of odor rises, and she slowly nods. Her hand passes over her hair, a silent question rising with it when she looks at me.

"You took it off when you got hot."

"Oh."

"Are you okay?" I angle my neck, trying to investigate what is happening here. Her pupils are dilated, and her mouth hangs open as her fingers press into her temples. "Do you still want to shower?"

"Yes, shower and then sleep."

She blinks rapidly, the fog of confusion clearing as she reaches a hand toward me, and a wave of relief washes over me as she seems back to normal. With the utmost care, I help her to her feet, supporting her unsteady frame as I open the shower door and close it behind us.

I adjust the temperature of the water to a warm and soothing level while steam fills the room. With my back to the water, I turn to Molli and give her a reassuring smile.

"Why don't we switch spots, and then I can turn around to give you some privacy?"

She's already leaning against the wall, clutching the niche to hold herself up. I move behind her, giving her some needed privacy to undress.

"You've seen me before. I don't care if you see me again."

She sighs while tugging at the hem of her sweatshirt, damp from the water spraying off the walls. She barely has one arm out before she sinks to the floor. "I'm so tired. Just leave me here."

My heart sinks as I watch Molly struggle, her strength waning after being so violently ill. Even the simple act of showering is overwhelming her.

"I can help. If it's okay," I whisper, her chestnut eyes boring into me with an unreadable expression.

I keep telling myself that I'd do this for anyone, my fellow man of the street, but the reality is, I'm doing it for her because I still care about her. The old feelings I thought were dead and gone are rearing forward at being able to take care of her like I used to do. If she'd let me, I'd wash every inch of her, dress her and tuck her into bed, knowing she finally needs me again.

She doesn't answer, merely tugs at the sweatshirt in a useless attempt to get it over her head. Without hesitation, I step forward to support her, wrapping my arm around her waist and dragging her to her feet. Her body trembles against mine, her skin pale from the stress of everything.

"I got you," I whisper, the tuff of her short hair dusting my unshaven beard. She struggles with the other arm and gives up, leaning her entire body into mine for me to take over.

"I can't."

"Do you want me to do it?"

I will if she lets me. I need her permission. I don't want to mess up with her or make any misstep that could put more space between us than already exists.

"Okay."

"I'm here for you every step of the way," I blurt out, wanting to reassure her while releasing some of the pressure building with me.

I adjust my arm around her waist and slowly pull the end of the sleeve while she wrestles her arm out. Once that's done, I pull it over her head and toss it on the shower floor behind me. There is a smattering of tattooed stars, large and small, swirling from her waist to the tip of her shoulder blade. It looks both expansive, expensive, and painful to have gotten done. And again, more questions float through my mind.

I pull her toward me. Her skin is cold and clammy against my chest, and I gently walk us closer to the water to warm up. I glance over her shoulder, noticing the same red ligature marks over the tops of her breasts. A murderous rage builds within me as I remember what she said. Some like it rough. This speaks to a length of time that is more than rough. This is intentionally inflicting pain at her expense, so the fucker that did this to her can get his rocks off. I'd love to cut his balls off and shove them down his windpipe.

I might just do that if I ever find out who did this to her. Is it just a customer that likes to play rough, or is it one of those guys that are after her? What if they tied her up to extract information? That's what this looks more like, not rough sex. I've had rough sex and enjoy it occasionally, but leaving marks is intentional and a reminder to the victim on purpose.

I reach for the shower gel in the niche to hand to her. The minute she opens the lid on the bottle, the fragrance spills out to counteract the smell of diarrhea permeating the shower. I am unsure if we should remove her sweatpants yet, so I leave it up to her.

"Um, the pants." She hesitates, holding the bottle while thinking about her predicament. "Can you turn around?"

I loosen my arm at her waist, my breath caressing her neck as I whisper, "Of course."

Her embarrassment kicks in, a welcome break from the hallucination she was having when I first entered the bathroom. Witnessing how fast she slipped in and out of it is shocking and disturbing. I figured they would come on slower or last longer. I've encountered many suspects high on different things when pulling them over or arresting them, but rarely have I had to deal with the withdrawals. That's left to officers like Shonda, who work in the jail.

My arm falls away as I turn around and face the back wall of the shower. The smell of body fluids rises with the steam as she removes the sweatpants and kicks them past me to the sweatshirt in the corner.

"You can turn around now," she says so lightly I almost don't hear her over the shower spray.

Bracing myself for what more I might see, I turn to find her body covered in more bruises, some fresher than others. Some are deep purple with red edges, and others fade from green to yellow. My hands roll into fists at my sides, ready to beat someone's ass for hurting her like this.

Her stomach is sunk in from lack of proper nourishment, with a star tattoo on each hip bone. Her rib cage is sharp and almost protruding from her chest, with smaller breasts than she used to have. Various scars dot her skin, a jagged one on her side—a stabbing, like mine, but not as long. A cigar burn is on the top of one breast and another on the side of her waist. Little red wounds, looking like the scratching and picking at her flesh from the withdrawal, cover the skin on her upper body.

Her legs are pin thin, the gap between them far more than healthy, with a piercing on each side of her lower lips. Were those voluntary, or did someone force her to get her labia pierced? Could that be for her benefit or her customers?

I can't think straight right now. Anger boils through my veins, my heart pulses in my ears, and I clench my jaw from asking her who did this to her. Now is not the time to demand answers, now is the time to be an understanding and supportive friend. Her shaking fingertips reach for me, connecting with the bumpy red healing scar on my left side and tracing the length of it.

"We both have battle scars."

Fuck. Battle scars. Mine from chasing an assailant that killed my friend. Hers from God knows what, and I close my eyes to push the fury into the pit of my sickening stomach. Be a supportive friend.

"Yes, we do," I murmur when I open my eyes.

Her gaze shifts to my leg, the scar hidden by the length of my board shorts, but the intent is still there. She wants to know about mine as I do about hers. It's only natural when you care about someone. Hopefully, in time, she will trust me enough to share.

Her fingertips remain pressed into my flesh as we share a moment, our eyes meeting and adding another block of trust that we are slowly building. It's a start.

She withdraws her hand, a glimmer of vulnerability crossing her features before she averts her eyes. There's a guardedness that I can understand, a need to protect oneself from further pain and exposure. It's a delicate dance between trust and self-preservation, and I'm willing to give her the space and time she needs.

She suddenly goes sideways, nearly fainting as I jump forward to catch her. Her eyes are glazed and unfocused, becoming dead weight in my arms. Pain shoots down my leg at the sudden movement, and her elbow hits the wound she just finished tracing. Panic replaces the pain as her eyes roll back, and she descends into another hallucination.

"Molli!"

My voice booms with urgency over the water pressure, her eyes fluttering as if trying to look up at me and failing. Her fingers roll inward, turning into claws that sink into the skin on her chest and stomach.

"Get. . . get off . . ." Her words are strained, choked with fear and desperation. She's panicking, flailing about, frantically scratching at her stomach, breasts, neck, and face, even scratching my arms. "Too many . . . too many!"

The raw intensity of her panic sends shivers down my spine. Adrenaline courses through my veins as I struggle to calm her down. I hold her tightly, trying to steady her trembling body and level my voice to a neutral tone.

"It's okay, Molli. I've got you. You're safe."

Her struggles continue, her mind ensnared in the torment of her delusions.

"Ekes . . . bugs . . . get . . .no, I can't . . . too many! Too many!" she screams repeatedly while hitting her head with her fists, and I try to block the blows. I fight against my rising panic, searching for a way to bring her back to reality. Wrestling with her body to stay upright and trying to catch her hands long enough to pin them to her sides is an impossible feat. I must try something else. With one hand, I reach for the shower control, gradually turning down the water temperature, hoping the ice-cold water will snap her out of the hallucination.

"It's not real. There are no bugs. None at all." I keep my voice calm and steady, eliminating any of the stress and worry rushing through me. "You're in the shower. Molli. In the shower with me. Alex. No bugs. Just you and me."

Her frantic movements gradually subside, her grip loosening as reality slowly seeps in. She blinks rapidly, her glazed eyes refocusing on my face. Confusion washes over her features, and she slumps against me, her body completely limp.

I hold her close, my heart pounding in my chest. The terrifying ordeal has shaken both of us to the core. She is almost trance-like when I call her name. The cold water has done the trick, and now goosebumps cover both of us. I reach and turn the dial back to hot and position her underneath the warm flow.

"Can you stand on your own, Molli?" I murmur close to her ear. "Turn around and hold on to my shoulders, and I'll do the rest?"

Her response is slow, her movements unsteady as she follows my instructions. With trembling hands, she turns around, gripping my shoulders for support. Her eyes remain averted, not out of embarrassment but in a strange fog that seems to overtake her as if she has become detached from her body while listening and obeying from afar.

With gentle care, I lather her short hair, my fingers massaging her scalp with soothing strokes. The warm water has already washed away the remains of her body fluids, and she watches the bubbles collecting under her feet. Careful not to startle her, I whisper what I need her to do, and it takes a few seconds for her to dip her head back in the warm water flow to rinse her hair free of shampoo.

"Can I?"

I lift the body wash and squeeze a generous amount into a loofah mom insisted every bathroom must have. I couldn't be more grateful. Although I don't mind touching her with my bare hands, she might find that too intimate. The loofah keeps a physical barrier between us.

She doesn't answer, just blinks and licks the bloody bottom lip that has clotted again. I lift her hand, cupping it in mine and placing the soapy loofah in her palm for her to do it. Uneasy, she slips her hand out and stares at me. She is detaching herself from her own body, which needs cleaning.

"If this is not okay, stop me," I say, wanting and needing assurance that doesn't come.

Time seems to blur as I start at the top of her throat and work my way down, keeping my strokes light and gentle, especially with her privates. The silence stretches between us. The sound of the water and Molli's soft sigh momentarily quiets the chaos in my mind. Eventually, I finish ringing out the loofah and placing it back in the niche while turning off the water.

"Uh, I forgot the towels. Two seconds."

I carefully detach myself from her and step out of the shower, grabbing two towels from the nearby rack. I catch a glimpse of her reflection in the fogged-up mirror. Her eyes, once vacant, now hold a flicker of recognition, and I take solace in that small sign of connection. She is back with me. I'll have to ask where she went in that shower when the time is right.

With gentle hands, I wrap one towel around her shivering body, ensuring she is covered and warm. I then use the other towel to dry my own body, trying to regain composure amidst the emotional rollercoaster we've been through.

I guide her out of the shower and into the guest bedroom. The air is cold against her damp skin, and she shivers when she sits on the edge of the bed. I grab the clean clothes from the bathroom and carefully help her into them, doing my best to avert my eyes in an attempt to help her maintain what remains of her dignity. With each garment I put on her, I can sense her regaining a bit of her own agency. Her hand catches my wrist, and she gazes at me.

"Thank you."

Her voice is barely a whisper, but the gratitude in her words resonates deeply within me. I offer her a small smile, my worry dissolving now that she's back with me.

"You don't have to thank me," I reply softly. "I'm here for you, and I'll do whatever it takes to support you through this."

Her grip on my wrist tightens for a moment before she releases it. I can see the battle she's fighting within, struggling to hold on amidst the chaos of her substance abuse.

"I'm so tired."

She looks past me at the pillows at the top of the bed before crawling up and collapsing against them. I watch as exhaustion engulfs her, her body sinking into the softness of the mattress, and I grab a blanket from the closet to drape over her. She pulls the blanket over her head, blocking me out entirely, and it's the oddest thing I've seen. Concern floods my thoughts, but I know she needs rest more than anything right now.

"Goodnight, Molli."

20

I awaken with a start, disoriented as to why I am on the floor, until the memory of last night floods back to me. Her slumber didn't last long, perhaps an hour or so, before the hallucinations started again. The bugs returned, and she started tearing at her skin, drawing blood with her long nails. Then she began mistaking her nails for snakes crawling up her fingers and trying to tear them off.

Without anything to remove the nails at my house, I covered them with band-aids to mask what she thought was attacking her. That did the trick until the cravings hit. She was running around the house, opening every cabinet, looking for drugs and alcohol, and throwing the contents on the floor when there wasn't anything she could use. When she couldn't find any, she got angry and violent, taking drinking glasses out of the cabinet, and throwing them against the wall, sending broken glass flying all over the kitchen.

I grossly underestimated the severity of the withdrawals, thinking the vomiting and diarrhea were the worst. Her violent outbursts and hateful words were like dealing with a completely different person. A possessed person, if I believed in such a thing.

When she couldn't locate any substances in my medicine cabinet, she cried and wailed at both the front and back doors, screaming that I was holding her prisoner while banging her head against the wood. With my leg and limp, I could barely keep up. The repetitive hitting of her head caused a lump on her right side and a small cut on her left.

Between the hallucinations and the intense paranoia, it was a challenge to keep her clothes on. She insisted on stripping naked and stood in front of the freezer to cool off. She cut her foot on a glass shard I missed when trying to sweep them up while also trying to keep her from slicing her wrists. She was oblivious to the cut and spread bloody toeprints all over the carpet. Every now and again, she'd snap out of it, coming to and being embarrassed that she was nude or with how trashed the house was. I assured her the house and clothes didn't matter so long as she was safe. That lasted a brief period before the cycle started again. It went on like this for two more days.

I was nearly at my breaking point while talking to Terrance and almost called an ambulance amid a highly combative episode of paranoia in which 'bad guys do bad things.' She ran around the house, clawing at the blinds to ensure they were closed, turned off all the lights, and attacked me in the dark.

I sit up, taking the other couch to be close to her after she insisted she was hungry, and then ended up passing out on the couch, only to throw it back up into a paper bag. Panic flashes through me as I realize Molli is not lying on the couch where I left her. I quickly scan the house, but she is nowhere to be found. My heart skips a beat, and my mind races with worry.

Fear grips me as I rush toward her bedroom, my footsteps and cane echoing down the hallway. Relief washes over me as I push open the door and see her asleep, nestled under the covers. I sigh, grateful she hadn't gotten out and wandered off in her vulnerable state.

The doorbell pierces through the quietness of the house, jolting me out of my thoughts. With a sense of urgency, I rush to the front door, my mind filled with questions about who it could be. As I swing open the door, I'm met with a concerned Dani, who pushes past me.

"Thank fuck, you're okay. I've been blowing up your phone, and when your lazy ass didn't feel like answering, I thought the worst, like you were dead or something," she barks at me, punching me in the arm as I quietly close the door behind me.

"Shh, I have a guest."

The last thing I need is Dani to wake Molli, and we start the cycle again. Her blue eyes glint, and then a slow smile creeps across her face.

"You sly dog, you finally got some. That's why you're answering your front door with no shirt on. Who is she?" She punches me again, a light tap compared to the stinging one from a second ago. "Is it that medic from last year? She was making eyes at you while slathering that crap on my head."

Her voice is light and teasing, a welcome distraction from the darkness of addiction.

"No. Keep your voice down. She's still sleeping," I warn, needing as much of a break as possible to get my mind together and devise a new plan.

"You hit it all night long. You son of a bitch. I never took you for a kinky mother—" she teases, then stops when she takes in the state of the living room.

Pillows are strewn across the floor, stuffing is everywhere, and the displaced cushions from the couch are scattered haphazardly. An overturned chair lies with its legs pointing toward the ceiling. The coffee table stands askew, its contents knocked over and broken on the floor. Every part of the room bears the marks of Molli's wrath.

"What the hell is going on because this looks like a robbery and not hot sex?"

Her hands plant on her hips, and her ponytails hit the side of her cheek when she twists her neck to look up at me.

"I assure you, it's not a robbery," I reply, rolling my shoulders back and stretching to ease the tension.

"I should hope not since you're a cop, and only an idiot would break into a cop's house. So, what gives?"

Knowing that I must come clean with Dani since she never lets anything go, I utter, "It's Molli. She's here."

Her eyebrows raise, and surprise replaces her sarcastic expression before she turns on her heel and walks down the hallway to the bedrooms. I struggle to keep up with her but see her stop in the doorway to look at a slumbering Molli. It's not but two seconds before she clasps the doorknob and gently closes the door.

The understanding actions catch me off guard. Not known for being compassionate unless it's dealing with Isla, her small consideration gives me the courage to ask for the help I need from her.

Motioning for Dani to follow me, I lead her into the kitchen, the only room spared from Molli's destructive rampage after I cleaned up the glass. The familiar scent of coffee fills the air when I attempted to make some for Molli to take the edge off before the paranoia hit.

"What is going on?" Dani whispers angrily, her eyes scanning the space beyond me, taking in the disarray of the den.

I lean against the kitchen counter, running a hand through my hair. Mental fatigue and physical exhaustion are pulling at my body. This situation is overwhelming.

"Molli's an addict."

Dani's eyes widen in shock. Her hand covers her mouth for a moment until she takes a deep breath and says, "Wait, she's the same girl from your childhood, the first love?"

She mirrors me in leaning against the counter and not waiting for me to answer.

"First love, prostitute, and an addict. Damn. But it makes sense."

Her shock is replaced with an understanding that even I need help putting together.

"How does that make sense?"

"Think about it. Could you turn tricks with rando guys on the regular? Think of how gross men are. Not to mention you guys' hygiene varies, all shapes and sizes, a few nice guys, most not. You'd have to be on drugs or strung out to let any dick that pays to climb inside your body."

Her description is vulgar and repulsive and sadly accurate. The ligature marks and bruising covering her body ignite the rage within me again. These are all things I keep pushing from my mind in my attempt to deny what she is and what she does.

"The real questions are how did she get here and why is she doing it? Women don't pick that shit. They are coerced into it or develop an addiction and sell their body for the next hit. That's what you have to find out about her. And how the hell is she here with you? Tell me that one because you had better not be a john, or I'll cut your cock off right now with that butcher knife over there."

That spark of anger returns as she twists the piercing in her mouth, her brain processing while tossing accusations at me. My fingers curl around the counter, irritated at her calling me a customer.

"It's a very long story, but I can assure you that I'm not a customer."

"Okay, then, why is she here?"

Dani is not one for letting anything go unless she decides it's done. I walk to the cabinet to retrieve a coffee mug and offer her one. She narrows her eyes and shrugs, which means she wants a cup too.

"I bailed her out," I reply, reaching for the cold coffee pot, pouring some in, and warming it in the microwave.

"Why? You trying to get back with her?" Her head tilts, and her eyes narrow, shooting me a disapproving look. "Because she's got to get clean first before she gets in any sort of relationship with you."

"No, she's in trouble, and I'm helping her out."

She has me on the defense, and I use the beeping microwave as an excuse not to elaborate, retrieving her cup and starting mine.

"It's a given that she's in trouble if she was in jail as a prostitute, but it still doesn't explain why you bailed her out and why she's here destroying your house. Help comes in lots of forms, and this doesn't look like the best of it. You know they have treatment centers and professionals—"

"She can't go, well, won't go," I interrupt, the guilt of not forcing her to see Terrance is eating me up. "Dani, look, you come in here and make a lot of assumptions, but you don't know what's going on. If you would just—"

"No, Hamilton. Don't get all pissy with me because I know that look on your face." She grimaces when she tastes the coffee but is content to resume giving me the third degree. "Bill, my stepdad, has it all the time dealing with my mom. Life with an addict is a constant struggle. You're not going to save her today. You're going to save her every damn day for the rest of your life. Do you realize that?"

She slams her coffee cup on the counter, the liquid sloshing over the side. What's one more mess in the sea of messes all over this house?

"Huh? What did you think? That you would bring her home and playhouse like you wanted all those years ago? Well, who's making assumptions now? You know this isn't going to work. You're not going to swoop in and save her from herself. She's got to be willing to do that. Bill does it all the fucking time, and that ghost of a woman just takes advantage of him. And I for damn sure won't let that happen to you. I won't let her turn you into another Bill. One is fucking enough."

She's shaking with anger, something not attributed to me but equally applied in her mind. It's when her eyes shift behind me that I groan inwardly.

I glance over my shoulder at Molli, standing in the doorway. Her face looks more drawn, the bruising deepening and the bags under her eyes are darker. Her expression is one of embarrassment and disappointment. Rarely do I want to throttle Dani for her candor, having grimaced when directed at other people, but having it directed at Molli when she's already struggling is out of line.

"Dani didn't mean any of that, Molli," I say apologetically, extending my warm cup of coffee to her as a peace offering.

"Yeah, I did. And don't speak for me, Hamilton," Dani insists, pouring salt on the wounds and being intentionally cruel. "Look, Molli, is it? I don't know you from Adam, but I know this guy, and he's one of the good ones. I've been through a string of assholes, so trust me, I know. He'll give you the shirt off his back. Well, it looks like he already did. But if you break his heart again, I'll break you. Capeesh?"

Molli's eyes widen, withdrawing into herself and hugging my sweatshirt to her body.

"Danielle Louise Winters shut the fuck up!" I roar at her. Molli startles, her eyes widen, and she backs away several steps while Dani remains unfazed at my anger and language.

"What a dumbass." Dani rolls her eyes. Her expression matches the sarcasm in her words. "You can't get all loud and blowhard in front of her like that. I swear, didn't they teach you anything at cop school? Aggressive behavior, loud noises, all that shit doesn't work."

Blame it on the lack of sleep, the lack of experience with this sort of thing, or that I'm genuinely in over my head, but everything feels like it's spiraling out of control. My efforts to help seem futile and it only adds to my mounting frustration. I rub a hand over my face, trying to shake off the weariness.

"Clean up this mess while Molli and I enjoy our coffee. Get to know each other and stuff." Sensing I'm struggling with handling their dynamically different personalities, Dani throws me a lifeline. "You got any donuts or something to go around here? Your girl looks like she hasn't eaten in well forever, and I haven't had breakfast since I was worried over your non-responding ass, but at least now I know why."

I'm slow to respond, my gaze set on Molli and gauging her reaction to Dani and her offer. It's quite the dichotomy with Dani threatening Molli and then wanting to be nice. It's something relatively new in that the first reaction is her true self firing forward, and her later reaction is the new version she's trying to be. It's usually entertaining to watch, but it's a disaster in this sensitive situation. I appreciate her attempts at growing and changing as a person, but it's brutal to watch sometimes.

Seeing that Molli remains unresponsive and gives no indication of her preference, I decide for her. I'll be in the same house. Dani won't intentionally hurt her even though she said she would, and I could use a break to regroup. Turning to Dani, I try to maintain a sense of normalcy amidst this new kind of chaos that only Dani can bring about.

"Um, yeah, there's some blueberry muffins in the pantry and more coffee if you want."

"Okay, I'll find it. Now go, you smell like puke, and it's grossing me out." Dani wrinkles her nose. I pinch my thumb and index finger into the bridge of mine, trying to keep calm while Dani is being that annoying gnat she accuses Rico of being.

I give Molli a reassuring smile before leaving the kitchen, almost certain I do smell like vomit. Even with her brash ways,

I'm grateful that Dani arrived this morning to help me out, even if she's going about it in all the wrong ways.

"My mom's an addict. You know, if you continue doing it, you could have a stroke and die. Or worse, live."

The first words out of her mouth have me cringing, and I almost turn around to walk back in there, forgoing my shower and kicking Dani out of my house.

"Go sit down before you fall down, and I'll get the coffee and muffins."

I listen for Molli's answer, waiting to see whether I need to charge in there.

"Okay."

Her reply is soft but an agreement to comply, and I exhale, knowing everything will be fine.

"Then you can tell me what's up with your hair."

21

My muscles ache everywhere as the scalding water glides down my back. The stress from the last several days has knots in my neck and into my shoulders. Usually, I'd jerk off to release some of this pent-up frustration, but with the two ladies sitting outside my bedroom door, it kills any desire. I couldn't get an erection if I tried, so I settled for stretching as best as my injuries would allow before getting out to get dressed.

Even though she's with Dani, I don't have the time to dilly dally should any of her symptoms start up again. Even though Dani is tough and very thick-skinned, I'm unsure how well she would handle it, given what she said about her mom.

I quickly open my bedroom door to find Rico perched on the counter, talking to the ladies in the breakfast room. My eyes zoom in on Molli to gauge how she's handling all the company we suddenly have.

"I didn't hear you come in."

"I like what you've done with the place," he remarks, raising a knowing eyebrow at me.

"Shut the fuck up and have some respect," Dani scolds,

tearing off a piece of her muffin and throwing it at him. It bounces off his cheek and lands in his lap before he plucks it up and pops it in his mouth. Molli gives me a guilty look before looking down at her hands.

"And what are you going to do if I don't? Punish me? 'Cuz we'd both enjoy that." Rico gives her a suggestive look. Their lighthearted bickering is a nice reset.

"Seriously, Hamilton, why are you friends with this neanderthal?" Dani exclaims, tossing a thumb in his direction. "Can you believe this dude?"

"He's always been like that," Molli says quietly, a half-eaten muffin sitting on a plate in front of her while her hand subconsciously floats to her head as she eyes Dani messing with her long ponytail. Dani's eyes widen, and her lip curls into a sneer.

"Wait, you know this guy?" She doesn't even give Molli a breath to answer before she's up and out of her chair, going after Rico. He jumps off the counter, putting the kitchen island between them. "If you're a customer, I'll rip your dick off."

Rico's eyes are blown out, Molli's head is in her hands, and I look at the ceiling for patience or guidance. Dani keeps faking left and right, chasing him around the island.

"Hell no. I'm above . . ." He stops mid-sentence, realizing it was probably something hurtful to Molli, and I intercede.

"Enough!" Raising my voice at her a second time today is more than I ever had in the almost year I have known her. "Can you take it down a notch? I thought Tomlin got you to stop fighting."

That has her stopping dead in her tracks and whirling around on me.

"How dare you! After all, we've been through, do you think I'd ever change for a man? I may love that guy with everything I have, but he'd never ask me to change." Her finger is so far into my face that I must lean back to avoid it touching me. "I'm a fucking phoenix rising from the ashes, and you'd best remember that."

Rico leans on the island, casting me a strange look, and I'm equally confused about this phoenix comparison. At least it gets her off Rico's case, and Molli seems entertained by Dani's outburst, which is more than I can say for myself.

"Don't you all have somewhere to be?" I say, pushing Dani's finger away as her blue eyes narrow when I step around her.

"I actually came by to talk to you," Rico blurts out, his eyes sliding to Molli, who thankfully doesn't see him from the kitchen island's angle to her breakfast room seat. "It's about that case we've been working on?"

I motion for Rico to follow me outside to talk away from the ears of both ladies. As we walk toward the front door, I hear Dani tell Molli that she took her first trip to Los Angeles a few months back, and Molli confirms she lives there. As interested as I am to hear that story, Rico's expression lets me know this is more serious.

"What's going on, Rico?" I keep my voice low as I close the front door and walk toward his truck parked on the street.

"Hers." He tosses his head toward my house with a grim look. "She mixed up with the Maldonado cartel."

"Fuck."

I run a hand through my hair and gaze down my quiet street, filled with retirees and young families. Not the neighborhood used to this type of crime.

"Yeah, apparently, she's the captain's girlfriend, Joaquin Amado. He's tearing through the town, looking for her. He knows she made bail, and it's only a matter of time before he finds someone who's been around here long enough to make the connection that you two used to be a thing."

"Shit."

My brain ticks through all my options which aren't many. She's in danger. In bigger danger than Rico and I both realized, which puts me and those around me in danger. Mom, Pops, Rico, and everyone I know, including Dani and Tomlin, Eli, Ronald, and Isla.

"And the Chief isn't too happy about you getting her out. Something about the state agency is involved since the distribution of drugs is crossing state lines and is most likely coming up from the Mexican border."

Rico's hand on my shoulder is reassuring, opposite his grim expression. It's clear that we need to take immediate action to protect Molli and mitigate the risks to ourselves and those closest to me.

"We can't let the Chief get her. He'll hand her over so he won't have to deal with all the red tape." I run a hand over my face, trying to deal with this added complication. "We need to find a safe place for Molli, somewhere they can't find her. The fewer people who know about her whereabouts, the better."

Rico nods, his gaze focused and resolute. "Agreed. But where?"

I contemplate the possible options, knowing that time is of the essence.

"I have no idea. No one I know has a second house, and I can't stay with someone else, putting them in danger either. A hotel for now. Maybe head out of town?"

"They will check the hotels for sure. Camping? Like we used to do on the back of the mountain? It's not ideal. You could set up some traps. Before that, you'll need to make sure Molli understands and will cooperate because that house of yours doesn't look like she's fully complying." His grip tightens on my shoulder before releasing it.

"Substance withdrawal. It's been rough."

"It looks it. What kind of substance abuse? Drugs or alcohol?"

"All of it."

I level his gaze, sympathy passing across his face.

"I called Terrance. He gave me some information, but after what we've been through, I was going to take her in to get medical help."

"Can't do that now. First place they will check for her unless the Chief wants to put a guard outside her door, which he won't do since he wants to wash his hands of this situation as fast as he can. She's not safe here, either. You're barely able to protect her. One hit to your leg and you're down."

I exhale, the situation getting worse with each passing moment. He's right. I cannot fully protect her, even if I want to. I run a hand through my hair, frustration and worry intertwining within me.

"Then where?"

Rico's gaze is steady, looking past me. I turn, seeing Dani hauling ass our way.

"If y'all are done gabbing like girls, Molli's inside throwing her guts up." She tilts her head, her eyes dart between Rico and me, trying to assign blame for our delay.

"Shit, it's starting again." The withdrawal cycle is going to be a challenge while in hiding. "I got to go. I'll think of places if you can too."

I turn away, walking toward the house to help Molli, and overhear Dani ask him, "What were you two talking about?"

Her violent retching echoes through the house, and I quicken my pace. When I enter the bathroom, she's huddled in front of the toilet, her body trembling with each convulsion. She raises her head, her water eyes piercing into me.

"I can't make it stop," she says as an apology. Her raspy voice is hoarser from all the stomach acids passing through her throat, and I feel so helpless. "It wasn't this bad last time."

Last time. I file that away—another question to ask her later. A wave of empathy washes over me as I kneel beside her, gently touching her back.

"It's okay," I whisper, offering whatever comfort I can. "This time, you got me. Whether you like it or not."

A half smile flickers across Molli's face, briefly lighting up her weary features. It's short-lived, interrupted by a gaseous burp that bursts from her lips and a round of vomiting into the toilet. I quickly grab a washcloth, wetting it under the tap, and gently place it on the back of her neck while flushing her breakfast away.

She raises her arm, coiling it around the seat and leaning into her shoulder. The same position as the other night when this first started. Her chestnut eyes slide past me, and I glimpse Dani in the middle of the hallway behind me.

"I'll be right back."

Leaning on the counter for support, I stand, carefully closing the bathroom door to give Molli some privacy. I follow Dani into the den, still looking like a tornado hit it when she whirls around to face me. Her shock is evident by her mouth falling open.

"She's mixed up with a cartel?" Her eyebrows disappear into her hairline while her hands plant on her hips. "And you're hiding her here?"

I grit my teeth. A surge of anger courses through me at Rico. How could he have divulged confidential information to a civilian, even if she's a friend? We don't need this added complication. I take a deep breath, trying to remain composed despite the frustration bubbling up in me.

"Yes," I begin, my voice steady but tinged with an underlying urgency. "Molli's in danger, and we're doing everything we can to protect her. We can't trust anyone else right now."

"Who's we?"

"Rico and me. He's the one that is digging around and finding out things for me while I'm on leave."

I wave a hand toward the other side of the house, where the

muffled sounds of Molli vomiting continue. She takes a step closer, her eyes searching mine for answers.

"I know it's a lot to take in," I continue, my tone earnest. "But Molli's life is on the line. We're keeping her here until we can figure out a safer plan. We're her only hope."

As I speak, I can see the wariness in Dani's eyes, the conflicting emotions warring within her.

"He said they are out looking for her, and it's only a matter of time before they find you and her. Probably in this very house, from the sounds of what's going on with her," she says, unwavering in her resolve, that I'm doing something foolish that is jeopardizing my life too. "What if they already know about this place?"

As Dani's words slice through the air, her concern for my safety clashes with my determination to help Molli. The impending danger is closing in on us, and I can't help but question my judgment.

"They don't. It hasn't even been a few days."

Her expression morphs into one of murder, my murder. Her hands clench, and I brace myself in case she lets them fly. Instead, she whirls around and begins pacing, her steps short and crisp, like a predator assessing its prey.

"You had Isla here yesterday, and now Molli. The girl with cartel ties? You're as dumb as that idiot I talked to outside. You're not only putting yourself in danger, but you're putting all of us in danger, especially my new family. Are you fucking nuts?!?!" Every word is a slow build to the rhetorical question. I look to the ceiling to keep from yelling back that I fucking know it. "After everything that Isla has been through. And don't even get me started on Eli. He'll have a fucking heart attack from the worry alone."

Guilt, frustration, and anger surge through me. Everything has been getting progressively worse. I haven't had a chance to properly think about the danger I've suddenly invited in when bailing her out.

"Fucking idiots," she continues yelling and pacing. "Well, you're not bringing this shit to their doorstep. You had better pray that they don't know your association with them, or else I'll murder your ass instead. You don't have to have a cartel to do it." She shakes her head. All those threats would be empty if she really knew the full extent of what we're dealing with. "Fucking men. She must have a golden pussy for all this."

I let that comment slide, knowing she's talking out of protective anger, the same protectiveness I feel for Molli.

"Clock's ticking, bro. Where are you going to take an addict going through withdrawal? Rico said the hospital won't take her." She stops pacing long enough to glare at me, and I'm surprised.

"You know she's going through—"

"Yeah, dude. Turns out good 'ole Jessica got a secret stash that Bill found, and I had to take care of Dylan while she went through this," she sneers, the hatred for her mother unwavering. "Is that what this is? Paranoia and shit?"

She twirls a finger in the air, signifying the ransacked room, and my lips press into a thin line.

"Well, you've really screwed the pooch on this one." She huffs, swiping a couch pillow off the ground and tossing it on the recliner with a ton of force that I think was meant to be a replacement for sending her fist into my jaw.

"Yes, it's more complicated than I thought," I finally reveal, my voice firm but weary. "I thought it was just a motorcycle gang or maybe a jilted pimp seeking revenge, but if it truly involves the cartel, which Rico is investigating, then we're dealing with something entirely different."

"You can't turn her in?"

I take a moment to lock eyes with Dani, searching for understanding, but the truth is apparent in her expression. She can't fathom why I wouldn't consider turning Molli into the authorities, especially given the escalating danger surrounding us. My commitment to protecting her but it goes beyond any rational decision. It stems from a deep sense of responsibility and an emotional attachment that started over two decades ago when a skinny girl walked into vacation bible school at my parents' church.

"No, I can't," I reiterate, my voice laced with emotion. "I promised to protect her, and I can't go back on that now. It's not just a matter of duty. It's something deeper. I feel responsible for her, and I want to see her through this, to give her a chance at a better life."

"Hamilton, I get that you want to help her, but what about the risks? Damn, man, you're putting everyone at risk, all for a chick you haven't seen since you were a teenager? It doesn't make sense. What am I missing?"

I run a hand over my beard, the scruff sounding in the quiet room, and I notice Molli's retching has ceased.

"What if we can rekindle what we were?" I whisper, glancing over my shoulder to ensure she hasn't entered the room unnoticed like she did earlier.

"Bingo." She points at me when I reveal the secret. The secret I wasn't ready to admit to myself. "You still have feelings for her. And if you do all this and she leaves? Splits town?"

Her concern remains, and her question hits hard. I shrug. Dread for the dangerous situation her presence has put us in is the same as the dread of her leaving and never seeing her again. The truth is, I can't control Molli's choices, but I can control mine, and I have to try, hoping it will all work out better than before.

"Then she leaves. I'll accept that. It's a risk worth taking."

Dani watches me momentarily, her eyes searching mine as if trying to decipher the truth of my words. Finally, she sighs and shakes her head.

"Where are you going to take her? Especially like she is?"

"I don't know. Neither Rico nor I have a second home, and the motels in town would be the first place they'll check. My initial thought was to take her out of town—"

"My place. You guys can stay there." She bites her lower lip as she thinks, determination set on her face. "Yeah, it's the only way. You protect her, dumb ass, and I'll protect you. But if this blows up in your face and you end up dying, I'm going to be so pissed at you."

I ignore the latter to concentrate on the former. "What do you mean, your place? I thought you lived with Tomlin up in the mountains."

"Oh, Grandma Hamilton, the place that started it all." A slow smile spread on her face as if holding a secret. "My garage apartment. Naturally, Lars would have to clear out the cars and take them to the mountain house to work. You're not bringing this shit to his doorstep either, he has a family to protect, and I won't let you fuck with that."

I pause, staring at her with such surprise that she continues while my mouth hangs open.

"Tomlin added a shit ton of security, cameras everywhere, bulletproof glass, and a massive fence around the whole thing. Ya know, bad neighborhood, worried about our safety at night, blah, blah, blah, but it's perfect when you think about it. Sort of like a compound, one way in and one way out. At least until you get this shit figured out or get her a lawyer, I don't know which. Why am I always the one having to figure shit out around here? Sheesh, do your part, man."

I'm familiar with his improvements to her garage, having gone to her small grand opening for the few clients she had procured in the short months since the show. Tomlin didn't spare any expense with all the security measures he installed. I joked about getting an off-duty security job there if he needed it, and he seriously considered it before Dani swatted at his chest, saying she didn't need a rent-a-cop cluttering up the lobby or parking lot.

"But that's your garage. Your livelihood," I protest, not knowing how long we'd be displacing her.

"What are you talking about? We don't have clients coming through the front doors. We have two projects underway that will take a couple of months, but nothing I can't handle at the mountain resort. We have all the same equipment up there, so we can keep working, and Lars is not in danger."

She's racing through this solution faster than I am. I am speechless, astonished by the extent of her generosity for someone she threatened to kill in the kitchen earlier this morning. The thought of staying in her garage apartment, with all its reinforced security measures, intrigues and unsettles me.

"And Tomlin? He'll be all right with this?"

She snorts, waving off my worries with a dismissive gesture before answering.

"It's my garage. I'll do what I want with it." She widens her stance in defiance, always challenging authority.

"Sure, but doesn't he have a say, or do you need to tell him?" I voice with concern, not wanting to get into the dynamics of their relationship. But he must know in order for all this to work. I can't get in that guy's crosshairs while dealing with this situation.

"You sure have an old-fashioned outlook on relationships, bro. I don't need his permission. But you have to tell her."

Dani points behind me, and that's when I glance back and see a very frightened Molli standing by the wet bar, shaking like a leaf.

22

I turn around, a knot tightening in my stomach as I take in her frightened expression. She's going through so much with the symptoms and now the threat on her life. The weight of it all could easily crush her. I walk toward her while Dani pulls her phone out of her back pocket and walks toward my bedroom for privacy.

Taking a deep breath, I meet her gaze and begin to explain. "Your boyfriend, Joaquin Amado?"

Her head shakes frantically, and her arms wrap around herself as her eyes widen with fear. Tears drip down her cheeks and she quickly wipes them away.

"He-he's not . . . no . . . he's a very bad man," she stammers, slowly backing up until she hits the counter behind her. I slowly descend on her, an overwhelming pull to comfort her as I'm not finished telling her the news.

"I know. Rico's been looking into it, and there's reason to suspect he has ties with a cartel out of Mexico."

Her eyes widen in disbelief, and her voice is barely above a whisper when she says, "No . . . no, um, that can't . . . it can't be true."

I cross the kitchen, reach her and gently coax a trembling hand away from her waist to hold in mine.

"There weren't things you saw that didn't make sense? Men coming in and out? Drugs? Perhaps guns or other women?"

She looks away, ashamed, and pulls her hand away to hold the bruised area of her face when I mention men coming in and out.

"I . . ." She shakes her head, not finishing her sentence.

"None of those matters. We need to leave. Right now."

I hate springing this one her, but we have no choice. We've lost valuable time that's giving them the advantage of finding her, and we're sitting ducks here.

"But. . . your house and my . . . problem."

Her hand courses over her short hair as if searching for the wig she pulled off last night. A frown mixes with the panic on her face.

"It's not ideal. But Rico has reason to believe that Joaquin is looking for you and—"

She stops tugging at her short hair to stare at me. "He-he's here?"

"Yes." Then it occurs to me that he's not from here. "Where is he from? Where does he operate out of?"

"Los Angeles," she whispers, her hand falls away. "But this is your home. Your life. I'm putting you in danger."

"I chose to help you. I left you in that jail when you refused my help, remember? Then I came back. It was my choice to bail you out."

It wasn't my finest moment, and it fills me with shame to think that I let her sit in there, suffering, all because my pride prevented me from helping her back then.

"I was blitzed out of my mind. I don't even remember what I said to you." She frowns. "Where do we go? Joaquin must have connections here. Why else is he here?"

"Joaquin may have connections, but we can't let that stop

us. Dani offered up her place. It's a commercial garage on the other side of town, with lots of security and far more than I have here. It's safer. Anyone that's looking for you won't know about that place. It buys us some time to plan our next move."

Apprehension wrinkles across her face before she looks for Dani in the den and then returns her gaze to me when she doesn't see her.

"I don't want to put her or her family in danger. I'm already doing it to you, and that's bad enough. I never meant for you to get involved," she murmurs, guilt in every word while she swipes her tongue across her busted lip. It's having a difficult time healing with all the vomiting.

"Don't worry about her. She's going to move to another location for the time being. I need you to gather your things while I coordinate with Dani and pack myself."

I step back, giving her physical space and the emotional distance needed to process all this. A mixture of emotions flickers across her face, and she nods slowly.

"And your parents? Will they be safe if he figures out our connection?"

The blood drains from my face. It's already challenging enough to put myself at risk for her, but asking Rico is an even worse decision. And now, getting Dani and my parents involved? It feels like a cascade of dominos falling against me.

"Fuck!" I yell, startling her as I storm off to the opposite end of the kitchen.

"Yeah, that didn't go over so well," Dani says casually, walking out of the bedroom and across the den, extending her phone to me. I meet her in the den, giving Molli more space between her fear and my frustration. "He wants to talk to you."

I look from her to the phone, and seeing Tomlin's name on the screen, I take it from her.

"Yo, Molli, let's leave them to work out the details while we get you packed up," Dani hollers next to my ear, and now I'm retreating into my bedroom for privacy.

"Hello?"

"What the fuck is this that I hear about hiding a fugitive at Dani's garage? And for an indeterminable amount of time!" Tomlin's voice pierces through the phone, taking me back to when I had to restrain him from attacking Mr. Wilson at said garage. Those days were simple in comparison.

I take a deep breath, trying to steady myself as I prepare to address his anger.

"I know this is unexpected, and I apologize for Dani volunteering in the first place. If I had somewhere else to take her, anywhere else, I would. But Molli's safety is at stake here. She's in danger, and I have to take whatever precautions to protect her until I figure this out."

There's a brief pause on the other end of the line, and I can almost feel the tension in Tomlin's voice as he responds.

"Hamilton, I understand that you want to help your old girlfriend, but this situation is serious. You can't just bring someone with potential cartel connections into Dani's garage. Not only does it put her at risk, but it also puts her family, her brother, Isla, and everyone she cares about at risk. You're essentially asking me to allow you to jeopardize Dani's safety. And she's my family. How do I say yes to that? You may not realize it, but that woman is my entire world. If something were to happen to her . . ."

A ragged breath escapes through the receiver, and I know how deeply he cares for her. It's evident in every smile, glance, and gesture he shares with her. It's enviable—something they have. Mom and Pops have it, which I desperately want too.

"Putting everyone at risk is the last thing I want to do. You have to believe that, but I don't have any other options. When Dani offered her place and mentioned the added security, I thought it would work long enough for us to get more information on this Joaquin Adamo guy and get her an attorney. She's terrified, and with my injuries still healing, I need every advantage I can get. My house makes us sitting ducks, and I can't let that happen either."

I grab a bag from my closet and start stuffing clothes in it. If I can't take her to the garage, I'll take her to a motel or figure something else out.

There's a heavy silence on the other end of the line, and I can sense Tomlin's internal struggle. I continue packing, my hands rushing as I gather only the essentials, including my gun, holster, and badge. Both desperation and determination fuel my actions.

"I understand that you're in a tough spot," Tomlin finally speaks, his voice heavy with concern. "But bringing Dani into this is a risk I cannot afford to take. I cannot risk my family's safety because of this."

I pause for a moment, my mind racing to find an alternative solution. I can't leave Molli exposed, but I also can't disregard the safety of those I care about. My grip tightens on the bag, the decision boring into my skull, where a headache is forming.

"I understand. I won't put Dani or anyone else in harm's way," I respond, my voice firm despite my turmoil. "She said she can move operations up to your cabin in the mountains, but if that won't work or is unsafe, I'll figure this out. Even if it means finding a different place to stay. I won't leave Molli unprotected."

There's a tense silence before Tomlin's voice softens, a hint of understanding seeping through.

"Listen, I know you're doing what you believe is right. I trust you to prioritize everyone's safety. Let's regroup and discuss our options at the garage but pull into a bay so if they have your vehicle's description, we can conceal it. We'll find a way to keep Molli safe without jeopardizing Dani's well-being, or Lars's for that matter. He's a family man too."

I release a breath I hadn't realized I was holding, grateful for Tomlin's willingness to consider alternatives.

"Thank you, Tomlin. I appreciate your understanding and support."

"I don't like your actions, but I can respect them. I might also have connections with a criminal attorney, but let's save that until I get there. I'm in Denver, so it will take a few hours to wrap things up and head there."

"All right then, we'll meet you at the garage."

With renewed determination, I zip up the bag and head into my bedroom, where Dani's leaning against the doorway.

"And Hamilton, keep Isla and her family out of this. If something happens to that girl, Dani will kill you and that girl you're harboring. Not only is she my world, she is her brother's also," he gives me a final warning before ending the call. And yes, I don't think it would bother Dani one bit to spend her life in prison if it meant protecting or exacting revenge for a loved one. She'd probably start an auto repair program for the inmates while in there. I chuckle at the thought.

"What's so funny?" she asks, kicking off the door frame to walk further into the room.

"Nothing."

Absolutely fucking nothing is funny about this situation.

Dani raises an eyebrow, clearly sensing the tension from that phone call. She takes a step closer, her gaze searching mine.

"What'd he say?"

"He's upset about the situation and wants to discuss this at the garage," I explain, handing her the phone and setting my bag on the bed. "Beyond that, he might have some connections with a criminal attorney."

"Yeah, he gave me an earful," she says, sitting on the bed beside my bag and absentmindedly touching the leather.

I doubt he gave her an earful. Even with her threats and

outbursts, he's always kept his calm demeanor with her. He possesses extraordinary patience when dealing with her, so this meeting will be interesting.

"I do appreciate what you are doing, Dani. If I knew of another way, I'd take it," I confess, shaking my head, trapped in an endless cycle of thoughts that offer no new insights. "Where is Molli?"

"She's getting the few things she has, but she needs clothes, decent shoes, toiletries, and skin stuff. You name it, and the girl needs it." Dani clicks her piercing against her teeth, looking away briefly before speaking again. "I'd say she could borrow my stuff, but we're not exactly the same size."

No, they are not. Dani is petite and curvy. Molli is taller and emaciated, as evidenced by her spine protruding down her back as I took in the massive number of star tattoos.

"Yep, I know. Are you ready to clear out of here?" I ask, hoping I got enough for the next few days until I can return here to get more things.

"You're not going to clean up this place first? You look like a victim of a burglary." Dani abruptly stands, walking toward the doorway as I grab my bag and swipe my keys, wallet, and phone from my dresser, ignoring the missed calls and text messages from her, Terrance, Rico, my parents, and the Chief.

"Nope, I got to get her moved before any other symptoms start again."

I follow her out of the bedroom and start closing the blinds. She notices my actions and follows suit. After securing the front and back doors and ensuring the deadbolts are engaged, Dani grasps my arm to prevent me from gathering Molli.

"She mentioned your parents to me. What are you going to do about them?" Worry etches a line between her brows, and I exhale deeply.

"I don't know."

23

Molli's quiet the entire trip to Dani's. Maybe old memories are haunting her as they are me, taking me back to when I drove her around town on Friday nights after playing in the football game and the gang all meeting up at Burger World. I intentionally pass it on the way to the garage to see if it evokes a response from her. It doesn't. She continues gazing out the window as we pull through the gate of Dani's garage. She's already waiting for us with a giant man standing beside her.

I understand Tomlin's concern for her safety. This area has seen its better days about fifteen years ago. However, the security measures he installed are over the top and draw more attention to the place than I would've preferred. Assuming the price tag of these cars warrants the added security, I think it's more about protecting the tiny thing with her hand cupped over her eyes in the bright sun than the hundred-thousand-dollar vehicles.

"She's not lying. This is more secure than I thought."

She turns to face me, her bruising looking much worse in the bright daylight, and puts her hand on the dashboard.

"Thank you for this. I don't know how I'll ever repay you," she murmurs, the warm air from the heater blowing against some dangly earrings she fished out of the pocket of her fur coat. The very one she's bundled in now, over my sweatshirt and pants.

She said this before—gratitude or guilt speaking now, perhaps both. Either way, I wouldn't think twice about doing this for her.

"Don't thank me yet. I don't know if this is going to work."

She doesn't say anything else when she releases the dashboard and turns to open her door. I cut the engine to my truck and collect my things before slipping out the driver's door.

Dani is crossing the parking lot toward us before she spins around and hollers, "Lars, close the gate for me, will ya?"

As the tall wrought iron gate begins to slide closed, Dani drops her hand and points to the building.

"Tomlin said to pull into the bay, so Lars cleared the spot if you want to pull through the open door. Molli, you can come with me inside. I have the best coffee in town. It's this cool expresso . . . heck, I'll show ya." Dani's already in charge, her no-nonsense demeanor taking over immediately now that we are on her property.

Molli gives me a weary look but complies, meeting Dani halfway through the parking lot and exchanging handshakes with Lars on their way inside the lobby of the building. I maneuver through the open bay with Lars at the helm directing me onto the iron lift that holds their cars while they work.

Once parked, he's beside my door, making introductions as well.

"I'm Lars Myers. It's nice to meet you after all this time."

He grips my hand, squeezing the shit out of it and catching me off guard. Not in the douchebag way of trying to see who's stronger, as many men do, but in a way that he must not realize his own strength.

Lars Myers. I've heard many good things about him from Dani, and she's right that his size doesn't match his demeanor. The Academy would love someone built like him for the force and as an instructor for new recruits. If he ever decided to stop this venture with Dani, he could have a long career in law enforcement.

"I've heard Dani say so many great things about you that I feel as if I already know you," he continues, his voice as welcoming as his offset smile. Rarely do I have to look up to a man, but I certainly do with him. How he works in the tight spaces of these cars is beyond me.

"I feel the same."

I release his hand and look around the improved garage. It's had a significant upgrade since I was here last year discussing the assault charges with Dani that the jerk she worked with could have filed against her. He tried to file something out there against her when she hit him. They came across my report, and I had to set the local PD straight when they called. They weren't interested in pursuing charges. I never did tell Dani that.

"She's sure fixed up the place, hasn't she?" I say, looking around the remodeled lobby, upgraded interior, and more bulletproof glass between the lobby and the garage.

"Yup, got full air conditioning, so it's comfortable while we work, surround sound speakers separate from the lobby so we can jam, and customers can't hear us. Not that we get many anyway. That glass really blocks out a lot. And the breakroom is always stocked with snacks. It's great. We even added a punching bag and a gaming system on the big screen upstairs, so if you want to crash and take a break, you can be more comfortable on the couch. It's a pretty cool place to hang out."

His voice is full of pride, obviously happy to be working for her, and it's nice to hear that Dani makes it a great work environment for him. I'm glad she's paying it forward in her new management and ownership role.

"Sounds like a real man cave," I say, trying to lift my voice to the same enthusiastic level as his but not coming close.

He tosses his head, trying to get his long brown hair out of his eyes, when he sweeps toward the glass door separating the two spaces.

"It is, have a look for yourself. I've got to get these cars loaded on the trailer to take them up to the mountain house. Dani says we have to move out of here asap since there is some fumigation going on that will last several days. Something about a rodent's problem or nest, but I haven't seen anything."

Ah, that's what she told him—smart move to protect him while keeping our secret. Never one to put anything past Dani, I'm glad she's as protective of her loved ones as I am with mine. Except for Mom and Pops, I still need to figure out a solution before calling them. Pops won't be as easily convinced as Lars, which brings dread into my stomach again. He'll demand to know the whole situation and want to contemplate various solutions, which we don't have time for.

"Thanks, I'll check it out. And good luck with the cars. I hear it's treacherous getting up the mountainside."

His smile spreads, and then he winks. "That's just the excuse Dani uses to go slow. She calls you a grandma driver when she's the real grandma. But don't tell her I said that, or else she'll dare me to a race on the backroads in her truck which wouldn't last two seconds against mine."

He chuckles, a lightheartedness that is enviable. I can see why he works here. If he has any talent to go with that good nature, he'd be an excellent employee and probably a good friend.

"It'll be our secret," I assure him, pushing through the door and walking down the hall toward Carl's office, which is now a breakroom. When I find it empty, I continue to the back of the building and follow the voices as I climb the stairs.

Memories of climbing these flood into my mind. Dani was

standing on the landing when she opened the door in her bra and underwear while Tomlin glared at me for looking her up and down. I quickly surmised that Dani was the girl from the bar that had caused him to speed off. When I got up here, he was staking his claim and making it known that she was his, even if she called him a pest and wanted him to leave.

How things change. I push open the door to her old place. Gone is the peeling wallpaper and secondhand furniture, replaced with a completely remodeled interior, including modern furniture and sleek chrome appliances. Besides the old punching bag hanging from the rafters where her little break-fast table sat, the place is brand new, from the textured ceiling to the sanded-down and refinished hardwood floors.

"Wow, this looks—"

"Awesome, huh?" Dani says, clutching a steaming mug while leaning against the kitchen counter. Molli's further behind her, sipping her drink and content to let her gaze wander from us to the finishes beyond.

I was going to say different. Dani rarely has this excitement level, so I don't want to dampen it with the wrong word choice.

"Yes, awesome."

"I know. Lars and I battle for supreme dominance up here, and the loser must clean the tools and soak the rags at night."

She points to an under-cabinet television stand with a few different gaming consoles and a large screen mounted on the wall. Opposite is a couch and a couple of stylish chairs that seem more like Tomlin's influence than hers.

"Anyway, I was showing Molli around. Shoot, if this place looked like this when I lived here, I'd have never moved out."

The second the words leave her mouth, a strange expression passes over her face, and she clacks her piercing a time or two until it passes. I'm not the only one haunted by my old memories. Hers probably goes on for days, but I'm glad she finally received the credit and accolades she deserves.

"Do you mind if I take a look around?"

"By all means," she offers, walking over to the cabinet, setting down her mug, and starting up on one of the consoles. "Come play me, Molli, while Hamilton does that cop crap of checking the locks and looking for escape routes."

I try my best to ignore Dani's comments, knowing she's just trying to alleviate the tension in her own way. Molli seems hesitant to join in, her discomfort evident as she slowly moves away from the kitchen.

"I don't know how to play," Molli admits, her voice filled with the same uncertainty as her actions. Even though there's only a six-year age difference, it seems like decades with what Molli has been through.

"It's fine. I'll teach you. Sit there." Dani points to the other small chair beside her. "Gotta pass the time somehow until Tomlin gets here."

Molli glances at me, seeking reassurance, and I offer her a gentle smile before walking to the window. I peer through the blinds, surveying the surroundings, focusing on security and Tomlin's impending arrival.

Leaving Dani and Molli to their game, I proceed down the hall to the bedroom. There's only one bed. I should have figured as much. If Tomlin does allow us to stay here, Molli can take it, and I'll take the couch. It worked out just fine when I slept on one last night.

I take a moment to myself. This day has already been stressful with visitors and finding out about her boyfriend. Ex-boyfriend, she alleges, which would be convenient if it's not true. I didn't doubt Rico, but he seemed sure she was his girl. The thought has me clenching my fists and looking at the ceiling to calm the jealous streak overtaking me.

She's not mine. Nor does she need to be with all this going on. That should be the furthest thing from my mind, but it was nostalgic when I held her in my arms. The ride over here, as quiet and slightly awkward as it was, reminded me of the fights we used to have where we were too proud to give in and make up. I need to shove all these renewed feelings aside to keep my head straight for what lies ahead.

"You, okay?" Molli whispers from behind me, and I turn to face her as she removes her fur coat to cup her arms. Her chestnut eyes flicker to the bed for a moment, and I wonder if she's worried about there only being one.

"I'll take the couch."

A small breath comes out when she smiles as if finding amusement in that. "I wasn't worried about that. I was thinking you should turn me in."

"What? No! It's not safe for you and—"

"It's not safe for them either. Before all this, I wasn't your problem, and I shouldn't be now. I shouldn't be any of these nice people's problem. They seem to be good people. You've done well for yourself here. I can see that. I can't mess that up. I already did it once before, and I won't do it again."

Taking two steps, I take the coat from her arms and place it on top of the dresser before reaching for her hand as she looks like she will cry.

She hesitates but relents, slipping it into mine. I cup it lightly and say, "It's too late to turn back now. We've already got a plan in motion, and it's a good plan for now, Molli. Can you see that? I need a couple of days to lay low and think over all our options, and if we can stay here, it will be better."

"But—"

"Look at this place. It's ideal. The part of town it's in, the security, no one would suspect you're here. And you've got me. Don't you think I'll protect you? Is that what's bothering you? Because of my injuries—"

She moves closer, her hand squeezing mine and resting against my chest, her touch comforting and familiar. It's a gesture she used to do when we were together, a simple act that always calmed me down. Damn her for doing it now and knowing it still has the same effect.

"I know you can protect me. I've always known that. But who protects you? And who's going to protect them?"

Her questions hang between us, creating an undeniable tension that crackles with my unspoken desire. As I gaze into her chestnut eyes, I feel the electricity building, drawing us closer together. Her lips part ever so slightly, a subtle invitation that sends a surge of longing through my veins.

At that moment, everything fades away—the dangers, the uncertainties—as my focus narrows on her. I'm transported back to when it was just the two of us. When the connection between us was pure and effortless. The memory of her soft lips against mine, the warmth and passion we once shared, floods my senses.

The room feels charged with anticipation as I lightly grasp her waist, my fingertips pressing into the soft fabric of the sweatshirt. I lean in slightly, a silent invitation for her to close the remaining distance between us.

A gentle smile plays at the corners of her lips, teasing and inviting, but her head tilts to the side, her expression unreadable. Time seems to slow down, each heartbeat echoing loudly in my ears as I hold my breath in anticipation of her response. It's a delicate dance, a moment of suspended possibility, where every move and decision holds immense significance.

But then, in that fleeting moment, she exhales softly, her breath mingling with mine. The moment passes, breaking the connection. I release a sigh, disappointed. We both know that now is not the time for indulgences, but the longing reminds us that our connection is still alive.

It's bittersweet, but with a gentle squeeze of her waist, I withdraw my hand and step back. Her hands fall to her side, and a flicker of disappointment passes through her expression.

"How's the gaming going?" I ask to chase away the remnants of desire between us.

"I'm not—"

"Molli, are you taking a dump or what? Because I can't keep playing for you."

Dani's impatient voice bellows through the small apartment, eliciting a chuckle from me.

"I think you're being summoned," I say, still smiling.

"Is she always like this?"

This is the question I have been expecting from her all day, but with Dani around, it couldn't come until now.

"This is the mellow version of her, compliments of her boyfriend. Wait until you meet him. It's quite a pairing."

"This is mellow?" Molli raises an eyebrow, and I nod.

"Yo, Molli. Quit making out with Grandma Hamilton, and get your skinny ass out here. I can't wait all day!"

"Wow," Molli whispers, inhaling sharply out of embarrassment. "Grandma Hamilton?"

"Long story."

"I'd better go before she starts a revolt."

"Consider it her way of accepting you. And consider yourself lucky because she's slow to trust anyone."

Confused, she says, "But she threatened me."

"Yeah, she does that. Pretty much all the time, but she hasn't acted on her threats in a long time." It sounds less and less reassuring the more I say. "Remind me to tell you how we met when she's not around. It will make sense then."

As she turns to make her way to the other room, she stops, clutches the doorframe, and says over her shoulder.

"I'll hold you to that."

I can't see her face, but her tone is lighthearted, and I exhale in relief. I can't help but feel a twinge of hope amidst this mess. Our reunion has brought back a flood of emotions and memories. Even though I don't know what will happen, at least she's back. I'm going to do everything in my power to not only keep her safe but to win her back.

With renewed determination, I turn my attention to the bedroom window and locks, peering through the blinds and seeing the front gate slide open for a black Porsche. Tomlin's here. He made record time. Let the games begin.

24

As a bell rings from downstairs, Dani springs up from the couch, a blur as she darts toward the staircase just as I emerge from the bedroom. Her footsteps pound on the steps until she reaches the bottom.

"Her boyfriend is here," I say to a bewildered Molli, who's playing Call of Duty, which is a terrible choice of game considering what's happening. She looks from me to the open door while her character gets shot up, spewing blood all over the large screen. "Why don't we shut this off?"

"I didn't want to be rude." Molli slowly places the control on the side table and shrinks into the armchair. "Oh my God, my hair. Alex, I need my wig. I feel naked without it."

Her hand glides over her short hair, her fingertips resting against a bald spot at her neck and the small amount of stubble growing back. She pushes out of the chair with a frantic expression as she looks around the room.

"Shit, we didn't bring our stuff in." She licks her lips, her hand still absentmindedly stroking her head. Her large chestnut eyes settle on me, a plea in them. "Will you please go get it? And hurry before he sees me."

Her sudden panic catches me off guard as she didn't care that Rico, Dani, and I saw her without it. I can't make heads or tails of her request.

"Of course, I'll go get it for you," I assure her, realizing this must be a security blanket for her. I pat my pockets, locate my keys, and nod at her.

"Stall them. I can't meet her boyfriend like this!" she says after I turn to leave.

I pause for a moment, unsure how it makes me feel. Does she know who Dani's boyfriend is? Does she want to impress him or something? A streak of jealousy surges through me, and I tamper it down. She's not even mine to be possessive over. But why does her wig suddenly matter?

"I'll do my best," I say casually, masking the storm of emotions brewing inside me at the thought of her wanting to get dolled up for a guy who's already taken while I'm available.

I jog down the stairs, letting out some of my frustrations on the creaky wood, and rounding the corner to see Tomlin leaning against the counter, smiling at Dani in adoration as she tells him about my best friend, Rico. When he catches my gaze, he straightens up and crosses the room to shake my hand, something he always does upon every greeting.

"I hear Dani's meet her match with this Rico fellow," Tomlin says with amusement while Dani plants fists on her hips behind him.

"Hardly, he's like Tweedle Dumb to this guy's Tweedle Dee. He's a match for no one."

She snorts in offense, and I merely shake his hand, getting a whiff of his subtle cologne. Another thing he's never without. This guy is always on and must be part of the celebrity life.

"Where's Molli? I thought she was coming down too, or was that just you trying to break every one of my stairs on the way down here?"

I release his hand with a guilty grin that has nothing to do with 'breaking her steps' and everything to do with Molli wanting to impress this already impressive man.

"She needs a moment of privacy, and I've got to get something from the truck for her." I point toward the front door as both are blocking my way. "If you'll excuse me."

"Ah, she's taking another shit, huh?" she says, turning to Tomlin. "She must be constipated from all the drugs because she was holed up in the bathroom when I was trying to teach her Call of Duty."

Tomlin chuckles, his deep voice muttering that it's not an appropriate game when I walk past and head out to the truck. Glad we both feel that way. It's good to see they are both in a jovial mood. Perhaps it will make them more likely to allow us to stay for a few days while I devise a plan. I'm certain Dani's on board, seeing how Lars is loading another car onto the trailer parked on the street. Tomlin is the challenging one, and I can't blame him. I'd be the same way if the roles were reversed.

Grabbing her bag from the truck, I forgo getting mine. I don't want to appear too presumptuous even though we're here and Dani's already making provisions to her workload. The bell on the front door chimes as they walk arm and arm out to Lars, who's coming up the drive and wrestling a hardy handshake out of Tomlin, who claps him on the back while Dani beams at both guys.

It gives me a warm feeling that everything has turned out for her, something I didn't think was possible when I met her at the truck stop. Life is funny that way. Sometimes you're in the shitter, and it turns around. Other times, you're minding your own business recovering from an injury, and your past grounds out a cigarette in front of you. I stride back into the shop and head upstairs but don't see Molli.

"Molls, where are you?" I ask, closing the door behind me to allow her more privacy.

"I'm in the bathroom." She pokes her head out into the hallway, and her eyes light up when she sees her bag in my hand.

"There you go," I say, offering it to her. She steps out to retrieve it, shrinking the narrow hallway around us.

She pauses, her eyebrow pitching when she asks, "Did you just call me Molls?"

"Uh, yeah, I guess I did," I reply, taken aback as I didn't realize I nicknamed her new name, which is already taking time to get used to. "It just slipped out."

"Just like when you used to call me Mar."

A hint of a smile tugs at the corners of her lips as she reminisces. This is good, but it pulls at that place in my chest where nostalgia from the old times and desire for her now reside.

"Those were good times," I murmur, suddenly hot and sweaty as I dip into dangerous territory.

Her not remembering me was hurtful and made me hesitate to bring up the past. But letting little slips like this happen helps me gauge if I'm the only one caught in the memories of a fond past. One moment turns into two and then three, then too many, and then I feel foolish for saying it in the first place.

As her chestnut eyes gaze up at me, she says, "Molls. I like it."

Not acknowledging what I said, but also not getting visibly upset. I'll take it as a small win for me. Her fingers graze mine when she takes the bag and disappears into the bathroom, closing the door behind us.

It reminds me of a slow dance. The kind we used to do at the annual harvest festival held every autumn underneath the twinkle lights strung across the old man Miller's barn. The band would be feisty with some folk or heritage song and then slip into a classic country ballad. I'd remove my hat, press it against her waist, draw her close, and breathe her in.

I fell for her so many nights like those, too many nights. As more time passes, I see glimmers of her old self that have me hoping to fall again. However, this time, it needs to be one hundred percent reciprocated because, as Dani already told her, she won't break my heart again. I won't let her. I no sooner step away when she throws open the bathroom door in a complete panic.

"It's not there."

Her voice shakes, and she starts picking at her skin like she did when she thought bugs were crawling all over her. It makes me panic because I need her to hold it together long enough to meet and talk with Tomlin. If she falls prey to the hallucinations or paranoia we've battled the last few days, it will all fall apart, and he won't let us stay here. I'll have to take her to a motel and risk them finding her.

"No, no, Molli, you must hold it together."

I drag her hand away from her neck, where her nails already put a long scratch in the delicate skin, holding it in mine. She uses her other hand to claw at her face, scratching up and down her jawline until the skin reddens.

"I have to have it. Alex, he can't . . . no. He can't see me," she stammers, her eyes filling with tears, and before I can catch her other hand, it slides into her hair to start tugging at it. Hard, painful tugs that hardily register as she's about to send herself into a full-blown panic attack that could trigger her other reactions and set off her delusions.

"It's okay, Molls. He doesn't care." I catch her hands, forcing them together in mine and squeezing them to assure her. "He's not like that. He won't mind about your hair."

"He will. Dani said he's famous." Her face morphs into fear, a haunted expression recalling something else that doesn't involve the here and now. "If he's a celebrity . . . someone important, I have to . . . don't you understand?"

I don't. I have no idea what Tomlin's celebrity status has to do with her reaction now. But I'm left to think quickly on my feet to prevent this from spiraling out of control with them downstairs waiting for us.

"I do understand. I promise I do." The lies spill out with ease. "He's not like that. He's not really famous. Just judo people know him."

Her head shakes unnaturally fast, her hands fighting to get out of my grip, but I refuse to let her go as I need to diffuse the situation before they climb the stairs at any moment.

"He's from Los Angeles. He could know people . . . he can't see me like this . . . he can't, he can't . . ." she murmurs repeatedly while slowly rocking back and forth as if in some trance.

I'm left scrambling, trying to understand what is happening and how to fix the situation. This is somehow tied to her past, each passing moment revealing layers of deep trauma and making me feel helpless again. I do the only thing I can think of. I pull her close, enveloping her fragile frame, hoping to bring her back to me, back here and not out of the dark memories she's trapped in.

"Molli." I don't know what to say as I hold her, her lips still whispering under her breath against my chest. She doesn't reciprocate, but she doesn't pull away, so I keep going. "It's okay. Shh, it's okay."

She fists my shirt, trembling in my embrace, and I lean my cheek against her head, her short hair tickling my nose. I feel her pain and fear, and I wish I could take it all away. But all I can do is hold and comfort her, let her know I am here.

"I'll go down and talk to them," I murmur when her whispering stops. "But Molls, I can assure you that he only has eyes for Dani. He will not comment on your hair or lack of wig."

She ducks her head further into my chest, seeking more comfort. This vulnerability is so different from the tough front she put up when I confronted her in the parking lot. It's almost as if it was an alter ego to protect the real Molli I'm experiencing now.

"I can't . . ."

Her voice is muffled but persistent in not being seen. As delicate of a state that she is in and weary of pushing her if it triggers her withdrawal symptoms, I acquiesce.

"Okay. Just stay up here. I'll be back."

I grip her tightly, shifting my head to press my lips against her hair. Unexpectedly, I find myself lingering there, anticipating her reaction—whether she would stiffen or retreat. She doesn't do either. She slips her arms around my waist and returns the embrace. A mix of emotions runs through me. Hope, happiness, and guilt for taking advantage of her vulnerable state in my desire to win her back.

When my overwhelming guilt becomes too much, I slide my hands to her shoulders and gently ease her out of my arms. Her eyes are puffy, rimmed with a pink tint that matches the bruising changing colors as it heals. Unshed tears remain at her lower rims as she subconsciously brushes a hand over her head, her lips still trembling at leaving behind her wig.

"Um, can you go back . . . ya know, to get it?" Her voice is small and hesitant, knowing it's not a good idea, but unable to comprehend living without it.

"I don't know if that's such a good idea."

It's insignificant to me but everything to her. Even though it pains me to tell her that, I need to be honest with her. The risks are too great at this point. If I knew it meant so much to her, I would have ensured we had it before we left.

"I know it's asking a lot, but when can we return there? How long will we be living like this?"

Her questions fall one after another as her arms wrap around her small frame again to self soothe. It's something I notice happens a lot now that the drugs are out of her system. I must figure out how to get her the help she needs, as we can't stay holed up in here the whole time without addressing it.

"I honestly don't know when we can return, and again, I'm unsure if this is where we will be staying."

The truth is harsh, but it's the only way it will work between us. The brutal truth. No less than that.

"They are waiting for us. I will talk to them and get this sorted out."

She steps back, followed by another, until she sees herself in the bathroom mirror and frowns. The thinness of her lips increases as she rolls them together. And once again, her hand ghosts over her hair with her fingertips stopping in the patch of stubble she usually caresses.

She doesn't say anything in response now that she's lost in her appearance. I release a deep breath before turning away and heading back downstairs. I find them in the break room, Tomlin's sprawled out on a small chair with Dani next to him, showing him pictures on her phone.

"This is the new one I was telling you about. It's a real heap that the owner is pulling out of this old yard in Tennessee. Do you see that damage? And it's a 1970 Dodge Challenger, First Generation. Can you believe that?" Her eyes sparkle when she glances from the phone to him and back. The love for this job is pouring out of her while talking about this car. "You know how much I love this decade of—hey, where's Molli?"

Dani's eyes dart to mine, as do Tomlin's. His arm drapes across the back of her chair, and his thumb strokes up and down her arm until he sees my expression, and his smile fades.

"She's upstairs," I say, clearing my throat and debating if I lead with the truth. It's best for everyone if I do. "I guess she heard from you, Dani, about Tomlin's celebrity status and is a little overwhelmed."

A half truth is better to gauge their reaction first. Tomlin's frown deepens, and his eyebrows pinch together in displeasure. Dani huffs and then closes her phone to place it on the table.

"I surely hope that is not the case," Tomlin murmurs, straightening up and pulling his arm back as if to stand.

"Please don't get up. This is best solved between us anyway. She doesn't need to know all the details. Frankly, I'm not sure she can handle them right now."

A bit of despair sinks into my words. I'm usually quick to assess a situation and make the right call. However, considering Molli and her feelings is causing me to second guess myself.

"I'll go get her." Dani pushes out of her chair and jumps to her feet before I stop her by holding up my hand.

"That's not the only reason if I'm being honest."

Dani looks from me to Tomlin, where he motions for her to take a seat, and in true Dani fashion, she ignores him to plant her hands on her hips instead.

"Out with it," she demands as if I'm hiding something salacious.

"I don't understand it, but she left her wig back at my place. Something about needing it and that she can't be seen without it. She had a very emotional breakdown about it."

I lower my voice in case Molli decides to come downstairs and is listening around the corner. It feels almost a violation of trust to talk about her like this to Tomlin, but I also don't want Dani charging up there after her.

"Something about you being from Los Angeles and knowing people? I can't make sense of the connection she's making since you're from Denver."

A bewildered look passes over his face and only intensifies when Dani looks at him. Their shared confusion matches mine. A few second of silence passes before Dani's mouth opens and closes, still thinking about it.

It's Tomlin who speaks first.

"Dani said she's from Los Angeles. That's your friend has been living out there in her, uh, profession." There is trepidation in his tone, as if he knows what he wants to say but is leery of saying it.

"I assume she's been there the last ten years, yet I don't know. Why? What are you getting at?"

A knot forms in the pit of my stomach as I try to process the implications of his words. Molli's past, her connection to Los Angeles, and the potential connections it may bring to our current situation.

"Does she think I could be a . . . client?" My mouth and Dani's fall open while Tomlin's eyebrow curls upward. "I don't partake. Dani, as you know. But others do. It's widespread, depending on her status and ability of her, uh, handler, to access the elite in that city."

The knot hardens, and Dani looks murderous while I feel sick.

"That's fucking disgusting," Dani blurts out, taking the words right out of my mouth. "And if you decide to 'partake,' I'll cut off your dick." She uses air quotes when she uses his word.

A smirk plays on his lips when he looks at her before outright winking. The nature of their relationship is still a mystery to me, as her threat of violence plays into his amusement. Odd, for sure.

"And what about reporting it?" she demands, bearing down on him. He drags his index finger to his face in thought, the amusement gone instantly.

"I have, and I do if they somehow slip past Rex and the security team, which has only happened once. Years ago." Having anyone slip past his security team is a huge breech, so I can understand how he's insulated from the problem. "As you are, I have a difficult time making the connection of the wig. Perhaps to conceal her identity, which is important to her. Or shame?"

"That's bullshit. She doesn't have anything to be ashamed of. She already told me about the deal with her hair, trickasomething-mania, but who cares? Some bald dudes always walk around like big shots, and it doesn't bother them. Sometimes, mine's a hassle, and I debate cutting it short but deny the world these cute pigtails, not a chance."

She grabs one, then glares at it and starts messing with the pink holder midway up when she sees it's not even with the other one.

"Trichotillomania," Tomlin replies with a snap of his fingers. "It's a compulsion. I don't know much about it, but a fellow contender had it at one of my first Worlds competitions several years back. I asked my trainer about it during practice rounds when the contender suddenly shaved it before the competition started. I believe it's a means of handling stress, and the act of pulling the hair is a physical release of the anxiety they feel. I'd liken it to the relief one may feel when exercising."

He pokes Dani in her side, giving her a knowing smile.

"Do it again, and you lose the finger. No matter how many times you ask, I'm not working out with you. Sex and cars are enough of a workout for me," she threatens without missing a beat or looking up from her hair.

I could have gone without hearing that, but I appreciate Tomlin's insights on the other matter.

"I've not heard of that before, nor has she confided that in me. I—"

"Well, duh," Dani interrupts, tossing her hair over her shoulder when done with it. "She's walking on eggshells around you. It's so obvious."

Completely bewildered, I counter her. "What are you talking about? I've been nothing but nice to her. You should have seen her the last several days. The withdrawals have been terrible. I've held, bathed, cleaned, and fed her around the clock. Most of the time, she was out of her mind imagining things that were not there or not happening."

I can't help my temper flaring with my frustrations. I've had no outlet for them, and I'm ready to burst. I may take a few swings at that punching bag they have hanging upstairs before this is over.

"I'm just calling it like I see it."

She raises a shoulder, sounding indifferent, and I take a step closer to her, about to lose it. Tomlin's up and out of the chair in a moment, stepping between us, and I turn away, running a hand through my hair.

"Dani, why don't you give us a minute? I'm sure Molli would appreciate the company since it sounds like she's struggling and doesn't know us or this place."

I don't bother turning around, choosing to grip the countertop while taking deep breaths to calm myself down.

"I know what you're doing, and it won't work. I'll check on her because I want to, not because you ask me to."

Her voice has an edge, and he murmurs something that escapes me when her sneaker squeals on the concrete floor.

"I don't know how you keep your cool with her sometimes."

I know it's out of line to say to him, but I can't help it. She can be too much sometimes.

He has a generous smile when I turn around but doesn't respond directly to my comment. Instead, he walks over, grabs a small white cup from the cupboard, and presses a couple of buttons to get the machine to swirl and grind.

"Do you want a cup?"

His hand hovers on the cupboard handle, waiting for an answer before closing it.

"Sure."

I turn around, flip the faucet to cold, and splash water on my face. The droplets are refreshing to my overheated skin. I towel off my face, feeling a slight tingling sensation that distracts me from the tension in the room. I ball up the paper towels, toss them in the trash can at the end of the counter, and turn to Tomlin while the machine is still going.

"I'm sorry, that was uncalled for." I have enough guilt over this situation. I don't need to pile on more, talking bad about the person stepping up to help me. "I shouldn't have said anything about her, nor should I have stepped up to her."

"Thank you. I appreciate that."

He walks over and grips my shoulder, easing the tension I created between us.

"Why don't you have a seat and tell me everything from the beginning."

When the aroma of hazelnut coffee fills the air, he releases me, steps to the machine to retrieve a cup to set on the table, and makes another cup. I take the seat Dani vacated and unload about our past, skipping over the night I got shot and including seeing her at the truck stop until now.

He's silent, the steam from the coffees rising between us when he joins me. I brace myself for the onslaught of questions when he surprises me by leaning back in his chair, scrolling through his phone, and setting it face up on the table before me.

"You're going to need to call him. It's the same firm handling Isla's pro bono case, but this guy handles federal cases. Not sure if this will rise to that level, but he'll be able to help you and Molli from here on out."

I stare at the phone screen, my mind reeling with gratitude. Tomlin's immediate assistance catches me off guard, and I'm momentarily speechless. I glance at him, searching for any signs of ulterior motives or hidden agendas, but all I see is genuine concern and a willingness to help.

"You don't have to do this, Tomlin," I finally manage to say, my voice filled with both hesitations. "I mean, it's already a lot that Dani is moving the cars out, and I'm not even sure if you're letting us stay, and now you're offering legal help too? It's too much."

"I had to hear it for myself. Dani's fiercely loyal, as you know, but it comes at a cost. One I'm not always willing to bear, even though she thinks she can take care of herself. Like I said, she is my family, and I will protect her over everything else. As I'm sure you feel or are beginning to feel yourself. However, now that I know firsthand the trouble Molli is in, I want to do whatever I can to help. Consider it my way of looking out for your family too."

Family.

Molli is not my family. And even though I want to correct Tomlin on that term, I don't because it does something to me. My chest tightens, and an uneasiness settles within. I want to win her back, but will I look at her like he looks at Dani? Would I protect her above everyone else, as he's saying? I don't think so. I did once, and it almost ruined me. I doubt I'll ever fall that deeply in love again. The first time was a free fall. This time there is a net. Never mind the circumstances are entirely different—innocent, first love versus damaged, experienced, second chance love.

His words resonate deeply, though. Family. I've always known I'd be a family man. I had a good example with Mom and Pops, but could she and I be the family I longed for? It's something I'll have to consider, as it seems like a million miles away from where we are now. That's what I need to focus on.

I reach across the table and firmly shake his hand, overcome with gratitude.

"Thank you, Tomlin. I can't express how much this means to me and Molli. I'll contact this attorney today and see how he can assist us."

Tomlin nods, his expression turning serious as he releases my hand and texts me the guy's contact information.

"To confirm, you and she are welcome here. That said, Dani

doesn't know this yet, but for the foreseeable future, I'm putting a private security team up there with them. Lars has a family to protect, as well as do I. If you need one here, I can add it to the contract."

"No, I don't think we'll need additional security," I respond, considering the implications of Tomlin's offer. "I appreciate the gesture, but with all the additional security you've added to this place already, and with the one entrance, we should be good until I figure this out."

Tomlin nods in understanding, a hint of skepticism flickering in his eyes. "And your injuries?"

"Healing." It's a fair question and one I've asked myself. "I'll be okay."

"All right, I trust your judgment. Remember, don't hesitate to reach out if you need to reassess the situation. Safety comes first."

"Thank you again," I say, downing the expresso and getting a massive jolt from the deep, concentrated coffee grounds. "That has a kick to it."

"Expresso. Dani's latest addiction." He chuckles, his skepticism easing into a more relaxed demeanor. "She can't seem to get enough of it. She tells me it keeps her fueled throughout the day."

I shake my head, still feeling the caffeine coursing through my veins. "Well, it definitely woke me up. I could use the boost."

"What can't I get enough of?" Dani blurts out from the doorway, her eyes narrowing at Tomlin. Molli lingers behind her, attempting to conceal herself behind Dani's short statue. Her hand rests on her neck, near her bald spot, and it falls to her side when she catches me watching her.

"Me," Tomlin chides, standing and collecting his coffee to hand to Dani when I realize he never took a sip. He made it solely for her.

"I thought you were talking about my beloved coffee. Best damn expresso machine in the world. I got one here and one at home."

Dani is across the room in a second to retrieve the cup, leaving Molli looking too exposed for her liking. The wooden table creaks under my weight as I use it for leverage to scramble to my feet, my healing thigh protesting at the sudden action. Tomlin passes his girlfriend to make introductions.

"Hello, Molli. My name is Tomlin Takahashi," he says, extending a hand toward her. Molli is instantly put at ease by his warm and sincere voice, enabling her to respond carefully.

"Nice to meet you," she replies softly, her eyes briefly flickering toward me before focusing on Tomlin and her hand ghosting over her head, missing the wig. The room feels momentarily suspended, waiting for this encounter to unfold as I intently watch her reaction for any sort of breakdown.

"Everything good?" I ask, checking in to let her know she's safe with him and that I'm here if she needs me.

She nods, her tongue nervously swiping across her lips as Dani moans into her coffee.

"You sure you don't want one?"

"Uh, no, thank you. I don't usually drink caffeine," she says quietly, moving toward me once Tomlin steps back to stand beside Dani. There is quite a bit of height difference between them, which Molli seems to be taking in.

"What? No caffeine?" Her mouth falls open in shock as she openly stares at Molli. "Then what do you take to keep yourself going? Awake and ... ya know, never mind."

She catches herself, and Tomlin puts a subtle hand on her shoulder, which I am learning is how he also communicates with her.

"Why don't we head up to the cabin? Help Lars get things settled," he suggests, pressing her into the side of his body in a warm embrace. A smile drifts across her face as she gazes up at him, then hums when she takes a drink.

"Um, Alex?" Molli's voice is delicate and faint, opposite Dani's brash and direct voice. "What about your parents?"

"Shit!"

I hate that I keep forgetting about them. Trying to get Molli and me situated is enough. Having to go to Pops and explain what happened and then wonder what to tell Mom is dreadful.

"What's this?" Tomlin turns toward me, breaking away from Dani with a curious look.

"Molli and Dani mentioned it earlier, but it slipped my mind." I run a hand through my hair, wondering what I will tell them and where they will go until this blows over. Neither will like this, but that old farmhouse is not the safest compared to this place. "If they make the connection that I have Molli, they could easily find my parents. It's not hard, they live in that old historic landmark near downtown, and Pops was the former police chief. Everyone knows who he is and where he lives."

Molli crosses the room to stand next to me, putting a hand on the middle of my back.

"They are really good people, and I would kill myself if anything happened to them on account of me."

Her choice of words is disturbing. Given that I don't know her as well as I once did, I'm unsure if she's exaggerating or would do it. Either way, Tomlin's eyebrows move up, and Dani lowers the cup from her lips to cradle in her hands.

"Do they have someplace secure to go? One that cannot be traced back to them?" Tomlin asks, his expression as perplexed as I feel. A sigh loosens from my chest as Molli's hand lifts from my back.

"My mom has a sister in Manitou Springs. That's not too far from here."

Thinking of the ease and speed with which I can get them moved and settled without too much disruption.

"That might not be far enough. And with it being an even smaller town than here, how likely is it that everyone will know your aunt the same as everyone knows your parents here?"

"Pretty likely. Unless I move them into a motel."

My mind flitters through the conversation of convincing them to leave their large, comfortable home to hold up in a one-room motel where Mom would have a heart attack about sharing bed linens with others.

Tomlin's brow furrows as he considers the situation.

"They could stay with Dani," he says slowly. "There is plenty of room. Lars and Dani would be working during the day and would be good company. It's far enough from the city, secluded and secure. No one knows about it except for a select few. We can arrange for your parents to stay there until things settle down."

"That's a great idea," Dani says, setting her up on the counter beside her while leaning toward us. "But let me tell you, he has this white carpet all over the house. It's a real nightmare with how dusty and dry it gets up there. I swear, who puts in white carpet?"

Tomlin shakes his head, ignoring her last comment when he says, "With the extra precautions I am taking, they would be quite comfortable for the duration of this thing. At least until we know more when you talk to the attorney."

"What attorney?" Dani's eyes narrow when looking at him.

"Someone I referred to him that could help. Same firm as Isla's," he replies with a smoothness that instantly erases her defensive tone.

"Good," she directs at Tomlin before turning back to us. "What do you think? Will that work?"

I'm not one to look a gift horse in the mouth, and I appreciate their offer. If only I didn't have to tell my parents the truth. I take a moment to consider it. The safety and security of my parents are paramount, and the cabin in the mountains seems like a viable option. Despite Dani's complaint about the white carpet, I know their intentions are genuine, and their willingness to help is sincere. Now I must tell my parents and get them to go to a stranger's home under terrible circumstances.

"Yes, I think it will work," I reply, meeting Dani's gaze with a determined expression. "It's a temporary solution that provides a secure location while ensuring their well-being and keeping them away from potential danger. Just pray that I can get them to go."

"Shoot, let me talk to them. Old people love me," she exclaims, causing me to worry when I think of my conservative parents living with a loud, brash girl who barely wears any clothes and sports a tongue piercing.

"Pray for me." I chuckle, and she retaliates with a swift punch to my ribs on the healing side. I immediately hunch over, cupping my hand over my side. "Damn."

As I wince in pain, Molli bends over with me, her expression filled with concern. Her hand returns to my back to comfort me, and I can't help but appreciate her genuine worry for my well-being.

"Are you okay?" she murmurs, but Dani answers instead.

"He's fine."

"Dani," Tomlin scolds as I straighten up, still holding my side but feeling the pain subside. "That was uncalled for."

She whirls on him, asking if he will get punched next, and he casts her a very long stare. Molli steps back, using my body as a buffer between her and Dani.

"Don't worry about it, I'll survive," I say with a weak smile, grateful for Molli's concern and Tomlin's reprimand of Dani.

She angrily swipes her coffee cup from the table, downs the rest, and shoves it at Tomlin before storming out of the breakroom, leaving us all bewildered. Tomlin takes a deep breath, his eyes following Dani as she storms out of the breakroom.

Confused, he shakes his head, clearly taken aback by her sudden outburst.

"I don't know what that's all about," he mutters, turning to watch her walk out the front door when the bell chimes before addressing us. "Regarding your parents, please text me when you have spoken with them so I can prepare everything. I do have a housekeeper who comes by weekly to handle the cleaning and groceries. I'll need to notify her of the guests and advise her to procure anything they want stocked in the kitchen."

I nod, grateful for Tomlin's willingness to take in my parents. This situation has upended many lives, and it's about to upend the most important ones to me.

"Thank you, Tomlin," I say sincerely. "I appreciate all that you're doing for us."

He gives me a reassuring smile.

"Of course. We'll get through this. Help yourself to whatever food and drinks that Dani keeps here and upstairs. I'll text you the address to the cabin. Otherwise, I need to go."

Still standing beside me, Molli offers a faint smile of her own. Despite the lingering tension, her concern for my well-being hasn't wavered. I can sense her gratitude for Tomlin's support as well.

Tomlin nods, his gaze shifting to her. "Nice to meet you, Molli."

"You too." The words are faint from her, and she gives a nervous wave before she turns and retreats after Dani.

It's a victory securing this place for us, yet it pales compared to the next feat I need to pull off. Convincing Mom and Pops to leave with no timeframe in sight.

"I could use a beer right now." The words are out of my mouth before I realize what I just said. "Sorry, I didn't mean—"

"I could too."

25

Tension coils in my stomach. The knot residing there continues building on the drive over to my parent's house to talk them into leaving immediately, as the snow returns to the forecast after taking a few days off. It's beautiful outside, with the dusting of white blanketing the landscape as I pull down the long driveway. Pops's truck sits at the top of the circle drive, the passenger door perfectly aligned to the front door to make it easy for Mom.

As I park my truck behind his, I take a moment to run through what I need to say and how I will convince Pops. Especially when he hears who it's for and why it's happening. I reach for my phone and quickly send a text to Tomlin, informing him that I've arrived at my parents' house and that I'll keep him updated.

Taking a deep breath, I step out of the truck and cross the grass, crunching under my shoes, to the front door. I can hear the muffled sound of the piano from inside as I approach. Mom is probably practicing for Sunday service. The light from the living room lamps cascades onto the wraparound porch outside, the warmth of the home contrasting with the cold reality I'm about to bring into their lives.

I push open the front door and step into the familiar entryway, greeted by the comforting scent of my childhood. Mom emerges from the living room, her face lighting up with smiles as she sees me.

"Alexander! What a surprise!" my mother exclaims, wrapping me in a tight embrace. "We didn't expect you."

"I know, Mom," I reply, returning her hug.

"I have a pie cooling by the window if you want a slice. It's not your favorite apple pie, but you don't mind blueberry, do you?" Her hand clasps together when I release her, beaming with happiness to see me. "I have a fresh pot of coffee made too. The dark roast kind we got in that gift basket from the white elephant exchange last month."

"Sure, pie would be nice," I relent, wanting to make her happy and lessen the impact of my news over sugary sweets.

She pats my arm and leads the way to the kitchen, still warm from the oven despite the cool air from the cracked window. With behaviors like an unlocked front door and an open window, they are not safe if those criminals track us down.

"Mom, where's Pops? There's something important we need to talk about."

She stops tugging on the oven mitts in the middle of the kitchen to look at me standing near the kitchen table.

"Alexander, is everything all right? Are your injuries not healing properly?" Her head shakes while questioning me. As if subconsciously answering her questions since she never wants anything to go wrong for me or my life. "You're not walking with your cane, so that must be good?"

I drag a chair away from the table, the legs screeching across the old floors, and sit down with a huff.

"No, everything is not alright. Has nothing to do with my

injuries and everything to do with an old friend in trouble that I'm helping."

Her eyes widen as worry settles into the weathered lines of her face, and she removes the oven mitts from her hands.

"Let me go get your father."

She quickly turns and rushes to find him, leaving me alone in the kitchen, smelling cinnamon and blueberries. The seconds tick by slowly as I wait for their return, my dread and guilt increasing.

The sound of approaching footsteps reaches my ears, and my parents reenter the kitchen. My father's strong presence fills the room as he stands tall, his eyes fixed on me. The concern on his face matches Mom's as she stands beside him.

"Alexander, what's this I hear that you're in trouble?"

Ever observant, his tone is as serious as the situation, and I motion to the chair across from me, indicating he should sit.

"Not entirely me, Pops, but perhaps you should sit because you won't like it either way." His brushy eyebrows lower, the same way they did when I was a kid, and the feeling inside me is not too far off from how I used to feel back then. "Mom, you too."

"Okay, but nothing that a little slice of pie and coffee can't solve," she chimes in, moving toward the cabinet to retrieve the dessert plates while Pops pulls three cups from the cupboard to place on the table.

I'm very certain this will not be solved over pie and coffee. However, breaking bread while delivering bad news is practically a tradition in this house. Therefore, I'm well versed in the practice. As Mom prepares everything around the kitchen, Pops joins me at the table. I struggle to find the right words to convey the danger surrounding Molli, me, and them.

"Mom, Pops, a situation has arisen, and I need you both to listen carefully."

Pops's expression changes as he leans forward, planting his

elbows on the table, while Mom sets the plates and forks on the table. I wait as she bustles back and forth, cutting the pie, setting it down for us to dish up, and pouring the coffee.

"This doesn't sound good, son," Pops says, sliding a piece onto Mom's plate before doing the same to mine and his.

Mom joins us at the table, taking her seat and giving me her undivided attention. Her green eyes, filled with worry, meet mine.

"No, it's not. It involves an old friend, Mary Ann Higginbotham, and she's in danger."

My heart beats faster when I mention her old name, waiting for the recognition to fall on their faces when they remember. Pops is first, his eyes glinting as his fork sinks into the pie.

"Who is that dear?" Mom says, her glasses fogging when she sips her coffee.

"The secretary's kid with the deadbeat husband," Pops responds faster than I can. "The one that couldn't keep a job, but you'd see all around town buying new things they couldn't afford." Disdain edges his words as he looks at Mom.

"Oh yes, the family that would send her unbathed to vacation bible school and then leave her sitting on the curb in the hot sun," Mom chimes in with her own story of recognition. Neither of which I knew or had heard before. Neither is boding well for my cause right now.

"Well, she's fallen in with some dangerous people connected to criminal activities in Los Angeles. And I'm helping her out, and—" I say as delicately as possible, choosing my next words carefully when Pops jumps in.

"What does 'helping her out' mean?"

The disapproval is in both his face and his actions when he stops eating and sets his fork against his plate. Mom mirrors his actions, and I sigh, knowing I'm not getting away with this unless I tell the whole truth of how all this came to be. I explain the situation, from the truck stop encounter to making her bail and the threat that looms over her. I speak of the danger that Molli is in. The need to keep her hidden and protected until I talk to the attorney. I emphasize the importance of their safety and the possibility of being targeted if our connection is discovered.

Mom's eyes widen in shock, her hand instinctively reaching for Pops's across the table while he glowers at me. He's not one for running from a threat, and he's divulged a few over the years. He appears more angry than frightened. I understand his long law enforcement career may prevent a healthy fear of this situation I am thrusting them into, but he's not a spring chicken anymore. Indeed, no match for younger cartel men who bring a brutality rarely seen in these parts.

Pops releases her hand, pushing his half-eaten pie to the center of the table before slamming his fist in the center and sending the delicate dishware rattling. The coffee sloshes over the edge of the rim.

"Oh, Alan," Mom gushes, startled by his out of character outburst. She quickly dabs at the spilled liquid, frowning as it absorbs into her white tablet cloth faster than she can help it.

"This is a damn fine mess you have gotten all of us into. And for what? That no good woman that left here all those years ago. Good riddance then and good riddance now," he yells, his voice getting louder and louder until he stands. I stand too, not to be scolded like their son, but to take it on the chin. "I thought you learned your lesson with her, Alexander. No! Now you're right back where you were with her and dragging your poor mother with you. Not to mention your friends."

He storms away from the table, fury rolling off him in waves.

"What the hell is wrong with you, son? Putting your mother's life in jeopardy over a prostitute?" He slams his fist down on the kitchen counter while Mom's eyes fill with tears, torn between her fright of the situation and the divide it's causing between the two men in her life. "We didn't raise you like that."

My hands curl into fists as my temper flares.

"Yeah, Pops, you did. You raised me to do the right thing. The honorable thing. Boy Scouts, Eagle Scout, community service on the weekends, front row at church every damn Sunday, church camp every summer, you name it, I did it. I did everything right—everything you wanted me to do. I was perfect. The perfect son to the perfect parents," I yell at him, ignoring the tears rolling down Mom's red cheeks as she grabs a napkin to dab at her nose. This blow-up has been a long time coming. Years in the making. "The police chief's kid. The Sunday school teacher's son. Star quarterback. Salutatorian. First in my class at the Academy. My whole goddamn life has been leading up to this very moment."

He steps toward me, using the few inches of height advantage to intimidate me as Mom's sobbing gets louder.

"Alan, don't hit him," Mom calls out through her tears, her arms reaching toward him, but the wide table prevents her.

Stunned that she would think such a thing, Pops's face contorts into hurt. I raise my hand, palm out, and shake my head.

"No, Mom, he's not going to hit me. He's never laid a hand on me before, and he never will. We might be angry, but we're not going to resort to violence," I defend in honor of Pops, who looks like she slapped him.

He takes a step back, glancing from me to her and then covering his mouth with his hand, trying to recover and calm down. I take a breath, using it to lower my anger.

"Growing up, you'd always ask if this was the hill I wanted to die on. Well, I guess it is."

I'm not going to admit I never anticipated the blowback reaching them, but now that it has, I must protect them too, even if it means upsetting them both. Something I hate doing, as evidenced by the tightening of my gut. But keeping them safe is the hill I want to die on.

His eyes darken, recognizing the phrase that was always a stopping point. Where I'd pull back and say no, I can't recall ever saying yes until now. We glare at each other, long seconds tick by with Mom's sobbing echoing in the room.

"She should have stayed gone," he mutters, turning on his heel and walking out the back screen door, letting it slam behind him.

As Pops's hurtful words hang in the air, I feel a surge of anger and sadness watching him retreat. It's as if a chasm opened between us, and I'm left feeling a profound sense of loss. Mom's sobbing intensifies, her body shaking with each cry. I rush to her side, wrapping my arms around her to offer comfort.

"Mom, I'm so sorry about all of this. The last thing I'd ever do is jeopardize the safety of you and Pops."

She clings to me, her tears soaking into my shirt. "It's not your fault. He's scared, just like I am."

I rub her back, saying, "We all are. Molli wants to turn herself over to the Chief without protection, and I can't let her do that. I can't lose her to save us, just like I can't lose you, Pops, or my friends to save her. It's a no-win situation, but I have to try."

I hold her tighter, feeling horrible. I realize how much I still want Pops's approval, and perhaps I did all those things to win it from him. Maybe I'll never make him proud. Maybe this is the crux of our relationship, a turning point, as I know, I must follow my path, even if it means disappointing him.

"I'll find a way to fix this, Mom. I won't let this tear our family apart. I love you both, and I'll do whatever it takes to keep all of us safe."

Mom's grip on me tightens, and we stay like that for a while, finding solace in each other's presence. The pie remains untouched on the table. Sometimes things can't be solved over pie and coffee, no matter how much she wants them to. I make a vow to mend the rift with Pops, to find a way to show him that I'm not abandoning everything he taught me but rather using it to serve and protect as the oath we both took demands. When Mom pulls out of my arms, she dabs the wrinkled napkin against her face and takes deep breaths.

"Where is the poor girl, now?"

It's best that they do not know, or at least Mom doesn't know, in case something was to happen.

"She's in a safe location, Mom," I reply, choosing my words carefully. "Somewhere secure where no one will be able to find her. As I mentioned when I explained everything, I need you and Pops to leave tonight for the secure location I lined up."

Mom's eyes widen with concern as she processes my words. Her hands twist together before busying herself with clearing the table and taking the coffee cups to the sink to rinse out. I follow her with the coffee pot, returning it to the maker and watching her as her nervousness keeps her bustling around the room.

"Alexander, asking us to leave our home is too much. Your father isn't going anywhere," she says, her voice filled with determination. Still holding my untouched slice of pie, she hesitates before placing it back into the pan. "I've always felt secure with him, and he can still protect us in our home."

I sigh, understanding Mom's reluctance to leave their home and her trust in Pops's ability to keep them safe, regardless of his age. It's difficult to ask, but I know deep down that it's the best course of action. I walk over to Mom, gently placing my hand on her shoulder.

"Mom, I understand your concerns and know how much this house means to both of you. But this situation is different. It's not something that Pops can handle on his own. We're dealing with dangerous people, and I can't bear the thought of anything happening to either of you," I explain, my voice filled with quiet desperation.

She looks up at me, tears glistening as the pie plate starts to shake in her hands.

"But, Alexander, we've faced challenges before. Your father has always protected us, and we've managed to overcome them."

I take the pie from her and set it on the counter. "I know, Mom. But Pops's older now, and this is bigger than anything he faced in his career. These people are relentless and will stop at nothing to find her. I need to convince you so you can help me convince Pops. It's only temporary until I can get ahold of the attorney and figure out what to do."

She takes a deep breath, her hands stilling for a moment. "If you truly believe this is necessary, then we'll go."

Relief washes over me as I hear her words, and before I know it, I'm wrapping my arms around her again.

"I do. Thank you. All I want to do is ensure you both are safe." She returns the embrace with a squeeze of her own and a pat on my back. "Now help me convince the old man."

"I will just promise me you'll stay safe as well." She pulls back, her hands holding mine and squeezing her love into them. Her green eyes, which I inherited, are bright from the tears.

"I promise. I'll take every precaution to ensure my safety. We'll reunite soon once this is all over."

"Then let's go get your father," she says with a determination much larger than her five-foot-three stature.

26

After going over it several times about Dani, Tomlin, and the secluded cabin with hired private security, Pops relents, grumbling the entire time he's packing. Mom insists on emptying the fridge into my truck so things will not spoil while I'm gone. It's a welcome surprise, as I still need to get food for us at the garage.

I double check that all the doors and windows are securely locked while walking around the house's perimeter. It's a routine Pops has followed countless times, but this time, it carries a deeper sense of urgency, so I do it. The quietness of the neighborhood is comforting as I take in the familiar sights, knowing it may be a while before they return.

Memories flood my mind as I glance around each room, thinking about the moments we've shared within these walls. It's both a goodbye and a promise that they'll return unharmed, a temporary farewell to the place they've called home. As I make my way back to the truck, I find Mom standing by the front door, tears streaming down her face. I walk over, wrap my arms around her, and hold her close.

"It's going to be okay, Mom. We're taking the necessary

steps to ensure your safety, and you'll be back before you know it."

She sniffs, clinging to me. "I know, Alexander. It's just . . . leaving everything behind and the uncertainty of it all, it's difficult."

I squeeze her tighter, sympathizing with how difficult this is for her.

"I understand, Mom. You'll be back to this old farmhouse soon enough. I've heard Tomlin's cabin is very nice and you'll be comfortable there. And Dani, well, Mom will need to look past her clothes and language choices. She's been through a lot but does have a heart of gold underneath all that toughness."

She nods, slipping from my embrace as a silent Pops passes with suitcases in both hands.

"If she's a friend of yours, I'm sure she's lovely."

Lovely.

That is not how I would describe Danielle Louise Winters, and that thought makes me smile. As Mom walks to the truck, Pops remains noticeably distant, his anger still smoldering beneath the surface. The tension remains thick between us, and I don't want this between us before they depart.

"Pops," I call after him while he's shoving the luggage in the back cab.

He slams the door with more force than necessary, muttering under his breath as he turns toward me. His eyes meet mine with a toughness I only used to see on the job. Never has he had to flee a case and me asking him to do that now only adds to his fury. I take a deep breath, maintaining my composure amidst his simmering resentment.

"I understand your anger, and I'm sorry my involvement caused so much turmoil. But Molli needs help, and I couldn't turn my back on her."

He scoffs, his face etched with frustration. "Putting her over your friends is one thing. Putting her over your family is reprehensible. Asking your mother to leave her beloved home—"

"Alan, please," Mom interjects, her voice a plea compared to the thunderous boom of his. "We need to support Alexander. He's doing what he thinks is right. Think of it as a little getaway at a fancy mountain hotel."

God bless that woman for trying to put a positive spin on this shitty situation. Pops shakes his head, his brows furrowed in stubborn defiance.

"I can't just ignore my anger, Margaret," he says, addressing Mom by her full name, which is only reserved for the most serious of situations. "You've made your choice, son. Let's hope it's the right one."

My shoulders slump and the knot in my stomach tightens at his words. He moves away, holding open the passenger door for Mom, who gives me a solemn look before patting my chest. After kissing her cheek and whispering that I love her, I ask her to text me when they get settled. As I watch her get into the truck, sadness creeps in, with his words echoing in my head. I hope I made the right choice too.

As Pops closes her door and rounds the front of his truck, I call out to him.

"I love you, Pops."

He nods. His expression softens for a brief moment before turning away. He slips behind the wheel, and the engine roars to life as they slowly pull away for the cabin. When the truck disappears from view, I feel a sense of emptiness wash over me. It's bittersweet, knowing that I'm doing what I can to keep them safe while hating the divide I've created between us.

Once I ensure the porch lights are burning and the front door is locked, I text Tomlin that they are on their way. Then I climb into the truck, find the number for the attorney, and brace myself for the unknown as the ringing echoes through the cab. Finally, his voicemail answers on the other end of the line, and I leave a brief message, name-dropping Tomlin Taka-hashi to ensure he responds quickly. When that call ends, I scroll through my contacts to find Terrance's number, and he picks up on the first ring.

"Alex, I've been worried about you. You haven't returned any of my calls or texts." Every word drips with worry, and I realize it's unfair of me to call him with a crisis and then not call back with an update.

"Hey man, I'm sorry I haven't called you back. It's been a little wild these past few days." That's a gross understatement.

"Okay, wild we can handle." Relief permeates through the receiver. However, his wild and my reality are two different things right now. "How is she doing? Did you change her mind about coming in? We have the space."

"I'm not going to lie. It's been rougher than I thought. The paranoia and hallucinations are the most unsettling. Aside from the picking at her skin and the rapid change of emotions, I'm hoping we are past the bulk of the withdrawals, but I'm always on."

"Hmm, sounds as if you might be out of the physical depen-dence period. However, the mental and psychological will always be there."

Her sudden insecurity comes to mind. The girl from the truck stop couldn't give a shit about me, but now she's self-conscious and withdrawn—a different version of herself.

"Let's talk about her environment. What's that like?"

I can almost picture his hand at his chin, eager to hear what's happening with her. I can't get him too involved if someone questions him. The less he knows, the better at this point.

"What do you mean?"

"Does she have access to fresh air, lots of exercise, nutritious food, things of that nature?"

I mentally tick through his list. Fresh air, locked doors, and her clawing to escape. Food—nothing that will stay down. And exercise if fits of rage count. None of that will change now that we'll be holed up at Dani's place for the foreseeable future.

"Yes," I simply answer.

"Good. The cravings will always be there, and you'll need to learn her triggers to support her through them when they arise. She can tell you most of them, but some are behavioral, such as smoking cannabis after a hard day, or environmental, such as seeing a highly frequented nightclub and remembering getting high before going. Those she might not remember herself to tell you. Those can sneak up on you both, and when the cravings hit, you'll need a diversion or a manner to redirect her to a more positive stimulant."

I shift in my seat, my thigh pulsing from so much activity, and finally getting a break. My elbow digs into the console as my truck idles in the driveway, wanting to finish this conversation before getting on the road.

"I'll talk to her tonight about triggers and diversion techniques."

"Right, then therapy, we discussed that, but I believe you're exploring some options around that."

Shit. We did discuss it, and I did have some ideas. All that went to hell in a handbasket now that she's in danger.

"Yes. I haven't started yet, but I will get on that."

The streetlights flicker on, illuminating the edge of my parents' property and romanticizing the slow, easy living of their lives. Something I look forward to when all this is over.

"I completely understand. You've probably had your hands full." Terrance's voice carries a note of understanding. "Lastly, Alex, you must take care of yourself too. If you're not good, you're no help to those around you. I see this all the time with my caregivers. They are so busy caring for their loved ones that they wind up in the hospital themselves. You can't let that happen, or she could relapse too. I've seen that as well."

I'm sure Terrance has seen all scenarios at this point, but I appreciate both his honesty and his worry for me.

"I hear what you're saying. Put my mask on before helping anyone else on the plane," I jest, trying to lighten the mood as fatigue washes over me.

"Something like that. Now, do you have any questions?"

"As for questions, I think you've covered everything for now. Terrence, I need to warn you about something related to this girl. If someone should ask if you've talked to me or heard from her, can you do me a favor and say no? I know I'm asking a lot, but it's for your protection and hers."

There is a brief pause, the sound of the hospital in the background growing louder and demanding his attention when he whispers an instruction to someone else.

"I know it's a big ask, but trust me, you don't want to be involved."

"Is everything okay?"

"No, but it will be. I need you to deny talking to me." Another person to protect.

"If that's what you need, then of course. But please take care of yourself," he whispers his assurances, and I thank him before ending the call.

I scrub my palm down my face to wipe away the weariness and put the truck in gear to head back to Molli. She assured me everything would be all right to leave her alone. Even though I felt extremely uneasy about it, I couldn't afford to bring her around my parents, at least not yet. It's impossible to reach her without her cell phone, something I think she unintentionally left behind at the jail. I try Dani's garage line, yet it rings repeatedly until her answering service picks up, asking if I want to leave a message. It was worth a try, even though I doubt she's felt comfortable enough to answer any person's place of business phone.

The aroma from Mom's leftovers causes my stomach to

growl. It's a nice treat given that we haven't eaten all day with the displacement happening. Even though I didn't have any pie at her house, I will tear into it after dinner with Molli.

As the slow country tunes from the radio float around me, I feel myself relax for the first time today, settling further into my seat as I navigate the slick roads and think about what needs to be done when I get home. Call Eli to warn him of the situation and to keep Isla away for her own protection. Check in with Dani or Tomlin to see how the welcoming went, and lastly, check in with my parents to get their side of the story.

The more tension leaves my body, the more fatigue sets in until I blink a little slower than I should. My eyes are burning, and I switch the station to classic rock, blare it, and pick up the pace to return to her place. The last thing we need is for me to fall asleep at the wheel.

27

As expected, the garage lobby is dark when I pull into the last bay, and the roll-up door closes, the gate rattling behind my truck. I push through the glass door leading to the breakroom with my arms loaded with bags of food. The breakroom is also dark, with the only light coming from the back stairs where Molli left the hallway light shining in the otherwise dark building.

I climb the staircase, the sound of Call of Duty blaring past the closed door, which surprises me. We agreed it's probably best for her not to be exposed to more violence. A brown paper bag starts to tear when I shuffle them to one arm to reach for the handle that I find unlocked. We must talk about that and other safety precautions, such as an exit strategy, should we be caught here by Joaquin or his guys.

When I swing the door open, she's dancing in the living room and yelling profanities at the screen while trying to shoot the characters. Empty beer cans are strewn everywhere, and my heart beats in double time. With everything on my mind, I neglected to check if Dani kept this place fully stocked. By the looks of it, she does. I cross the threshold, taking in the scene.

Molli's still in my sweats, but she cut the arms and legs off, turning them into some of the tiny outfits Dani runs around in. It's far too cold outside for what she is wearing, but being drunk off her ass, it won't matter. She won't feel it.

"Alexxx, baby," she squeals, her voice higher than a cartoon character as she sways toward me, dropping the controller on the table with a loud thud. "Momma was waiting for her sugar to come. Give me some sugar, sugar."

Her words are more than slurred, almost indistinguishable as they melt together. She giggles, stumbling toward me, and wraps her arms around my neck. Her touch is warm, but her breath is harsh from the alcohol. The bags are smashed between us, breaking open the one that started tearing, and she giggles even louder.

"Oops."

Her pupils are dilated, leaving tiny chestnut irises above a playful smirk.

"Molli, lend a hand, please?"

I attempt to guide us toward the kitchen counter, but she abruptly pulls away, causing everything to teeter precariously in my grasp. With a sudden jolt, she stumbles and lands heavily on her backside. Instead of startling her into reality, she bursts into laughter, and containers scatter across the floor. Irritation bubbles up in me as I bend over to see if she's okay.

"Are you okay?"

I crouch in front of her, lifting her chin as she stares at the floor.

She lifts a finger to her lips when focusing on me.

"Shh."

Her mouth tightens around the word until it falls into a frown and another laughing fit. I take a knee, knowing I need to get her off the floor and into a cold shower to try to sober up while I run down to make another cup of that expresso. My hands cup her elbows, applying gentle pressure for her to rise with me when she leans forward and plants her soft lips on mine.

A jolt of electricity courses through my entire being, and I can't help but let out a soft gasp of surprise. Her tender and warm touch ignites the fire that has always burned for her, even after all these years. Her closeness is intoxicating, and I feel an overwhelming desire to pull her even closer, to explore every inch of her being.

With a rush of emotions flooding my mind, I notice her eyes flutter closed as mine widen. I've imagined kissing her again, even masturbating to the feel of her again, but not like this. Never like this. When she's intoxicated and vulnerable, unaware of her actions. I reluctantly force her away until she realizes what I'm doing and jolts back in offense.

"Come on, Alex. You know you want it. Every man does."

Her unsettling words pierce my heart. She forcefully shoves my hand away as anger sours her giddiness. I'm left grappling with my desire for her while wanting to fix all the hurt from everyone who came before me. To mend what's broken.

"You've had too much to drink. Let's get you into the shower while I clean this up and get dinner for us." I stand, creating distance to avoid her advances while helping her.

"What? I'm not good enough for you? Are you saving yourself for some churchgoing, good girl? Someone that your father would approve of?" she accuses, her eyes slitting as she attempts to remove her top. "That's why you don't want any of this?"

I quickly intervene, reaching out to stop her as her arm slips out, exposing her left breast. Gently, I guide her arm back through the armhole, realizing that she must have cut the sweatshirt while intoxicated, revealing too much.

"It's not about being 'good enough' or not," I reply firmly, trying to keep my voice level despite the rising tension between us. "You're not in the right state of mind. You've had too much to drink, and I wouldn't take advantage of you like that. I care about you too much to do it."

Her anger gives way to vulnerability when her eyes well up with tears.

"I just . . . I don't want to think about anything else right now. I want to forget."

"I know you do." I cringe at her pain. If I could take it away, I would. I've got to find her help and fast. "Numbing the pain with alcohol won't make it go away. It'll only make things worse for us right now. Remember the last few days? The bugs, the itching, the hallucinations? All that will come back if you go down this road again. And I won't let you do it. I can't stand by and let you do that to yourself again. I know it's hard. But you're stronger than this."

She looks away, clearly struggling with her conflicting emotions.

"I can't handle it. The knowing . . . the memories . . . the nightmares. It's too much. I don't know how to deal."

"Hey, you don't have to face this alone," I say gently, holding her hand. "I'm here for you. We'll get through this, okay?"

She hesitates momentarily, her grip tightening on my hand as if seeking comfort and support. "I'm scared, Alex. Scared of what they'll do if they find me."

"I won't let them hurt you again."

Tears spill from her eyes, and she looks back at me.

"Promise me you won't leave, Alex. Promise."

If promises were kept, she would've never gone away. Never had me waiting by the flagpole at the front of school to walk into graduation together. Never had me look for her in the crowd, holding my breath when they called her name and realizing she was gone. If promises were kept, she'd have never experienced the things that brought her nightmares and turned her into an addict. If promises were kept, she would've been my wife.

"I'm here, and I'm not going anywhere."

Every word stabs my heart. I used to believe in promises until she promised to stay and then left. Her tears flow freely now, and she pulls me into a tight embrace, burying her face in my chest. I hold her close, my words a heavy commitment to the same ones I spoke all those years ago. A reminder of all the broken promises and shattered dreams that led us to this moment, and as much as I want her back, a piece of me still hurts from her betrayal.

I'm unsure of how long she clings to me, crying. But as I sit on the floor with her, I cradle her in my arms until her tears cease and her body stops trembling. We remain that way until all that fills the air is silence and the distant chirping of a video game waiting for a player.

"Molli, why don't I make us something to eat?" I say softly, nudging her side to move her head off my chest. She moves slowly and lifts her face. Her eyes are swollen and bloodshot.

"I'm so tired. I just want to sleep."

She falls against me, her head hitting my shoulder and her eyes closing. It's been a long day for both of us, and as much as I'd prefer something in her stomach, I'm not sure she'll eat it anyway, feeling the way she does.

With one last try, I ask, "How about some of Mom's leftovers? She gave me some lasagna and pie or homemade chicken noodle soup. Doesn't that sound good?"

I shift, forcing her to sit up, and her hand stays on my chest. Her gaze is unfocused, her eyelids drop, and it's the effects of the alcohol causing her to want to pass out.

"Hamilton . . ." I wait for more, and she blinks a couple more times before nodding off.

"All right, off to bed. I'll help you."

I slowly get to my feet, then assist her to stand and walk to the bedroom. Once inside, I gently guide her to lie on the bed. She curls up under the blankets, still looking exhausted and emotionally drained. I grab a glass of water from the kitchen and hand it to her.

"Here, drink some water," I say softly, hoping it will help with the effects of the alcohol. She takes a few sips, but her eyes droop, and it's clear she's ready to drift off to sleep.

"Rest now," I whisper, tugging the bedding over her bare shoulder. "I'll be right here if you need anything."

She murmurs something before surrendering to sleep. I watch her for a moment, my mind a mess of the ups and downs of this day, and Pops's words filter through my head again.

I hope you made the right choice.

I feel a sense of clarity and conviction within myself. I know I made the right decision by standing by Molli's side. My priority is to protect her and those I love. Once she's asleep, I quietly leave the room, catching the door closed behind me, and make my way to the kitchen to pick up the food strewn around the floor. As I stoop over, a deep groan escapes my body while collecting the various containers.

My body aches, and my thigh protests with every movement. I try to move carefully, not wanting to make any noise that might disturb Molli's rest. I gather the containers and clean up the empty beer cans before putting some lasagna on a plate to warm in the microwave. As I stand in the kitchen, I feel a sense of exhaustion wash over me. It's been a long day, emotionally and physically draining.

I glance at the clock on the wall, realizing it's well past nine o'clock. The hours have slipped away without notice. I reach for my phone, seeing a text message from Tomlin that they are there and settled in. I thank him again for their generosity and move on to Dani's text, saying Mom looks like Mrs. Claus and she can't wait for her home cooking. It makes me smile, and I'd be curious to hear what Mom thinks of her.

Mom left a voice message, and I hit the button to listen. She's marveling over how lovely his place is, how expensive everything looks, and that he's famous. The cheerfulness in her voice is nice to hear. I'm relieved that part went as planned, aside from Pops. Mom doesn't mention him, which is intentional, knowing he's still angry about this situation.

The microwave beeps, indicating the food is ready, and I quickly thank Tomlin for putting them up before grabbing my food and a soft drink from the fridge to eat in front of the television. I reach for the controller to turn off the game, turn down the volume, and switch it to Sports Center. Sitting on the couch, eating dinner, and watching sports highlights seems reminiscent of my regular life, and I relish the normalcy of it.

Almost an hour passes before I clean up, check for unopened beers to pour out, and put away the dishes. Before doing my security checks, I return to the bedroom to check on Molli one last time. She's still sleeping peacefully, and I'm glad for that.

I quietly gather some blankets and pillows from the bedroom closet to set up a makeshift bed on the couch. Once it's arranged, I head downstairs for a quick perimeter check to ensure the exterior doors and garage bays are locked before returning upstairs. With a quick brush of my teeth, I settle down on the couch and pray for strength and guidance. I pray we can overcome the challenges ahead and find a way to safety and peace. And as I drift into sleep, I hold on to the hope that tomorrow will bring more answers.

28

The piercing shrill from my phone on the kitchen counter jolts me from my slumber. The garage apartment is bright, with sunshine streaming through the sides of the blinds and casting a long beam across the wall beside me. I jump to my feet and wipe the sleep from my eyes, careful not to wake Molli if she's still out. I race around the furniture to snatch the phone off the counter and plaster it to my ear, not even looking at the screen.

"Hamilton."

My voice is as rough as I feel. When I glimpse myself in the microwave glass, my beard is scruffy, my hair is going in all directions, and my eyes are puffy. This week wears on my face.

"Hello, Officer Hamilton. This is Brooks Tyler speaking. I'm a friend of Tomlin Takahashi," he says with a smooth graciousness that is both enthusiastic and hopeful.

"Nice to meet you, Brooks. I left you a voicemail yesterday."

Not wanting to communicate everything that needs to be said in case she is awake, I walk to the door and head downstairs to make a cup of coffee in the breakroom.

"Ah yes, why don't you walk me through everything? I have

my legal assistant with me as well to take notes. Do you mind if we record this?"

He switches the phone to speaker and a soft female voice chimes in with a greeting.

"I don't."

I take a deep breath, steadying my voice as I explain the circumstances and the urgent need for legal guidance. As I provide more details about Molli's situation and the potential threats, he becomes more engaged, asking pertinent questions and outlining the possible legal avenues we can explore.

With each passing minute of our conversation, I am hopeful. He exudes confidence and experience, garnering my trust in his ability to navigate the complexities of our situation. He assures me that he will do everything in his power to protect Molli and guide us through the legal process once he finds out if it's a state or federal interest in Joaquin and his accomplices.

As the call ends, I sit silently, staring at the empty coffee cup I pulled out a while ago as I mull over everything he said. Tomlin's top-notch for this, and when I asked about the retainer and legal fees, he waived it off as pro bono since the firm dedicates so many cases a year. First, Isla's case is pro bono, and now this one. It's remarkable the connections Tomlin has.

Now that I'm up and the wheels are turning on what still needs to be done, I make Molli and me a cup of coffee with the blueberry pie. It's not the best breakfast, but I'll go to the store later today to stock up on groceries. As the machine grinds away, I make my way toward the lobby, where the sunlight streams through the expansive windows, the sky free of clouds. The light snow from last night is melting, with a few random patches scattered about. I scroll my phone to find Eli's number to explain the situation. It rings a few times in the stillness of the closed garage before he picks up.

"Good morning, Alexander, you're up early. Are you going to rehab?"

I flick my wrist, looking at my sports watch to see it's only half past eight. I didn't realize how early the attorney called. He must start all his calls to accommodate his court schedule.

"No, that's not what I am calling you about."

I let the seriousness of my voice convey it's not a social call.

"Oh no. This doesn't sound good. Is everything all right?"

His words are rushed as keys jingle in the background, and the squeak of a car door can be heard. I pause before answering as it sounds like he's leaving for the pet shop.

"Is Isla with you?"

"I'm alone. Why?"

"Good."

I fill him in on the pertinent details of what has happened while protecting Molli's privacy about her line of work and substance abuse. He gasps when I tell him that I have to leave my home, take over Dani's garage and that they have relocated to Tomlin's cabin with my parents.

"Oh my God, Alexander. This is . . . this is . . . so serious and sudden. We were just over there." His worry ripples through the receiver. "Wait, they don't know about Isla, do they? Because—"

"No, I assure you that they don't. You all being there happened before I got Molli out, and even if they connect me and Molli, they can't connect me to Isla as I am not on her case other than a prosecutor's witness, and there is a convenience store full of them. "

"Then she . . ." Emotion clogs his voice, and there are several rapid breaths through the phone while he collects himself. "I don't know what I'd do if something . . ."

I turn away from the large window, shaking my head and looking down at the new floor Dani put in. I'd never endanger them, and I hope Eli understands that. I can hear the fear in his voice.

"I know. That's why I am calling now. I need you to stay

away from my place or any association with me for now. Should anyone ask, you've not seen or heard from me. Make up some excuse about being occupied with Isla or responsibilities, but let others think we no longer talk. I'm not sure who all this guy is connected to but if someone asks, say we lost touch and then let me know who's asking."

"Oh no. This keeps getting worse," he confesses, his voice unsteady. "I need to pull over. This is . . . a nightmare."

A horn honks on his end, and he mumbles something I can't make out.

"I know it's frightening, Eli. I wish there were a way to shield you from all of this. But right now, I need you to be careful more than ever. I can't risk putting you, Isla, or Ronald in danger." My throat tightens, and a streak of guilt races through me.

"But what if . . . if something happens to you?" I can hear the fear in his words. "Alexander, you're still healing. Are you even off your cane? You relied heavily on it when we were over there the other day."

"I'll be fine. I'm off it and will continue to get stronger."

"This is just . . . is Tomlin protecting Dani and your parents? I mean, Lars's there. Although he's a big guy, he wouldn't hurt a fly." Eli's worries are rapid fire. "I'll tell Isla you're on vacation, there is no cell service, and you can't get messages. I'll have to tell Ronald the truth. Well, both want to know you are safe."

"Tomlin hired security for them. They are safe, the same as Molli and I are." I try to sound confident despite my doubts. "I appreciate your help to maintain distance from all of this."

"I feel so helpless, unable to do more for you."

"You're doing enough by keeping your distance and I'm sorry for dragging you all into this mess," I say, bothered by how upset he is. "But having you on my side, even if it's from afar, means a lot."

"Of course, Alexander. Please be safe." His voice is barely above a whisper.

"I will."

My throat tightens, and I clear it loudly after I hang up. Eli's a good man, the best for Isla, and a wonderful friend. I know he'll follow my instructions and simultaneously give himself an ulcer from worrying.

"Everything okay?"

I turn to see Molli, having changed into something more modest of mine. It reminds me that I need to grab her and me some more clothes when I run out to get groceries—her hand trails over her head, a slight frown on it. The bruising on her face is fading fast. Her busted lip is healing, and the crusty scab is gone when she puts her soft lips on mine.

"Sure." I sigh, knowing I need to update her on the attorney, but I need more coffee before unloading all that. "Would you like some coffee? I was thinking of having a piece of Mom's homemade pie to go with it." She continues walking toward me with a glint in her eyes.

"Before that, I want to say something."

Her fingers catch my wrist, pulling my arm until my hand is in hers. I curl my fingers over hers, wondering what she will say. Bombshells keep dropping left and right, and I could use a small break before the next one falls.

"About last night—"

"Don't worry about it, Molls. Relapses will happen, and it's only been a few days anyway. I wouldn't even call it a relapse, more a way to forget everything of late. I even said I wanted a beer, so it's okay."

I squeeze her hand, ready to release it when hers tightens to keep it there.

"I wasn't talking about getting drunk. I was talking about the kiss."

Her chestnut eyes bore into mine. Her petite frame so close

to me, bringing up that kiss, plus the morning wood I always have is not boding well to have this conversation now.

"It's fine. We've all had too many drinks and done things we regret," I say, gently letting her off the hook with a shoulder shift to feign indifference.

"That's just it, Alex. I knew I was doing it. I wanted to do it. That and much more. I wasn't using it to forget you. I kissed you because I wanted to go where that kiss led."

She releases my hand, stepping too close for a friendly hug as she plants her palms on my chest. I flinch in response. My resolve is so damn low right now. If she made the first move, I'd make all the rest, and that's the last thing we need to confuse this situation with my lust and wanting of her.

"Molli," I warn, searching her face to see if she's too hungover to realize what she is doing. "This is not a good idea. We need to keep a clear head about this. I know what you are thinking, but this is not the answer."

"We've always been good this way, Hamilton."

She rolls up on the balls of her feet, trying to reach my lips. Fuck. She's right. Whenever we were at odds, sex was the way back to each other. But we're not teenagers with raging hormones anymore. We're grown adults with responsible brains and severe outcomes.

"Molli, things are different now."

She steps back, her hands slipping away to fall to her sides.

"Because of my past."

I close the distance, taking her hands and putting them back where they were. Both wanting, needing, and missing the connection we shared so intensely.

"Because of *our* past. I survived you once. I don't think I can survive you again."

Her hand slides out from under mine to cup my face, her thumbs caressing the edges of my beard to the dry skin of my cheek.

"So don't survive me again," she murmurs, her hand slipping behind my neck, pulling me toward her.

The desire in her eyes matches what is flowing effortlessly through my veins, and I don't want to stop this. I want to feel every part of her, memorize every tattooed star on her body, and make her mine again. My heart races as she pulls me closer, the intoxicating familiarity of her touch makes my dick hard, and my hands slide around her waist, closing the distance. Where her lips were soft and hesitant last night, mine are firm and demanding, meeting hers with such force that she gasps before surrendering and letting me devour her lips, opening them wide to welcome my tongue.

It's intense, a hunger burning for years that's finally releasing. I gently cradle her butt, lifting her as her legs encircle my waist. Her body is plastered full length against mine as the tip of my dick strains against my pants.

Her elbows lock around my neck, a vice grip to keep kissing her with a hunger that surprises me. Her hand tangles into my hair, pulling it almost painfully as I tilt my head to dive deeper. I'm demanding, insistent on making her mine again in this very moment when logic should prevail but doesn't. She matches my vigor, grinding her horny body against mine and using the friction to get off. I love it. It reminds me of the times she used to do it before football games, behind the building, just before I had to head out to play.

I swallow her moans, their heightened intensity absorbing into mine and begging me for more. My skin burns with heat, my cock wants to explode in her, and all I can think about is laying her on the bed upstairs and keeping her there for days. It's only when she rips her lips from mine, leaving us both panting, that logic prevails. I touch my forehead to hers, my hands still wrapped around her body and she stops moving against me.

"Why are you stopping?" Her arm loosens as she leans back in my hold to gaze into my flushed face. "You have regrets."

A flicker of pain crosses her vulnerable face before hiding it.

"No, I don't regret that. Not in the least." I adjust my neck, moving it back to allow us to talk. "I'd like to do far more than that innocent kiss."

A sly smile slowly spreads on her face. "That was hardly innocent."

"It is compared to the obscene things I want to do to you," I grit, lowering her slightly so she can feel my hard cock against the bottom of her butt.

"So do it. We're grown adults. No more sneaking into your bedroom or off camping in the woods like we used to." She grinds her butt against me, teasing an already starving man with the one thing he's been denied for years. "Why are you hesitating? I'm clean. If that's what you are worried about. I know it's hard to believe, but I test regularly, and they took them at the jail too."

It wasn't what I was worried about, but now that she said it, it's crossing my mind. The drugs, the prostitution—maybe I should be concerned.

"I keep condoms in my truck. That's not what I'm worried about."

I struggle between giving in to the pull of desire and the history we share and listening to the voice of reason. The passion and history are overwhelming, but I force myself to set her back on her feet gently. Her eyes are filled with confusion and longing, and I can see the hurt in them.

"Molli, you have no idea how much I want to be with you right now," I admit, my voice strained with the effort to resist her pull. "But I can't let us fall back into old patterns. We both know how destructive that can be."

She takes several steps back.

"But we can be different this time. We've both grown and learned from our mistakes. We can make it work. I know we can."

She looks so fucking sexy with her swollen lips pleading for me to take her. It's killing me inside not to do just that. I take a deep breath, running a hand through my hair.

"I'm not saying it's impossible, but we must be sure. We can't rush into this without thinking it through. There's too much at stake right now."

Her eyes glisten with unshed tears. My heart aches at the sight, wanting to save her from this mess.

"I thought you wanted this too."

"I do, but we need to get past all this, Molls," I reply, trying to steady my racing heart. I rush to her, wanting to show her how I feel but I must remain strong and clear-headed. "Let's just take it one step at a time. Can we agree to that?"

She nods, tears streaming down her cheeks.

"I understand. I just thought . . . I thought maybe we had a chance."

"We do have a chance," I say, reaching out to wipe away her tears. "I promise."

She gives me a small smile through her tears, and I hug her gently, wanting to comfort and hold her. The hug is fleeting when she leans against my arms, encircling her, and says, "We have homemade pie?"

29

Mom's food is generous but won't last long. I go shopping after checking the kitchen, break room, and bathrooms for any substances that could tempt her. The grocery store is busier than I anticipated after going by Walmart and picking up some clothes for us. It feels a little odd buying undergarments for her. As much as I try not to picture her in them, I can't help but choose what I'd like to see. Given the situation, they're probably more lacy than practical, but if they're not suitable, I'll buy more later.

Clutching the grocery list as I shop, I round the corner to the meat section when my phone vibrates in my pocket. It's Rico. I move to a deserted aisle, lean against the handle of my basket, and lower my voice when answering.

"Hey, man. What have you been able to find out?"

"Where are you?" he whispers, above a bunch of racket on his end that makes it hard to hear him.

"I'm at the grocery store." I press the volume up on my phone and smash it to my ear. "I can barely hear you."

"That's because it's a shitshow over here. The Chief is

looking for you and sending a squad car to your place today."
The scrape of a chair cuts through his words and the voices
start to fade as if he's walking away. "Sup, yeah, gotta take a shit.
I'll be back."

Sending a car for me? My pulse quickens. I straighten,
wondering what happened to escalate the situation.

"You at the station?" I murmur, looking around to ensure
I'm still alone on the aisle when an older couple stops their
basket at the end cap to look at something.

"Yeah, but I need to get out of here. Can you meet me at the
dive bar we went to after the funeral?"

His keys jingle near the receiver and I look at the groceries I
have to see if I check out and get over there in time.

"Yes, I'm at the grocery store, so I need to pay and will come
straight there," I say, swiftly turning my cart around to grab
some meat with all the sides and veggies I have. "I can be there
in fifteen minutes or so."

"Good, park at the back of the building and don't get out. I'll
pull in beside you."

He doesn't wait for my response when he ends the call. I
quickly go through the grocery store, gathering the items I need
for the week. My mind is racing, thinking of what could have
happened to escalate the situation with the Chief looking for
me. As I reach the checkout, I fumble to pay for my groceries
while my heart pounds.

With my bags in hand, I hurry to my truck and load everything inside. As much as I'd like to speed there, I can't risk
getting pulled over and hauled into the very place that's looking
for me. I make sure to park at the back of the building as
instructed by Rico. Sitting in the driver's seat, I keep the engine
off, the cold winter air enough to keep my groceries for a bit
while I anxiously await his arrival.

A few minutes later, I see Rico's truck pulling into the

parking lot. He parks his truck beside me and aligns the driver's window so neither can be seen. I see the tension in his expression as his window glides down and he kills his engine.

I lower my window, the cold air brushing my heated skin when I ask, "What happened?"

Rico leans against his window frame, glancing around to ensure no one is around.

"It's bad, Alex. The Chief got wind of you helping Molli, and he's furious. He's convinced you're hiding something and that you're a part of what she's mixed up in. He's not giving up until he finds out what it is."

I clench my fists. My anger and frustration are building after being with the department for almost six years.

"What does he think I'm hiding? I'm just trying to help an old friend in trouble."

Rico shakes his head.

"I don't know, but he's on a warpath. I only heard about the squad car from the rookie because he saw some suits go into the Chief's office and having put two and two together, they're looking for you."

"Who are the suits? Internal affairs?"

"I don't know. I wasn't there."

I take a deep breath, my eyes gazing out the windshield to process who they could be. Either way, if this is being escalated out of his jurisdiction and they think I'm somehow involved, it only makes sense to locate me. Things have escalated quicker than I had imagined they would.

"I'd assume internal affairs as quickly as it's escalated," I murmur, looking back at Rico.

"Fair assumption. You probably should start considering getting a lawyer involved with how quickly the Chief turns. It's odd though. With your sterling record and recent accolades over the shooting, not to mention the former police chief's kid, you'd think he'd denied your involvement to everyone who stepped in the place. Unless something's not right with the investigation into Matt's death?"

"Why do you say that?"

"I don't know. Just a feeling. Or the Chief could be dirty or somehow involved in this? He is turning this over awfully fast if you ask me."

My eyebrows move up in surprise.

"You think the Chief is dirty? Who would he be in bed with? No one cares about this little town."

Rico shrugs, his expression thoughtful.

"I don't know, but something about this situation doesn't sit right with me. The Chief is going after you like this, especially after everything with Matt. The timing is too coincidental. Something's off."

I ponder his words, the pieces of the puzzle slowly coming together.

"You might be onto something. There's more to this than meets the eye. Could it somehow be related to the truck stop? It was our jurisdiction, and it's been a known problem for years. I remember Pops even talking about it when he was the chief and having busted that place numerous times. Maybe the Chief is somehow involved in it, getting kickbacks to look the other way. Maybe he has something to do with the blue light and knows I was poking around in that."

Rico chews on his lip, thinking.

"Perhaps Molli knows more than she thinks."

"Leave her out of this."

My instinct to protect her shoves forward and Rico frowns.

"Not what I mean, Alex. She may not have realized that she's met the Chief. If she was around Joaquin and his operations, then what is she doing back here? Have you asked her that? It seems highly unlikely that it's a coincidence she happens to show up in her hometown all these years later.

There must be a connection, and not to you or her past, something we're just missing. But I think she could have the key piece of information we're looking for."

Rico's words strike a chord within me, and I can't help but consider the possibility that Molli might hold the key to unraveling this complex situation.

"You might be right. I need to talk to her. I've been careful not to ask anything of her. I didn't want to trigger anything."

"I understand, but you don't have that kind of time. We need answers and we need them now," Rico insists, his urgency stirring a new worry within me. "And I know you don't want to believe this, but she could be involved with Joaquin's operations. It's possible she knows exactly what's going on and is too scared that you'll turn her out if you find out she's guilty. Either way, we need to get to the truth."

"She's not involved," I say, my anger sparking at the very hint of her impropriety. "What about Joaquin? Is he just walking about town right under the Chief's nose?"

Rico's mouth sets into a line and I already know the answer.

"Not exactly. He has his guys out looking for her. I ran into one coming out of the motorcycle shop. I was bringing my bike in for repairs and bumped shoulders with one of them. His neck tattoo gave it away. Luckily, I wasn't wearing my badge, but the shop owner was nervous and more than happy to see me. He said to me that he suspected they were bringing in stolen bikes. He's too scared not to work on them. I asked if he filed a police report and he looked at me as if he'd seen a ghost."

"Yeah, something is up. Can't deny that there's a connection."

The Chief, Internal Affairs, Joaquin, drug trafficking, Molli, bikes, and this small town. I can't seem to bring it all together. How are they connected?

"But they have been making the rounds. I'm seeing more bikes around town than usual, and not touring bikes. It'd be very unusual for this time of year. It's why I'm putting mine in the shop. It's too cold to ride, but bikes are an easier getaway than a car or truck."

"Get away from what?"

"Oh, robberies are up. Sky high and, with how short staffed we are, it's impossible to cover them. There's a pattern there but no resources to work on it."

I prop my elbow on the truck frame, laying my hand against my face as I wonder about more connections.

"Robberies of what?"

"You name it. Liquor stores, gas stations, convenience stores, gaming rooms, and here's an odd one, a laundry mat. What is someone going to do with all the quarters?" Rico shakes his head in amusement. "Strippers won't take quarters."

As Rico mentions the recent rise in robberies and the unusual pattern, my mind starts to connect the dots. The thought of gaming rooms and a laundry mat being targeted raises a red flag. Joaquin is involved in illicit activities, and these robberies may be linked to his organization in some way.

"You mentioned gaming rooms and a laundry mat being hit. Those places deal with a lot of cash transactions, right?" I ask, my mind racing with possibilities. "It could be related to money laundering. The quarters from the laundry mat could be used to conceal the illegal proceeds from other criminal activities."

Rico's eyes widen in realization.

"You think these robberies are a cover for money laundering?"

"It's a possibility worth looking into. If Joaquin's crew is involved, it could be their way of cleaning their dirty money. And with the Chief involved, it's no wonder the cases are being buried and understaffed," I theorize, the puzzle pieces starting to fall into place.

Rico nods, a serious expression on his face.

"Well, damn. And you keeping Molli is jeopardizing it all.

She could be a snitch and rat them out, ending everything, and the players would fall like dominos."

"Fuck," I gasp, my mind reeling from the revelation as my hand grips the side of the door.

Our once peaceful town is now a cesspool of corruption, and Molli's life is in far more danger than we both realized. Rico and I stare at each other.

"We've got to keep you two hidden. More now than ever. You're at that hot chick's place, right?"

"Yeah, Dani's garage. Don't worry, it's secure." I think about the cameras that Tomlin added around the place and need to get access so I can monitor them from my phone. "She moved up to her boyfriend's cabin in the mountains. I also convinced Mom and Pops to go there, so the old house is locked up tight."

"Nothing can link them to that place? They will be safe up there?"

Rico's concern is all over his face, as my parents are his parents too.

"Yeah, it's pretty secluded and her boyfriend hired a private security team."

He scoffs, "Rent-a-cops are not what they need."

"He's incredibly wealthy. And famous. I'm fairly certain they are carrying. Trust me, he tries to save Dani from herself so he won't let her be unsafe. I'm surprised she hasn't called me already bitching about it."

"She gets bitchy a lot? You know there's a good way to handle that."

He wiggles his eyebrows and I smile.

"I don't want to hear it." I pat the side of my truck. "Is that all for now?"

"Hey, how did Pops take the news?"

"He's not talking to me. But at least he's safe. Can you imagine Mom around Dani? That's something I'd like to see." I infuse my humor and then release a long sigh. "Tell me I'm doing the right thing, Rico. Pops said he hoped I made the right decision. I'll do everything I can to keep Molli safe, but I can't help feeling guilty for jeopardizing everyone else, including you."

He reaches out and touches my arm.

"You know you're doing the right thing. When all this is over, you'll be the hero who took down a corrupt Chief, which should make the old man proud. As for me, I'm just the station idiot who thinks my best friend is a guilty bastard who skipped town."

He chuckles. Then his face turns serious when he removes his hand from my arm to retrieve something from the seat next to him.

"Here."

He hands me a manilla envelope.

"What is this?" I flip it over, looking for any markings, and then gaze back at him.

"Everything you need to know about your girl. It's all in there."

Rico glances at his watch, the seconds ticking away like a countdown.

"Why?" I grip it tighter, the contents thicker than I wish they would be, which speaks to more than that rap sheet Shonda had shown me.

"Because you deserve to know where she's been the last ten years."

Rico grips the steering wheel tightly as he says it, indicating he's read all through it, and it's not good.

"I don't know how to thank you. It's too—" I start, emotion swelling through my windpipe. Rico offers a reassuring smile.

"Shut up, man. I've had your back ever since we had to share that sleeping bag at the Father-Son Campout, and Gloria felt sorry that her *mijo* didn't have a dad when yours stepped in."

I chuckle, the memory so faded I don't remember the campout, but I do remember the sleeping bag being too small for the both of us.

"We've been through too much together for me to bail on you now. Besides, we both know you'd do the same for me."

I nod, agreeing with him. "Without hesitation."

"Alright, get out of here. I'll text you when I know more."

I nod, putting up my window and watching him be the first to pull away. Settling into my seat, I turn on the engine, stare at the envelope, and let my curiosity get the better of me. I rip off the seal and open it. The first piece has a yellow sticky note with a drawing of a dick. I tear that off and look at the paper it's attached to. Molli's medical report from the jail, listing her injuries from when they first brought her in and then her blood work in the pages behind it.

Apparently, this is what Rico saw when drawing the dick. To borrow Dani's phrase, 'what a moron.' She is clean, as she said. It's a slight relief as I turn to the next page, and a picture of a guy falls into my lap. I flip it over to see Rico's scribbled handwriting with Joaquin's name.

He stands around six feet tall, with a muscular and intimidating build, hinting at the years of physical exertion and not the gym kind like me. His eyes are black, a steely gaze glaring into his mug shot while his hair is shaved off.

A few scars trace over his face as does a couple of teardrop tattoos and some woman's name on the side of his neck. A smirk twists his mouth up as more tattoos snake over his collarbones and disappear down his shirt. His arms are a patchwork of inked illustrations and symbols depicting allegiance to gangs and criminal ties, both as a mark of pride and a warning to rivals. They continue onto his hands, where gnarled knuckles have 'HARD LUCK' inked across them.

"What a real piece of work," I mutter, wondering how Molli got tangled up with this guy.

I flip through the rest of the pages, tons of reports and more pictures I'll need to sort through in greater detail. But getting out of this parking lot and across town to Dani's place undetected is a priority, especially if the Chief has my buddies back at the station looking for me.

30

The bay door rattles closed behind me as I pull in and kill the engine. Molli is standing in the doorway, the glass door against her back, and wearing those cut-off sweats from last night. Her legs are long and thin, too thin from all she has been through, but with some of my home cooking, I can get some weight back on the both of us. I'll put Dani's punching bag to good use in the next day or two. If I can't go to rehab, I'll have to do it here, and maybe Molli can help if she's so inclined.

"Aren't you a sight for sore eyes?" she hollers, walking barefoot across the garage, which is not the best idea and why I picked up some white tennis shoes for her.

I remember her doodling on hers in school with a Sharpie, so I bought one too. It's probably not good living so much in the past with her, but it's the only time we were great, and I'd like to relieve some of that now if I can get away with it.

"I don't know about that, but I got enough stuff to feed us for a while," I reply with my door open, shoving the manilla envelope into my glovebox before she reaches me. "Bags are behind me."

She cautiously opens the door, careful of my left leg dangling out the side. It's one thing I've noticed about her. Her actions and how she handles things are delicate and a light touch. Opposite of Dani throwing this around and making a lot of noise. Molli handles everything gently, almost dainty, which I can't recall her being like in the past. Her touch was almost hesitant when she kissed me last night and again today. She used to be more like Dani. I guess people change in more subtle ways.

"All this?" she says while loading bags on her arm, and a small smile appears as she takes in the entire back seat. Growing up with Mom, she always kept a full kitchen to make anything at a moment's notice. I guess I inherited that from her.

"It looks like a lot, but it's not that much, just the staples and stuff from the list you made me."

I close my door, edging by her to scoop up the rest so she doesn't feel overburdened to carry them. She's still frail, and with beer for dinner last night and pie for breakfast, she won't get stronger that way.

"Did you have any of the leftovers while I was out?"

"I did." Her eyes widen as she takes a step back to look at me. "Was I not supposed to? I didn't know."

"Oh, no, it's fine," I reassure her, not wanting to make her feel bad. "Of course, you can have them. I just wanted to ensure you had enough to eat while I was out."

I give her a warm smile, trying to ease her worries. Something in the way she reacts makes me curious about her past. Was it from that guy, Joaquin, or her parents? So many unanswered questions. She relaxes slightly, a hint of relief in her eyes.

"Okay, I couldn't eat much anyway. I guess I'm still getting used to everything and not used to having options."

"Options?"

I loop the rest of the bag handles over my forearms and bump the truck door to close it while she walks toward the lobby. I'm not sure if she heard me, but either way, she heads in without answering, leaving me to wonder what she meant.

Once upstairs, we work as an efficient team, putting things away. I take the kitchen. She handles the clothes and then opts for a long shower. When I have everything put away, I start seasoning the chicken, deciding to go with chicken picatta for a fast and easy meal. After boiling the pasta and cooking the chicken, I call Mom with a quick question about the sauce recipe. It barely rings before she answers.

"Alexander, how are you?"

Her voice is light and happy, revealing nothing about their situation or how it's going.

"I'm fine. But I was calling to check in on you and Pops."

Nerves fill my body, and I hold my breath to hear it's a disaster and that Pops is moving them back home.

"Oh honey, this place is marvelous. Just marvelous. Your father is in Heaven with those two kids out there. He's putzing around, getting in their way, and being nosy. He's even letting Dani look at his old truck. They were discussing plans of possibly restoring it together. How darling is that?"

Well, knock me over with a feather. Maybe she's better with older people than I thought since Pops refused when I offered her help.

"I think he knows every detail of both their lives. Not to mention grilling Mr. Takahashi about his fame and philanthropy. He's been a dream host. Last night, he grilled steak on his outdoor kitchen, and we danced in his sock-hop diner. It was more fun than your father, and I normally have."

A pang of jealousy runs through me that they are having more fun with them than with me. I shove that immature thought away as they are happy and enjoying their mini vacation.

"Sock hop diner?" I say, flipping the sizzling chicken to brown the other side.

"Yes, his car showroom is based off an old diner. It's the cutest thing. I'll have Dani text you some pictures. He's even got a jukebox that doesn't need quarters. It plays anything you want, can you imagine that?"

I imagine Tomlin can afford whatever he wants.

"And Pops? He's not mad?"

"Oh, you know your father, he grumbles and then takes his coffee out to bother the kids while they work. He spent most of the day out there. I think he will teach Dani how to play chess, which might help her temper." The cadence in her voice picks up, both amused and worried at the same time. "She's a live wire, that one. Did you know she got her tongue pierced to stop her from cursing? I can assure you, dear, it's not working. She cursed a streak of words I've never heard when she hit her head and got blood on the carpet."

I shake my head, only imagining how that went over. Crap was a bad word growing up with them. Dani makes that word seem normal in comparison.

"Luckily, nothing a little club soda didn't fix in getting the stain out. She was more worried about the carpet than the gash on the back of her head. It's my turn for dinner, and Dani asked if I knew how to make pot roast. Can you believe such a question?"

"The gall of her," I jest, smiling into my phone. "I'm glad everything is going well. I wish Pops understood my decision."

The phone is silent for a moment before she responds.

"Your dad is a proud man. Asking him to flee from danger isn't in him. He understands that he's older and may be unable to react as he once did. But no one wants to feel helpless and that's essentially what you did."

Even though her voice is compassionate, her words and

message aren't. It hits me right in the gut, and my guilt grows more.

"Yeah, I guess you're right."

"And Alexander, you're a proud man too. You can dig your heels in and be as stubborn as a mule. Both my boys can. It makes you strong and reliable, but sometimes, you both need a hand to the head to convince you to work this out. Just give him time. He'll come around."

I can be just as stubborn as my father, refusing to see things from a different perspective. But her mention of my pride and comparison to Pops hits me hard. Maybe I'm more like him than I care to admit.

"Now, how's it going on your end? Learn anything new about these guys after Mary Ann?"

I'd never tell Mom what I know now. I don't want to worry her, and that's all she'd do if I relayed what I learned today.

"Kind of quiet over here. I'm making chicken picatta right now. I use chicken broth or chicken stock to make the base?"

I pick up the box and hope it's the right one as I dump it into the pan with the other ingredients to simmer.

"Stock, and don't forget to brush the chicken after it browns a little. That's the real secret to locking in the flavor. Chicken picatta sounds delicious. Something I haven't made in a long time because your father and I don't need the calories. Now that I'm cooking for a full house again, I might need to bring out our favorite recipes. Especially with that young boy, Lars, he eats more than you ever did."

He's also almost twice my side. Maybe Dani is right. Mom is as wholesome as Mrs. Claus. A connection I never made having lived with her but realizing it now.

"I think they'd love the old recipes, Mom."

Keeping her happy will keep him happy and everything up there safe and away from the dangers here.

"I think so too. Well, I'll tell your father that you called, and hopefully, he'll call you on his own soon. Thanks for checking in, dear."

She hangs up while I stir the pasta, temporarily distracted until I see Molli has changed into her new outfit. She does a little twirl for me at the entrance of the kitchen to see, and it tugs at my heart. This feels like a dream of what our life could be like if Rico's right in that we can get past it all.

"You look lovely," I say, and she returns my smile.

"Were you talking to your mom?" she asks, stepping into the kitchen as I tuck my phone away and turn down the heat.

"Yeah, everything is good with them."

"That's a relief." She rubs the center of my back, a comforting gesture as she must sense my worry for them. "Whatever you're making smells good. Do you need any help?"

I smile appreciatively at Molli's offer and enjoy being here with her.

"Thanks, but I've got it under control. Just finishing up the sauce."

She leans against the counter, watching me with a contented expression.

"You're quite the cook, Hamilton. I never knew."

I chuckle, stirring the sauce before turning off the heat.

"I guess you learn a few things when you're living alone. Oh, and growing up with Mom."

"Impressive," she teases, a playful glint in her eyes. "I'm lucky to have a personal chef."

The compliment warms my heart, and I walk over to her, wrapping my arms around her waist.

"Well, it's my pleasure to cook for you, especially when you've been through so much."

She rests her head on my shoulder, her arms slipping around my neck.

"You've been through a lot too. I don't know what I would have done without you."

I tighten my embrace, savoring the feeling of having her in my arms.

"We'll get through. And when it's all over, we'll figure out what comes next."

She looks up at me, those chestnut eyes filled with hope.

"I'd like that."

Before I can respond, the timer for the pasta goes off, and I step away to drain it. Molli joins me at the stove, and we finish preparing the meal together. As we sit down to eat, I can't help but feel a sense of trepidation regarding the difficult conversation I'm having with her later tonight.

31

Dinner comes and goes with the dishwasher quietly whirling in the background and some show on the TV. I look at my watch, noticing that time is slipping away and it's getting late. Molli and I share the couch, her legs draped on the coffee table, creating a peaceful atmosphere I'm about to ruin.

"I need to talk to you about something," I finally mutter when the show flips to a commercial.

She looks at me, reading the seriousness on my face, and drags her legs off the table. As she reaches for the remote to click it off, I shift on the couch to face her directly. She does the same with a sullen expression.

"This doesn't sound good."

She curls her legs underneath her while resting her arm the length of the couch, narrowly touching me as her hand drapes over the back.

"I met up with Rico while I was out." I lick my lips, watching her reaction. "He has learned more, and I need to ask you some difficult questions."

The entire dinner is mostly silent as I ran through different ways to start the conversation. I decide there isn't any good way except to come out with it.

"Okay," she says slowly, her hand raising to scratch her neck, and I mentally prepare for an episode tonight.

"How did you get mixed up Joaquin?"

Molli's face tenses, averting her gaze momentarily before finally meeting my eyes. I can sense the hesitation, and it worries me even more.

"It's . . . I didn't start off this way."

"I know you didn't, Molli. I assume you left here to follow your dreams," I say softly, trying to keep my hurt and rejection out of the conversation.

It's not her problem. She lets out a shaky breath and stills the hand at her neck.

"Joaquin was big time. Or so I thought. I met him in LA. He was charming and persuasive, always had money, and got us into the best clubs and parties. People didn't mind his tough appearance. The tattoos were his thing if you know what I mean."

I for damn sure don't know what she means. He looks like the criminal he is. I don't know these Hollywood types, but if they let a guy like that into their parties, it's seedier than I thought.

"Go on."

Her face lightens a slight smirk that makes me think she still misses that lifestyle.

"I was young and naïve, and this guy really took an interest in me. He wanted to help me become a star. He was the one who told me to change my name. So, I picked Molli Sitara."

She does that same sweeping motion she did in the truck stop. A dreamy look on her face for several seconds as she looks up at the imaginary name in the air until her expression changes, and her hands fall into her lap.

"It was right after that story broke of that 'casting couch' producer who made women sleep with him to get part. You remember, right?"

I would have murdered the guy the second I found out my girl had to do that to get work in that fucking town.

"I don't but proceed."

She nods and shifts uncomfortably.

"Well, it sort of still continues but more discreetly. In their homes or hotels booked under different names to avoid getting caught by law enforcement." I raise an eyebrow, and she shakes her head. "Well, anyway, there was this part . . . the leading role, to be the star, but you know."

She shrugs, and I know precisely what she's saying this time. Her hand returns to her neck, scraping long strokes down the side and leaving a trail of red skin. This could trigger something, and as much as I hate putting her through it, I need to get to the bottom of this tonight. I have ideas on what needs to happen next, and this is a critical piece in the process.

"I can assume," I murmur, placing my upturned hand on her leg to comfort her, as I assume this will only worsen. She looks at it but doesn't move either hand toward it. That's fine. I leave it there as an open invitation for when she needs it.

"Joaquin arranged it all. It was in the Hollywood Hills, a nice place, decent guy, and it wasn't that bad. He made it comfortable for me."

She bites her lip, pausing to look away. My blood thickens as it throbs slowly into my ears. I don't want to hear this, but I need to hear this. It's essential to set aside my feelings to be there for her regardless of how hard it is to listen.

"Turns out I didn't get the part." She gives me a weak smile. "He didn't even know about the film. He was someone that Joaquin was involved with. Owed a debt to. Later, I found out that I was the payment."

Tears spring into her eyes and her fingers scratch harder

against her skin. The slow throbbing of my heart rockets into shock as I hear what those pieces of shit have done to her.

"Molls," I utter, reaching toward her with my arms wide open. She glances at me briefly and gently crawls into my lap. I hug her tightly, my hand slipping to her nape as her head lays against my shoulder.

"I'm so sorry."

"I should have known. The parties, the drugs, older guys, and younger girls. It was right there in front of me, and somehow, I thought I'd be different." She sniffs, clutching as tightly to me as I am to her. "I wanted it so badly. I didn't even realize what was happening."

She cries into my shoulder. Her body racks with grief and sorrow from the nightmares that haunt her now.

"You were only eighteen. How were you to know?" I lean my cheek against her head and rub her back. "It's not your fault. It's all those fucking men."

My body trembles with anger, wanting to hunt every one of them down and make them pay for what they did. It wasn't her fault. She was young, beautiful, and innocent. They were sick bastards who knew precisely what they were doing.

"No."

Her head jolts up, nearly hitting me in the nose to look me dead in the eyes. Her stare is hard and intense through the watery tears.

"Don't become angry and turn into one of them. I've seen too much violence and too much violence to lose you to it. I know what anger and revenge do to people. I've seen it and can't lose you to it."

Her words pierce through my anger. It's the truth. Becoming consumed by rage and seeking revenge won't solve anything right now. It will only perpetuate the cycle of violence and cloud my judgment when deciding how to get her truly free and away from Joaquin. I cup her face gently in my hands, wiping away the tears from her cheeks.

"I won't become like them. I won't let them ruin us. But I won't let Joaquin or anyone else get away with this. We'll do this the right way together. We'll bring them to justice and make them pay."

Her eyes soften, and she nods, her hands resting on top of mine briefly before pulling them off her cheeks to hold in her hands. Two more tears drip down her cheeks while she takes a few calming breaths and continues her story.

"From there, it just seemed to spiral out of control. The bigger Joaquin got, the wilder the parties became. And Hamilton, the amount of drugs . . . coke was everywhere." She shakes her head and looks away, returning to that time. "The things I did . . . what I . . ." Her body begins to tremble, violently shaking as her hands untangle with mine and simultaneously scratch her face and neck. "No one . . . no one should ever go through that."

The anguish in her eyes mirrors the turmoil in her soul. My heart shatters at the thought of all the horror she's endured. The helplessness I feel is overwhelming, crashing over me like the grief crashing over her. Whatever residual pain lingering in me from her leaving is instantly benign—scattered into nothingness at hearing how horrible her life has been all these years.

I pull her into me, her body trembling violently in my arms and her tears soaking my shirt as if each drop carries a fragment of her pain. I hold her as tightly as possible, wanting to shield her from the world and protect her from the darkness that engulfs her. My fingers gently trace down her spine, from her neck to her waist, in a feeble attempt to soothe her.

As her sobs echo in the quiet room, I feel a deep ache in my chest, a primal urge to protect her at any cost. I want to take all her pain away, to carry the burden for her, but I know I can't undo the past. All I can do is be here for her now, to offer my unwavering support and love that's always been there for her. She was mine then, and she's mine now.

"You're safe," I whisper, my voice raw with emotion as tears flood my eyes. "I promise I won't let anyone hurt you ever again. I'll protect you with everything I have."

Her grip on me tightens. I want to show her that the love we shared never ended, that it's still there if she wants it. If she wants me.

"You're the bravest person I know," I murmur, my lips brushing against her ear. "So brave."

"I got to . . ." She stirs in my arms, wanting loose, and I comply when I see her blotchy face. "I'll do whatever it takes, too. Whatever you need me to do to stay here and be with you. I made a mistake a long time ago. I won't do it again."

I cup her face, the words I've wanted to hear for so long whispered at her most vulnerable moment. And the look of desire amidst both our tears has me slowly connecting my lips to hers. A hesitant kiss, different from the one this morning. This is tender, filled with the forgiveness of what happened before us, resolving past hurt to clear a path for our future. The one she just spoke life into.

I taste her salty tears on her lips as I deepen the kiss. A contented sigh escapes her as she draws me closer, wanting me as eagerly as I want her. I grasp her butt, tucking it against my pelvis for her to feel my hard cock. She smiles against my lips before plunging her tongue into my mouth and feeling every bit of me.

My hand traces up her back to rest on her head, encouraging more of me into her mouth as our tongues switch places. Her hips move above me ever so slowly, grinding into the stiff shaft that would explode the second it's inside her. She moans, the sound vibrating into my mouth and feeding the lust building in my balls.

My fingers dig into her ass cheeks as her grinding gets faster and more feverish. I'd love to make her come, to hear her scream my name and fall apart under me like she used to. And with the place to ourselves and all the time in the world, I don't hesitate to scoop her up and break our kiss. Our breaths come in ragged gasps, taking in the same air as I hold her the same as I did downstairs. Her legs tighten around my waist, her ankles interlocking, and everything about it is so right.

"I know I told you this is not a good idea right now, but fuck," I plead, trying to remain levelheaded but only thinking with one head. The one that has wanted to be inside her ever since he saw her at the truck stop. "I only have so much resolve."

"Then stop holding back. I want to be with you."

She releases my neck to tug off her shirt, exposing her small breasts to me, and I look to the ceiling to regain my composure.

"Are you sure?"

Never in my life have I asked a woman if she's sure she wants to have sex with me, but this is Molli. A woman as fleeting as the stars she's chasing and the ones dotted all over her skin.

"Make me yours."

"Fuck yeah," I utter, snatching my wallet off the counter as I carry her to the bedroom and tossing it on top of the dresser.

I forgo the overhead light and click on the bedside lamp before gently laying her on the bed. She looks so fucking beautiful, laid out, waiting for me. Something I've fantasized about hundreds of times. Now, to have her within my grasp, in my touch, I want to love, punish, own, and destroy her in countless ways.

"Take everything off," I say, my voice thickens with desire. She bites her lip, a playful teasing when I move closer, the light cascading across her half naked body.

"Some things never change. You always loved being in charge."

Her thumbs loop into the top of her waistband, wiggling them down and raising her hips, revealing a pair of the black, lacy panties I couldn't resist buying for her. When she tosses them on the floor, she lies back down, completely ignoring what I said.

"You have no idea, sweet Molli," I say, stretching my shoulders and neck to ease the tension that's become a permanent fixture there.

"Are you trying to intimidate me or something?" She has an easy smile when she says it, tucking her hands behind her head to watch me and stretching the star tattoos on her hips upward. "You always loved to scare people with your size."

She pokes my thigh with her big toe, causing my muscle to flex immediately out of defense.

"It didn't work on you back then, and it doesn't seem to be working now," I mutter, catching her foot and massaging it.

"Not in the least. You may play rough, but you'd never hurt me."

Her hands loosen from her head to slide over her skin and pluck at her breasts, getting the nipples as erect as possible. Like a welcome gift to me, one hand slips past her stomach, traces each star before slipping past the seam of her panties and rubbing little circles. She uses her foot as leverage, pushing against me to raise her hips to show me what I am missing. I watch, entranced at her getting off so quickly in front of me. It's hot as fuck, both her mental and physical teasing. It's part of the chemistry between us, one giving and one taking.

"That may be true, but you don't listen very well. I distinctly told you to take everything off, yet here you are still in your panties."

My hand tightens around her foot, taking a step forward and placing it against my chest so she can shuffle out of her little panties. She continues swirling her fingers underneath them, moaning in pleasure instead of acting on my instructions. A wicked little grin slowly spreads across her face, taunting me and making my dick rock hard.

"Then you take everything off," she challenges, dragging the balls of her feet down my shirt to tuck into the top of my pants.

I fucking love this about her. She's a tease, always has been. She does what she wants when she wants. Consequences be damned, and that's the same in the bedroom. She'll go far beyond any woman I've ever been with and enjoy every damn bit of it.

I'm quick to bend over, grasping the edge of the string panties and sliding them down her legs before she even has a chance to respond. She gasps in surprise and then raises an eyebrow as a further challenge to me. I take the tiny threads of fabric, twist them in the middle, grasp her hands, and string them through until she's bound up in makeshift handcuffs.

"Next time, you'll obey," I tease, loving how easily I have her hands bound and resting over her head.

A delicious little smile teases at her lips, her chestnut eyes locking with mine when she murmurs, "Touché."

As much as I've drawn this out, I can't wait to get my cock inside her, to ram it in and drag it out repeatedly, knowing she's always been able to take my larger size. It's always driven me crazy, watching her pink pussy swallow my dick and then shrink back down, only to take it deep again.

That perfect view of watching my dick fuck her will have to wait as I take her on her back, wanting to watch her face and see the ecstasy I bring her when I fuck her right. Her toe stabs me in the stomach, poking me a couple more times.

"What's the hold-up, Officer?"

Goddamn that mouth, I will stuff it one day, but not tonight.

Tonight, I'm taking her in every way I can until we're both satisfied and exhausted.

"Not a damn thing."

I grab the back of my shirt, yank it over my head, and throw
it aside, watching her eyes size me up. Since high school, I've
packed on more muscle and lost a little through rehab, but I am
still bigger than I was. We'll see how well she can handle me.
My pants and underwear are next, widening my stance for her
to appreciate what's about to be inside her repeatedly.

She eyes my cock, subconsciously licking her lips in appreciation as it points directly at her. Excitement courses through
my body, feeling my veins, muscles, and skin expand in anticipation of a passionate night ahead. My mind is racing faster
than my heart. Do I take her slowly, savoring every inch of her
or do I slam into her, fill her to the hilt, and get us both off
quickly?

"Fuck it."

I reach for my wallet, pull out the remains of the strip of
condoms, and tear one off, all under her watchful eye. She
hasn't moved any inch from where I left her, and I fucking love
how easily she gives up control to me. It makes me want to
destroy her even more.

"Right to business then," she taunts, her lips curving into a
knowing smile while I tear open the package and roll it on.

"Yes, ma'am."

She inhales, the actions shoving her nipples even higher.
Not wanting to forget this, I gaze at her, ready and waiting for
me. Her legs widen, inviting me into where I always felt best—
inside her. I climb onto the bed, the mattress squeaking under
my weight, eliciting a giggle from her. It becomes a moan when
I swipe my tongue over her pierced lips, drinking in her
wetness and ending with rapid circles to her clit.

"Ohhh."

I love catching her by surprise, and her bound hands come

down to push my head further into her mound. She smells of the fresh soap in the shower, expensive stuff mixed with her scent, which is highly arousing. She watches me as I pleasure her with my tongue and moans occasionally. I wink, using the scrape bristle of my beard to run across her lips, trying to nip at the silver studs sunk into the plump skin and over her clit.

"Again," she commands, light and airy.

I shake her hands loose from my head, catching her arm and putting them back over her head. She doesn't need to do anything. I'll do it all and make us both feel amazing. A smile ghosts across her face, and I reward her obedience with another round of intense sucking, a swipe of my beard, and a gentle blow across her hard clit. My cock couldn't get any tighter in this condom, nearly cutting off the blood supply as desire sucks my balls tight to my body.

Sweat breaks out over my skin as I execute the motions repeatedly, watching her body clench and her hips elevate to my mouth. She's close. So close that I'm almost willing to let her have it if I wasn't so selfish, wanting her first orgasm to be all over my cock.

"Alex." She wiggling her hips and shoving her mound toward the ceiling when I back off. "I was about to come."

"I know."

My thighs are astride her while I slip an arm under her back to move her to the top of the bed. She uses the closeness to lick a trail across my pectoral muscle and leaves a lingering kiss. I duck my head to dust one over her lips, her head raising for more, and with a slow shake of my head, she knows it's not kissing time.

"Are you ready?"

I don't know why I am asking. Every part of her body wants my body, but a small part of me wants to confirm that she wants me. Not because she's horny or wants to feel good, but because she wants to be with me again. Her former lover and boyfriend, and this is the entry point in getting back what we used to have.

"Always."

Her chin raises, meeting my gaze with desire and acceptance, and it quiets the final doubts in my head.

"Good."

I grab a pillow from beside her head, quickly stuff it under her hips, and kneel between her legs. With her hands still bound, her chest panting lightly, and her mound glistening like my wet mouth, I slowly put the tip inside her. It's been so long. I close my eyes, trying to hold back my orgasm as goosebumps flood my skin. I thought I wanted to slam into her, be rough, and make her take it. Instead, I take it slow, feeling her inch by inch until I'm settled at the very base of her cervix.

It's incredible, warm, and smooth, gripping my cock and sucking it in further. I open my eyes to see the most contented smile on her face with her eyes shut and savoring the moment.

It's a welcome back and a welcome home all rolled into one. The memories of then and now mix about the room with us, swirling into the nostalgia of yesteryear and the future promises. I want to make this last. I want to live inside her, where nothing exists beyond us. All the problems that led us here fall away, and the only thing that matters is her and us— giving pleasure, receiving pleasure, and sharing our bodies, minds, and hearts.

Her eyes flip open, and a curious expression passes her face before she asks, "You going to move, or have you forgotten how this is done?"

That sass. The one I loved back then that I thought I lost to substance abuse is returning to the bedroom. I fucking love it.

"You're going to pay for that."

I clutch her thigh, tuck it into my side and smack her bare ass. The crack is loud, echoing in the small room, and she laughs.

"You always loved to smack my ass. Now get moving, Buster. You owe me an orgasm or ten," she says, grinding her wet pussy against my cock to make something happen.

It's right there, and then, I realize I fucking love her, never really stopped. Sure, it faded as I was forced to put her out of my mind, but now that she's back and agreed to be mine, it's game over for the both of us.

"You better hold onto more than just that pillow."

I ease a few inches out, then slam back into her. She gasps, a look of awe on her face as I repeat it. So much for not slamming into her. Her bound hands come out, reaching for the top of the headboard and not quite making it. I untwist the panties with my finger and set her free. She tosses them to the side of the bed, scoots her hips further into me, and hikes her legs to her chest.

"Fuck," I groan, getting in even deeper until I hit her cervix with every thrust.

It's so fucking good, it rockets my orgasm to the front. I fuck her like a runaway train, fast and furious. Moans spill out of her until she screams my name. It's a glorious fucking sound, knowing I'm doing it to her. I'm making her feel this good, and it feeds my ego.

My breath increases, and sweat drips from my forehead onto her legs as I keep going, wanting to make her come repeatedly. Make my name fall from her lips so she knows she's mine, and I'm hers. Her eyes are closed, her mouth parted, breathing in and out as I pound into her. Her hands slip loose from her knee, her leg falling to the side before I catch it and hold it in place. Her face contorts into pleasure, with her eyebrows pulling together and her back arching as she comes hard. Awe coats her features, a smile plays at her lips, and my name escapes them again.

A sated, breathy annunciation that is forced out of her. I come with a deep groan. My orgasm explodes out of my cock, sending sensations through my nerves and all over my body. Her body tightens one last time, coming again and riding out our orgasms together. It's incredible, feeling the warmth and pulsing of her pussy all around me, pulling every ounce from my cock as her knees fall to the side and I collapse on top of her.

Her hand traces down my sweat covered back, pinching my ass, and I jolt, my cock shoving in deeper, and she moans. Our shared pants fill the room. The only sound as the garage apartment is quiet, and the surrounding commercial buildings are closed for the night.

"You still got it, Hamilton," she says, pushing against my chest for me to let up and allow space to breathe. Finding her compliment humorous, I chuckle and bury my face in her neck. She's sweaty, not as much as I am, when I lick her salty skin.

"Good to know," I murmur when her short hair tickles my nose. "I wasn't too rough?"

She twists her head, forcing me away from her neck to look me in the eyes.

"No, why?"

"I was in there pretty deep."

The fleeting thought of busting through her cervix crosses my mind. That can't be good. She continues to gaze at me, a fondness in her expression that I hope one day will become love again. Her hand slips up my back and over my shoulder to cup my cheek while her thumb strokes my beard.

"You're fine."

That is such an odd word choice. Not I'm fine. But you're fine. It could mean several things, and I want to demand what it means to her now. Are we still talking sex, or is she thinking something else when her eyebrows draw together in concentration?

"Now let me up. I have to pee, or bad things will happen down there that we don't have time for."

She smiles, the haunting expression gone as she pokes me in the ribs on my good side. I roll off her and watch as she scoots to the side of the bed then turns to me.

"Do we have any more pie?"

Both surprised and pleased she wants more food, I smile and swing to my feet, needing to handle the used condom anyway.

"I think we do. You want some?"

She smiles brightly at me from the bedroom doorway, the light slicing over her skinny frame and highlighting the visible ribs on her left side.

"And coffee. The stronger, the better if you keep me up."

She disappears toward the bathroom, not waiting for my response, and I'm left dumbfounded. This feels like something I used to wish for when I lay in bed after she snuck out of my parents' house. When I used to envision what life would be like after we got married and got our own place, it made me happy and scared the shit out of me.

"I'm so fucked."

32

I took her two more times until she begged off for sleep, more coffee, or just a break from my cock. All her words. After she fell asleep, I conduct the perimeter check and ensured all exit points are secure before retrieving the envelope from my truck to go over the contents.

Her rap sheet is long, spanning a speeding ticket in Nevada that was somehow dismissed without prejudice even though she didn't appear in court. On graduation day, Pops clapped me on the back and suggested we go inside to the ceremony as whoever I was waiting for didn't seem to be coming. She was already in another state when she knew I'd be waiting for her.

I shove all that old pain away as I have her now, and that's all that matters. The charges continue, mainly in Los Angeles and the surrounding towns. Some were dismissed while others have guilty pleas with time served. Each time, she was out in a day or two, bonded out and allowed to walk free regardless of all her priors. It gives credit to the little bit she told me last night about this guy being connected in that city.

If it were here, she'd still be in jail. And then it hits me, and

I fall back against the couch. I'm dumbfounded. The realization is so sudden and shocking that it steals the air from my lungs. We wouldn't have let her out. Short staffed or not, she would have been flagged in the system. Too many priors, missed court dates, flight risk, and even a couple of charges for contempt of court. She should not be out unless the Chief orchestrated it all from the start.

And Rico? Did he play Rico too? Knowing he's like a brother to me, is he using him too? Or is Rico on the take? No. No way. Rico likes to operate on the edge at times. Keeping one foot on both sides of the law enforcement fence, such as smuggling out this file, which is against the law. He couldn't be. He absolutely isn't.

I look for a pattern, anything to piece together what Joaquin and his crew could be planning, and other than running drugs in these parts, I got nothing. I run my hand over my beard, the whiskers scraping as I think, until the hallway floorboard creaks, and Molli is peering out, wearing my shirt from earlier. Her eyes dart around the papers, taking them all in and slowly stepping into the room.

"What is all this?"

Her voice is low, given it's the middle of the night. However, the look in her eyes is more uncertain, and her finding me like this worsens it. I should have told her about Rico giving me her file when I got home.

"Molli."

I stand, my hands out defensively as she strides to the papers and starts picking them up, seeing her name one after another and letting them gently float to the floor around her. There's an eerie quietness as her eyes track back to mine. The chestnut irises are on fire as her head tilts, a silent question I'm slow to answer.

"NOOO!"

She lets out a gut-wrenching scream and violently snatches

the remaining papers, clutching them to her chest. They are turned every which way, crinkled in her hands as she goes ballistic, trying to shield them from my eyes. She's mumbling under her breath and heaving as panic overtakes her. I step closer, reaching out, but she pulls away, her eyes filled with tears and fright.

"Please let me explain," I plead, my heart breaking at the sight of her so distressed.

She slips on a page she let float to the ground, falling on her butt and scrambling away from me when I try to help. I keep my hands where she can see them and try to remain calm even though it feels as if my pulse is racing a thousand miles an hour.

"Here . . ." she continues mumbling and scooting away until her back hits the wall, tucking herself into the corner by the gaming console. Her eyes are wild and unfocused as she rocks and mutters.

"Molli," I implore, my voice gentle and soothing as I take a cautious step closer, trying not to startle her further. "Let me explain."

Her breathing is rapid and shallow, and her hands clutch the papers to her chest like a lifeline. It's clear that she's spiraling into a state of panic, and I know I need to approach her with extreme care.

As I draw nearer, she retreats deeper into her shell, and the realization that she's frightened of me kills me, especially after what we just shared. Deciding not to press on, I halt my steps and ease onto the floor, bringing myself to eye level with her. She continues whispering and rocking, the papers scraping the wall as she clutches them tighter.

"I should have told you about this. I'm so sorry."

She doesn't acknowledge me, and I continue, keeping my voice steady.

"Rico thought it would help. Please help me to understand

what you've been through. It was wrong. I should have talked to you about it. Should have let you continue telling me what happened rather than letting myself get carried away and do what I just did with you."

I wave a hand toward the bedroom, feeling like a selfish prick for having sex with her. I put my need to be reconciled with her, to be on the path towards being a couple, above her need to tell me everything, and it's reprehensible.

Her gaze finally settles on me, tears streaming down her face as she scratches at her neck. The same long, hard strokes, as usual, leaving blistering red marks down her delicate skin. I can't let her hurt herself any more than my betrayal already has.

"Molls." I scoot closer, and she panics, looking around the room to escape. I instantly stop. "Please. I won't hurt you. You don't have to fear me."

Her head shakes rapidly, causing her hand to scratch her face instead, and it spooks me that she's not registering what is happening. Her whispering increases. I duck my head, putting my ear closer to her to make out the words she's saying—something about here.

"Here? What about here? You're safe here."

I lean closer to make out what she says until she suddenly stands, throws the papers in the air, and bolts for the apartment door. They scatter in the air like confetti. My heart lurches with panic as she throws it open and runs downstairs.

"Wait!" I call out in desperation, sprinting after her.

My footsteps pound down the stairs as I race down the hall and spot her on the ground by the front door. She claws at the bulletproof glass, sobs racking her body as tears flow in furious streams down her cheeks.

"Can't stay here. Can't stay here. Can't stay here," she cries repeatedly, her words a broken record of her trauma.

Her trance-like state is freaking me out, and I skid to a stop, my heart racing. She's lost in another world, and it sends chills down my spine. When she's unsuccessful in clawing through the glass, a hand snakes into her hair and starts pulling it out to ease the stress she's enduring. I quickly run to her, fall to my knees, and I try to comfort her with a soft touch to her shoulder.

"Molli?" My voice shakes, and I clear my throat to try again. "It's okay. You're okay."

Her chanting lowers, her lips mumbling over the words as she shakes my hand off her shoulder and continues pulling out strands of her hair. I reach for her hand to stop the self-harm, and she slams me away, her terrified eyes not exactly meeting mine when she does it.

"You're hurting yourself."

I try repeatedly, and she slaps at my hands, chest, and face to get me away from her. I'm in over my head, not knowing what to do. If I bear hug her it could send her over the edge and my words don't seem to work. Then I remember what a therapist did for a little boy taken into the facility from an extreme abuse case. I adjust to sitting with my back to the wall, facing the lobby as she faces the glass, murmuring and sobbing. My thigh presses against her shin, the only thing she hasn't slapped away, and I begin.

"Hey, where did we go?"

My voice cracks, sounding terrible in the quiet building, but I continue, watching her face intently for any recognition.

"Days when the rain came. Down in the hollow. Playing a new game. Laughing and a running."

It's a subtle change as she sniffs, her eyes glazed and unfocused, one hand tugging her hair and the other pressed against the glass.

"Hey, hey, skipping and jumping."

I keep my voice low, pouring all my emotions into the song, hoping the familiarity brings her back to me.

"In the misty morning fog with our, our hearts a-thumping and you."

She takes a shuddering breath, and I pause, waiting for a response or any other movement to let me know I'm getting through to her. When nothing happens, I continue.

"And you, my brown-eyed . . . girl."

My voice thickens with emotion, and the last word is barely a whisper. I clear my throat and wipe the tears from my eyes, catching her attention as she looks at me. Really looks at me, not locked in or vacant, but stares those brown eyes at me. And it causes my breath to catch as my chest aches.

"And you . . . my brown-eyed girl."

Her whispering stops, and I look up to thank God almighty that this is working. The same as it did for the little boy rocking himself in the middle of the playroom.

"And whatever happened to Tuesday and so slow. Going down the old mine with a transistor radio."

The progression happens as I keep singing. Her hand pulls off the glass, bracing herself as she slides closer to me and slowly lies her head in my lap. A shuddering exhalation comes out with the lyrics. My pulse races as I hope this will keep her calm until I figure out what to do next. Her hand is still pulling her hair, it's not the worst thing, and I don't try to stop her this time. I keep singing and slowly, she chimes in so softly I feel her hum on my thigh rather than hear the words.

She always loved this song.

It was our song.

I sang it off-key to her when I drove her around town. The windows were down, her feet on the dashboard, and her hair carried off by the wind. It's a beautiful memory that I can see even now, beyond the physical and psychological trauma that she has endured. That carefree, beautiful, brown-eyed girl is still in there, slightly beyond reach.

The lyrics continue to flow, a quiet duet of comforting words that mean everything to me, the same as they meant everything to her back then. Her humming blends with my singing, creating a soothing melody that brings her back to the here and now, where I stoke her skin and assure her everything is fine. That I've got her. I will take care of her to the best of my ability. The fear and panic in her eyes are gone, replaced by a sense of tranquility as she leans into my touch, finding solace in the middle of the night in the quiet lobby.

As the song's last notes linger in the air, she whispers loud enough for me to hear, "My brown-eyed girl."

I still my hand, leaving it to rest on her arm as she looks up at me. Her gaze is focused and direct, her look piercing and intense. Not anger, not sorrow, not any emotion I can really put my finger on. Simply watching me and, I release a soft smile, tilting my neck toward her as I start stroking her skin again. There are no words that need to be said, no explanations or solutions to be found at this moment. All that matters is that we're here, together, and that's enough.

"I'm tired," she says after the longest time, shifting on the floor to sit up.

I nod, my hand falling to the cold linoleum, having seeped through my briefs to numb my butt.

"Let's get you back upstairs."

I swing to my feet with a groan, twisting to crack my back, and do a few shoulder rolls to release the tension. I offer my hand to help her to her feet. She brushes off her butt and legs, and I do the same, even though Dani keeps this place spotless.

As we make our way back to the apartment, I can't help but feel a sense of relief. We've had a difficult and emotional night, but somehow, we've made it through and overcome another hurdle. I'll need to deconstruct what happened and where I went wrong. Not telling her was my biggest mistake, and I won't ever hold anything back from her ever again, no matter how hard it is or how I think it could be for her betterment. I'm understating now that surprises are the worst thing for her, and her reaction speaks to all the uncertainty she faced with Joaquin and whatever else happened in Los Angeles.

If I tell her directly, we can deal with it together, and even if the short term is hard, it's better, in the long run, to help build that trust between us.

We enter the apartment, the papers flung about catches her eye, and, without hesitation, she turns her back to them. As if physically turning away from her old life that she's trying to escape. I'll clean it up and tuck it out of sight to avoid this occurring again after I put her to bed,

"You're brave, Molli. I hope you know that," I say softly, my hand on her back as she leads us down the hallway to the bedroom. I catch her by the arm and kiss her forehead softly before she crawls into bed. She mumbles something into the pillow, and as I turn to clean everything up, she calls out to me.

"Come to bed with me, Alex."

She flips back the covers and scoots to the middle of the bed, a clear sign where she wants me. I smile, genuinely happy at how much she reaches out to me. It makes me feel both wanted and needed, gateways to eventually being loved.

The scattered papers lay forgotten as I join her. Her head rests against my chest, her fingers tracing gentle patterns on my skin, and I hold her tight. I press a soft kiss to the top of her head, and she sighs contentedly, relaxing fully into me.

With each passing moment, the seriousness of what just happened fades as I match my breathing to hers and will my body to relax. The pending harm will be there in the morning, and I need to learn the rest of the story from her before I make my next move. A move that will likely blow the lid off this entire thing.

If I begin to think about it, I won't get any sleep as it fills me with both dread and trepidation. I push it from my mind for tonight, close my eyes, and relish the feeling of my brown-eyed girl asleep on my chest. Sometimes dreams do eventually come true.

33

A jab to my ribs awakens me, and I groan, rolling away from the morning sunshine streaming through the open window. My eyelids squeeze close, and it's peaceful again until she's yanking on my shoulder, my name falling from her lips teasingly. I blink my eyes open, still half-asleep and turn toward the source of my annoyance. She's lying next to me, a playful grin on her face as she pokes a finger into my rib cage.

"Come on, lazybones. It's a new day."

Her voice filled with excitement. I groan again, putting my back to her. Considering last night, I'm relieved she's in such a good mood, but I'm not. I refrain from using her phrase 'I'm tired' and select one of my own.

"It's too early," I mumble, my voice muffled in the pillow despite being husky from our interrupted evening. She giggles, her fingers tugging the blanket from me, and the cool air prickles my heated skin.

"It's already 10 o'clock and your phone is going berserk."

I squint at the clock on the bedside table, realizing she's right. It's so damn late. I can't recall ever sleeping this late. Then again, I've never had a night like last night. Even though I have a lot to do and plan for, I roll onto my back and throw a hand over my eyes to block the bright sunlight.

"Fine, fine," I grumble, "I'm awake."

She wiggles next to me, then settles against my side and resumes her previous position of laying her head on my chest. This time, she isn't drawing patterns on my skin. She's letting me wake up slowly.

"I'm glad you're feeling better."

I peek from under my arm to look down at her. She shifts her head to gaze up at me and sighs, giving me nearly the same look as last night when she lay on my lap and I sang to her.

"I had time to think while you were sleeping."

"And?"

"And I'm sorry about last night."

My arm swiftly moves off my face to cup her body, holding her in place because this is the first time she's been forthright with me about her past. Offering to talk about it first rather than me having to force it out of her. And I want to be as encouraging as possible if she wants to open up. I rub the sleep from my eyes with my fist before giving her an encouraging smile.

"Go on."

She takes a deep breath, inching closer and moving her leg between mine.

"Last night was . . . bad."

I open my mouth to say it wasn't that bad, to not add to her guilt, when she places a timid finger to my lips and quickly moves it away.

"Don't, please."

She licks her lips and continues, "I don't understand what happened. I don't know why I just snapped like that. It was like I was trapped. I didn't see you, Alex. I saw him. Him coming toward me, him chasing me down the stairs, and me trying to escape him."

I squeeze her flesh, my arm tightening so she knows I would never do anything to harm her. If I can't tell her that right now, I want her to physically feel my support.

"Those papers—it all flooded back." Her voice wavers with emotion, and I lift to give her a little kiss. "I'm trying hard to forget it, but I realized today that I can't keep running from them. I need to face them, to share them with you."

"It would help. To understand so I know how to help you," I quietly inject, hoping my interruption doesn't stop her from continuing. She pauses, her lips twitching in the corners, trying to decide whether to smile or frown.

"I was with Joaquin for a while, but it wasn't by choice," she whispers, her eyes glistening with unshed tears. "He forced me into that life, and I did things . . . terrible things that I'm not proud of. I was scared. I didn't know how to escape. I felt trapped like there was no way out. He threatened . . . threatened to kill me if I ever left, and I believed him."

She buries her face in my chest, muffling a sob. I stroke her back, knowing this is hard but necessary to get it all out. We can't have a repeat of last night, not if I can help it. It's several minutes of comforting her before she raises her watery eyes to mine and gains enough composure to continue.

"Take your time, Molls."

"No, I need to tell you. I have to because it's ruining what we are starting, and I won't let him win again."

Her resiliency is remarkable, and I couldn't be prouder of her fighting spirit raring back. She sniffs, wipes her nose with the back of her hand, and starts again.

"I saw things." She shakes her head, her gaze boring into mine as she details her nightmares. "Things he ordered and things he did himself. I know what he's capable of. Horrible, horrible things, Alex."

"I'm so sorry."

I slide my hand over her shirt to trace her delicate jawline with the tip of my finger.

"When you showed up, God. I knew you. I knew it was you, and I was so embarrassed. You were so shocked when I said I didn't, but I did. I . . ." Her lips roll together while tears drip down her cheeks. "And you . . . you called me."

A sob catches in her throat and her hand covers her mouth as she cries harder.

"Mary Ann."

I catch each tear with the back of my index finger, my heart clenching so hard it aches.

"I didn't know."

"No, no, Alex. You don't understand."

Her voice gets stronger, and she sits up, her knee pressing into my side while she wipes the remaining wetness from her face. I pull myself up to lean against the headboard to give her my full attention.

"It was shocking and sudden and everything all at once. It was me and you, strangers, but not really. I had a hard time processing it, so I appeared nonchalant. You on top of him, I couldn't deal with it. And then Rico comes along, and it was like, whoa, everything was happening so fast. I didn't know how to react, so I pretended not to know you, to keep my secret buried deep. But I did know you, Alex. I remembered you from that night, from my past life before Joaquin. And when you called me Mary Ann, it shattered me. I realized you had known me too, and I felt like a fool for pretending otherwise."

Her voice trembles as she shares her inner turmoil, and everything clicks into place.

"You were a reminder of the life I had lost, and I was terrified of facing that pain on top of what I was already dealing with. Of course, I was drawn to you, the only person who has ever shown me love and kindness. But I was tainted, am tainted. You're everything right in this world. When you said you were a police officer, I was so happy inside. You did it. You made a great life for yourself. It's also why I pushed you away at the jail."

"I thought you didn't care. Didn't care at the truck stop or the jail. It killed me to leave you, but you left once. I thought you'd leave again. I didn't want to be hurt again," I confess, frowning because I still regret leaving her in that jail cell and Rico having to convince me to get her out. I'll regret that and Matt's death to the day I die.

"I know I hurt you, Alex. I saw it then, that cold night, and every day since. You hold yourself back." I open my mouth to argue that I'm not holding back to protect myself. I'm holding back to give her time and space to heal before committing to me wholly.

"Let me finish. It's okay. Trust takes time. But Alex, when you came back and held me with the bars between us, you saved me from that nightmare. I can't thank you enough for getting me out and away from him."

Her hand finds mine, her fingers intertwining, seeking comfort and reassurance.

"You don't have to thank me. And we're not out of the woods just yet."

"I know, but I want you to know that I'm sorry for lying to you, for pushing you away when all I wanted was to be close to you. I was just so scared, Alex. Scared of my past, scared of my feelings for you, scared of losing the one person who had brought light into my life."

She looks into my eyes, her gaze pleading for under-standing.

"Can you forgive me?" I caress her cheek tenderly and then cup her face in my hands.

"There's nothing to forgive. We've both been through so much already, and once we get past this, things will be better.

And if you still want me, you'll have me. It's really that simple."

She nods, relieved before she leans forward and presses her soft lips to mine. The kiss is slow and gentle, a testament to our deep emotions. It's a kiss of forgiveness and acceptance. As our lips move against each other, I feel a sense of peace wash over me, knowing her thoughts behind her actions when we initially reunited. It helps clear the lingering doubt from my mind. The larger question of why she left lingers, the same as the last ten years. One day, when she feels comfortable sharing, I'll finally have closure.

She pulls back, resting her forehead against mine as we catch our breath. And in this moment, I know that I'm exactly where I'm meant to be – with her, my brown-eyed girl.

"Now, who's hungry?"

She leans back, smiling with a warmth about her face that's brighter than the sun filling this room and making me feel lighter.

"What are you in the mood for?"

She gives me a mischievous look, climbs over my legs, and stands by the side of the bed. She's still wearing the shirt from last night, her lean legs looking tempting when I run a hand up the back of them and caress her bare ass.

"I could go for this."

I sneak a finger between her legs, and she jolts back, leaning on the dresser just out of reach.

"No, sir. I need food before we do that again. And a shower."

My grin widens as I fold back the covers and watch her slide down the dresser before playfully darting out the door.

"Catch me if you can, Hamilton," she taunts from the hallway.

I chuckle, feeling a surge of happiness and playfulness in the air. With newfound hope and a sense of renewal, I chase after her, my thigh protesting, but her infectious excitement makes me happy. As I catch up to her, I scoop her up in my arms, her giggles echoing through the apartment.

"You're mine, Molli Sitara," I say, my heart full of unspoken love for her. "And I'm never letting you go."

She wraps her arms around my neck, her eyes sparkling with happiness.

"I wouldn't have it any other way."

I can't help but notice that she's taken care of everything. The papers are neatly stacked on top of the manilla envelope on the coffee table. Setting her gently on her feet, I release her waist to walk over to them. I pick them up, flipping through to see they are in date order, and her hand traces over her head to rest at her usual spot.

"You cleaned up." It's meant to be a question. "You didn't have to. I know this is hard for you."

One arm wraps around her waist, her elbow resting on it as she gently pulls her hair.

"I wanted to. Everything is hard right now."

I drop the file on the table, walk to her and pull her close.

"I'm proud of you, Molls."

She doesn't hug me back and I don't need her to. This embrace is to comfort her as she's facing difficult tasks head on and to let her know she's not alone.

"Breakfast is ready too," she whispers against my chest, and I look over her head to the kitchen counter with plates of scrambled eggs, sausage, toast, and fresh fruit. My heart swells with love for this woman who has faced so much darkness yet still manages to bring light into my life.

"You've been busy." I kiss her forehead. "Thank you."

She blushes and looks away, but I can see the happiness on her face.

"You're welcome."

34

With the dishes cleaned and put away, showers taken, and ready for the day, I sit down with my phone to see a slew of calls and text messages. Molli is content with watching television while I read the text messages.

> I hope everything is going as well as can be expected. Isla asked about you and I said you're heading out of town. I hate lying to her after all she's been through, but this is for her own good. Stay safe. I'm worried about you and your friend.

I smile. Eli is always diplomatic. His use of the word 'friend' is considerate. When all this is over, I'll introduce them to my new friend as she'll be a permanent fixture in my life.

> I appreciate it. Hopefully, this will be over soon, and we can get back to our normal lives.

The reply will come later as the pet store has long since

opened and demands his attention. I scroll through Dani's multiple text messages.

> First of all, why have you been hiding your parents from me? You ashamed of me or something?

> Your mom made me beef roast over noodles and this gravy. I nearly died. It's so good. Tomlin said I was being melodramatic. Eves. The dude only eats healthy shit so he wouldn't know. Lars had three plates.

> Tomlin got us security. SECURITY?!?!?! As if this place doesn't have enough security. He got us additional security. Did you know about this?

> What the hell's going on? Why haven't I heard from you?

> Bruh

> Call me!

> That's it. I'm driving over there once I sneak past these security dudes.

I'm shaking my head, Molli casting me a curious gaze, and I merely say, "Dani."

Glancing at the time on the phone, her last text was about ten minutes ago, and quickly I dial her number. As soon as she picks up, she starts yelling into the phone.

"Hamilton, where the hell have you been? I've been trying to reach you for hours! I'm so worried!"

"Are you on the road yet?" My pulse quickens, needing to stop her from coming here.

"Hell no, Tomlin blocked the door. He needs to go back to

Denver if he thinks he can do that shit. I swear, he's been so fucking overprotective and smothering, I want to scream or rack him like I did before."

A bird calls in the distance. I'm glad she's outside, so neither her boyfriend nor my parents hear her cussing. Although, it sounds like it's going well for all parties.

"I'm sorry, Dani," I say, trying to calm her down. "I've been dealing with some things and couldn't get to my phone. We're okay, though."

"Okay?" she snaps, and I move the phone away from my ear. "Okay doesn't cut it! When you're in deep shit and hiding out Hamilton, you need to answer your phone so I know you're alive. I swear if you die in my building, I'll resurrect you from the dead and kill you with my bare hands!"

I chuckle at her complete lack of decorum while Molli's eyebrows raise. Only Dani would blurt that out regardless of the seriousness of our situation.

"And don't even get me started on that loser friend of yours blowing up my phone. It almost makes me regret transferring my business number to my cell because of that idiot," she grumbles when a piece of equipment roars to live in the background, drowning out the rest of what she's saying.

"I can't hear you," I say, putting the phone back to my ear when the machine shuts off.

"Call your friend!" she yells, blowing out my ear drum. I wince and quickly pull the phone away from my ear to put it on speaker.

"Okay, okay, I'll call him," I reply, trying to appease her. "Besides security, everything else is fine? Mom and Pops?"

"Yeah, your mom is Mrs. Claus, like I said." Her voice calms, taking it down a notch from out of control to very annoyed. "I might never let her move out. She's making a turkey tonight. Actually, a whole Thanksgiving meal since I've never had one before. She got all teary-eyed and hugged me when I told her my dad, and I would have those frozen TV dinners for the holidays."

I genuinely smile at my phone. That sounds exactly like something Mom would do.

"And Pops?"

"He's definitely like you. He walks around grumbling and mumbling but hangs with us in the garage. He taught me a shortcut on a gasket, so that was cool. I looked over his truck. It's a lot newer than what I usually work on, but we've been tinkering with a few things. Oh, and get this. He wanted to teach me to play chess. Fuck that. It's boring as hell, and I don't have the time to stare at a checkerboard. So now, he plays with Tomlin. Apparently, no one can interrupt them when they start playing. Did you know a game can last for days? Days?!?! What a snooze fest. Anyway, Lars really likes him. I think it's that father figure stuff because they sit on the back patio and talk about life and shit while staring at the mountains."

It bothers me to hear that he's bonding with another man and has yet to forgive me for keeping them safe.

"Has he mentioned me at all?"

"No." Her answer comes fast. "Why? You guys fighting or something?"

My gaze falls on Molli, listening intently even though her eyes are on the television.

"No, just a difference of opinion."

"Want me to ask your mom?" Dani's voice softens, and I can tell she's trying to be understanding.

"I'd prefer you don't," I say quietly, hoping she listens when the heavy equipment rattles again. Figuring she's about to yell, I put it back on speaker to say goodbye. She says something, but the call ends, and I'm left staring at my phone.

"She's certainly a force to be reckoned with." Molli looks amused by Dani's scolding when I turn my attention toward her. "How old is she?"

I tilt my head at the odd question. Molli's skin tinges pink as if she shouldn't have asked, and I reply, "Twenty-two."

"Wow, she's younger than I thought." She shrugs a shoulder, looking very uncomfortable. "She's very pretty too."

I chuckle.

"And Dani knows it. Trust me when I say she rides my ass nonstop when she wants to, and not in a good way."

Molli turns the volume down on the television when a commercial comes on. She looks deep in thought for a moment before asking,

"You like your ass getting ridden in a good way?"

I burst out laughing, the sound echoing through the apartment. Molli is grinning wider than I have seen since she's returned, and I must give it to her. She pulled it off with such a serious expression.

"You sold that for a moment." I laugh and lean back in my chair to press a hand to my diaphragm.

"I'm an actress. Of course I can sell it."

The smile slowly fades when she references the life that took her away from me and became the thing her nightmares are made of. Scared to lose her again to the haunting of her past, I immediately lean forward and clasp her hand dangling over the arm of the chair.

"You're definitely an actress with that performance. We can find you work here when all is said and done."

She'll always be a star to me, but with the sad expression on her face, that might not be enough. She looks down momentarily, then back up, her eyes searching mine when I squeeze her hand.

"I won't go back."

I release her hand to cup her cheek, and she leans into my embrace. The panic in her gaze makes my heart ache. "Father Michael does a Christmas and Easter production every year. Maybe you can start there."

"The church?"

Her laugh is bitter as she pulls my hand from her face and curls into the corner of the chair.

"They'd never let someone like me in that place."

I hate how she categorizes herself as unworthy, as if all the parishioners of that church are water walkers except for her. It couldn't be the furthest damn thing from the truth. Growing up in that church, front row pew every week with my mom as a Sunday school teacher and, at times, the director, I know where all the skeletons lie and whose closets they lie in. Every person in that place is a sinner. Molli may have had her sins visible to the outside world, whereas everyone else is hidden, but make no mind that they're all the same as her, and I, for that matter.

"We'll just have to see about all that when this is over."

Her hand grips the end of my sweatshirt to pull it down over her knees like she used to go in high school, and I love that some of her mannerisms are still the same.

"You sure are making a lot of plans for after this and after that, but what are we doing in the here and now besides me freaking out, fucking up or getting drunk, and you picking up the pieces every damn time?"

That cynical tone is back. I dislike it, even if she's right with what she's saying.

"Glad you asked, that's my next call."

I ignore the calls from the station, knowing it's the Chief, and call Rico. It rings a few times before he picks up, speaking Spanish like I'm his mom. Understanding he's probably not able to talk, I remain silent as he rattles on about why he hasn't been over and that it's not a girl keeping him away but work. It makes me glad he taught me Spanish growing up.

I can't help but admire his quick thinking, even in the face of danger. It's a tense situation for him, knowing where I'm at and collecting information at the same time. There's a brief silence on the other end before he switches to English.

"Hamilton? Sorry about that, man. Had to play it safe."

"I understand."

"Molli there?"

"Yes, you're on speaker."

My eyes dart to hers as they widen, looking worried as she glances at the phone in my hand.

"Good, I'm heading there now," he begins, his voice low and serious, "I found something big. Really big. There's more to it than what we talked about the other day. The Chief is definitely involved. I've got pictures."

Fuck.

I keep my composure as best as I can, even though the shock and gravity of Rico's words hit me like a ton of bricks. The Chief's involvement in robberies and money laundering or with Joaquin? Any of it is possible and goes way beyond anything I could have imagined. Molli's gasp beside me only amplifies things. Her eyes are wide with concern, and I reach out to squeeze her hand reassuringly.

"Are you sure about this, Rico?" I ask, my voice steady despite the turmoil inside me.

"Positive. I've been digging deep. He's in bed with some seriously dangerous people," he replies, his tone grave. "We can't trust anyone in the department. I've seen too many signs of corruption now that I have the evidence."

"How about I meet you by the river at our old fishing spot? No one knows about that place but us," I suggest, worrying he'll be tailed if he's suddenly leaving the station and his post. "They could be tracking you."

"I already swept my truck for trackers. Remember that thing I bought that detects air tags, GPS trackers, and other stuff?"

I hum my acknowledgment, recalling the device Rico had purchased while dealing with a clingy ex-girlfriend that he thought was stalking him. Turns out she wasn't. Her brother lived in the same apartment complex.

"It's clean as of this morning when I pulled in, but I'll park at my mom's and take her car over. She's out of town at a funeral with her sisters. No one knows that, so we're good."

"Text me when you're close. I'll open the gate and a bay for you to pull in and hide the car. Never can be too careful."

"Okay, see ya in half an hour," Rico whispers, then suddenly switches back to Spanish, his voice raising as though he's arguing, and I hear the station chatter behind him. I quickly end the call, my heart beating fast as I stare at the blank wall across the room.

We're so fucked.

35

His text comes through at the same time I spot his mom's maroon Cadillac slowing on the road and waiting for a car to pass to open the gate. I move to the side as he pulls into the open bay beside my truck before pushing the button on the wall to lower the door. He cautiously opens the driver's door while glancing out the side window to ensure he has proper clearance.

"Does Gloria know you took her prized possession?"

I roast him when he swings to his feet, an envelope under his arm as he gently closes the door.

"No, and I plan to keep it that way. Although, she probably keeps a mileage book somewhere I don't know about, and I'll be caught either way."

Gloria humbles him. Someone has to or else his ego would never be in check. His eyes wander all over Dani's place, taking it all in and letting out a low whistle.

"She's got a nice place here."

"Yeah, she's doing well for herself." My tone turns serious as I give him a welcoming handshake. "Are you sure no one followed you?"

He shakes his head, shooting a worried look at his watch before meeting my gaze.

"We're in the clear. How are you holding up?"

"I'm hanging in there." I exhale my frustrations, knowing I can let it out with him while Molli's waiting upstairs. "This whole thing is a damn nightmare."

"Yeah, it's like we're swimming in shark-infested waters, and we don't even know who all the sharks are." Rico nods grimly, and his jaw clenches. "And Molli? How's she doing?"

"As well as can be expected, but I need to figure out counseling options." I look past him to the spot in the lobby where she was clawing, trying to get away from the hallucination of Joaquin. "At times, I'm in over my head."

"Well, shit's about to get worse. So much worse. They're running them across state lines, up to Canada." He blows on his hands and rubs them together. "Can we get out of this cold garage at least?"

"Yeah, let's head upstairs."

He grabs my arm to stop me by the breakroom.

"Did Molli tell you anything? Because if we can't trust her, this isn't going to work." Rico's dark eyes bore. His concerns are valid, ones I've pondered before I experienced the last several days.

"She's been trying to escape him for a long time. She's scared to death of him, but we can trust her. She wants out, Rico. You were right for making me get her. Don't go against your initial gut instincts. You're right, and you've always been right about her. She needs our help, now more than ever."

He mulls over my words, his face cloaked in doubt. "And you're sure she should be a part of this conversation? See the pictures I've got in here?"

He swipes the envelope from his arm and shakes it in the air. I snatch them up, flip on the breakroom light, and sit at the table. I open the envelope and pull out the stack of pictures, my pulse racing with each image. The first picture shows the Chief, his face stern and unyielding, standing with a group of shady-looking individuals outside a warehouse. The crates are piled to the ceiling behind them.

"Drugs?" I ask, pointing to the crates.

"Yep."

I whistle.

"That's a lot."

In the next set of pictures, I see the Chief again, this time in a dimly lit alley, exchanging money with more suspicious-looking characters. Fear is in their eyes. They're handing over cash out of desperation rather than willingness. It's clear that the Chief is using his position to extort money out of these guys.

As I continue to flip through the pictures, my stomach tightens. There are images of brutal murders, bloodied faces, broken bones, and mutilated bodies.

"These are damning." I'm filled with rage and disgust. "If we go public, it could bring down the entire department."

His expression is tense as he works his jaw back and forth.

"That's why we need to be careful. We can't trust anyone in the force right now."

He's right. The corruption runs deep, and we can't afford to make any mistakes.

"Where did you get all these?"

He looks everywhere but me as I gaze up at him. I catch the edge of the chair and shove it away from the table, indicating he needs to sit and explain.

"Where, Rico?"

Rico takes a deep breath, sits, and finally meets my gaze.

"I've been working on this for months, ever since noticing some suspicious activity within the department. Guys transferring or suddenly retiring, it didn't sit right. I was at the station late one night, parked my bike in the back, and was putting on my helmet. I saw the Chief talking in the alley with a guy that looked similar to this Joaquin guy. I knew something was up, so I've been digging, gathering intel, and following leads. It's dangerous work, but I couldn't turn a blind eye to what I was uncovering."

His eyes dart to the pictures spread out on the table.

"I managed to get a hold of some guys willing to point me in the right direction of the Chief's involvement. They provided me with leads, and I got the pictures as evidence. But don't even ask them to turn informant because they won't. I've already tried."

I pound on the table, my anger and frustration grow with each passing moment. The betrayal is hard to stomach from my own best friend.

"Why the hell didn't you tell me?"

He takes a deep breath, looking remorseful. "I didn't tell you because I wanted to shield you from this. It's been my mission to take down the Chief for a long time, and I didn't want to drag you into my mess. I didn't think it was fair to involve you in something that could potentially ruin your career or put you or your parents in harm's way."

I raise an eyebrow, surprised by his answer.

"You think I can't handle it?"

"That's not it, man. I know you're more than capable, but I also know how much this job means to you. I didn't want to risk you losing everything over my vendetta."

I lean back in my chair, digesting his words.

"And Gloria? Aren't you putting her in harm's way?" I ask, worried for his family's well-being.

Rico's expression softens. "Of course I am. That's why I've been extra cautious, trying to keep her away from me. I know it's a dangerous situation. That's why if something happened to me, it would die with me, and you'd never know about it."

My anger flares, and I can't help but abruptly stand, causing my chair to clatter to the floor. I begin to pace the breakroom, my frustration evident in every step.

"So, you were just going to keep this to yourself? Leave me in the dark while you put yourself in danger? Bullshit! You're my best friend, my brother, fuck, man!"

Rico jumps to his feet and looks regretful, with a hint of defiance in his eyes.

"I was trying to protect you, Alex. Protect your parents too."

"Well, newsflash, Rico," I snap, unable to contain my anger. "I'm a grown man. I can make my own decisions. We're partners, and that means we face these dangers together. I trust you, and you should trust me."

He sighs, running a hand through his hair.

"I know, and I messed up. I should have trusted you enough to include you from the beginning. I'm sorry."

I pause in my pacing, my anger still coursing through my veins.

"I get that you wanted to protect me and my parents, but you can't do that by shutting me out. We're brothers, Rico. That means we always share everything, the good and the bad. If I can't trust you, who can I trust in this world?"

"You're right." Rico nods, his expression contrite. "But there's one other thing."

"Fuck." I scratch my beard, trying to make sense of all this. "What?"

"I didn't want you involved in case you took over as Chief." I open my mouth and his hand raises between us. "I know you wanted to go into the FBI, but your Pops killed it."

"You knew about that?" I ask in astonishment. When I told Molli, I thought she was the only person to know.

"Not in so many words, but I have a connection up there. He said you put in an application and withdrew it." My hand falls away from my beard, rolling into a fist in frustration for all the secrets he's kept from me. "Chief is the next best thing to the

FBI. You can't bust the current Chief and expect to make interim until the election. But if I do it, that clears the way for you."

I'm flabbergasted at how Rico's seeing a path to my future before I even saw one for myself.

"Why?"

His eyes cast down briefly and then return to mine with a guilty look.

"Because I want to make detective. Turns out I'm pretty good at this stuff." He extends his hand to me. "I didn't know how to tell you that I wanted to move on, move up, and further my career without leaving you behind. We've always done everything together. I didn't know how to bring it up without hurting you."

"Maybe Dani is right that you're an idiot. We're not kids anymore, Rico. We can pursue other paths and still be broth- ers." I grab his hand, using it to pull him into a tight embrace. "I'll always have you back."

His arm wraps around my shoulders, pulling me into him, and my anger fades. He did this to better himself, better me as well, and was too afraid to tell me. Who's protecting who here? I'm grateful to have him in my life, regardless of what unit or agency we work for. We've been through too much together to let something like this tear us apart.

"And I have yours."

"I'm sorry for getting so worked up," I say, my voice softer as I pull away. "I just didn't see this coming, you know?"

"Yeah." He flashes me a half smile while stepping back from the embrace.

"Am I interrupting?" Molli says softly from the doorway. I hold my hand out to her, welcoming her into the room, when Rico takes us by surprise to hug her.

"How ya doing, Mary Ann?"

She bristles slightly at her old name. Something Rico is not fully aware of as he's not had a chance to talk to her as much given the sudden events. I wait for her to correct him, and when she doesn't, I do.

"She goes by Molli now. Molli with an I."

As he stands there, his back turned to me, I catch her eyes flickering toward mine. Her lips curl into a slight smile, silently acknowledging her gratitude for my correction. Rico remains unfazed by this subtle exchange even though it's important to her. Upon releasing her, she steps forward and freezes when she sees the pictures scattered on the table.

"What is all this?" she asks quietly, her arms wrapping around her body despite the warmth of the heat in this room. It speaks to her discomfort and bravery of staying here to face this head on when I'm sure she'd prefer to run away upstairs. Rico turns around, facing Molli with a serious expression.

"This is the proof I've gathered against the Chief."

"He really is involved?" Molli's eyes widen with shock, and she takes a step closer to the table, looking at the pictures.

"Yeah, he is. Has been involved for quite some time and appears to be expanding his operations. I haven't figured out how he got involved with Joaquin, but they are together."

"This is . . . intense," she says, her voice barely above a whisper. A picture catches her eye, and she steps forward. It's the one with the Chief meeting a suspect in the dark alley. "I know him."

Her finger points to the picture before she picks it up, her hand trembling slightly. I move to her side, touching her neck to comfort her while she stares at the photo. Her pulse hammers against my palm as her skin heats up.

"Who is he?"

"He's part of Joaquin's gang." Her words are faint. "His name is Miguel Ortiz. They call him Razor because of what he does to his victim with a switchblade."

She shivers, the photo falling out of her hand and onto the

table as her back presses against my chest. My mind races with the implications of what she's saying. Razor is part of Joaquin's gang, the same violent and ruthless group that kept her in this life she escaped from. Is this part of the things she said she saw that Joaquin ordered? I instinctively move my hand to rest against her waist, but she seems too stunned to notice.

"He was one of the enforcers," she continues, her voice still shaky. "He's merciless and completely devoted to Joaquin."

Rico's eyes narrow with concern as he looks at her.

"You're saying you can pick this guy out in a lineup?"

We exchange a look as she moves out of my touch to pull the other photo from behind the envelope to see the victim. She nods, her fear evident.

"I ... yes, but if he recognizes me ..."

She's scared, and I don't blame her. Facing someone from her past, someone who had inflicted so much pain on her, someone who is so violent, is the last thing she needs right now. I shake my head emphatically.

"She's not going into that station to identify him."

"He did this." I take the picture from her hand as she points to a carving on the body's flesh. "See the 'M'? He does that to all his victims."

She turns away, walking to the opposite side of the table and picking up the toppled chair. Her hands clasp the top of it, her knuckles turning white as she watches Rico and I search the other photos for his signature marking.

"Razor is dangerous, and if he ... if he is working with the Chief ... it's ... it's impossible. I'll never be free."

"You will, Molli." My voice is steady despite the nerves gnawing at me. "I'm going to give the Chief what he wants most. Me. I will turn myself in and pretend to offer my loyalty to him. It's the only way I can get close enough to gather evidence against him and expose his criminal activities."

Molli's eyes widen in shock, and she shakes her head.

"Alex, it's too dangerous. You can't go in there alone."

I place a reassuring hand on his shoulder.

"I won't be alone. Rico and I will have a plan in place, and he'll be watching my back. We'll set up some sort of signal in case things get too dangerous, and he'll step in to get me out."

Rico nods in agreement.

"He's right, Molli. We need to do this carefully and strategically. It's the best way to catch the Chief, and he doesn't suspect anything so far. It's the perfect guise for Hamilton to say you skipped town, skipped out on bail, and that he's been out looking for you because it's his neck on the line. His reputation."

"Exactly, and in this small town, where the former police chief's kid is an angel, my reputation is everything. The Chief will understand that I don't want it tarnished by a runaway prostitute I once knew and will blackmail me to work for him. Force me to carry out his activities." My voice strengthens with conviction as the plan starts to form. "As far as everyone in town knows, my parents are visiting her sister, which explains the only other noticeable absence. He doesn't know about Dani. Eli and Isla are going about business as usual."

Rico's eyes light up as he grasps the full scope of the plan.

"It's the perfect way to get close to the Chief without arousing suspicion."

"And don't worry, Molli. I won't do anything illegal. It's all just a ruse to get close to the Chief and expose him for what he is."

Her gaze shifts between us, worry etching on her face.

"But what if something goes wrong? What if he figures it all out? What if Razor kills you?" she whispers the last part while pulling on the hair on the back of her head.

I walk to her, taking her hands in mine.

"I won't let that happen. I'll be careful, and I'll play my part convincingly. Rico's gathered a lot of evidence against him already, but I need to gather the rest to ensure it's an airtight case against the Chief and Joaquin to ensure you will be safe."

"We're going to need help, Alex," he says with his phone in hand. "You and I are not enough. Especially as large as this thing is."

It's the biggest risk I've taken yet. One of last resort that I never thought I'd have to consider. Loyalty is ingrained in us, a code we live by, and I'm about to turn coat on that for the greater good. It's an easy decision, but the repercussions can't be undone.

"Make the call."

Rico nods, turning away from us as he dials the number to set this dangerous plan in motion. I release Molli and step toward Rico as he puts the call on speaker for us to hear.

"Colorado Bureau of Investigations, Public Corruption hotline. How can I help you?"

Molli looks at me in shock, her eyes widening in realization.

"Yes, this is Officer Ricardo Rodriquez with the Cañon City Police Department. I have some information about my boss, Police Chief Reynolds, that I'd like to report."

The voice on the other end becomes more official, asking for details before transferring him to the investigator assigned to our jurisdiction.

"Agent Hunt."

A bright smile appears on his face.

"Robyne. Rico here."

His voice deepens, oozing charm, and I glare at him. Now is not the time to hit on a female officer, least of all the very one who is the gateway to the help we need.

"Why are you calling the hotline again?" she says in exasperation. "I told you to call my line directly."

"I would, but you don't return my calls."

I try not to roll my eyes at Rico's flirtatious banter with

Agent Hunt. This is not the time for his antics. We have much more important matters at hand. He puts the call on mute.

"Oh, didn't I tell you that I know someone who can help?" he says slyly. This is another one of the secrets he's been keeping. He unmutes the line and continues, "We used to go out, but I told Robyne I'm focusing on my career and don't have time for a commitment."

"It was one time, Rico. Last I checked, that was the excuse I used on you," she grumbles. "I'm going to hang up now."

"Wait!" I interject, snatching the phone out of his hand. "Ignore Rico. My name is Officer Alexander Hamilton. We need your help. There's corruption in our police department, the Chief of Police specifically."

"Give me all the details."

Agent Hunt's tone shifts from annoyance to seriousness, becoming fully engaged in the conversation. Rico takes a deep breath before delving into the tangled web of corruption he uncovered. He provides names, dates, and any other information that might be relevant, making sure to be as precise as possible. As they go back and forth, Molli pulls on her hair again and I slide my arm around her waist. She leans into me, breaking the desire to self sooth by absorbing my touch instead.

Once Rico finishes, there's a brief pause on the other end of the line before Agent Hunt speaks again.

"This is what you were working on when we met at the bar."

"Yeah, but I didn't know the Chief was connected to Joaquin at the time, Robyne. Molli also identified Joaquin's enforcer just now when she stumbled upon the pictures I shared with Hamilton because it involves him too."

"Because he made her bail," Robyne asks while papers shuffle on her end. Not entirely. Rico and I exchange looks over the phone.

"Yes. Molli was my former girlfriend in high school. The three of us grew up together. Naturally, I'd bailed her out before I knew all this."

Molli clutches my arm, unwilling to let her go during this difficult conversation. She needs to know and feel my unwavering support.

"And you had no idea about her connection to Joaquin then?" Agent Hunt continues probing. I take a deep breath, preparing to share the whole truth.

"No, I didn't. I only found out about it after. She's been trying to escape that life and leave Joaquin, but he wouldn't let her go. He threatened to kill her if she ever left. They want her now because she can identify them. She's already identified Razor's signature on two of the victims' bodies."

Molli's grip tightens on my arms, her nails digging into my skin, but I don't flinch.

"Hamilton's with Molli now," Rico adds, setting the phone on the table and moving to sit down. I release Molli and we both follow suit. "Tell her your plan."

Agent Hunt remains silent as I share my plan with her. A strained sigh rattles through the phone as she speaks.

"It's a risky plan, Officer. You'd be putting yourself in a lot of danger." Agent Hunt's concern is evident as she continues, "We can't let you go in there alone. I can get a team together to provide backup and surveillance. We can also wire you up to monitor the conversations and get him to confess to working with them, where their operations are, and where the money is going."

"I'll be with Alex too," Rico says, shooting me a stern look.

"Then you'll be wired, Rico. Close enough to act but not enough to tail them."

"I'll send you what I have gathered so far, Robyne. But Alex will be our best source. He has a vested interest to have this go right."

His eyes fall on Molli as she looks at me. I give her a reassuring smile and reach for her hand.

"We'll do everything we can to support you both. Safety is the priority. If things get too dangerous, we'll pull you out."

"I'll get what we need," I say with conviction. I didn't just get Molli back in my life to die trying to keep her. "I know the angle I have to play with the Chief. He's disliked me from the start because of who my dad is."

"And to state the obvious, your family cannot know about this." Pops won't know as we're still not talking. "No one can know about this," she adds.

"Molli has some pending charges against her. I want those expunged in exchange for my cooperation." Rico slowly nods while Molli tugs on my arm, whispering that it's not necessary. "She has an attorney in Denver that represents her interests."

The line goes silent for several seconds before she finally says, "Have him give me a call and we'll work something out."

Satisfied with her answer, I press her for one final favor and the most crucial detail.

"Who will protect Molli while I'm on this assignment?"

The three of us exchange looks. If there were someone else I could trust as deeply as I do Rico, I would ask them. I can't ask Tomlin and Dani to take on more risk as they are already protecting my parents. Eli and Ronald are out of the question due to Isla. Agent Hunt takes a moment to consider my request before responding.

"I understand your concern, Officer Hamilton. We'll do our best to ensure Molli's safety while you're on this assignment. I can assign a couple of men to keep a close eye on her, and we'll make sure she's well-protected."

I stare at Rico, wondering if Molli would be so trusting of complete strangers and immediately knowing she won't. She retreats into herself as the terror of being separated from the only two people she knows and trusts sinks in.

"Thank you, Robyne."

Rico snatches the phone off the table and stands up, heading out the door to finish the conversation. A sense of anticipation and anxiety swirls within me as we sit and wait for word to come.

"I'm scared," Molli whispers, her hands twisting in her lap.

"I know. We all are."

I wrap her in my arms, setting my chin on the top of her head and praying it all goes down without anyone getting hurt.

"I wish I could get high."

36

After seeing Rico off, I return to the breakroom to find Molli sitting there, her fingers nervously scratching at her neck. Given her last comment and the tense conversation, it makes the air in the room feel heavy. I walk to her and take a seat beside her, wrapping an arm around her shoulders to offer comfort.

"You okay?" I ask gently, sensing her unease.

Molli lets out a shaky breath and nods, but her eyes betray her anxiety.

"Yeah, I'm just . . ." wanting to get high. It's understandable. That's how she survived her world of danger and uncertainty as long as she did. "The whole plan, it's a lot to take in."

I give her a reassuring squeeze.

"I know, Molli. That's why we need to call Brooks. I want him to get it in writing from Agent Hunt that my participation in this plan will dismiss your charges. I'm asking him to make them forgo your testimony in exchange for my cooperation so you won't have to go through this anymore."

"No. You don't have to keep doing everything for me. I can testify."

"No, Molli. You can't have another night like last night. I won't let them do that to you. And I understand that it might happen again. Something unforeseen could trigger another episode, but not if I can help it. I'd hate myself for standing by and allowing them to use you like that with no regard for how it impacts you. And testifying could put you back in that dark place as they pick through the details of everything you saw."

"Alex." Her hand finds mine, gripping it tightly.

"I'm set on this. I'll testify. Not you."

"Okay."

Her body sags in relief as I pull my phone out of my pocket, scroll for Brooks's contact, and hit the number. As it rings, I move my arm from her shoulders to lean my elbows on the table and place my phone in the middle as Rico had done. Molli leans into the side of my body while her knee bounces against my thigh.

Brooks answers on the third ring, his voice crisp and professional.

"Alex, what can I do for you?"

"Hey, Brooks," I begin, trying to keep my voice steady. "I'm calling with an update on Molli's case, and I need a favor."

"Is she there with you?"

She immediately straightens to lean forward and speak into the phone.

"I'm here, Mr. Tyler." Her voice is light and somewhat timid as it comes across. "I haven't told you, but thank you for taking my case."

"It's nice to meet you, Miss Sitara, and you're more than welcome."

Brooks's manners prevail over mine. I feel slightly guilty that I haven't made formal introductions between them, but we haven't had time given the situation.

"Tell me what you have, and we'll go from there."

I nod and glance at Molli, who's steadily watching me

before I explain everything that happened with Rico, the pictures, and the conversation with Agent Hunt. He listens intently without uttering a word until I finish giving him all the details.

"Agent Hunt says she's on board with the plan, but she also said not to tell anyone about this. That right there is a conflict. I want to create a written record to ensure that Molli's charges are dropped. As you know, saying and doing are two different things in law enforcement. I'm also asking for her testimony to be waived in exchange for my cooperation."

There's a brief pause on the other end of the line before Brooks responds.

"That's a big ask. You know how serious this case is, and they will want all the evidence they can get."

"I know, but Molli has been through so much already. I don't want her to go through the trauma of testifying in court, especially as this could drag on for years. She's been trying to leave that life behind, and this could be her chance to start fresh. If she must go back and testify after seeking counseling, it could set her back. Her wellbeing is my top priority."

Brooks sighs. "All right, I'll see what I can do. But you need to understand this is not a guarantee. The decision ultimately lies with the prosecutor and the judge."

"I understand," I reply, anxious and wanting to bounce my knee alongside hers. "Just do your best. I want to get their sign off before I go undercover so that if something happens to me, Molli is still protected." Molli gasps and clutches my arm. I lean over and give her a quick kiss.

"I'll call Agent Hunt right now and see if we can work something out. But you need to be prepared for all possibilities. They may balk at giving us what we're requesting until after you get the evidence for them. That's typically how things are done."

"I know and appreciate you trying," I say firmly. "Thank you, Brooks."

"I'll call you as soon as I know more. I'm not speaking as your attorney since I don't represent you, but you must weigh your options closely. This could blow back on you and end your career in law enforcement. Albeit a noble cause and the right thing to do, some will deem you a traitor for breaking your code. We have whistleblowers and hotlines for reasons such as this, and corruption is illegal by courts of law at all levels. However, it will be a media frenzy when you are successful and the story breaks. You'll find yourself at the center of it all. Ensure you have a strong support system for you and Molli, as it will be rough for a while."

I appreciate his warning and optimism of saying when I'm 'successful.' The media scrutiny I can handle. It's getting what we need, keeping her safe, and turning them in that worries me more.

"Let's cross that bridge when we get there," I mutter as my closing thought.

"Good enough. I'll be in touch shortly."

I hang up the phone. The apprehension builds as I hit the voicemail button and listen through the ones left by the Chief. What he says is not what I expect.

"Alex, I haven't heard from you since I visited you at the hospital. How's the recovery going?" His tone is cheerful, unnaturally so, and even Molli shifts away from me in surprise. "I'd like to talk to you about that awards ceremony now that the funeral is out of the way."

I frown. He made a spectacle of himself at Matt's funeral, turning it into a political event of clapping people on the back and shaking others' hands as if campaigning for his next term. He wasn't sorrowful in the least, appearing jovial and smiling as he interacted with the Cañon City elite.

"Unbelievable," I murmur as that call ends and another starts.

"Hamilton. It's the Chief again. I heard you missed your rehabilitation appointment, and I wanted to check on you since I never heard from you about the ceremony." The same false concern, with a slight edge to his voice. "I'll send a car over to check on you. Ensure you didn't fall and hit your head or something of that nature."

I grit my teeth, seething with anger at the Chief's audacity of checking into my hospital appointments, which violates privacy laws. His reach is far greater than I anticipated, and I'm glad I warned Terrance about the possibility of being inquired about.

"Officer Hamilton, it seems you disappeared on me. Your neighbor said your squad car is in the driveway but didn't see you leave. We had to do a wellness check and enter the premises, which appeared ransacked." The cheerfulness is gone, replaced by an accusatory tone. "If you're in trouble, call my direct line at the station or even my cellphone. Wouldn't want anything to happen to my finest officer, would we?"

His veiled threat heightens my anger, and I'm out of my seat when he mentions my parents.

". . . seems they went to visit your family in Manitou Springs."

This time, I am pacing, fury in my veins as he's done everything I suspected Joaquin and his gang to do. They're working together.

"Calm down, Alex. This is what you planned for. It's why we're here and your parents are there."

Molli stands, grasping me by the hand to guide me back to the table to sit with her as the final call ends. I take a deep breath, trying to quell my rage.

"You're right," I say, my voice steadier than I feel. "He's

trying to draw me out before we're ready. But I won't let him. I'll stick to the plan, turn myself in, and expose his corruption."

I swipe my phone off the table, and she looks at me with a playful smile.

"If you're really that angry, I know a way to relieve it." The innuendo is blatant, and when she slides onto my lap, it's obvious what she wants.

"Seriously?" I ask, tilting my head as my hands cup her ass.

"I want to get high, you want to beat his ass, let's take it out on each other."

"I'm not sure that's the best idea." Her playfulness continues as she tweaks my nipple and I slap my hand over hers when she tries to do it again. "I hate that."

"I know," she taunts and does it to the other. "What are you going to do about it, Officer Hamilton?"

The desire in her eyes is unmistakable. When she nips my lip with her teeth, it's all I can take to hold back the tsunami of lust racing through my body.

"You're going to get it now," I mutter, standing suddenly with her in my grasp until I set her on her feet. "Put your hands on the table where I can see them and don't move a muscle."

"Yesss, sir," she slurs in a sexy little voice and complies perfectly. I jog out of the room to my truck, grab more condoms from the console and run back in to throw them on the table.

"Hold on tight."

She gives me a wicked smile and wiggles out of her sweats. I smack her ass, and she jolts, covering both cheeks to prevent me from doing it again.

"Not so hard, Hamilton."

"I told you to keep your hands where I can see them and to not move," I jest, taking my sweet time to stalk around her before squatting behind her. "It's called corporal punishment."

I tap her leg, feeling goosebumps break out over her skin in eager anticipation, and I fucking love it. She steps out of the rings of fabric long enough for me to toss it onto the other table beside us.

"No, it's called police brutality," she huffs, glancing over her shoulder to see what I'm doing.

"Face forward, ma'am, and put those hands back on the table." I intentionally lower my voice, the one I use when dealing with unruly criminals, and she fidgets until I clamp a firm hand around her ankle and move her leg to where I want it. "Spread 'em wide for a full cavity search."

She laughs in a lighthearted cadence that echoes in the small room but complies, even wiggling her tiny butt in my face.

"Is this wide enough?"

"I'll be asking the questions around here, got it?"

I hold an ankle in each hand, giving them a light squeeze as my lips connect with her chilled skin. I drag them back and forth, breathing lightly as my tongue darts out, sucking some spots, biting others, and blowing on everything I make wet.

"I'm ticklish there."

She giggles and I repeat the action to the opposite leg. Doesn't she know I remember it all? Every damn spot of this body and how it reacts. She might have adorned it with tattooed stars, but I will make her remember all my favorite spots.

"I know."

She tries to flinch away when it gets to be too much, but my hands at her ankles keep her where I want her. The heat from the ceiling vent skates down her back, keeping her warm against the goosebumps growing more prominent the longer I tickle her. She wiggles and whines, complaining and laughing until I bite the red cheek with my handprint still on it.

"Alex!"

I slide my hands up her legs until they cup her waist, my chest pressed into her back as I check in with her.

"Too hard?" I murmur against the shell of her ear, then nibble on it as I wait for her response. She smells good and I'm convinced. I'm buying that same shower stuff for our house when this ends.

"No, it just surprised me," she says sweetly, turning her face into mine for a little kiss and trying to turn around when I click my tongue at her.

"Please turn back around, ma'am. I'm not done."

I catch the hem of her sweatshirt to whisk it over her head. She immediately shivers against the coldness and my body presses into her. Her hands never lift from the table as I nuzzle her neck and let my fingertips drift over her stomach to caress her clothed mound. A little sigh escapes her throat as her head falls back and her eyes close. She's wet already. Teasing is always a great precursor, but this is next level soaking, and I love how responsive she is.

"Are you planning on stripping me naked while you're fully clothed?"

Her eyes flicker open, catching mine briefly before I take a knee behind her.

"That's how strip searches work."

I hook my thumbs into the lacy panties I bought for her, still proud of my purchase, and drag them down her legs. A light scent lifts from her body and I close my eyes to memorize it until she wiggles her ass again. My eyes open to the most beautiful sight. Her standing in only her bra and the smattering of stars on her back while my face is perfectly aligned with her pussy.

"Push out," I instruct, ensuring her pussy hits my face straight on.

She gasps when we connect and jolts forward before I grab her hips and bury my face between her cheeks. I guide her further back, causing her sweaty palms to squeak across the table. My thumbs separate her flesh, and I give a long lick front to back, savoring every last drop until I dive in and tongue the softest part of her. She moans, her body moving in unison to my delicate flickers against her clit. When her muscles tighten, I pull back and watch her sweet pussy contract inward, inviting me to fill her up.

"Again."

Her command is light and airy, full of breathy desire and a smile. I love how she sounds and how her body clenches for me. I appease her, going into an expected cycle of a long stroke across everything, tickling her clit and fucking her slit with my mouth. It's endless and fucking fantastic.

My cock is hard as possible, straining against my pants as sweat collects on my back. I want her totally naked as I fuck her with my mouth. I want her split open and vulnerable, totally open to receiving the pleasure only I will give her from now on. The only man to ever see her like this again. It sends my pulse racing and my cock about to burst to know that I own her entirely as she has always owned me.

"Ham . . . Hamilton."

She pants as she comes on my face. I continue fucking her slit, her soft walls clenching against my tongue. She tastes so fucking sweet that I can drink her in the rest of my life. Her knees buckle, nearly falling back on me as my drenched beard smears against her back. I catch her, pride swelling within at the effect I still have on her.

"Ma'am, I will need you to resume your position." I keep my voice low, seeing if she'll comply, and she turns to face me.

"My legs are like jello."

Her tone is serious. Her face is soft, but damn if the lust in her eyes doesn't tell me everything I need to know. In seconds, I toss her over my shoulder, snatch the condoms from the table, and take the stairs two at a time up to our room. She's silent the whole time until I toss her on the bed.

"My turn."

She scrambles to the edge, rips my pants down, and has my hard dick in her mouth before I can say otherwise. Her eagerness is a huge fucking turn-on. No whining about sucking cock. She has me down her throat in a second and I'm about to bust a nut.

"Too much."

I cup the back of her neck, trying to pull her back, and she's relentless. Alternating between sucking the skin off my dick and swallowing it down her throat until she grips my balls, squeezing them at the bottom, and I'm coming uncontrollably. It's the fastest I've come in years.

"Fuck!"

She moans as my release keeps coming, sending so much intensity all over my body that I feel like my legs are also turning to jello. Her head pulls back long enough to look me in the eyes and trace the head of my cock around her lips.

"Ah, too sensitive."

I push my hips backward, relieved she's not clutching my buttocks and restraining me like I had done to her. Her mischievous smile taunts me while she attempts to get sneaky licks in, and I keep her at bay by gripping her shoulders.

"Beware, Officer Hamilton, two can play your game," she taunts, kneeling on the bed and puckering up for a kiss. It takes me by surprise, and I tighten my hold on her shoulders.

"You don't want me to kiss you. I licked your ass."

She brushes my hands away from her shoulders, gets to her feet, and stands on the bed. Her eyes sparkle with desire as a playful smirk plays at the corner of her lips.

"I know, I was there."

Her arms envelop my neck, drawing me in closely until her lips meet mine for a passionate kiss with plenty of tongue. We savor each other enough to taste each other's cum, and it couldn't be hotter. The kissing continues until we are left breathless, eventually parting with our eyes locked in a meaningful gaze.

"Now fuck me properly because what you did downstairs wasn't enough."

"Yes, ma'am."

37

My hands encircle her forearms, her skin cool against my sweaty palms, and I love the contrast. She was always cold, and I was always hot. It was a perfect fit. She'd cuddle up to me, stealing the heat radiating from my body. Her icy fingers would find their way under my shirt and nestle against my skin, and I loved it. I smile against her flesh knowing I have that again.

I press my lips against the tender skin above her elbows, feeling the soft texture beneath my touch. The harsh stubble of my beard contrasts with the gentle kisses, eliciting a faint shiver that sends goosebumps dancing across her skin.

She reaches for the back of my shirt, eager to pull it over my head and toss it on the floor behind me. I follow her lead, unclasping her bra and letting it fall to the floor. We are finally skin to skin, equals in our passion to please each other.

She tilts her head slightly, and our lips find each other again, engaging in a tender yet fervent kiss. Her back arches slightly, pressing her nipples against my hard chest, and a soft gasp escapes her lips when my finger finds her wet clit.

"Fuck me," she murmurs, her cheek nuzzling my face as I plant kisses across her narrow jaw. "I want you inside me."

Her words are puffs of air against the heated skin on my neck and shoulders as my lips leave hers.

"How bad do you want it?"

I nip at the delicate skin under her earlobe as I swirl my finger in the opposite direction until she falters, shifting back, and I know she's getting close. My hand braced at her shoulder blade drifts down her creamy skin to press against her ass, forcing her right back where she was against my finger and not relenting.

"Tell me, Molls," I tease, loving the little breaths and sounds coming out of her. Her hands roam my chest, dipping in and out of my muscles to try and tickle me. "It doesn't work like that. You're the ticklish one."

My finger continues working her clit, while I stuff two past her swollen lips, and she moans, loud and long, her head falling back and her eyes closing. She leans heavily into my arm, transferring her weight so she can enjoy the sensations my fingers are creating. It's a fucking lovely sight. She is pliable and welcoming, willing to take whatever I give her and enjoy it without question or demanding to know what's next. This is why I love it when she surrenders to me. Her expression is one of awe. Her mouth parts, alternating between a smile and taking a breath. It's the one I think of when I masturbate.

"You're so fucking beautiful."

My fingers work her wet pussy until her body tenses. I glance up to see her face drawn, a serious look that has her pushing my soaked hand away from her body. Confusion pushes through the cloud of my lust for her as she steps down from the bed to stand beside me.

"What's wrong?"

"You don't have to say that Hamilton." She picks up her bra

from the floor and begins to put it back on when I stop her. "You were going to get laid anyway."

I'm still so fucking turned on by her that I'm trying to catch up here, but I'm still not putting two and two together.

"I don't understand. What are you talking about?"

She attempts the bra again, and I take it from her, balling it in my fist to stop her from getting distracted.

"Calling me beautiful. I know I'm not. You don't have to lie to get your rocks off," she spits out with so much hate and venom that her accusations nearly knock me over. "So typical."

She rebuffs my hand when it reaches for her, stepping around the corner of the bed and just out of touch. Anger runs through my body at a feverous pace if this is how she feels about herself. She feels this way due in large part to those motherfuckers who treated her like a possession that could be bought and sold without any regard for her emotional and psychological state. I throw her bra on the floor behind me, stalking her like prey so she gets one thing straight about me and us right from the start.

"I'm not one of those guys, Molli."

Her eyes darken as I round the corner of the mattress and she steps back.

"I've known you almost my whole life. I knew you when Kevin Spelman told our first grade teacher that you raised your dress and showed him your underwear. Fucking little liar. I knew you when you were picked to play in the Princess in the Pea in third grade, but you got sick with the flu and couldn't be the Princess. I knew you when you tried out for cheerleading and didn't make it because you couldn't do a flip-flop. I knew you when you fell asleep on the catwalk above the racquetball courts at the church lock-in so you wouldn't have to go to midnight mass."

A sob catches in her throat. Tears form in her eyes and drip down her cheeks as her arms wrap around her midsection. I continue stalking toward her. She retreats until her back hits the dresser, and she has nowhere to escape.

"I knew you when you dumped me on my ass and ran off into the night while the sirens drew nearer. I knew you when you came by the next day and laughed at me doing your community service. I've known you thousands of days and hundreds of ways. Never once, Molli. Not once did I ever think you weren't beautiful. You're the most beautiful woman I've ever known. No matter what you've done or been through. Nothing will change that in my eyes."

Emotion clogs my throat as she's bawling and caving in on herself as if the weight of what I feel for her is doing it. I reach her as she's about to collapse, hold her in my arms, and gently carry her to the top of the bed to place her on it.

"I'm going to show you how fucking beautiful you have been and always will be to me."

My heart bleeds for this woman. If I die on this mission, I'll die a happy man because she is mine and I am hers. How it was always supposed to be. As I draw the covers back, she continues to cry and takes her time to get under them. When she's settled against the pillows, I slip under the sheets, collect her in my arms, and hold her until the tears and sobbing subside.

Only when she's ready, do I slip her underneath me and gently make love to her. The love I've always felt for her. The love that threatens to burst my heart and mind open because I'm so fucking happy to have her back for good. Her face is splotchy, her eyes are the lightest shade of brown I can ever recall seeing, and I kiss her face repeatedly.

"My brown-eyed girl," I murmur against her jawline and trail kisses up her cheek, across her temple to linger on her forehead.

I lean to one side, adjusting my hard cock to rest in between us as I take my time with her. She sighs, content and at peace, her eyes closing as she drinks in the loving words spilling from me into her hair, her flesh, and everywhere my lips connect with her body. Her hands lazily caress my back, running in opposite parallels down the sides of my body from butt to neck and back again. It strokes a fire in me so hot that I would love to plunge into her, as I did yesterday.

My want of her is secondary, pushed to the back for me to focus on showing her how much she means to me. As my lips wander over her neck and collarbones, nipping, sucking, and kissing, her hand catches the back of my head to push me further into her flesh.

My body tightens over her, tucking her closer and trapping her legs between mine. I want her to feel every touch, kiss, caress, and whisper to her skin before I penetrate her. Even then, I'll ease in so slowly she'll sigh in contentment. It takes everything in me not to burst, to come all over her stomach like I did when we were young and pulling out.

I tease her nipple, sucking, blowing, and rolling one between my teeth as she whimpers and twitches, keeping her hand on my head and guiding me to the other breast when she's ready. It's a collaboration of coordinated movement, her guiding and me following. A rare and opposite power exchange between us. If she needs to lead, to feel in control, to feel beautiful, I'll sit the fuck back and give her pleasure on her terms, the way she wants it every damn time.

When I travel lower, her hand lifts from my head to clutch the bedsheets beside us. I crane my neck to see her reaching for the strip of condoms and coming up short. With my long arm span, I easily grasp them and place them in her hand, following her lead when she's ready for me.

"Now," she moans, as my tongue flattens against her clit with slow and precise licking to feel it hardening before circling each piercing. I glance up to see her tear open the package and hand me the ring.

I kiss her stomach, her thighs, the little stars at her hips, and everywhere but where she wants before sitting back and rolling the condom onto my dripping dick. She moves her legs from between mine, reaching for my cock to guide me slowly into her. I pause at her entrance, taking a mental picture of how sexy and desirable she looks right now, with flushed cheeks and hungry eyes.

"You're beautiful, Molli. Always have been."

My nose burns and I blink back my emotions as tears stream down her temples to get lost in the pillows. Her hand releases my cock and pulls on my arm to draw me close, to kiss her deeply as I slide into her pussy.

Home. It's what she called it a long time ago when I said I could live in her pussy. It was an endlessly hot summer with a rare cool breeze through my window. We had the house to ourselves that weekend and she slept over. I don't recall how she got away with it by her parents, but I had her every way I could.

She was buried underneath me as she is now, the movements the same, but the feeling more intense now. She called her pussy sliding home as a baseball analogy, laughing in my ear as some guys strike out and some make it all the way home.

We move together, moans and pleasure escaping her mouth when it unlatches from my skin, only to latch on somewhere else. Her legs wrap around my waist, locking at my lower back while I cradle her head in my hand and thrust slowly and deeply into her. I take my time, filling her up, vacating her, and pushing back in. The feeling is incredible—something I want to go on forever as I stare into her eyes.

But she's wrong. Her pussy is not a baseball analogy. It's not home plate. It's home. A home where she and I blur into one person. Where my love overflows onto her and into her, consummating everything good and right between us. Where she laughs at me, teases me, taunts me, and gives as good as she takes.

Home. Warm and inviting, the only place I want to be after a hard day. The place where our love starts, our family is born, and our lives merge. She's my home. My only home and I'm hers. It's the most beautiful word from the most beautiful girl I know. Home is where the heart is, and she owns mine wholly.

Her body tightens, her hand falls away, and the back of her head presses into my hand as she orgasms. It's fucking awesome to watch, and mine is not far behind, spilling into the condom and wishing it was spilling into her. Children are in our future. Hopefully, a half dozen little girls that look just like their momma, but only when the time is right. Only when she says it's right will I expand the home I feel with her to share it with others.

"You're awfully quiet."

Her hand cups my face, her thumb stroking my beard with an intensity in her eyes that's hard to take. I bury my head in her neck and lower my body to feel every inch of her skin.

"Was that not good for you?"

I breathe quietly into her skin before pressing my nose against her while her arms hug me tighter.

"It was perfect."

38

Time fades away as I lose myself in her. Every touch, thrust, kiss, and embrace burned into my mind. I'd stay buried in her with her underneath me as long as she'd let me if it wasn't for her insistent finger poking me in the ribs.

"We already talked about this, Hamilton," she jests, her panting long since recovered, much to my dislike. "Let me up."

I groan, going on record that I dislike it even though I need to, once again, deal with the condom. With a few parting kisses, I collapse onto my back, my hand swiping across her sweat covered skin as she climbs over me.

"Don't act like such a big baby. You'll be back in there soon enough."

She shakes her head as she walks out of the room, a line of cum clinging to her inner thigh. It makes me proud as hell that we're so compatible in bed and out.

"Are you cleaning up?"

Her voice travels the short hallway to me, and I swing to my feet, chuckling at her. When I enter the bathroom, she has the shower going and is stepping inside. I wiggle my eyebrows right as she snaps the curtain closed.

"Don't even think about it. I need a break and food," she hollers over the blast of hot water and rising steam to the ceiling as I clean up in the sink.

"Alright, alright," I reply, trying to suppress the playful grin that threatens to spread across my face when I think about joining her in the shower. "I'll get started on something. So take your time."

I walk away from the door, giving her the privacy she needs as I grab a pair of shorts from the bedroom to slide on. My mind is still filled with the image of her suds covered body standing under the warm cascade of water. I can't help but feel a magnetic pull toward her, especially after what we just shared.

I head to the kitchen, munching on some snacks while I whip up some stir-fry and set up a makeshift workspace on the coffee table. As I wait for her to finish her shower, I go over the plan in my mind, making sure every detail is in place. I need to be prepared for anything that might happen, especially if the Chief suspects my involvement in protecting Molli and not her jumping bail. When she finally emerges from the bathroom, her hair is damp, and her skin is flushed from the shower's heat.

"Dinner is ready on the stove. If you grab the drinks, I can dish us up and meet you on the couch," I offer. She peeks over my shoulder as I lift the lids and hums her with satisfaction. "I could get used to these home-cooked meals."

She turns away, not waiting for my response, but I murmur, "I could, too."

Molli goes to the living room to get comfortable on the couch. As I serve the stir-fry, I hear her faintly singing our song from the other room. It brings a smile to my face, and I can't help but feel a sense of contentment. With two plates of steaming stir-fry in hand, I join her on the couch. She's sitting cross-legged, and her eyes light up when she sees the food.

"Dinner is served," I say, setting the plates on the coffee table.

"Looks delicious." She licks her lips when picking up the fork. I join her on the couch and reach for the remote when she touches my arm.

"I was hoping we could talk about the plan. Or should we wait until after we've eaten?"

I set the remote back down, pop the lids on both soda cans, and take a long drink. She balances her plate on the arm of the sofa and mixes the rice before turning and looking at me.

"What part did you want to discuss? The whole thing, or was there something bothering you?" I ask, scooping up a forkful of it and shoving it in my mouth. I know I should be nervous, as she obviously is, but it's necessary to put this to bed once and for all.

"I'm worried, Alex," Molli says, setting her fork down and clasping her hands together in her lap. "There's so much at stake, and I can't help but think about all the ways this could go wrong."

I set my fork down to give her my undivided attention.

"It's completely normal to feel that way. What's bothering you the most?"

She looks at me, her eyes filled with worry.

"I'm scared that something might happen to you. I messed up by leaving. I can't fix that, but I don't want to lose you. What if the Chief figures out the plan? What if he sees through the ruse and hurts you, or worse?"

Her voice drops to a whisper, fear infused in every word. It's understandable. I'd be petrified if the roles were reversed and she had to walk into a setup that could endanger her life, regardless of how much training she had. I reach out and gently squeeze her hand reassuringly.

"I know, and nothing will happen to me. The state police know what they are doing. They will have everything carefully planned out and we'll be as prepared as possible. As for the Chief, I'll be cautious and vigilant. Having Rico there at the station will help. He'll be both the eyes and ears for me and the state police, so I'm not going in completely alone."

She looks down at our hands, her grip tightening on mine.

"I want to believe everything will be okay, but it's hard. I've seen Joaquin's deals go bad, and it can get very bad."

I pull her closer, wrapping my arm around her shoulders. Her body relaxes slightly against mine.

"You heard Agent Hunt herself. They will pull me out if it gets too dangerous. It's not in anyone's best interest if I were to be killed. It would draw too much attention to Joaquin, the Chief, and their operations. That should bring you some assurance. And Rico has thoroughly investigated, and we have a solid case. Even if something goes wrong, we'll find another way to expose him. We won't let either of them get away."

She looks up at me, her eyes searching mine.

"Do you trust the police with me? I'll be here alone with them, I assume."

She hits on the one part of the plan that I don't like. I didn't want to mention it to her downstairs, knowing she's relying on me and my experience to give her strength through this.

"They won't lie to you and then hand me over to Joaquin or Razor, would they? Especially after Mr. Tyler calls them wanting me not to testify?"

She pulls out of my embrace, her hand clutching her neck and rubbing that spot.

"I mean, they don't need to protect me then. Only you, really, since you'll be their star witness."

Her doubts are real, if a little unfounded.

"I don't think they'd go back on their word."

"Alex, I'm a prostitute. Women get murdered every day at

the hands of their pimps or johns. If I were to end up murdered, I'd be another statistic. No one would care," she says, biting her lip to keep from crying. I hate that everything she's saying is true.

I scratch my beard, my gaze meeting hers as my temper flares.

"*Were*. But, no, you're right, Molli. Too many women are statistics, and the murderers bond out. It's what's wrong with our system."

We sit in silence for a few moments, grappling with how trustworthy they will be with her and how she could have it all wrong. The risks are too great for me to place her in the hands of someone I don't know, even if they are fellow law enforcement officers. She sits back, our food growing cold as we deliberate this piece.

"Let's at least eat. That will give me a chance to think."

She nods, and we eat in silence. The flavors of the stir-fry are dull in my mouth. My mind is occupied, racing down our options and coming to the same conclusion. I steal glances at Molli, noticing the furrowed brow and how she absentmindedly pushes the food around her plate.

"I didn't know you knew all those things about me."

"What things?" I ask as she takes a bite of her food, leaving the fork against her lips while she finishes chewing.

"The play and the lock-in." She shrugs, scooping up more on her fork and leaving it dangling in front of her mouth. "All the things from when we were kids. I don't even remember them. I barely remember anything besides us in high school."

This is treading into dangerous territory, as she's never told me why she left me by the flagpole that day. I wanted to know the answer before, but not now with how she looks at me. I don't think I ever want to know.

"You don't remember me sitting behind you in fourth grade and always asking if you needed your pencil sharpened?"

I polish off my plate and stand to get seconds. I point to hers, still overflowing with food, and she waves me off.

"That was this fat little kid with freakishly green eyes?" she blurts out and slaps her hand over her mouth in astonishment. "Nooo."

"Our eyes fade as we age. You should see Mom's," I justify, keeping an eye on her as she registers through the myriad of emotions crossing her face.

"You were so fat, though."

My cheeks flush, feeling amusement at her candid remark.

"Yeah, well, I guess I had a bit of a chubby phase back then. Blame Mom's cooking," I admit with a chuckle. "But hey, look at me now, all grown up and in shape."

Molli's hand drops from her mouth.

"You turned out pretty good, I must say. Still, those green eyes were quite a sight, even back then."

I can't help but smile as I walk back into the kitchen, scooping up another generous serving on my plate before turning to face Molli.

"You gave me a paper heart on Valentine's Day. Red, I think," she says with a playful glint. It was actually pale pink.

"Yeah, I remember," I reply, my heart warming at the memory. "It said I love you."

Molli chuckles, her laughter filling the room with joy.

"Did you seriously love me back then?"

I pause for a moment, looking into her eyes. "I must have. I wrote it."

She turns away with a serious expression as she looks down at her plate.

"Maybe one day you'll love me again like that."

I never stopped.

My chest aches and my fingers clench the plate so hard I wonder if it will break. Professing my love for her now will only complicate things. Could send her into another episode of fear and panic over my safety while I'm gone. I can't be selfish right now. As much as it kills me not to tell her, I know I can't. Not until this is over with. I duck my head and say nothing when I return to the couch.

As we resume eating, the atmosphere feels heavy. Molli flicks on the TV, finding some mindless show to watch, but the laughter from the screen doesn't quite reach her. A lingering sadness refuses to dissipate as she curls into the cushion away from me after setting her plate on the table. Internally, I'm dying to profess my love to her, to even get down on one knee to propose without a ring. Externally, I do nothing but set my plate near her and wish things were different.

As the show ends, the silence returns, and we both seem lost in our thoughts. Molli lets out a soft sigh when I reach for her foot and start massaging it. Another show starts as my hands move past her ankle to rub the back of her calf. She says nothing as she pushes her other foot into my lap, wanting the same treatment. I work both throughout the next show until her eyes droop and her face nestles into the couch cushion.

I don't dare move for fear of waking her, but my mind wanders over the day. It seems endless as if we smashed three days into one. It's not surprising that she's already asleep. The stress alone would cause anyone to crater except a planner like me.

The screen flickers, throwing different levels of light over the room's walls as I contemplate what to do to ensure Molli's safety. Carefully, I disentangle myself from Molli's feet, ensuring not to disturb her rest. She mumbles something. Otherwise, she remains right where I leave her as I head downstairs to retrieve my phone and her clothing from the breakroom.

There's another missed call from the station, a text from Mom, and one from Dani. I ignore them as I sit at the table, my fingers drumming a rhythm into the woodgrain while the phone rings. It's late, well after respectable hours, to call, yet that doesn't deter me. He's my only choice. God help me for that, and it will cost me big time. Trepidation causes me to be jumpy, wanting to hang up and wishing I could, but I remain on the line until he finally picks up.

"Hello?" His tone is quiet and gentle, exactly what I expect from a man of the cloth.

I take a deep breath, press the phone to my ear, and cradle my head in my other hand.

"Hi, Father Michael. It's Alex Hamilton."

"Alexander?" Father Michael's voice carries a sense of surprise as he responds, "It's quite late. Is everything all right?"

"I'm sorry for the late call, Father. I know it's not ideal, but everything is not okay."

He'll assume my parents or my injury. He'll never realize I'm bringing back the girl he once made an exception to the rule so she could acolyte on Easter Sunday with me.

"Oh dear, is it your folks? If so, your mother already rang that she wouldn't be at church on Sunday because of an illness in the family." It would be like Mom to call him ahead of time to not leave him in a lurk for Sunday school. "I believe it was her sister, your aunt."

I scrub a hand over my weary face as I hunch over the table, trying to figure out how much I need to tell him versus how much I want to tell him.

"No, it's not them. They are fine and with my aunt."

No need to blow their cover, even though he's bound by oath, the same as I am, albeit a slightly different one. He sighs, and I imagine him taking off his glasses to clean them as he used to do in his sermons, for effect I used to suspect.

"Alexander."

I brace myself for the conversation I've been putting off for quite a while now.

"God still loves you, even if you have gone astray. It happens in our youth, and even though you have put your back to the church, we are still here for you. I am still here for you."

"I know."

"I had hoped to have had time to talk to you at your folks' home or the funeral, but you slipped away each time. One could think it was intentional."

He always delivered his pointed innuendos with such certainty that it was a battle not to feel like a guilty son of a bitch.

"I know, Father," I repeat, wondering how I'm going to ask the favor I need to ask if it keeps going this way.

"I don't mean to pry or judge. It's just that I care deeply for you and your well-being. I care for all of God's children, even the little lambs that wander off after the wrong shepherd." His voice softens, a touch of sadness in his words. "Regardless, you will always be a part of our family, and I want you to know that you're never alone in this world."

"I appreciate that," I reply sincerely, leaning back in the chair and staring out the breakroom door to the dark lobby beyond. "And I know I've been distant. I have a lot going on right now, and it's a lot to handle."

"I understand, my son," he says softly. "Life can be over-whelming, and we all face adversities that test our faith. But remember, God's love is unconditional, and we are here to support you, no matter what."

I take a deep breath, trying to find the right words to ask my favor, and decide to be direct with it.

"Father, that's what I'm calling about tonight. There's something I need to ask of you. It's about Mary Ann Higginbotham."

There's a moment of silence on the other end of the line, and I can sense Father Michael putting his glasses back on while he thinks. Finally, he speaks with a firm yet compas-sionate tone, "Stacy and Mark's daughter?"

"Yes."

"Oh my. I haven't heard her name in years. Her parents stopped attending several years back. I tried to visit them, but they wouldn't return my calls. Hmm, Mary Ann. Last I knew, she was in Hollywood, an actress, I believe."

His voice lifts. A genuine fondness when he says it, causing me to clench my teeth as I prepare myself to share what happened and how he can help.

"Not exactly, Father. And that is why I am asking you this favor."

I let the seriousness of the situation drip into every word of the story, telling him all of it. He listens intently, his shock and concern evident in his voice when he gasps while I recount the dangerous and disturbing events involving Mary Ann. As I share the extent of her troubles and the web of corruption she's entangled in, I can feel his genuine empathy and caring nature emanating through the phone line.

"My goodness, this is truly a distressing situation," he says with a heavy sigh. "I can't believe Mary Ann has fallen into such perilous circumstances. It breaks my heart to hear of her struggles."

"I know, Father, and that's why I'm contacting you," I reply earnestly. "I need someone I can trust to protect her while I work on a plan to bring down those involved in this corruption. I have no one else. I promise I am not bringing trouble to your door either. They will not connect her to you or the church if she stays hidden. She also needs someone to provide emotional support and guidance through her addiction. I'm worried the stress of this alone could make her relapse. The state police could turn her over to a facility if they have to deal with some of what I've encountered."

The request keeps expanding, piling up with more and more requirements from him. My guilt increases with each addition as I realize I have abandoned him and the church for years, and now I am burdening him with our problems.

There's a moment of contemplation before Father Michael speaks again.

"You can count on me, Alexander. I will do whatever I can to help Mary Ann and ensure her safety. I'll also pray that she finds her way out of this darkness and back to a path of light."

"Thank you. Your support means more than I can express," I say, relieved that he will take care of her. "I'll call you from this phone when the wheels are set in motion and then drop her off before heading to the station."

"I will be by her side, offering whatever guidance and comfort I can," he reassures me. "And you, my son, remember you are not alone in this fight. God is with you, guiding your steps and giving you strength."

I shake my head, overwhelmed with his generosity to help her and me, even though I strayed from the church. It's unbelievable that there are compassionate people who care like Father Michael and are ready to extend a helping hand when needed most. One day, I'll return the favor.

"Thank you again."

"Alexander, if you will hang on the line a moment longer, I'd like to pray with you."

I feel a lump forming in my throat, moved by his offer.

"Of course, Father. I would be honored."

As I bow my head in prayer, I can't help but feel a sense of peace wash over me. At this moment, it feels like a weight is lifted from my shoulders, knowing that he will shelter, feed, protect, and guide her while I am away. I listen as his soothing voice prays. His words are a source of comfort and solace amid the chaos surrounding us. He asks for protection and guidance for both Molli and me and for strength and courage in our challenges. My mission and her recovery.

After the prayer, I thank him again, genuinely grateful for his understanding and willingness to be there for us.

"Your words mean a lot, Father. Thank you for everything."

"It's my duty and privilege to be here for you, my son," he replies warmly. "I'll await your call."

With a heartfelt goodbye, we end the call. I sit in the break-room, reflecting on the day's events. Now that I have every base covered, I have renewed my determination to take down the Chief, Joaquin, and everyone involved.

I rise from my seat, tidying up the space by pushing in the chairs, grabbing her clothes, and turning off the lights. Returning to the apartment, I gently lift Molli into my arms and carry her to bed, receiving a drowsy thank you as I tuck her snugly under the covers. With efficient movements, I swiftly clean the kitchen, lock up the place, and shower before joining her in bed.

As I snuggle close, wrapping my body around hers, memories of Father Michael's unexpected compassion flood my mind. Inspired by his kindness, I utter a prayer of gratitude and protection before falling asleep.

39

I run after the assailant down the dark alley, my footsteps echoing in the cold winter air as I shout commands into my shoulder radio. Each step I take echoes like the past, the sounds of pursuit taunting me. And then, as if the nightmare itself has come to life, there he is, the Chief aiming a gun straight at me. Shock paralyzes me for an instant until a shot shatters the silence, and the pain strikes me. I stumble back, my body colliding with the unforgiving pavement. It's like a cruel twist of fate to face the one person I should've been able to trust. Betrayal burns like acid while the bullet has me struggling for breath.

My gun clatters feet away, too far to reach, when the Chief stands over me and says, "You were always too much trouble, Hamilton." He sneers, his voice dripping with malice. "I should've taken you out a long time ago."

Fear courses through me, and I can't believe what I hear. This nightmare, this twisted version of reality, has me trapped, and I'm struggling to escape his clutches.

Summoning all my strength, I gasp, "You won't get away with this."

The Chief chuckles darkly, his gun still trained on me.

"Oh, but I will. Who's going to stop me? You're nothing but a nuisance, and once you're gone, no one will dare challenge me again."

I can feel the cold, hard pavement beneath me and the blood pouring out of me, but I won't die. Molli needs me. I scan my surroundings, looking for any advantage, any opportunity to turn the tables. And then, my hand brushes against something cold and metallic. It's my fallen radio. With a surge of adrenaline, I reach for it, knowing that this might be my only chance.

With one swift motion, I press the emergency button, summoning backup. The Chief's eyes widen in surprise as he realizes what I've done. But he's not one to back down. He raises his gun once more and empties the chamber into me. Reality and my nightmare blur, the lines between life and death blending into the afterlife. My soul hovers overhead, looking down at Molli's distraught face as she clings to Rico for support at my funeral. It's a surreal and heart-wrenching sight, witnessing the pain my absence has caused her.

"I'm so sorry," I whisper, unable to reach out and comfort her.

I jerk awake in the middle of the night. My heart pounds in my chest, and the relief of being alive washes over me like a tidal wave.

"Fuck."

It was a nightmare, seeming so real that I'm right back in it when I close my eyes. Even if it's a glimpse of a possible future, I won't let it become a reality.

I shift to my side, facing Molli, still asleep, unaware of what I've just experienced. I gently caress her cheek. Thankful Father Michael will keep her safe when the time comes.

"Death won't take me that easily. I'll fight for us, Molli. I'll fight for our future together."

I won't let the Chief's threat linger in my mind. I'll be vigilant and focused on this mission, knowing I have more at stake than ever. Far more to lose now that I have her and a life to look forward to.

Drawing her closer, I press my lips softly against her forehead, and she rustles, murmuring incoherently before rolling over. As I lie there, embracing Molli's warmth, I realize that every moment with her is a gift, a chance to rewrite our destiny. I won't take it for granted. I'll cherish every second.

"I love you, Molli."

I close my eyes, wrap my arm around her waist, and drift off to sleep. A moment later, my phone is ringing, waking both of us with a start. I'm on my feet and crossing the bedroom, hunting down my phone from where I left it, charging in the kitchen. It's an unknown caller, and my stomach instantly tightens.

"Hamilton."

My voice strains from fatigue as I look at the clock on the stove and see that it's just after six in the morning. When I turn to face the window, a blueish hue is coming through the side of the blinds. The sun isn't even up yet.

"Officer Hamilton, It's Agent Hunt. We got intel today that a big shipment is being moved, and we're bringing you in early. Our agents can't infiltrate quickly enough, but I believe this is our chance to get you in and—"

"I'm in. Tell me the details," I interrupt, my mind racing from the urgency of the situation.

Agent Hunt briefs me on the mission, providing critical information about where it's at, what they are transporting, and who they expect to be there. She continues with the Chief's suspected involvement, the meeting tonight, and the address of the motel that the team is rendezvousing at today. I listen intently as Molli's soft touch slides up my spine and she leans her cheek into my shoulder.

"And Rico? Does he know?" I ask, frowning when I see the fear in Molli's eyes.

"He's the one that got the intel after being at the station all night."

"Right. I'll pack up here and be there within an hour. There is something I need to do first."

Molli's expression turns curious, but she doesn't press for details while I wrap up the call.

"I understand. Send me the address of where Molli is at, and I'll send two agents over right now."

I murmur my agreement and end the call rather than get into all that with Agent Hunt. Taking Molli's hand in mine, I lead her gently to the couch, her curiosity and concern evident in her eyes. I know she wants to ask more questions, but I need to tell her what I have in mind so we can leave quickly.

"There is something I need to tell you," I start, and she looks instantly worried. "There's someone I trust who can keep you safe."

"I thought you wanted me to stay with the agents they are sending over?"

She shakes her head, extrapolating her hands from mine.

"I know you're uncomfortable with that idea and I can't say I am one hundred percent either. And you may not like this idea any better, but I believe it to be in your best interest in many ways," I explain, hoping she'll understand. "You'll stay with Father Michael."

Her eyes widen in surprise, and I can see the hesitation in her expression.

"Father Michael? At the church?"

"It sounds odd, but I already talked to him last night." She stands, crossing the room to stare at me. "Please don't be mad. I told him everything."

I stand, moving toward her as hurt appears on her face.

"But will he . . ." She licks her lips, tears surging into her eyes as a hand rests against her chest. "With my past . . . and everything . . . did he even agree to help me?"

Pain and embarrassment fill her words. I know what she's thinking as I felt anxious about calling him.

"Yes. He wants to help you. I didn't hold back with him either, Molls. He knows about the addiction, Joaquin, all of it. I thought it was important for him to know so he understands the risks, but more importantly, he understands you and your needs."

Her lips roll together as the tears collect them.

"I've already spoken to him about it, and he's more than willing to keep you hidden and safe. He won't judge you for your past. He's a compassionate man. Very compassionate, in fact. He prayed for us while I was on the phone."

"But Alex, it's been years. I have done so many things that there's no way he'd let me in."

"He will, and he is. He's waiting for my call and is preparing a room for you. You know that rectory has all those old quarters. Mom says they sit empty unless a visiting priest is in town."

She shrugs, seeming not to remember that part of the property.

"But this is the best option we have for now. It's Father Michael or the police officers." I tilt my head, imploring her to choose the church.

She exhales loudly, wipes away the tears, and stands taller.

"Father Michael."

Relief washes over me as she agrees he is the better option. Knowing she understands the gravity of the situation.

"Thank you. I'll drop you off with him and then head to the motel."

She approaches me, pulling me into a prolonged hug.

"I don't want you to do this."

Her short hair brushes against my chest, and I lie my chin on top of her head while holding her.

"I know, but it's the only way you're free of all this," I mutter, feeling wetness against my skin and knowing she is silently crying. "Once this is over, we'll be together and never have to deal with this again."

"Okay," she says, trying to be strong for my sake. She's reluctant to leave my arms and I understand completely. I'd hold her forever if that solved everything.

"Can you be ready to go in ten minutes?" I ask, hoping to make the transition as smooth as possible.

"Yes," she replies, taking a deep breath. "I'll be ready."

I wait until she's out of the room to call Father Michael. He picks up on the first ring and I tell him it all got moved up and we'll be there in twenty minutes. With surprise in his voice, he assures me that he's ready and that she'll be in excellent hands, the Lord's hands. I thank him and silently hope he is right.

Molli moves silently around the garage apartment, and I can't help but feel a heaviness between us. She carefully packs her few belongings, looking at each item before placing it in the bag. I quickly change into a more plausible outfit for being out of town and swing her bag over my shoulder. The last thing she grabs is her fur coat, holding it over her arm as she looks around the bedroom. Her eyes settle on the bed, where I made love to her while telling her she was beautiful. With a deep sigh and watery eyes, she turns away and leaves the room.

"I didn't see the appeal when Dani lived here, but now I do. It's a cocoon away from the world," I say, turning off the lights and taking my own last look around.

"I'll miss this little place," she whispers, her hand drifting over her hair and then falling to her side when she catches me noticing the action. I lock the door and we go downstairs toward my truck. I hit the button to open the bay door and the cold air swirls past us. Fresh snow blankets the ground, and the winter chill causes Molli to dart to the passenger door.

I climb into the cab, set her bag between us, and start the engine, the sound breaking the heavy silence between us. Molli slips on her fur coat before buckling her seat belt. Her breath comes out in visible puffs as she clutches the handles of her bag tightly and moves it onto her lap. I adjust the heat settings to get it warmer for her.

As we drive, the snow drifts gently across the windshield, adding to the melancholy atmosphere. The world around us seems quiet and peaceful, opposite the tension and apprehension we're stepping into. I take the long way to the church, savoring every moment of our time, even though we're both quiet.

"You remember that day it snowed like this our senior year?" Her voice breaks the somber silence, and I turn to face her, a sad smile forming on my lips. "And they finally canceled school?"

"Yeah," I reply softly, my heart tightening. This is the first time she has brought up a memory of us.

Molli nods, a wistful expression crossing her face.

"I remember we built a snowman together, and it was so silly and lopsided, but I loved him anyway."

"It was." I think back to that happy time as the snow continues falling. "The nose was your lipstick tube."

"And it wore your baseball hat." Her fingers brush against the window, where snowflakes gather, and she sighs. "We were laughing and playing like children."

"We did." I glance at her to see if she looks as melancholy as I feel. "Then you threw a snowball at me, and the snowball fight began."

Molli chuckles softly, sounding like pure happiness.

"You were so competitive. I think you took it more seriously than I did."

I smile, remembering how we gleefully ran around my front yard, ducking behind our snowman or the trees for cover. Pops called us idiots, and I was the biggest idiot for her.

"I couldn't let you win that easily. But you had this mischievous glint in your eyes that made it all the more fun."

She nods, her grip on the bag tightening.

"It was one of the happiest days of my life, Hamilton."

"It was for me too," I admit, my voice softening when hers moves down to a whisper. I rub her shoulder, the coat collar pressing against her cheek as she looks at me. "I'll give you another day like that. We'll make as many snowmen as you want. We'll make a whole damn family in my front yard."

Molli's eyes glisten with tears, holding my gaze for a few seconds before turning away to gaze out her window.

"It really was magical."

I remove my hand from her shoulder, forcing it back on the steering wheel as we drive the rest of the way in silence. Luckily, with the earliness of the morning, patrols are light, so I don't have to worry about the Chief having a colleague pull me over. With the staffing shortage, I can almost guarantee I'll make it to the motel undetected as well.

We pull into the back parking lot, my headlights flashing across the old stone building where the rectory is located. The heavily arched door swings open to reveal Father Michael, already dressed in his clerical clothing for the day. He gives a small wave as he smiles warmly at us. I turn off my truck and open my door, Molli following suit to accommodate Father Michael waiting at the front of the truck. She slips out, quietly closing her door and holding her bag in both hands to avoid his outstretched hand. I quickly round the front fender to shake it, and he doesn't seem bothered by Molli's unintentional snub.

"Welcome, my children," Father Michael greets, his voice gentle, making this as easy and welcoming as possible for her.

Molli forces a smile, trying to mask her emotions, but I can see the worry etched on her face. Father Michael's perceptive gaze doesn't go unnoticed, and I know he can sense her discomfort.

"Thank you for taking care of Molli."

As the snow continues to fall, I wrap my arm around her.

We follow him inside the old church providing both stability and sanctuary.

"It's my duty to provide refuge and guidance to those in need," he replies, his hands and eyes raising to the ceiling as he does during his sermons. "You can rest assured that she'll be safe here."

Molli nods, her eyes glancing between Father Michael and me, her emotions evident. "Thank you," she murmurs, her voice slightly choked.

Father Michael offers her a reassuring smile.

"You're welcome, my dear. You can find comfort and strength in the Lord's embrace during this time."

She doesn't respond, choosing to meander the old hallways we used to run down when trying to find a place to hide during the high school youth lock-ins. Her footsteps echo in the quietness, a contemplative look on her face that makes me curious to know what she is remembering about this place.

"I know you have a hard task ahead of you," Father Michael says to me, his hand touching my shoulder as we watch her wander away. "Remember that the Lord's guidance will be with you every step of the way."

I nod, appreciating his words of encouragement. "Thank you, Father. Your support means a lot to both of us."

A faint smile crosses his face when I look at him. "I'll take good care of her, my son. You focus on your mission, and we'll be praying for your safe return."

She doesn't turn around. There's no good luck, no last hug or kiss. Her aloof behavior confuses me as she leaves me standing there bewildered by her distant demeanor. I brought her to a place of safety and solace, but she appears haunted and distant instead of finding comfort. As if blaming me. It makes little sense.

As I watch her walk away, a knot forms in my stomach. I want to call out to reassure her that I'll be back and that I love her, but Father interjects, "Sometimes goodbyes are difficult for the ones that love us the most. Especially with what you have told me about her past. It's important to understand that she's not abandoning you but is trying to escape the anguish and heartache that saying goodbye brings. It is also an effort to shield herself from the potential devastation she might endure if any unfortunate event were to befall you. Sometimes, you have to let people walk away from you for them to realize they should be walking toward you."

Sadness creeps in as I register his words. She didn't say goodbye when she left me at the flagpole—shielding herself from the pain, the same as now. I never thought of it that way, but it's the only explanation. It's not a reflection of her feelings. It's a defense mechanism she deployed all these years to keep herself sane. She walked away then and didn't walk toward me until fate forced her to. She's walking away now, but will she choose to walk toward me when I return?

"I'll respect her need for space and distance, and if she feels like talking, I'll be there for her. Bringing her here was the right decision. I believe that some quiet contemplation might help her confront her inner turmoil. I'll be supportive and help her navigate through the challenges she's encountering."

When she rounds the corner and her footsteps fade, I glance at the stone floor. With a heavy heart, I turn away, knowing that the mission ahead is challenging, but it's what needs to be done. I'll face whatever comes my way, determined to return to her.

"Thank you again," I shake his hand, sympathy in his expression as we walk to the back door together.

"You're welcome, Alexander." His voice is filled with understanding and compassion. "Remember, Deuteronomy 20:4. For the Lord your God is he that goeth with you, to fight for you against your enemies, to save you."

I nod my appreciation and step outside. The door closes

and bolts behind me as the snow falls heavier, blanketing the ground in a soft, white layer. The cold air stings my cheeks, and I pull my jacket tighter around me. I look back at the rectory and make a silent vow that I will return, and she will never need to shield herself from the pain again. I'll be her shield and sword from now on. With that, I look at the sky, the snowflakes hitting my face, to whisper a prayer of safety and courage before returning to my truck with trepidation coursing through my body.

40

As I drive, I pull out my phone, dialing Rico's number and wanting to get more information about the deal going down at the warehouse tonight so I can be better prepared. I have my service piece, of course, but I wonder if I should pick up a couple of extra guns from my house.

"Rico, what did you find out about the deal at the warehouse tonight? Is it drugs or guns or both?" I blurt out before he can even greet me.

Rico's voice comes through the line, calm and collected as always.

"It's drugs. A big shipment of heroin and fentanyl coming in. Big enough to make a significant dent in Joaquin's operations when we bust them."

The roads are slick with collecting precipitation, and I navigate them carefully while listening.

"They were unloading the semi-trucks in the middle of the night. The place is filled, and they are moving it in smaller shipments tonight. We've already got eyes on the place."

"Good work, man." He deserves this promotion and will get it if everything goes as planned. "And the Chief?"

"Sitting fat and happy in his office, looking for you. He already cornered me this morning. I covered. Said you were communing with nature as part of your recovery and will be back today. He didn't believe it but didn't press me on it either. Oh, and he's had a squad car parked outside your place when I drove past your street this morning."

"Imagine how pleased he'll be when I walk into the station today," I say with a sneer, my hatred for the man growing with every passing minute. I grip the steering wheel harder and accelerate to get to the motel sooner.

"I'll be there, brother. Every step of the way."

There is a loud crash on his end, followed by cussing, and I worry where he's at.

"Where are you?" My pulse quickens if he's still at the station.

"At the motel with that sexy Agent Hunt," Rico replies, then muffles the phone, but I can still hear him defending himself to her in the background. "She agreed to go on a date with me to celebrate our victory."

I hear her holler that she did not. I chuckle, marveling at Rico keeping his sense of humor at a time like this.

"Just get your ass over here already. This wiretap shit itches like hell."

I nod, even though he can't see me. "I'm almost there, and if you weren't so hairy, then it wouldn't be a problem."

The banter is a welcome reprieve from my sadness leaving Molli behind.

"Fuck you, man."

He ends the call and my smile fades as I think of her. She's in excellent hands with Father Michael, safe and cared for. This mission is critical, and I can't afford to be distracted. I release a deep breath and steel myself for what's to come. Putting on my game face, I pull around to the back of the building, park next to Rico's motorcycle, and rap on the door. He throws it open with a huge smile and says, "Welcome to the party."

The motel room is small and dimly lit, with peeling wall-paper and a musty smell that hangs in the air. In one corner, a small table is cluttered with surveillance equipment and laptops displaying live feeds from various hidden cameras around an unknown address. Wires and cables snake along the floor, connecting the devices to a central control panel manned by two state police officers. The room buzzes with activity, agents speaking into headsets and typing furiously on keyboards.

Agent Hunt stands in the center of the room, a commanding presence with her sharp features and piercing blue eyes. Her dark hair is pulled back into a tight bun, and she wears a stern expression as she hunches over a map, talking to an agent. Despite her serious demeanor, an air of confidence and authority about her demands respect.

The other agents are spread out around the room, each focused on individual tasks. Some are monitoring surveillance footage, while others are analyzing data and communicating with agents in the field. The tension in the room is high, a sense of anticipation and readiness for what's to come.

Rico moves aside to let me slip into the room and then walks over to stand beside Agent Hunt, trying to look tall and opposing, which goes unnoticed by her. As I approach Agent Hunt and Rico, she looks up from the map, meets my gaze with a nod, and extends her hand.

"Officer Hamilton, I've heard good things about you." Her eyes set on me with fierce determination, and I recall Molli's comment about my vibrant green eyes being startling in my youth. Hers are having the same effect on me as they sit in stark contrast to her nearly black hair.

"Hopefully not from this guy." I thumb at Rico, who's

scratching his chest, and the muffled sound echoing through the room.

"Quit messing with that," she snaps, her nerves already frayed with him. I raise my eyebrows as he grumbles about the razor burn, making his chest itch. "Now let me show you this."

What I thought was a county map is actually a schematic of a property with a few buildings on it. It takes a few moments to realize what I'm looking at.

"This is the old prison farm." I tilt my head to get a better look and then glance at Rico for confirmation. He beams, and Agent Hunt nods.

"Pretty slick, huh?" Rico says as I look around the room to see the footage from the feed showing a remodeled interior of a building abandoned long ago and fell into disrepair when Rico and I were kids.

"That place has been closed for decades, a haven for drug users and vandals. It's caught on fire more times than I can remember and last time we were there, the roof had caved in from the elements with a chair oddly sitting on top of the rubble." The memories of that place pour out of me, wayward adventures from our youth. "But the State of Colorado put up a formidable fence around it. We no longer get calls to go out to that place."

Rico's eyes dance with excitement as I put it all together. Agent Hunt intently watching both of us.

"And when was the last time either of you took an emergency call there?"

"Rico? Help me out. Maybe five or six years. I went out there with my FTO when I first joined the force. He warned me then to be careful where I stepped because of the piles of needles everywhere." I scratch my head, trying to recall being out there and coming up with nothing.

Rico says, "About the same. You don't notice where you're no longer called out to."

"That's state-owned property," Agent Hunt interjects, her eyes narrowing with realization. "With the wall and it being off the grid, away from prying eyes, no one would suspect a drug operation in a condemned building like that."

I point to the screen nearest me. "That doesn't look condemned. They built that or rebuilt it from the looks of the exterior."

I crane my neck to get a partial view of the exterior on another monitor. Her eyes narrow at my realization.

"Exactly. They kept what remained of the original building, reinforcing the walls from the inside and adding an almost undetectable roof because of the incredibly realistic tree coverage they had attached over it. To do all that—that takes years."

I shake my head, not believing how long this has been going on. Was the Chief dirty this whole time, and we just didn't suspect it? Or did he somehow get dragged into it? Not that I believe him to be innocent, but could they be black-mailing him?

"Pulling the emergency records and backing into the calls, we're suspecting about five years," she confirms, shocking both Rico and me as he turns around and lets out a string of cuss words in Spanish.

"How could we not know?" I mutter the words when I want to cuss like Rico.

How does this happen in our small town? The citizens count on us to keep them safe and away from all the troubles of big city living. We are aware of the regular addicts who use drugs, as well as catching the occasional tourist doing it recreationally. However, it's still a mystery how this happens in our small town. This is so much larger than anything we are equipped for. The size of it is too large for our understaffed department to handle if someone stumbled upon it.

"Fuck, this is the perfect set-up. Right under our fucking noses."

I finally let my temper blow. Pops would never let this happen in his town. He had an eagle eye on everyone and ran criminals and their operations out of his town more than once. Agent Hunt's expression darkens, mirroring the shock and frustration I feel.

"They operated with extreme caution and precision. This kind of underground operation evades detection, especially in a close-knit community like yours. They kept a low profile, only involving trusted individuals who were part of their inner circle.?

Rico's jaw tenses as he glares at the warehouse in disbelief. "I can't believe we missed this. All those years, and we never suspected a thing."

Agent Hunt places a reassuring hand on his shoulder. "Don't beat yourselves up. These criminals are experts at what they do. They knew how to hide their tracks, and the Chief's involvement likely provided them with the perfect cover."

I clench my fists, anger welling up inside me. "The Chief . . . It's hard to believe he could be involved in something like this and do this to our hometown."

Agent Hunt nods solemnly. "It's not uncommon for criminals to have someone on the inside. It gives them access to information and the protection they need to operate freely."

"Could he be blackmailed into it?" I wonder aloud, trying to make sense of it all.

"It's a possibility, but we can't jump to conclusions just yet," Agent Hunt replies. "We need more evidence before determining the extent of the Chief's involvement. So, are you ready to get in there?"

"More than ready. Wire me up." I want to murder the Chief and everyone who's been a part of this for the last five years.

"Good." She nods, and an agent walks over with the equipment I'll be wearing.

I quickly undress, shucking my jacket and shirt on the bed as he makes fast work of the cords and camera. Rico rolls his eyes at my shaved chest, something I've always done to measure my muscle definition in the gym, and it seems to come in handy when he scratches at his chest again.

I can't help but feel a surge of adrenaline. This is what I trained for, and it's time to put my skills to the test. The agent finishes wiring me up and tests all the connections. I put my clothes back on, trying to calm my racing heart and prepare for the mission ahead. Rico gives me a reassuring pat on the back, knowing how important this is.

Agent Hunt briefs me one last time, reminding me of where they will be in proximity to the warehouse and that Rico will be with me at the station. Upon my agreement, I embrace Rico and whisper that I love him. He pushes me off and says to stop being a girl, even though I hear a huskiness in his voice. He grabs his heavy coat and helmet and winks at Agent Hunt before leaving out the door with me on his heels. It's crucial that he get to the station before I do, so it appears as though we haven't been in contact.

I step outside, the snow continuing to fall, and I barely notice the cold air biting my skin as my burning rage focuses solely on the task ahead. Rico's motorcycle fires up as I round the corner of the building. His helmet is already on when he gives me a thumbs up and then revs the engine, peeling out and sending ground snow into the air. His back tire fishtails until he straightens out and then speeds off toward the station.

I fire up the engine, the sound drowning out my thoughts momentarily as nervous excitement courses through my veins. Knowing I can't make a misstep, I role play the various scenarios the Chief can throw at me, preparing myself as best I can for the unexpected. The drive to the police station feels like an eternity as I go over my plan in my head repeatedly. I must stay one step ahead of the Chief, anticipate his moves, and remain calm under pressure.

As I pull into the parking lot, my mind is racing, but I force myself to take a deep breath and calm the fuck down. I check the equipment one last time, ensuring everything is working. The wires are concealed under my clothes, and the camera is hidden but effective.

Walking into the station, I nod to familiar faces, trying to appear nonchalant while my heart pounds. I can't afford to let anyone sense my nerves or suspicions. I greet some fellow officers as they welcome me back, exchanging small talk with Shonda as Rico makes a big production of hugging me. It's over the top but effective in getting the Chief's attention in his office across the room.

His beady little eyes squint when they see me, a flash of hatred until he wipes it away and paints on a fake smile. Rico moves to my right, having a full view of the Chief while I see him get to his feet out of my peripheral vision while Shonda talks us up. I hum and comment, looking completely engrossed as he makes his way over to us.

"Showtime," Rico murmurs, subconsciously scratching the mic secured to his chest.

Shonda swiftly interjects, "No, it's not on Showtime. It's on HBO."

She shoots him a disapproving glance for interrupting her enthusiastic rant about a new show she's binge-watching. There's no chance that she's part of this corruption.

"Hey, Chief Reynolds, look who's back? Well, not back back, but back today, at least." Her voice carries louder than necessary, and he grits his teeth, trying to play nice while we know otherwise. "Why are you here, Alex? Bailing someone else out? "

Her innocent yet probing question is the perfect set-up as I turn to the Chief to answer.

"The Chief wanted to discuss the awards ceremony. I just returned to town and thought I'd swing by before heading home." I keep my voice neutral, watching his face redden at my blatant lie. "He sort of discussed it with my Pops while I was in the hospital."

I throw another log on the fire, watching the hatred in his eyes build as they shift from me to Rico and then back.

"Oh my God, how is your dad? I miss him so much. Did you know he recruited me out of CU Bolder in the first place? And how's your mom? I miss her baking." Shonda keeps lining them up for me to hit out of the park. "And where's that apple pie you promised me?"

"They are good, enjoying retirement. At the moment, they are out of town visiting family. And you'll have your pie when she returns."

"Appears all the Hamiltons are out of town at the same time. That's highly unusual," the Chief remarks before looking sternly at Rico. "Rodriquez, don't you have some work to do rather than standing here breathing down everyone's neck?"

"Shonda loves it when I breathe down her neck."

Rico smirks, unable to resist a playful response. She playfully slaps his arm and laughs.

"You're a fool. Now, the Chief's right. I got work to do, so you guys have to go."

She shoos us away, even the Chief, by returning to her computer and humming a song. The atmosphere appears friendly and lighthearted to anyone unaware of the Chief's corruption.

"Hamilton, come with me," the Chief barks, and I expect him to walk toward his office. However, I'm taken aback when he heads to the front door instead.

"Sir? Aren't we headed to your office?"

I toss a casual thumb in that direction and try to appear nonchalant. An odd expression pulls across his face.

"I assume you'll need to include Susan since she normally handles these sorts of things," I continue, hoping to probe further without giving away my true intentions.

I glance at Susan, his longtime assistant who's kept his calendar for years and knows all his appointments, the legitimate ones at least. She's busy talking on the phone and oblivious to the activity at the station.

"I thought we'd discuss over breakfast. You eat breakfast, don't you?" he questions, turning toward the front of the station again without waiting for my response.

My heart pounds harder as the Chief's unexpected request sends alarm bells ringing in my head. Breakfast? This isn't part of the plan. Why is he deviating from his routine? I exchange glances with Rico, who raises an eyebrow in silent questioning.

"Yeah, sure. Breakfast sounds good," I reply, trying to keep my voice steady despite the nerves swirling inside me.

My mind races trying to figure out the Chief's motives. They are moving the drug shipments tonight, under the cover of night, and it's still early morning. As I follow him outside, I spot the telephone company van the state agents are using, parked discreetly nearby. I tuck my chin into my coat, pretending to be cold in the blistery conditions, and cast a long side glance toward the van while the Chief walks to his driver's door.

"Get in."

His demeanor changes now that no one is watching. My pulse races, wondering where exactly he's taking me, and sweat collects at my waistband, holding my gun.

My boots crunch against the snow-covered path leading to his car. I settle into the passenger seat as the Chief starts the engine. The tires grip the icy surface, creating a muffled and rhythmic sound. Yet the moment he takes a left out of the parking lot, the hairs on the back of my neck stand on edge.

Something is off. This is not the route to any diner in town. Instead, he driving us out of town. My knee bounces against the door, and my hand rests against the window's edge as I try to appear unconcerned.

"Chief, this isn't the way to the diner." I keep my voice level, nearly monotone, when I follow up with, "Where are you taking me?"

He glances at me, his eyes holding a calculating look. "Change of plans, Hamilton."

The landscape outside the window transforms from familiar streets to vast open spaces, and my mind races through every scenario. Are we heading to some secluded location where he could expose my undercover status? Hand me over to Joaquin, or worse, have me killed? The Chief knows I can take him, but a gang of criminals would outnumber me.

Amidst the tense silence, the Chief suddenly demands, "Where is Molli?"

Shit.

"Gone. She skipped bail on me." As I utter the rehearsed response, trying to infuse it with anger and frustration, I catch a flicker of suspicion in the Chief's eyes. "It's why I didn't return your calls."

I need to be cautious about pushing too hard with the act. It's a precarious dance in trying to deceive him.

"So you weren't recovering in the mountains, as that goon said." Thank fuck he thinks Rico is an idiot. It will keep his ass alive.

"No, sir. I was trying to locate her. It's my ass on the line if she doesn't make her court date, and it's jeopardizing my job." Every word is a tightrope between truth and lie, deception and exposure.

"That's disappointing," he mutters, accepting my explanation for now, but I know he's not entirely convinced.

"Why, Chief?" My mind races, wondering how he knew she

was in the wind. It wouldn't come from Rico and it's a far leap to assume just by parking a squad car in front of my house. "How did you know she was missing?"

A disturbing smile pulls at the corner of his lips, his hands tightening on the wheel while his gaze remains fixed on the road ahead.

"You just confirmed it."

Fuck.

He outsmarted me. A puppet master playing with his puppet, and I walked right into his trap. The tension builds in the car with this realization that he is one step ahead of me, possibly many more. I have to turn the tables on him, especially if the snowy conditions worsen and could affect the wire communications back to the van. I ease forward, pretending to scratch my leg while looking in the side mirror, and no one is behind us. It confirms I am truly on my own and at the mercy of my own wits.

I could lunge at him right now, overpower him so easily with sheer force alone, and crash the car. It's so tempting my hand curls into a fist by my thigh. But then, Molli would never be free. She'd always been in hiding until they caught Joaquin, and even then, that could take years if I fuck this up from beating this old man's ass into the ground outside this car.

"Why are you asking about her?" I know the answer, but I want to hear his confession. Hear it from his fucking lips that he's a corrupt asshole working with that motherfucker that made her life miserable.

The Chief's smile widens as if he's already won.

"Why are you asking about her?" I repeat, my voice steady despite the turmoil inside me. I need to hear the truth from him, no matter how much it infuriates me.

He glances at me, a gleam of triumph in his eyes. "Oh, kid, you are just a pawn in this game, aren't you? I asked about her because I know how much she means to you. And I also know that she's your weakness."

I clench my jaw, the truth of his words stinging like a fresh wound. Molli's my weakness, and he's exploiting that.

"You think you're so clever, don't you?" I retort, my voice tinged with anger. "I won't let you destroy her life to protect your ass. I could end you right now, crash this car, and beat you to death."

"You could, but you won't." His chuckle is dark and menacing. "You don't have a choice, Hamilton. I hold all the cards, and I'll use them to bring you down if you don't do exactly as I say."

I glare at him, refusing to back down. "I won't be your puppet. You can't control me."

His eyes narrow, his grip on the wheel tightening. "You'll do exactly what I say, or I'll make sure your career is over before it even begins. You'll be lucky if you're not rotting in a jail cell by the time I'm done with you."

"You've got nothing on me. I have an exemplary record."

"You did until you decided to kill the rookie." He glances at me, shock registering on my face. "Ah, you didn't think I'd let my boys take the fall, did you?"

A chill sweeps down my spine at the mention of Matt's death, and I clutch the door harder, trying to contain my rage.

"What do you mean?"

"The store was mine. I moved a lot of money through it before that idiot kid showed up that night and ruined it. His patrol was across town. Why he was over there, I still don't know, but he fucked it all up and got himself killed. It just so happens that I have a report on my desk that says it's friendly fire from a bullet that logistics matched to your gun."

I grit my teeth, trying to control my anger at the Chief's callous words. Matt's death was a tragedy, and I blame myself daily for not protecting him. But I didn't kill him. The Chief using it against me, manipulating the situation to further his agenda, is repulsive, and I won't stand for it.

"You set him up?" I accuse. "Matt didn't deserve to die on the cold streets for your illegal activities."

The Chief shrugs, a sinister grin on his face. "It's a shame that my store was destroyed. But Matt? He was expendable. Just a means to an end."

I can't believe what I'm hearing. The Chief is not only corrupt, but he's a cold-blooded killer. He'll stop at nothing to protect his criminal activities, even if it means sacrificing innocent lives.

'You're a monster," I seethe, my hands trembling with rage. "Matt has a family. A new wife and baby. You destroyed his family. I won't let you get away with this."

He chuckles darkly.

"Oh, but you will, Hamilton. You don't have a choice. Either you do as I say and play nice, or your life and career are over." The butt of my gun presses into my back, tempting me to blow his fucking head off and take control of the wheel. "Not to mention the lives of his family."

I freeze with my mouth open as a cold sweat sweeps over me. My God. He didn't. I hid everyone close to me so he couldn't find them. He must have gotten Sarah and the baby instead.

"You son of a bitch," I growl, my hands trembling with anger and fear for their safety. "If you touch them, I swear to God . . ."

The Chief interrupts with a sinister smile. "You'll do what? You're in no position to make threats. Now, you have a choice to make. Play by my rules or watch his family die. It will be their blood on your hands, like the rookie's."

I clench my jaw, trying to think of a way out of this impossible situation. I can't let Sarah and the baby become pawns in the Chief's twisted game, and I also can't risk their safety by acting rashly.

"What do you want from me?" I ask, my voice steady despite the turmoil inside me.

"Now, that's what I have been waiting to hear." The Chief's smile widens, his eyes gleaming with triumph. "You're going to help me cover my tracks. Make sure no one gets too close to uncovering the truth. And if anyone gets too curious, you'll take care of them, understand?"

I swallow hard, my mind racing with possibilities. He wants me to murder for him. Kill more innocent people like Matt to continue his illegal operations. Fuck.

I have no choice but to comply, at least for now. I must play along if I want to protect Sarah and the baby.

"Fine," I say through gritted teeth. "But I won't forget what you've done. And I won't rest until you pay for it."

The Chief chuckles, clearly enjoying his control over me. "Kid, you're so predictable. Just like your old man. Too bad they were away when I sent my guys to their house. Remember, if you step out of line, the consequences will be dire. Let's meet my business partner, shall we?"

41

The snowy landscape blurs outside the car window, but the road to the old farm prison is unmistakable. With each passing mile, the snow falls heavier, obscuring the road ahead and making it even more difficult to transmit any communication back to the state police. Adrenaline courses through my veins rage through my body, and pure hatred through my mind. My hands tremble, clutching the door and my seatbelt, anything I can to keep my hands off his throat.

The road is a winding path, snaking through the dense terrain. The snow-covered trees flank both sides like silent sentinels until we approach the formidable wall with razor wire on the top. His car slows to a stop in front of the massive gate. Two guards in military fatigues step out of nowhere to peer inside the vehicle. The Chief doesn't bother rolling down the window, eye contact enough for them to recognize him, and waves to someone out of sight to open the gate. The old farm prison looms ahead, its weathered bricks and barred windows reminiscent of a bygone era.

My inner turmoil intensifies, and I feel as if I'm striking a deal with the devil himself. As we pull through the gate, I note the buildings with cameras mounted on each corner, capturing all angles that match the surveillance footage Agent Hunt's team has. They must have hacked the system. Knowing they have eyes on everything that is happening brings the slightest relief. I need to stall to draw this out and buy them time to assemble and dispatch since they were preparing to intercede twelve hours from now.

The road within the property wall is patchy, having deteriorated long ago from time and the elements. Keeping it in this condition deters unwanted attention, as a new paved road would tip off anyone flying over or investigating this place. Aside from the updated security system, the site looks worse off than when I was here with my field training officer. Some buildings are covered in graffiti, while others are being reclaimed by nature, with bushes growing over broken windows and vines threatening to consume the remaining structure. A burned-out building on the left collapsed in on itself long ago. The roof is smothered with a thick layer of snow, while the back wall of the building still stands high in the air.

"What is this place?" I murmur, knowing what it is and seeing if the Chief will bite. He smirks instead of responding.

There are no cars or trucks around. Nothing that can be seen overhead. Plenty of dead trees cluster around entryways, leading into buildings that are gone or caved in. It adds to the eerie feeling that slides over me as the Chief rolls to a stop in front of the largest building, where a mammoth roll-up door could easily fit the semi-trucks Rico talked about.

The door slowly moves, revealing crates stacked to the ceiling on each side of us as he slowly drives through. We pass row after row of wooden storage crates. The street value of this bust will be in the hundreds of millions. It's unbelievable and ghastly at the same time. If this represents a five-year operation, I can't fathom how much the Chief is on the take for. The crates give way to a large opening where several cars are parked, and this is how they mask their activities.

Three men step from the shadows, wearing all black. Joaquin in the middle, Razor on the right, and another man I didn't see in any of Rico's photos on the left.

"Who are they?" I ask, my pulse quickening when I see another group loading guns into a white cargo van. That must be their supply vehicle, and it could be crucial to escape this place once I find Sarah and the baby.

I scan the place for other exits. The catwalk hugs the roof and provides visibility to the entire floor's operations. The dim lighting hangs from the center of the ceiling, drowning the sides of the building in darkness.

"You'll know soon enough," the Chief replies, parking the car just short of the men staring directly at me. "Keep your trap shut while I do all the talking and Matt's family won't get hurt."

I force myself to maintain a stoic expression, nodding in response to his warning. As we step out of the car, I keep a close eye on Joaquin and his men. They have an air of confidence and arrogance about them, as if they're untouchable.

The Chief leads me toward Joaquin. Razor's unrelenting gaze dissects me, the other man's eyes just as invasive. If they find the wire, I'm a dead man. My pulse is a rapid rhythm echoing in my ears, and my sweaty palms turn clammy. I roll back my shoulders, my neck popping from the action. Joaquin smirks, his dark eyes gleaming with malice. They shake hands. The Chief is more eager to do so than his business partner, under the watchful eye of his enforcer, wearing a double holster with guns stuffed in each side, a gun on each hip of the other guy.

"Well, well, well, look who we have here," he says in a thick accent. "A recruit, huh?"

I force a tight smile. "Don't worry, I know what's at stake."

Joaquin chuckles, clearly amused by my bravado. "We'll see about that. Search him."

My pulse spikes, sweat floods out of my skin and I glare at the Chief to do something. The second they pat me down, they'll find my gun and the wire, and this will be all over with.

Razor steps forward. I step back and say, "What the hell, Reynolds? You gonna let them treat me like this? You gonna let me search them? They don't trust you?"

His decision is split second, realizing Joaquin is pulling the upper hand on him and instantly scowling. He steps in front of me to block the enforcer, irritated at being called out by me to intercede.

"Call your goons off, Joaquin. If I say he's with me, then he's with me."

It's a tense moment. The Chief is staring down Joaquin. Razor and I stare down each other until his boss slaps him on the back.

"Yo, he's cool."

Relief washes over me as Joaquin finally relents. The Chief shoots me a warning look, a silent command to play my part convincingly. I shrug, appearing nonchalant despite the adrenaline coursing through my veins and the sweat running down my temples.

While the Chief and Joaquin converse, I discreetly scan the area. The building continues past us, with stairs leading to the catwalk on the far wall and two exits, approximately fifty feet away, on opposite sides. The other guy whispers something in Joaquin's ear, and I shift my eyes back to them as though I wasn't looking around.

He stares me down, and I stare back, holding my own until his gaze returns to the Chief. I catch snippets of their plans. Twenty trucks are rolling in tonight to be packed and sent to various parts of the country. They seem confident it will go smoothly, having men manned every five miles on the route out of here until they get to the main roads.

Just then, Razor steps forward, eyeing me with suspicion. "I don't trust him," he growls. "He looks like a rat to me."

"He's on our side," the Chief interjects. "He's to me what you are to Joaquin."

Razor narrows his eyes at me, clearly unconvinced, and grunts in disbelief. I must think fast and find a way to gain their trust.

"I've got connections," I say, sounding as confident as possible. "I can help you guys navigate any potential roadblocks. Divert cops to other parts of town, so twenty trucks leaving here and traveling the same road, even under the cover of night, aren't noticed and stopped."

Razor studies me for a moment, then nods. "All right, but if you're lying, I'll be the first to take you down."

I nod, knowing that I've just bought myself a bit of time. The Chief seems content with my answer, convincing him of my loyalty. The tension in the air eases slightly as Joaquin accepts my explanation, albeit with a hint of skepticism still lingering in his eyes. Razor remains on edge, his hand never straying far from the guns holstered on his sides.

Joaquin and the Chief walk through the warehouse, and we file in behind them. This operation is massive, far more extensive than I could have imagined. It sickens me to think of all the lives they have ruined with their illicit activities. With my newly established role, I continue listening to their conversation, gathering as much information as possible. They discuss the shipment's size, destination, and delivery times, and I commit every crucial detail to memory. Joaquin and his men are on high alert, reacting to the slightest noise in the place.

As the conversation continues, I sense an opportunity to gain even more trust from Joaquin and his men.

"I can also provide you with intel on any upcoming police

raids or investigations," I add, sounding as helpful as possible. "I have connections with other agencies, state and federal, that will be loyal for the right price."

This is a stretch, pretending Rico's connections are my own that I can level for their activities. Joaquin's eyes narrow, considering my offer.

"That could be useful," he says finally, glancing at the Chief for confirmation. The stoic Chief nods approvingly, signaling his agreement with the arrangement. "All right, you've got a deal. You give us the information we need, and we'll make sure you're well taken care of."

Another calculating decision is made that keeps my cover intact for now. Before I can fully feel a sense of relief, everything changes in a horrifying second. Joaquin's expression transforms from calculated consideration to deadly determination. Without warning, he pulls out his gun and aims it at the Chief's forehead. Time slows to a crawl, and my heart hammers into my skull.

"No!" I shout, my voice echoing across the vast warehouse, but it's too late when Joaquin smirks and pulls the trigger.

The sound shatters the air. The proximity is so loud in my ears that I squint. The Chief's eyes widen a split second before he's hit, then turn glassy as his blood and brain matter splatter across my face and clothes. I watch in horror as his lifeless body crumples to the ground with a thud. I expect Joaquin to turn the gun on me, clenching my fists as I prepare to feel the cold steel barrel against my forehead as I recite the rosary in my mind. Joaquin hands the gun to Razor, who wipes it clean with a rag before passing it to me.

"Touch it, or you're next."

My mind is a whirlwind of fear, anger, and disbelief, but I refuse to show weakness in front of these dangerous criminals. My body is numb as I clutch the gun, pointing it at the ground. The act establishes my loyalty, as I could point it at Joaquin and blow his head off like he did to the Chief. My deal with the Chief is over, only to be solidified with a sinister twist of fate to the most dangerous man I've ever dealt with. It's a sickening realization.

"Why?"

I motion to the body, the blood rapidly flowing from his wound and running into a nearby drain. The burden of the gun is heavy in my hand when Razor grabs my wrist to take it from me. I wipe the arm of my jacket across my face to get his body fluids out of my eyes and off my nose and mouth while nausea settles into my gut.

"You got my girl."

His head tilts, his dark eyes boring into me with the recognition that he knew all along who I was. It's chilling how well he played both the Chief and me.

Fear washes over me, sending cold chills down my spine. My hands grow clammy, and my throat tightens, making it difficult to swallow. Joaquin's knowledge about Molli causes my whole body to tense. How could he know I bailed her out? Does he have any idea that I dropped her off with Father Michael?

My mind races, thoughts tumbling over one another as I try to figure out my next move. Should I deny any involvement with Molli or attempt to negotiate with this ruthless killer? The dead Chief lying there is a chilling reminder that negotiating is impossible.

"I don't know what you're talking about," I manage to say, my voice coming out more defiant than I feel. It's a weak attempt to distance myself from Molli, to protect her by denying my knowledge of her. It's the last attempt not to betray her or the trust she put in me. I'll die like the Chief on the ground before I let him get to her.

Joaquin's gaze pierces through me, and I can see the skepticism in his eyes. He's not buying it, and I know that lying to him could lead to even more dire consequences. I glance one last time at the dead Chief, my emotions in turmoil.

"Clean this shit up," he commands, his stare never leaving mine until he breaks it to look around at the crates before us.

It is a temporary truce as Joaquin talks about the Chief dismissively, waving a hand at the lifeless body while a storm of emotions brews within me. The Chief was nothing more than scum, responsible for the suffering of countless people, and he got what he deserved for his crimes.

Matt and Molli are innocent victims caught up in this dark underworld. Matt didn't deserve his fate of being caught in their crossfire. He had his whole life ahead of him, and it was cut short for the profits of these two pieces of shit.

And my Molli—forced into a life she didn't want and certainly didn't deserve. Her addiction is a cruel consequence of his blatant disregard for life. It ignites a fury within me to stay strong and see this whole thing through.

Joaquin walks away, leaving me behind with his men until he says, "She made me a lot of money in LA."

His words cut through the air as he pauses, turning to the side and giving me a long glance, implying I should walk with him, leaving them to dispose of the body.

"Kept many of my top customers happy."

The mere mention of Molli being exploited and used for profit by these criminals sends a surge of repulsion through me, and my hands instinctively coil into tight fists. The overwhelming urge to kill him here and now threatens to consume me. It would cause my death, but I know where I'm going when I die, and it would be worth it. And I know where Joaquin's going, and that's more than worth it. Unyielding, I lock eyes with him, closing the distance between us with unwavering determination. His words are like venom, designed to provoke a response, but I won't give him that satisfaction.

"You'll buy her from me. Work off the debt by, what did you say?"

He snaps his fingers, and I paraphrase about diverting cops and covering his tracks as we walk toward the van. His men have finished loading and are closing the doors.

"Starting with this one. It's heading to Denver. You'll ride with them, secure the money, and be back to arrange the rest tonight."

As we approach the van, I take a deep breath, preparing myself when I remember the Chief's threat from the car.

"All right," I reply, maintaining my composure when I make my demand. "I'll ride along and make sure everything goes smoothly. But I want to see Sally and the baby first. I want assurances that you will let them go before I leave here."

His dark eyebrows flicker, a lack of interest in his eyes.

"I know you have them," I insist, refusing to back down. "Sally and the baby. I want to see them now."

Joaquin's eyes narrow, and he scoffs, clearly irritated by my demand.

"You don't know what you're talking about," he retorts. "I don't have anyone."

I clench my fists, my patience wearing thin.

"Don't lie to me. The Chief said you're holding them hostage."

He leans in, his face inches from mine, his breath hot against my skin.

"I don't take kindly to threats."

"I'm not threatening you," I reply, my voice steady despite the fear bubbling inside me. "I'm demanding the release of innocent people. Sally and the baby are not a part of this and don't deserve to be caught in the crossfire."

"What the fuck do you think?" His voice drips with malice. "I'm not running a fucking daycare so you can have a little family reunion. Get your fucking ass in the van."

He shoves me against the side of the van, his forearm pressing against my throat, choking off my breath. Suddenly, a deafening explosion rocks the back of the building, sending shockwaves through the air. The force of it knocks Joaquin off balance, and I use the distraction to break free from his grip. Chaos erupts as the building is engulfed in flames. The sirens grow louder, and shouts echo from the catwalk. Police in camouflage swarm in, and the recognition of what is happening registers on Joaquin's face.

He curses and takes off toward the front of the building. His footsteps echo through the maze of towering crates, and I race after him, taking cover as he fires upon me. With steady hands, I retrieve my gun, my fingers wrapping around the cold metal. The sound of me cocking it alerts him of my location, and he fires again. Bullets ricochet off the metal surface, sending sparks flying as I gauge his movements. Squatting low to the floor and using the crates as a shield, I advance on him.

Gunfire surrounds us, the exchange between his men and the police adding to the chaos and making it harder to determine his location the closer they get to us. I duck my head around the corner. The row is clear, and I advance to the next set of crates, getting closer to the large opening the Chief drove through. I clear two more rows, spot his shadowy figure streaking across the back wall, and fire a shot that pierces his leg.

He yells out in pain and stumbles but doesn't go down. Instead, he turns and fires blindly in my direction, forcing me to duck behind the crates again. The adrenaline courses through my veins, and every second feels like an eternity until I can return fire.

I need a distraction, something to throw him off balance, and I notice the last warehouse light hanging directly over my head, giving him a perfect view of my position. I aim my gun and fire, shattering the bulb and covering my hands over my head as the shards rain over me. It plunges us into darkness, the only light coming from the fire burning at the opposite side of the building. Leveling the field, I rely on my tactile training, moving stealthily and navigating the remaining rows in search of him.

My breaths come out in short pants as I duck and weave, narrowly avoiding the bullets that hit the cargo above my head, sprinkling a fine dusting of powder over me. I quickly shake my head, blowing it out of my nose and mouth to avoid the exposure affecting my abilities.

My temporary distraction allows him to sprint away and vanish out a side door that clangs closed behind him. I race after him, easing the door open and waiting for enemy fire. A glance shows it's clear. The snow is falling with the intensity of a blizzard, creating a whiteout that obscures my visibility. The blistery wind clears more drug substances from my face as the hunt for him continues.

I crouch beside a clump of overgrown ice-covered bushes while searching for his footprints. The bitter cold bites at my exposed skin, and the snow crunches under my boot as I follow the blood droplets mixed with his faint imprints. He's trying to escape toward the back of the property, the wooded side beyond the crumbling buildings. With his injury, it will be impossible to scale the formidable wall containing this place.

I follow the trail, my senses on high alert and my breath visible in the freezing air as I push forward. I spot him up ahead, his figure darting between the trees at the edge of the property. His injury is slowing him down, and I gain ground quickly, my heart pounding in anticipation.

The blizzard roars around us. The snowflakes are swirling as he glances back at me with desperation written all over his face. He fires his final two shots, and the wind sends the bullets astray. I race toward him, the distance closing with every step.

He's cornered, and he knows it. I raise my gun. My hands

are numb from the conditions but still able to fire should he decide to attack. He glares at me. His eyes are filled with defiance, even though he knows there's no way to escape the consequences of his actions.

"It's over, Joaquin," I call out, my breaths come out in white puffs. "There's nowhere to run."

In one last desperate attempt, he raises the gun to his temple, his finger hovering over the trigger. With each step I take, the gun clicks ominously, but he's out of bullets.

With no other choice, he lowers his weapon, his shoulders slumping in defeat as his body sags against the wall. I approach cautiously, my gun still trained on him, unwilling to take any chances. I've been through too much to let him slip away now.

"You know this is not over." He raises his chin, the snow wetting his clothes and causing them to cling to his body. "This is far bigger than me and that guy."

"You're probably right, but at least I got the piece of shit that tormented Molli."

The men, exploitation, sexual assaults, police reports, beatings, arrests, addictions, withdrawals, breakdowns, hallucinations, fear, paranoia, and scars. The vile animal that did the culmination of all those things to my beautiful, brown-eyed girl stands at the end of my barrel—tempting me to put a bullet through his eyes. My finger lightly presses on the trigger as I contemplate killing him for everything he's done to her.

"Do it, man," he taunts, bracing himself against the wall, daring me to end his life. He spews more repulsive details of the heinous acts he and others did to her.

His filth-laden words fuel the fire of my hatred, pushing me closer and closer to the edge. Every fiber of my being screams for vengeance and for justice to be served. Killing him feels like the only way to truly protect Molli and all the others who have suffered at his hands.

My finger hovers over the trigger, the weight of the gun

pressing against my palm. I envision that bullet ripping through his skull, ending the life of the monster who tormented my girl. The temptation to seek my justice, to rid the world of this evil, is almost unbearable.

The snow falls heavily, swirling around us in a dance of white and gray as if nature itself is echoing the turmoil within me. His hands press into the wall at his sides, standing erect and lining up the gun to his heart. I jolt it up to aim at his head. One shot is all it takes. My heart is pounding in my chest, the rage and pain clouding any reasoning to uphold my oath as a peace officer.

I faintly register approaching footsteps as Rico emerges from the snowstorm, his eyes wide with worry as he stands beside us.

"Alex."

His voice is loud over the surrounding weather, his hands in a defense position mirroring Joaquin's as he hobbles closer.

"I know what you're thinking, and he's not worth it. You want revenge. It's understandable, but if you kill him, he wins. You go to jail and Molli's alone."

I look into Rico's eyes, the conflict in my own mirrored in his. I don't want Joaquin to win. I don't want him to take away Molli's chance at a better life. A life free from fear and pain. A life with me, healing from this, and chasing her dreams, better dreams, with me by her side.

"He deserves to pay for what he's done." My voice is raw with emotion.

"He will pay, but not like this. Not at the cost of Molli's future and yours."

My heart pounds in my chest when I take a deep breath, the cold air burning my lungs. The desire for reckoning claws at the edges of my mind despite Rico's wisdom.

Joaquin attempts to dive for the gun. Rico moves with lightning speed, landing a swift right punch that collides with

Joaquin's jaw. He crumples to the ground, his defiance silenced, and I can't help but feel relieved that I didn't kill him after all.

"What?" Rico shrugs. "It was self-defense. I felt threatened, didn't you?"

Officers run toward us, led by Agent Hunt, who quickly assesses the situation as Rico takes the gun from my trembling hand and gives it to her. Her sharp eyes study us both.

"Good work, Officer Hamilton," she says, her voice firm but with a hint of compassion. "You managed to capture Joaquin alive. That will go a long way in building a strong case against him and his accomplices."

I nod, trying my best to compose myself, but the adrenaline coursing through my veins makes it hard to steady my breathing. I did the right thing by not succumbing to my anger, but it's difficult to dismantle my need for vengeance.

Agent Hunt continues, "We'll take it from here. I'll need you to give a full report. Rico, take him to the van in front for ballistics to get started."

Rico wraps his arm around my shoulders and guides me away as they arrest Joaquin. I take a moment to glance at the abandoned warehouse, now illuminated by the flashing lights of the police cars and overrun with investigative personnel.

"There were tens of millions of dollars of drugs in there." Rico's voice breaks the silence, his eyes searching mine for a reaction.

"And guns." My mind flashes back to the van that was headed to Denver.

"How does it feel to be a hero?"

"Hero? That's what Molli called me when I was lying on the concrete after getting shot."

Rico's steps falter momentarily. "Like a premonition?"

"I don't know." I shake my head, unsure of how to categorize it. His arm drops from my shoulders as we trudge through the snow, the wind howling around us. "The Chief killed Matt."

"I heard," Rico confirms, and I am surprised. "You weren't out of range yet."

A bitter taste rises in my throat as I think of the Chief, the betrayal cutting deep. "Sally and the baby? Are they safe?"

"They were never in jeopardy. It was a ruse."

Relief washes over me, but it's quickly replaced by rage. The Chief manipulated me, leveraging my love for Molli and fear for Sarah and the baby's safety. It makes me sick to think of how easily he played me.

"I should have seen it coming," I say, my fists clenching. "I should have known he was capable of this."

Rico places a reassuring hand on my shoulder. His eyes filled with empathy.

"You couldn't have known. The Chief was cunning, and he had us all fooled. Of course, there will be an investigation into the station, but last time I checked, there is an immediate opening for an interim Chief since the last one got his brains blown out."

Ricos's dry humor is a little too much to take since said brains are covering my clothes.

"I just want to get back to Molli as soon as possible."

Thoughts of having her locked away in my room, making love to her for the rest of my medical leave, makes me smile.

"Then pick up the pace, slowpoke," Rico chides, elbowing me when we reach the broken pavement leading to the van.

42

R ico and I arrive at the church. The sight of the
magnificent building against the snowy backdrop is
a stark contrast to the chaos and darkness we've just
left behind. Its grand architecture and towering spires seem to
touch the sky and reach to the very God I prayed would keep us
safe.

We step inside, the air filled with the hushed whispers of
congregants seeking comfort and guidance from Father
Michael. The soft glow of candlelight casts dancing shadows on
the stained-glass windows, creating an aura of tranquility
within the sacred space.

Father Michael is tending to the needs of the altar when he
catches sight of me. His eyes widen in shock as he takes in my
appearance. He quickly covers his mouth in horror when he
sees the blood and matter still staining my clothing.

"Alexander."

He walks with purpose down the center aisle, ushering me
to the side and away from the few parishioners, saying prayers
and lighting candles.

"You've fought the demons of hell and have returned."

I manage a weak smile. The processing of the scene took all night. The property's vastness and the extent of the bust took hours of manpower to report to multiple agencies. The second they released me, Rico knew I wanted to come straight here and agreed to take me.

"It's been a long night, Father," I murmur, knowing the judicial process is starting and will linger over a couple of years, if not more, to get through all the trials and appeals procedures.

He nods before turning to Rico. "And with Ricardo in tow, I see."

"Every good demon hunter needs a trusty sidekick."

Rico extends his hand, warmly shaking Father Michael's hand, then claps him on the back in a gesture that seems too boisterous for the solemn environment. A disapproving look from a lady in the front pew prompts him to lower his voice as he speaks.

"Well, gents, I'm going to light a candle and thank the big man upstairs for my upcoming date with Agent Hunt."

"I . . . um . . . I'm not sure I understand," Father Michael stammers, confused. Rico grins mischievously and wiggles his eyebrows.

"Don't worry, Father. It's just Rico being Rico," I say with a chuckle, apologetically smiling at the priest. "You can't ever take him too seriously."

Father Michael looks bewildered but willing to go along with the banter.

"Ah, I see. In that case, I hope your upcoming 'date' with Agent Hunt goes well, Ricardo."

Rico winks playfully at him. "Thanks, Father. If all goes well, you'll hear about it in the confession booth."

As Rico heads off to light a candle, the smile fades from my face, and I ask, "Where is she?"

A worried look appears when he pushes his glasses up the

bridge of his nose before cupping my elbow and leading me out of the sanctuary.

"She's very different now, isn't she?" he says, not expecting an answer as we walk down the stone hallway back to the rectory side of the church. The morning light shines through the arched stained-glass windows, sending prisms of color to dance along the floor.

"She's been very quiet and reflective, which is good and a given for what she has endured. Yet, the change within is deep-seated, beyond the touch of any man, in hopes that the Lord above can do his work in her."

"Father, if this is your attempt to get me back into church—"

He holds up a hand to silence me, the long sleeve of his robe giving way to his clergy clothes underneath.

"No, my son. It's not. She's afflicted. I've seen it before in my addiction counseling and expressed my desire for her to attend our weekly meetings. But it's a myriad of her more recent past mixed with the past that you shared with her. Things you might not have been made aware of until now."

He continues walking again, his dress shoes clicking on the stone as I try to figure out what he's talking about.

"If you're talking about high school, we were great. It was the happiest time in my life."

"Of course, it would be for you, Alexander. You were an athlete, came from a loving family that doted on you, and attended this very church until you stopped. Your life was good, the American dream, if you will."

Me and God had a falling out when Molli left. Blaming him was the only reasonable explanation I could come up with at the time, and then it seemed to adhere over the years. Not that I'm willing to share that with Father Michael now.

"Okay, what are you saying?" I ask, eager to get to the punchline so I can see her.

Father Michael pauses for a moment, putting his index finger and thumb to his chin in thought.

"What I'm trying to say, Alexander is that Molli's past is more complex than you may realize. She's been through experiences that have left deep scars on her soul, and those wounds are not easily healed. She's been carrying this pain with her for a long time, shaping who she is today."

I listen intently, both confused and worried, as his words suggest there's much more to her story than I'm aware of.

"You see, Molli didn't have the same upbringing as you," Father Michael continues. "Trauma and hardship marred her childhood. An apathetic mother putting the well-being of her child underneath the priority of her latest husband. Unwanted by her mother, she endured neglect and emotional abuse and had to fend for herself at a young age. It's no wonder she built walls around her heart, pushing people away to protect herself from being hurt again."

"But she was wildly independent, free-spirited, and fiercely determined," I counter, having no idea that Molli's home life was so bad growing up.

"All cries for help. Her parents dropped her here as often as possible and were always late picking her up. Occasionally, they would forget about her, leaving her to go home with Mrs. Schneider several times."

"Mrs. Schneider, the church's secretary?" I ask in astonishment, rubbing my beard as I try to recall if I ever saw that happen.

"Yes."

I turn away, wanting to drive my fist into aged stone, as I hear Molly's life has been a shitshow at the expense of everything else. His hand rests lightly on my shoulder, drawing me back to him with sympathy in his expression.

"She faced challenges that most of us can't even fathom,

which has taken a toll on her mental and emotional well-being."

"So she feels loveless."

My heart clenches when I say that, wanting to right the wrongs over all these years. I wish I could go back in time and shield her from the pain. Father Michael nods sadly.

"It's going to be a long road for her, Alexander, and she needs someone patient and understanding by her side."

The revelation of her abusive and neglectful childhood has shattered my heart into pieces. I can't fathom the idea of not doing everything in my power to be there for her. I love her so deeply that the thought of her facing this alone is too much to bear.

"I want to be that person for her," I say firmly, my voice laced with determination. "I want to help her find the love and support she deserves. I won't abandon her like everyone else."

Father Michael smiles gently, a glimmer of hope in his eyes.

"I believe you can make a difference in her life, Alexander. Your love for her is clear, and sometimes that's all it takes to begin the healing process."

I know that the road ahead will be difficult, and healing won't come overnight. But I'm ready to face every challenge, to hold her hand through the darkest moments, and to be a beacon of love and support in her life. I already walked through hell yesterday and slayed the demons that haunted her physically. I'll help her slay the ones that haunt her psychologically.

Because loving Molli means wanting to be there for her in every way possible. It means being her safe haven, the one she can rely on, and the one who will never give up on her. I can't change her past, but I can be a part of her future, helping her heal and find the happiness she deserves.

I'll be patient and understanding, giving her the space she needs to heal but also being there every step of the way. I'll be her support, her rock, and her protector. I won't let her face this pain alone, for she is the one who captured my heart and never let it go.

"But I will say this, her desire for love and acceptance, I believe, is what sent her to Hollywood in the first place. If she had received it from her mother, perhaps when she was a child, the future could have been different."

His introspective thought bothers me deeply, like an arrow to the heart.

"But I loved and accepted her. With everything I had," I defend, feeling hurt that mine didn't matter and sent her on the path that turned out to destroy her.

"I know you did, Alexander." He lowers his chin, almost nodding his understanding before he continues, "I think by the time you came along, the feeling of unworthiness was already solidified, through no fault of your own, of course. However, I think she's more open to receiving the love you have for her now, and with some patience, your love will be returned."

That's all I want. To love her and be loved by her for all the days of my life.

"Where is she now?"

"She's working in the food pantry."

He waves a soft hand toward the end of the hall. I glance down at my filthy clothes, then Father Michael's pristine white robe, and with a grateful smile, I extend my hand.

"Thank you."

He takes my hand in both of his, genuinely happy. "It was my honor to help my children in their time of need, and when the time is right, I hope to see you both back in Church."

"Of course," I reply, releasing Father Michael's hand.

A thrill runs through me as I turn and jog away, taking the stairs to the basement and swiftly pushing through the double doors. There she is, working diligently to prepare meals for the homeless.

Her back is to me, and I pause for a moment to take in the

sight of her. Even in this humble setting, she radiates a certain beauty that captivates me. The soft glow of the overhead lights dances across her short brown hair that looks as though she trimmed it into a hairstyle.

I take a deep breath, my heart pounding with nervous excitement. I know this won't be easy, but I can't let fear hold me back any longer. I need to be honest with her and share my feelings.

"Did I ever tell you that my mom taught me how to dance? She said I was born with two left feet, but I wanted to learn so I could dance with you at our wedding."

I keep my voice low so as not to startle her, and when she whirls around to greet me, the smile falls from her face. Her hand clutches the middle of her chest at the sight of me. I probably should have cleaned up before I came, but I had to see her immediately. Her breath comes in bursts. Her eyes blink rapidly at the tears flowing into them.

"Is that ... Is that ..."

"I'm okay. I'm not hurt."

I curse myself for not thinking about how triggering this could be for her after all the violence she has been exposed to. I rip off my jacket, tossing it on the floor, quickly followed by my shirt, pants, and boots to make a necessary burn pile. The cold room nips at my skin, and I stifle a shiver as I stand in my underwear and socks and slowly turn around so she can see I'm okay.

"No new injuries."

"Oh, thank God," she whispers, running to me and collapsing into my outstretched arms as I grip her with a vitality for life itself.

Her tears soak into my bare skin as she clings to me, and I hold her tightly, never wanting to let her go. Her grip is so desperate and fierce that it feels like she's trying to anchor herself to me.

"It's okay."

She pulls back slightly, and her breath hitches when I lean over to reunite our lips. I pour everything I have into this kiss. Her past, my past, our past, and every moment in between. All the words and conversations from them and now and every emotion I've felt since she came back into my life.

She breaks the kiss, breathless, when she whispers, "I thought I lost you."

"You'll never lose me," I reply, gently wiping her tears. "I'll always come back to you, Molls. Always."

She clings to me tightly, her arms encircling my waist and fusing our bodies. I understand the depth of her fear, the trauma she's endured, and the scars that still haunt her. Our love goes beyond the physical. It's a meeting of souls, a reconnection of two hearts separated by time and circumstance worthy of being solidified once and for all. My hold never wavers when I reach for the twist tie from the loaf of bread, hastily fashioning it into a circle that will have to do for now.

"I love you, Alex," she murmurs into my chest, and my eyes close.

Tears run down my face as the words I longed to hear fall softly from her soft lips. My breath hitches, and my heart feels like it might burst with happiness. Every moment of pain and struggle leading up to this moment is worth it. I have her love, and I'll never do anything to jeopardize it. I press my lips to her head, silently vowing to protect, cherish, and love her for the rest of our lives.

"I love you too." My voice is raspy. "And I'll do whatever it takes to be the man you need and deserve."

I hug her tightly, breathing her in and basking in the moment. She pulls back, and I take that as my opportunity to take a knee in front of her. Her eyes widen, and her hand cups her mouth, muffling a sob as tears flow down her cheeks.

"Molls," I whisper, trying to stop the flow of tears to get this all out. "You are the bravest, strongest, and most beautiful person I've ever known. You've faced unimaginable pain and still have so much love to give. You deserve all the happiness in the world, and I want to be the one to give it to you."

My heart pounds in my chest, and my hand trembles with nerves as I hold out the makeshift ring up to her.

"Will you be my brown-eyed girl? Will you let me be the one to stand by your side, to love you unconditionally, and to share in all this life has to offer?"

Her tears spill over, and a radiant smile breaks through when her hand drops. A smile that holds the same hope and belief in our happiness that I do.

"Yes," she whispers, her voice barely audible.

A rush of relief and joy washes over me as I slip the makeshift ring onto her finger. I stand, pulling her into my arms once again, and this time, it's not just a reunion hug. It's a celebration of new beginnings, two souls walking a path together, hand in hand, and knowing we have and will over-come anything life throws at us.

She quietly starts humming a tune so familiar that I begin swaying and putting those old dance lessons to use in the small church basement in only my underwear and socks. She hums the entire song until I gently dip her low to the ground. Her head falls back, giggling as I smother her exposed throat in kisses as a newly engaged couple and murmur against her flesh, "You, my brown-eyed girl."

The End

BONUS SCENE #1

MOLLY SITARA POV

"Are you sure I look all right?"

I touch the side of my hair, grateful the Father has his barber set for when he cuts hair for the homeless ministry. It turned out better than I expected when he showed me how the back looked in the mirror, having covered a couple of my bald spots with how he applied the gel.

"You look beautiful."

His eyes dance in the bright sunlight reflecting off his dashboard when he smiles at me. For the longest time, I couldn't fathom how he could love me as much as he did. When he first asked me out, I thought it was a joke. A prank that football boys played on outliers like me, duping us into going out with them in hopes we would give it up sexually and have them brag about it at school. I turned him down no less than a dozen times until I couldn't take it anymore and erupted in the hallway. It caused a scene, but I was already dubbed the crazy girl anyway, so it didn't matter.

When he took me to the movies and didn't try anything, I thought he might be gay. Come on. It's the movies. Everyone knows what happens in the back of that dark place. When he took me to Burger World on our second date, after the football game with all his friends, I caught them exchanging knowing looks. I thought he'd at least force a kiss on me or sneak a hand up my skirt. When he didn't, I was convinced he was gay.

The following three dates were easy. I treated him like my gay best friend until he finally asked if he could kiss me. It was the sweetest and dorkiest thing I ever heard. When I agreed and felt his lips on mine and the explosive chemistry between us, I thought, 'I could get used to this.' That was that until it wasn't.

His strong hand squeezes my knee, never leaving it the entire drive up to the expensive home of Mr. Takahashi. I set my hand on top of his, still wearing the bread tie from when he proposed yesterday. He didn't want me to take it off when we made love amidst the mess I made at his place, nor when we got the shower to clean up and ended up going at it again. It's been wet and dried out too many times to count in the last day as we rediscovered each other repeatedly.

The soreness still radiates from my core as I sit in his truck. He didn't seem to care, giving me a proud smile when I told him the home was closed the rest of the day. Why he likes calling it that, I don't understand, and when I asked him to explain, he just smiled and kissed me gently. If he wants to have his secrets, so be it. I have mine, and he has his.

However, last night wasn't a secret. He told me everything from the night he got shot and lay looking at the stars thinking of me to resisting the temptation of killing Joaquin. The thought of losing him to prison for his murder had me clutching him harder, crying into his neck, and making him promise he would never think like that again. We have so many lost years to make up for that I'd be devastated if anything happened to him. I wouldn't want to live anymore, and once I spoke those words, he clutched me in return. The thought is horrible to both of us.

"Not too much longer," he murmurs when his truck shifts to climb the winding road up the mountainside.

The views are breathtaking. The fresh air is crisp and tinged with a faint scent of pine as if it seeps through the cracked windows. The mountain range is stunning, their snow-covered peaks a canvas of white and gold in the glistening sunlight. He slows the truck at a large entrance with antler racks spread across the top, oddly opposite his sleek appearance.

"This is his place?"

As we pass under them, I point to the racks, and he chuckles.

"Yeah, Dani said they're weird as fuck but very sentimental to him. That's a direct quote."

His relaxed smile lingers on his face, the one I love the most when he casts it at me. I worried myself sick that I'd never see it again. I couldn't say goodbye when he dropped me off at the church. It had been too many times in my life and one time too many with him. I figured he wasn't gone if I didn't say goodbye. As if he was running an errand and would be right back. It was the only way I could function that day, repeating to myself that he'd be right back.

"It will be okay, Molli."

He squeezes my knee, associating my quietness with avoidance. I had gotten good at transitioning to other places in my mind to take me away from reality. This was no different. Over ten years have passed since I saw his parents, and I'm not looking forward to this reunion.

"If you're nervous about my parents, don't be. I'll handle them, and you hang out with Dani. Lord knows she'll handle everything if things get out of hand."

My eyes widen, and I swallow hard. "Do you think things will get out of hand?"

"Bad choice of words. Things will not get out of hand. I'm

just saying if you feel uncomfortable at any time, we'll leave and go back home, okay?"

He doesn't know I'm so uncomfortable right now that I'm slightly nauseous. His mom has always been pleasant. It's his dad that I'm worried about. It's been many years since I've seen the police chief, and I could go several more without seeing him.

A few turns later, with the gravel road climbing up, his truck and expansive house come into sight. It's a green roof, and natural elements blend in with the surrounding environment, except for the large sheet of seamless glass. Its reflective surfaces catch the sunlight and blind us as we pull behind a black Porsche parked under the shelter of the roofline.

"Wow."

A house from the Hills back in LA flashes through my mind. The memory of the party, drugs, and waking sore next to an unknown man soured my appreciation of the place in front of me. What I wouldn't give if I could erase the last ten years from my brain.

"Mom said it was like a hotel. I can see why," he agrees, drawing me back to reality, when he opens his door, a gust of cold air races into the truck and blows away the past.

I brush a hand over my hair, feeling the bald spots to ensure the product still covers them. Hamilton helped me with it at home when I was about to put my wig back on. He held my hands, looked me in the eyes, and told me I was beautiful and didn't need it. Although I'm still getting used to his compliments, something that never changed from when we were together the first time, I wanted to believe him and set the wig aside. Now, I wish I hadn't, as it feels like I'm missing the armor needed for walking into this place.

He closes his door, walking to mine to help me out, something old-fashioned but cute. I slide out and give him a kiss of gratitude. He smiles brighter and weaves his hand into mine to lead the way to the front door. The long panels flanking each side of the door give way to the activities inside, beautiful furnishing, and luxurious finishes until Dani's face suddenly pops out to look at us.

Surprise mars her expression as she throws open the door to hug him tightly and then me unexpectedly. Her body hits mine so hard it knocks the air out of my chest while the scent of motor oil lingers on her skin.

"What the hell are you guys doing here?" Her voice is light when she releases me, and then she frowns. "They're fine."

I'm startled when I see two men approaching, guns lowering that we're previously pointed at our back.

"Some security they are. They should have stopped you at the gate." She rolls her eyes and widens the door. "Come in, come in. But shoes off, you know, that damn white carpet."

The floors are marble, the finishes are gold, and the whole place is shades of white. It's both pristine and inviting, with the entire back of the house a sheet of glass framing the mountain range. It gives the homes in LA a real run for their money in elegant simplicity and obvious expense. Tomlin sweeps into a hallway, barely dressed in tight shorts and dripping in sweat. I avert my eyes as it seems so surprising that none of them are prepared for our visit.

"Is everything okay?" he asks, using the towel draped on his shoulder to dry his incredibly muscular chest and abdominals.

"Did you not call ahead?" I poke Hamilton in the side, and he beams, happy and proud.

"Nope, I wanted to surprise everyone." He smiles, I frown, and Tomlin studies both of us over the edge of his towel. "The good news is that it's all over."

His arm wraps over my shoulder, drawing me into his side, where I place a hand on his ribs to steady myself. His comfort is needed when his parents appear behind Dani and Tomlin at the edge of the living room. His dad's eyes narrow, staring suspiciously over Dani's left shoulder while his mother claps her hands together and starts barreling toward us.

"Alexander!"

She's pushing through Dani and Tomlin in a flash so fast they are both startled, and I quickly move away when she hugs his middle. He releases a soft 'oomph' at impact and slowly wraps his arms around her. The height difference is cute, and her exuberance would be sweet if it weren't for his dad shooting daggers at me while he ambles into the foyer to join us.

"Oh, Alan, look who's here?"

Her voice is muffled, not bothering to look at him when she makes the announcement. I take a hesitant step back, my skin starting to crawl with anxiety as I look to Hamilton for guidance on what to do. His gaze remains firmly locked on his father, and when I glance at Dani, her steady gaze is fixed on me. At that moment, the desire to flee is overwhelming, and I start scratching my skin to distract myself from the discomfort. The scratching feels good, and the stroke and intensity are something I can control in this uncontrollable situation.

"Hey, Molli, have you seen Tomlin's badass trophy room? Dude's a legend!" Dani jumps to save me, grabbing my hand before I can even think. "Plus, he has to catch a shower, and we'll let the Hamiltons do their thing while we do ours. I can also show you the diner. Have you eaten? Do you like home-made pizza?"

I glance at Hamilton. His face is tense as he releases his mom, who's oblivious to the situation. His forest green eyes shift to mine, a mirror of his mom's faded green eyes, and his mouth loosens.

"That's very generous of you, Dani. Thank you," Tomlin responds to the easy compliment from his girlfriend's lip. "Like she said, I'll grab a shower and be out. Then, we can discuss lunch options while you explain what has transpired since we last spoke. Make yourself at home. I shouldn't be too long."

His graciousness is like a balm over this tense situation while they play referees between his parents and us. They're keeping the situation from growing more intense, and Dani offering me an escape is very kind of her.

"I'd love to see if it's all right with everyone else."

By everyone, I mean only one, and when he graces me with a subtle smile, I'm relieved. As we drove up here, I hadn't fully grasped how uneasy this situation might be for him, and even now, I'm determined to comfort him. With a gentle release of Dani's hand, I step forward, prompting his mother to take a step back and rub the spot between his shoulder blades.

"I won't be long."

In a swift motion, his arm encircles my waist, drawing me close for a fleeting kiss atop my head before he lets me go.

"Take as long as you want. I'll be in here catching up with Mom and Pops."

His voice is flat and neutral while his eyes bore into his father. Dani grabs my hand, yanking me away from Hamilton and running down a beautiful hallway that lights up around us like the grocery store's frozen section.

As Dani leads me into what she enthusiastically calls the 'badass trophy room,' I can't help but feel apprehension the moment the door opens. I'm overwhelmed by the sheer enormity of his achievements. Every wall is adorned with gleaming trophies, large polished medals, framed pictures of him in the center of the podiums, and Olympic memorabilia everywhere.

"He's a certified badass. I couldn't be prouder of him." Dani's voice is full of genuine admiration for her boyfriend.

"This is unbelievable."

I feel small in this room filled with all this greatness. The walls ooze with his accomplishments. Yet, he remains approachable and humble despite his remarkable achievements. It magnifies my own inadequacy, haunted by a past filled with actions I deeply regret, all in a world where I don't quite fit in. Why would Dani even want to be my friend when her life is on another level from mine?

She walks over to shut the door, then snaps those big eyes at me with fierce determination. I'm instantly uneasy. Not that she'd hurt me, even though she does threaten a lot, but being trapped in a room alone with her makes my anxiety spike.

"Stop pulling your hair and spill your guts," she says, standing a few inches shorter than me with her hands on her hips. I didn't even realize I was pulling on my hair, and I cross my arms to stop the compulsion. "Why are you here? What happened with that dude and all of it?"

I'd much prefer she heard it from Hamilton, but he's preoccupied with whatever is happening with his father. He didn't mention much to me, but something was wrong by the looks of it. I blow out a long breath, my fingers curling into my coat to prevent them from reaching up to my hair as I relay Hamilton's information. She asks one question after another, not letting me finish before she interrupts. She's way too direct, and I can see how Hamilton loses his patience with her rapid-fire questions. I answer them as best I can, but she still demands more information that I don't know.

The small space, her questioning interrogation style, and the tense situation when we arrived makes me crave a high. When it all gets too much, I scratch my neck, jaw, and chin until I finally break. "Can we get out of here and maybe go outside? I'm feeling a little . . ."

I don't bother to finish. The flush of heat sweeps over me, and I fan my face with my hand. Her eyes widen, a flash of recognition sweeping across her face as if remembering this feeling, and she throws open the door.

"Out the back! Hurry!" she yells, racing out of the room and glimpsing back at me to see if I'm following.

It's not this urgent that I get to wherever she's taking me, but I'm relieved when we finally wind through several rooms to make it out the back door. The air is cold and refreshing to my warm face, and I take big gulps, mimicking the breathing techniques she's demonstrating as if she's been through this herself.

"Whew, Molli. You had me scared you were going to be sick. This one time, on the beach. Girl, let me tell you. I was sick as a—"

She stops when we both hear their raised voices around the corner. She sneaks over to the corner of the deck, ignoring the million-dollar view and waving me to join her. When I do, Hamilton and his dad are arguing—about me ruining his life. I gasp, covering my mouth.

His mom is nowhere in sight, and they are both standing in the yard, gesturing and taking turns yelling.

"We should probably go back inside."

Dani tugs at my arm, trying to avoid the situation now that she hears my name, but I can't let Hamilton take the fall for my decisions. I step forward, out of her clutches, and walk toward them. Both are distracted until I'm in earshot and then his dad glares at me, clamping his mouth shut.

Hamilton glances over his shoulder and frowns, his expression both guilty and sorrowful. He meets my eyes and shakes his head slightly as if trying to convey that things aren't as they seem.

"Molli, it's not what you think."

Famous last words. I hate that Hamilton feels compelled to defend us in front of his dad this way.

"It's exactly what it is, Hamilton."

My voice carries a firmness that surprises me, starkly contrasting the swirling uncertainty within me. But I stand my ground as I press forward and take the stairs to join them in the grass.

"Do you want to tell him, or should I?"

His dad's glare falters, and he looks away with a steely expression. It's unbelievable that he never told his son what happened. All along, I thought Hamilton knew and forgave me while I was gone, and that's why he was so willing to take me back. His forgiveness has already been granted, but now trepidation swims in my stomach, knowing he's been lied to and the truth is still not out. I shouldn't have assumed when I returned. I should have discussed it with him before all this happened and before he proposed.

"Tell me what," he demands, confusion marring his handsome features as he looks from me to his dad and back.

I'm crushed, and my heart hurts when I slip the twisted tie from my finger, cup his hand, and set it in the middle. I refuse to lie to him anymore, and saying yes when he didn't know is the biggest lie of them all. Tears cascade down my cheeks, and I press my lips together, trying to get ahold of myself to end the best thing that's ever happened to me.

"I can't accept this. I thought when you asked me that you knew what happened." My voice wavers, and I clutch my chest, fighting back the rising tide of sobs threatening to break free. "I can't . . . I love you too much . . . to lie."

Panic floods his widened eyes as I gently close his fingers over the twisted tie, a silent plea for understanding. I release his hand, only for him to grab my wrist, his touch a desperate request for me to reconsider.

"Lie? Molli, what's going on?"

His voice rises, mirroring the panic now swirling in his forest-green eyes. I can't hold it together any longer. The tears flow freely, my sobs muffled by the palms of my hands. Without hesitation, he pulls me into his chest, his hand cupping my head and his arm tight around my waist, locking me against him.

"Pops, what is she talking about?" He is trembling in anger, while I'm shaking in sorrow and despair for losing the best things that have ever happened to me. "What did you do to her?"

I cry not only for the weight of calling off our engagement but also for the incineration of our cherished dreams and aspirations. Each tear carries a fragment of the future we were eagerly crafting, now reduced to smoldering ruins.

Amidst the tumult, his dad's voice cuts through, a futile attempt to rationalize the chaos.

"Now, son. You have to understand that you have a promising life ahead of you. And well, she didn't. I did what any father would do. I paid her to go away. It wasn't difficult, I might add. She took the money and was gone the next day. You already had a juvenile record because of her. I wasn't going to let it turn into a criminal record. I know you were hurt, but you overcame it and had a successful career."

My heart feels like it's been shattered into even tinier pieces. The truth is out, raw and painful, unraveling the delicate balance we once had. When I try to pull away, he releases my head but keeps his arm at my waist.

"Paid her off? Sent her away?" His voice trembles with restraint, the immense effort it takes to keep his emotions in check evident in every word. "You made that decision for me without even asking? Without considering what I felt or what she meant to me?"

The betrayal hits hard. The divide between father and son is growing bigger. Their strained relationship pulls apart the bond that used to hold them together. The pain in Hamilton's eyes is raw as he grapples with himself to not explode at his dad.

"I'm so sorry, Alex."

I lift my hand to touch his face, but he intercepts it, gently placing it against his chest and keeping it there.

"It's not your fault."

His voice is as cold and unyielding towards me as it is

towards his dad. I try again, desperation in my voice as his eyes remain fixed on his father.

"Alex, it is. I took the money and left. I walked away from you without a second thought. I'm the one to blame, not him," I plead, tugging on his shirt in a last-ditch effort to break through. He looks down at me, his gaze penetrating.

"It's not your fault, Molls," he repeats. His eyes are devoid of the warmth they held during our drive up here. The happiness present then has vanished, replaced by an overwhelming sense of guilt that crashes over me like a tidal wave.

"What's happening out here?"

His mom's voice cuts through the crisp air, and her arrival causes his grip on me to relax. I seize the opportunity to slip out of his reach, hugging myself for comfort. Behind her, Dani descends the steps, her expression a mix of confusion and astonishment, while Tomlin, who's changed into his nice clothes, lingers at the top of the stairs.

"Just chatting about Pops's web of lies and betrayal."

His voice drips with heavy sarcasm, a tone that's so unlike him. His hands curl into fists at his sides, and his chest rises and falls rapidly. Tomlin hurries down the steps, positioning himself beside Hamilton as a silent deterrent against any potential violence Hamilton's anger might have him take, even though it's our fault.

"I don't understand." Her gaze flitters between her husband and son and finally lands on me, searching for an explanation.

"I took money . . . from Mr. Hamilton to, uh, leave town . . . back in high school."

I mash my lips together as the tears turn his mom into a water blur. Dani stands next to me, not saying anything but bumping my side as if not knowing what else to do.

His mom is bewildered, her head shaking as she looks between the two men.

"Alan? What are the kids talking about?"

His father stands there with a stony expression, his eyes avoiding his wife's gaze. Her question lingers, the silence stretching on until it becomes unbearable.

"Pops paid Molli to leave town, Mom. To get away from me because she was damaged goods. He thought she was ruined when I got caught with the four-wheeler."

"Paid her to leave? Alan, is this true?"

His dad's jaw clenches, and for a moment, it seems like he might deny it. With a resigned sigh, he finally admits, "Yes, it's true. I thought it was for the best. Look how good our son turned out because of what I did."

His mom's expression shifts from shock to hurt. She turns her gaze back to me, her hands twisting in distress at her waist.

"Oh, Molli, I'm so sorry."

I appreciate her saying that, but I feel stripped bare in front of them all, and I want to run and hide. I can't keep my hand off the back of my hair, nervously tugging at the strands of hair that Hamilton had helped me style earlier. Dani looks troubled as she steps closer, her arm brushing mine.

"I cried myself to sleep for months, Pops. You watched me mourn her." His body trembles, the floodgates of his emotions now wide open. "I couldn't eat or sleep. I was a wreck, and you knew the entire time. You lied to my face every single day. Do you know what it was like for me that night I got shot and was lying on the cold concrete? I hallucinated that Molli was there, that she still wanted me while I was bleeding out. And you thought it was best for her to go away?"

Anguish pours out of him, recalling all those nights he suffered while I was off pursuing my dreams. It's hard to hear what I put him through, and the blame directed at his dad should be aimed at me. I didn't have to go. I didn't have to take that money and put my dreams ahead of his love, but I did, and now I understand how deep of a reserve that hurt is within him.

He steps back, colliding with Tomlin's chest. The truth laid bare for everyone to hear is overwhelming, and I understand his desire to escape it, to run from the painful revelation. I move forward, fingers intertwining, my hand reaching his. His grip on mine tightens, and his gaze briefly meets mine as I lean into his embrace. Our pain forms a connection between us, a shared agony — the pain I've caused and the pain he's been bearing all this time. It's a heartbreaking solidarity, a tragic and cruel bond that ties us together.

"When I told you she was coming back this week, you blamed me for choosing her over Mom."

His hand shakes within mine as the anger courses through his muscles and into me. I instinctively clasp my other hand over his arm, hoping my touch can offer solace and act as an anchor in this storm of emotions.

"You said you hoped I was making the right decision. Well, did you? Did you genuinely make the right choice—for yourself or me? Her return disrupted your perfect plan for me. But you know what? I didn't get the girl of my dreams until now, and I didn't get to follow the path to the FBI. So, maybe I should reconsider that option, given that I'm finally reclaiming my life."

Each sentence is a testament to his inner struggle and the turmoil building for so long. His voice carries so much hurt and bitterness that tears flow from my guilty conscience. His words are like bombs dropping, revealing the hidden truths that have festered beneath the surface.

His dad's posture reflects a readiness for this confrontation as if he's been bracing for this moment for years. His jaw is set, determination gleaming in his eyes, yet he remains silent, allowing Hamilton the space to pour out his feelings, to release the pent-up anger and resentment that have plagued him for so long.

"The FBI?"

His mom clutches her strand of pearls, clearly struggling with the truths, shattering her illusions of a perfect and loving family. The painful reality is destroying everyone in their wake, and Tomlin moves closer to wrap a comforting hand around her shoulders as tears stream down her cheeks.

"I didn't want our son to die in the line of duty. If he didn't go, that was less likely to happen," his dad defends, even though he's lost some of his vigor and appears regretful. The risk remains the same whether his actions were right or wrong. The very risk that took his friend's life. "Alexander."

Hamilton's eyes remain locked on his father. This has gone on long enough, and I must make this right.

"Alex." I'm terrified to make things worse than they already are, but his dad is not alone in the blame. I am responsible too. "I know you're upset with your dad, and even though you say it's not my fault, I can't deny my role in all of this. I can't just absolve myself of what happened years ago. I shouldn't have done what I did to you, and I carry that regret daily. But if I had stayed and hadn't taken that path, we might not be together now."

His forest green eyes hold skepticism, a battle between his feelings for me and his resentment towards his dad.

"Don't you see? If I hadn't pursued my dreams, even though I failed, I'd carry so much anger and pain and direct it at you, just as you are at him. You're blaming him for holding you back, just like I'd have blamed you for holding me back. We wouldn't have made it, Alex. That's what I am saying. We both did things that were not fair or right to you, but if we didn't do them, I wouldn't be standing here right now."

As I finish, he releases my hands and walks to the yard's edge, his posture reflecting his internal struggle. His need for space is clear, and Tomlin steps in with his characteristic diplomacy.

"Why don't we give these two privacy and wait inside?"

Tomlin's voice is gentle as he releases Mrs. Hamilton. "And Dani, did you want to discuss that matter you mentioned this morning with Alan?"

"Yeah, that thing I told you about earlier," Dani responds, picking up on the cue and smoothly guiding them toward the house.

The air is tense as the unspoken strain between me and his dad hangs in the space between us. Caught in this tangled web, his dad and I exchange a guilty look, acknowledging our roles in this intricate mess. With uncertain steps, he follows Dani and Tomlin, leaving us alone. I exhale, wrap my arms around my waist, and stand beside him as he stares at the magnificent mountain range. I don't know how long we stand together before he turns to me with tears burning in his eyes.

"Why did you leave me? I swore to myself that it didn't matter because I had you back, but that was before all this. All the things I said were true, but there was something I didn't say. I blamed myself. I felt like I ran you off. I knew I loved you more than you loved me, but I told myself it was okay. That's how every relationship was. But was it? My mom smothers me in her love, and I run away from it. Did I do that to you?"

His questions fall just as his tears do, and my heart is so destroyed for what I did to him that I curl inward, praying that his heartbreak kills me right here on the side of the mountain.

"Tell me, Molli. Did I love you so much that it drove you away?"

I cup his face gently, wiping away his tears with my thumbs. Those beautiful green eyes were as startlingly bright as they were in elementary school.

"No, Alex. Your love was never the problem. I just felt unworthy of it. If my mom didn't want me, then why did you? I didn't understand it at the time. I could not see that I was running away from something beautiful and real that would give me lasting fulfillment more than any motion picture or my name up in lights could."

He covers my hand with his, slowly removing them to hold between us when he whispers, "And now?"

"And now, I know that I love you and want something beautiful and real with you. But I can't say that I won't still struggle with self-worth. After everything I've done and seen, I don't feel worthy of how you look at me, but I'll strive daily to fix that. I'm just a brown-eyed girl looking at a startling green-eyed guy and asking him to sharpen my pencils and send me a lifetime of red Valentine's."

A tender smile tugs at the corners of his lips.

"It was actually pale pink."

The tension between us gives way to a deeper under-standing and a shared commitment that we will face the challenges together. And then, in a moment that feels like a lifetime coming full circle, he lifts me and gently kisses mine. It's a kiss of forgiveness, redemption, and the promise of new beginnings, where I know I am loved and love him in return. And the rest, with his father, will take time to forgive and heal from, but we'll do it together.

"I love you, Hamilton."

BONUS SCENE #2
MOLLI SITARA POV

T he warm spring sun streams through the church's stained-glass windows, casting vibrant hues on the polished pews. I position myself near the entrance, a silent spectator of the unfolding pageantry. A smile plays on my lips as I watch Eli and Isla linger at the front of the church, oohing and aahing at the dress rehearsal for the upcoming Easter pageant and reenactment of Jesus's resurrection.

When I first met Isla at Hamilton's house, he had her family over to grill out and catch up on what happened. He shared her history privately before they arrived, and sensing her discomfort with the conversation, I asked her if she wanted to help me water the flowers I had recently planted. She jumped at the opportunity to escape and take her little dog to nose around outside.

I complimented Anna's outfit, and that's when her demeanor changed. Suddenly, she came to life, talking with her hands and describing her ideas for various costumes and clothes. It hit me like a divine download to see if she could help with the Church's Easter pageant. At first, she was hesitant when I described what I needed and said she had to ask her Dads. I fully agreed, and before I realized she meant that moment, she was running back into the house with Anna.

By the time I caught up with her, Hamilton had a confused look, Ronald was frowning, and Eli was hesitant. They had some bad experiences in the past with their lifestyle and the church. After I set up a meeting with Father Michael to address their concerns, everything was a go, and here we are.

Eli's eyes shine with pride as he watches his daughter as she shares her vision and passion with the young actors. Isla is radiant as she moves among the group, offering encouragement and guidance. She has indeed poured her heart into this project, and Eli couldn't be prouder of her dedication. Isla's creative touch is evident in every stitch, every fold, and every finished seam. Having not grown up in the Church, Father Michael wanted to bring her to speed on Jesus' life.

Ronnie would drop her off, and we'd sit in the basement where Hamilton proposed the first time while they discussed the stories of the Bible as I worked in the food pantry. It was a quiet time that allowed me to listen and reflect on all the wonderful changes in my life and its new direction. She poured herself into the project, which showed in the blending of historical accuracy with her artistic eye. Eli was speechless when he saw some of her finished robes, throwing a hand over his mouth and choking back tears. Always her supporter, he scooped her up in his arms and fawned all over her, intently listening to every detail of the design process.

"You sure look beautiful," Hamilton murmurs in my ear while I am leaning against the wall, watching the scene play out. "That smile says you're happy."

I turn to him, those green eyes full of love, as he holds his hat in his hand and pries me off the wall for a discreet kiss at the back of the church.

"How could I not be? Look at all this."

I wave a hand at the production, so proud of all the time, effort, and commitment on everyone's part to make the pageant stunning.

"I am looking at all this."

He grips my waist, his hand sliding down to my ass to grab a handful, his eyes never leaving my face.

"Stop grabbing my ass. You had plenty of it last night. Any more, and you'll be in the confession booth," I mutter, swatting his hand away and straightening my skirt.

"I wasn't in your ass, but I could be if—"

"Hamilton!" I scold, uncomfortable talking about that kind of stuff here. "Aren't you supposed to be off doing police duties?"

His knowing smile falters when I ask about his job. It's been a rough road with the State investigation of the entire police force, Brooks negotiating the charges against me, Rico's interviewing to become a detective, and the still very rocky relationship with his dad. Although he tries to keep all the stress hidden from me, it is apparent when he crawls in bed with me each night. He insists on going to bed together and will wait until I'm ready. He either wants to have sex with me or cuddle me while I pry his day's activities out of him. He doesn't always want to talk, choosing to bury his face in my neck and fall asleep. I know it's his way of dealing with everything and his ongoing fear that I might slip away.

I reassure him countlessly that I'm not going anywhere, but after that day on the mountain, I know the reservoir of pain still runs deep. And I'll continue to reassure him of my love through my words and actions, and however else he needs me to be there for him. When he proposed again for the second time later that day, he swore he'd take me out to buy me a new ring. Any ring I wanted as he had been saving for it for, the last several years. However, I told him I wouldn't relinquish my twist tie until we were married. He looked down at the ground, smiled, and whispered his agreement. Even though we haven't even talked much about the wedding or setting a date, we both know it will happen eventually and are fine with waiting as we know we'll be together forever anyway.

"I heard there was a disturbance at the Church. Something about a smoking hot chick setting the place ablaze. I had to investigate for myself. Probably will need to place her in handcuffs and have my way with her down in the basement," he jests, his body moving forward to press his chest into my back, his dick hard against the top of my butt.

"You're insatiable." I turn in his arms, place my hand on his face, and caress his trimmed beard. "Now, what are you doing here?"

"Fine, but handcuffs for sure tonight." The desire eclipsing his irises is unmistakable, and I always enjoy being bound up by him. "Want to go to lunch?"

"Is everything okay?"

The desire slides from his face, and his gaze flickers past me as the chorus rises. His arms loosen around me, and he reaches for my hand to lead me to the narthex.

"They've asked me to be the interim police chief." His voice is resigned to a fact that we've been anticipating for a while now. Every day, the trepidation of them asking has been hanging over us until now. "Just until the general election in the fall. But then, they want me to run for the position."

"That would affect your application to the FBI," I state the obvious, knowing that I'll support him in pursuing his dreams wherever they lead him. He shrugs, his hands tugging at mine before releasing them.

"I'm not sure I want that anymore," he confesses for the first time. I can't hide my surprise as it's been a joint discussion at home. "Truth be told, Chief doesn't sound so bad if we're considering starting a family."

"Hamilton, that's not fair. I told you once that I'd like to have children, but not anytime soon." I lick my lips, uneasy having this discussion here. "We can talk about this when we get home."

He immediately pulls me into a hug, his strong arms tucking me against his chest, and his gun belt presses into my stomach when he drops his head on my shoulder.

"I know, I know."

I hold him for a long while, understanding he prefers physical touch to reassure him when things get complicated. And to borrow his words, if the truth be told, I've thought about starting a family more than I care to admit. He'd make an excellent father. I'm just worried I'd make a terrible mother like mine. That's what scares the hell out of me. I couldn't live with myself if I did to my daughter what was done to me. I doubt Hamilton would ever let that happen, but still, I need to work through some things before I think about becoming a mom.

"Alexander, what are you doing here?"

Eli's light cadence breaks the mood, and Hamilton slips from my arms to look at Eli with his arm draped around Isla's neck.

"The actors or parishioners, not sure what you call them, are taking a lunch break, so we thought we'd head out too."

They shake hands, Isla waving at Hamilton like she always does and then looking at her dad.

"We're about to do the same," he replies with a smile. "Join us. Then Isla can catch me up on all this pageant and costume talk that Molli constantly gushes about."

She blushes. Eli beams and kisses her cheek before saying, "Lead the way."

With the tension of our previous discussion melting away, we join Eli and Isla, falling into step as we head out. The spring sun bathes us in warmth, surrounded by friends and touched by the light of possibility. I find solace in the bonds that tie us together. And while the path ahead may still hold uncertainties, I know that with Hamilton's unwavering presence by my side, I'll navigate it with courage and love.

Turn the page to read Chapter One of Isla Frank's story in *Isla*.

ISLA: CHAPTER 1

ISLA FRANK'S STORY

Amid the vibrant pulse of city life, my cozy apartment emanates a sense of familiarity and coziness. The sunlight streams through the windows, casting a golden glow on the walls adorned with my sketches while Anna sleeps on my bed. The distant traffic sounds are white noise to my creative sanctuary, with Lily, my vivacious roommate, bursting through the door. Her eyes sparkle with excitement, clutching a colorful flyer in her hand as if it's a secret waiting to be revealed.

"Isla, you won't believe what I just found out!"

My attention lifts from my sketchbook, curiosity instantly ignited by her exuberance.

"What's up?"

Lily moves with a lively energy. She blames it on her mom's Turkish heritage, something I know nothing about but am slowly learning the longer we live together. As Lily crosses the room in animated steps, the flyer dances in her hand.

"An open audition for Travis Jackson's upcoming off-Broadway production! They're searching for new talent, and honestly, Isla, I can totally envision you shining on that stage."

While I highly regard Travis Jackson's work, stepping onto his stage feels like a distant aspiration—one that directly conflicts with my studies at Parsons.

"Lily, you're the thespian, not me."

Her grin broadens, undaunted by my excuses.

"You exude this old soul aura. Your mere presence could capture anyone's attention. Besides, it's just an open call. A chance to dip your toe in and see how things work."

I shake my head gently, a small smile curving my lips.

"You're the adventurer in this friendship. I'm more of an observer and content being the moral support." I tap my charcoal pencil against my lips. "Old soul aura. I like it."

As she continues prattling on, trying to convince me, my mind drifts back to that enchanting rooftop retreat and the promises we made up there. The rooftop was a tapestry of vibrant blooms and fragrant floral air, with potted plants lining the edges. A rustic wooden bench stood against one wall, where we sat daydreaming about making it big in the city that never sleeps.

Lily as a famous Broadway actress. Me—as a successful fashion designer. One day, collaborating, where I design the pieces for the show she headlines. From our elevated vantage point, the city skyline stretching out before us, we planned where we would live, what type of men we would marry, and how many kids we'd have. She said none, and I said some, undecided on the number. There is a yearning in me to prove to myself that I can be a better mother to my children than my mom was to me. That bar is set incredibly low. Anyone would be better than her.

Lily's touch on my shoulder brings me back to reality.

"Okay, maybe not an audition, but how about working on the sets or costume design? Ya know, get some real-life experience."

Her idea is appealing. Although she's more of a risk-taker

than I am, I need to step outside my comfort zone more often. This seems fairly safe with Lily there. I can sit in the theater and watch how everything is arranged, then decide. Worst case scenario, I bring my sketch pad and do my homework in a place other than my bed.

"All right, I'll go. But no promises on the audition, and I'm bringing my sketchbook, just in case."

I hold up my finger in warning. Triumph shines in her eyes, her infectious enthusiasm unwavering as she does arabesques around the room.

"Yay!" Lily claps with glee. "I just know it'll turn out great for both of us."

As she continues dancing and leaping about the room, apprehension swirls within me. The thought of going piques my curiosity. It is exciting to see how a theater works behind the scenes, but auditioning and being given a part terrifies me. She snatches my sketchbook off the bed, holding it at eye level to study my latest design, due tomorrow.

"The bow is in the wrong place."

I scoot to the edge of the bed, trying to reclaim it from her grasp. This scene is familiar. She often critiques my work, even though most of her advice is misguided. With other pressing assignments demanding my attention, I'm not in the mood to entertain her critiques. Her finger hovers over the illustration of the bow, and she nods with a knowing look.

"Just as I suspected, no bow."

She tosses the sketchbook back onto the bed beside me, sending particles of dust dancing in the sunlight.

"I'm heading out for brunch with my bestie from Connecticut. I'd invite you, but I already know you'll say no, as usual."

"I've got a ton of homework to finish, but if you pass by a salad place, I won't say no."

I glance from my sketch, gauging her reaction to see if she'll bring me back some food, which she typically does. She sighs, and her exasperation is evident in her tone.

"That's the thing, Isla. You're always buried in work. You're never going to meet anyone by holing up in here."

An overly dramatic sigh punctuates her frustration. I can't help but chuckle at her flair for theatrics. If this act keeps up, she'll definitely get a part.

"Love you too," I tease in response, deferring the whole guy discussion as I always do.

Although I'm lonely and the fantasy of my dream guy crosses my mind, given my history, the last thing I want is to get into a relationship and have to explain what I've been through.

With a huff, she flounces out of the room, leaving me alone. Irritation prickles within as the possibility that she might be right about my design lingers. I wait for her to exit the apartment before I mimic her action, placing my finger over the bow.

"Shoot. She's right."

My hand searches for the eraser on the tufted white comforter, finally locating it near Anna, which awakens her. Her sweet eyes fix on me, and her nose dips into the pillow. I crawl up next to her, smothering her in affectionate kisses.

"We don't need anyone else, right, Anna?"

She closes her eyes in contentment as I press my face against her fur. In moments like these, I find solace in her unwavering presence. She's always been there for me. The magnitude of how my life has evolved since the day I got her is nothing short of astonishing. The trial itself was grueling—a painful rehashing of my past, where I had to confront my haunting memories head-on. The courtroom became a battleground of emotions, made even more challenging when my mom made a chaotic appearance, her addiction evident as she pleaded with my parents for money.

Ever my protector, Dani jumped out of her seat, ready to launch herself at Rick if it weren't for Officer Hamilton holding her back and Uncle Tomlin escorting her from the courtroom. She was almost held in contempt of court that day.

Uncle Tomlin, the pragmatic one, devised a plan that she could put tally marks on a piece of paper every time she wanted to punch someone, then take it out later on the punching bag at her garage. As the days grew and frustrations mounted, her knuckles became redder and redder until one day, she came in with bandages on her hands. He quietly advised me not to inquire about it.

On the other hand, Officer Hamilton was far more subtle, leveraging his size and hard stare to communicate his feelings. Attending all my proceedings in his uniform helped paint the picture of an intimidating law enforcement officer while showing his support. Sometimes, Aunt Molli would attend, only long enough to make an appearance before the testimony made her nauseous, and she would leave. It didn't help that she was pregnant at the time. Another reason Officer Hamilton was so protective was that he was like the uncle I always wanted and never had.

The worst and most heartbreaking part was when my parents were there. They had to hear every detail of the abuse with my mom, her boyfriends, and Rick. Too many times during my testimony, I avoided looking at their faces, choosing to focus on the prosecutor as we practiced behind closed quarters. When the defense's line of questioning began, my eyes flickered between the defense attorney, my crying Papa, and my stoic Dad.

Always the more openly emotional one, Papa wore his feelings on his sleeve, crying into his handkerchief. He'd hug me and apologize for getting upset when we left each day after court, only to repeat it the following days. Meanwhile, Dad would envelop us both in his arms, murmuring encouraging words to calm us both—his quiet way of protecting his family. The difference in their personalities worked on so many levels. Something I appreciated as time passed, and I realized that both met my needs at various times.

Were it not for their unwavering love, Uncle Alex's quiet yet formidable strength, Dani's audacious defiance of conventional norms, Uncle Tomlin's attorneys' relentless pursuit of justice for me, and even Aunt Molli's involvement in those church pageants, which led to my first costume design gig, I wouldn't be standing where I am today—within the walls of my dream apartment and living my aspirations at fashion school.

"We're doing just fine because we've got each other. Like always."

With one last affectionate peck on her head, I sigh, my thoughts turning resolutely to the homework surrounding me. Clutching the eraser in my fist, I shift back to my sketchbook, making the change that Lily recommends while her audition idea floats around my mind.

**Read the rest of Isla Frank's story
in *Isla*.
(The Cañon Series, Book 4)**

Leaving behind a shadowy past marred by a drug-addicted mother, her mother's abusive drug dealer boyfriend, and the torment of a truck driver exploiter named Rick, Isla Frank is bound for the vibrant lights of New York City as a new fashion design school student with the love and support of her adopted dads.

Fate intervenes when her roommate persuades her to attend an off-Broadway audition. Little does Isla know that this single decision will alter the trajectory of her life. Caught in the crosshairs of the captivating and eccentric playwright Travis Jackson, she becomes the subject of his intense fascination. Drawn to her petite frame, the soft hues of her eyes, and her demure presence, Travis yearns to sculpt her into his next Broadway star and lover.

The enchantment of her playwright boyfriend's affection and the whirlwind success of her breakout role in his latest theatrical masterpiece is an intoxicating spell. Bliss reigns until an ominous night shatters the facade. Amid a drunken rage, Travis's hand strikes her delicate cheek, leaving a mark not just on her skin but on their relationship. Amid apologies and forgiveness, a pattern emerges — a relentless cycle of abuse that threatens to eclipse her newfound radiance and evokes the haunting memories of her difficult childhood.

A twist of fate intervenes when an ardent patron of the arts happens upon Isla's poignant performance in Jackson's ill-fated Broadway play. Captivated by her soul-stirring portrayal and oblivious to the torment she silently bears, Gabe Gannon discovers the truth backstage. Telltale bruises mar her body, hidden behind the heavy stage make-up and costumes, that he cannot ignore. He's driven to help, even though his intentions might not be as noble as they should be, considering their significant age gap.

Isla is a single POV, age-gap, forbidden love, damsel in

distress, enemies-to-lovers romance containing dark themes. Content warnings are available on the author's website.

Looking for steamy, naughty fun? Turn the page to read *Paolo*, the first book in my Cougars and Cubs Series.

PAOLO: CHAPTER 1
PAOLO AND TAYLOR'S STORY

My fingers dance across the keyboard, basking in the afternoon glow that floods my corner office every Friday. The skyscrapers outside my window stand tall, silent sentinels guarding the bustling financial district below. This view used to fill me with pride, but now it's a constant reminder of the lifestyle that holds me captive. Golden handcuffs are what they call it. Making too much money to walk away and with too much work to feel accomplished at anything.

The clock on my computer marches toward 5 pm. The echoes of colleagues granting well wishes for a joyous weekend fill the halls as they escape out the door to their family and home lives, leaving the corporate grind behind. It's another weekend, another trio of lonely nights in my high-rise apartment, a routine that's become all too familiar since my divorce a year ago.

The moment I opened that bedroom door and saw them entangled on our bed, my world tipped on its axis. My heart shattered into a million pieces, and the pain was excruciating. In the aftermath, I became a different person. I threw myself into my career with an intensity I had never known before, hoping my success would fill the void the betrayal left behind.

There are days when the questions still haunt me. How did I miss the signs? How could I have been so blind in the first place? The painful days are few and far between, but the loneliness is almost daily.

My phone buzzes, interrupting my thoughts. Glancing at the caller ID, I see it's Chloe, my best friend and colleague. I chuckle because she's probably still in the office too.

"Hey, Chloe."

"Taylor, I just heard Williamson's charging down the hall like a dark storm cloud," she whispers through the receiver. "He's looking for you."

By Williamson, she means Theodore R. Williamson III. Firstborn son and current Chairman of the Board of the expansive investment house that bears the moniker of his grandfather. Rarely is he on this floor. Even more rare is that he's looking for me.

My heart rate spikes as I furrow my brow.

"What for? He never talks to me, not directly, anyhow."

He goes through my boss, the Chief Executive Officer, who's a stickler for following the chain of command and never stepping outside of it. When I glance across the glass offices, the CEO is already gone for the day, and his secretary is packing her bags to leave.

"I'm buried with the quarterly filing due in two weeks."

Before I can continue complaining to her, Mr. Williamson bursts into my office. His usually impeccable gray hair is in disarray, and his face is a roadmap of bulging veins and angry red splotches.

"Taylor, just the person I wanted to see," he barks with an open collar and his tie hanging askew. "We've got a mess on our hands."

I replace the receiver in its cradle and gesture toward the guest chair on the other side of my desk.

"Please, have a seat."

Mr. Williamson remains standing, slamming a thick folder onto my desk. It hits with a resounding thud, startling me.

"This is Mr. Jacobsen's file, our most lucrative client. He's been with us for over a decade and is threatening to leave."

I blink at the name on the folder. Jacobsen & Associates has been a loyal client for years. They have an extensive real estate holdings company in addition to their oil drilling and mineral rights leases. I can't fathom why they'd want to cut ties now.

"What happened?"

"He's furious about some miscommunication regarding his portfolio. He's been trying to reach Jim all week about some recent trades he took the liberty of making into volatile international stocks, which directly conflicts with Mr. Jacobsen's risk tolerance. And now Jim isn't returning his calls." Mr. Williamson's voice drips with fury.

Fucking Jimothy.

Jimothy is what I call him. It's a disparaging nickname since he doesn't deserve the respect of being called by his proper name, Jim. The man is nearly twenty-five years older than me. He is a narcissistic egomaniac who regularly cheats on his wife with the country club beer cart girls. He broods about the office like he owns the place and treats me as if we are not equals when, in fact, we are. Something I remind my male chauvinistic boss of all the time since he continues to let Jimothy run amuck.

"I'm sorry to hear that, sir."

I'm not. I hope this is the straw that breaks the camel's back in getting him fired since the last three hostile work environment complaints against Jimothy haven't done the trick.

"I knew you would be. Since you're the only one of my senior executives still here, I will need you to get right on it.

Familiarize yourself with his portfolio and trades, then be prepared to present your recommendations on Monday on how we save this relationship."

My stomach churns. My inbox is overflowing with emails, and my calendar is a cluster of back-to-back meetings. I don't have the time nor the inclination to handle this just because I'm still here on a Friday afternoon or to save Jimothy's ass yet again.

"Mr. Williamson. With all due respect, I'd love to help. As you know, I'll do anything for the good of the company. However, I have my accounts to handle, and I'm double booked with the quarterly filings due in two weeks. Perhaps another executive . . ." I crane my head to look back to the row of empty glass offices, knowing full well I'm the only one here. "Or perhaps Jim could come in this weekend and work on it. Since he's responsible—"

"Taylor, he's in Mexico on vacation with his wife."

"Oh."

I haven't had a vacation all year, prioritizing work over everything, even my well-being. Now I have to clean up the mess made by this rotten, scheming, and lazy bastard.

"It's settled then." He doesn't look pleased by my objection. That makes two of us. I'm not pleased either. "You'll present first so we can open it up to questions before proceeding with the regular agenda."

I hate Jimothy for this. And right now, I hate Mr. Williamson too. Mostly, I hate my loyalty to this company that goes unacknowledged and unrewarded.

"I'll get right on it and reach out to Mr. Jacobsen." I reach for my phone when his waving hand stops me.

"No need, I already did. Just see what you can find. Then we'll regroup before approaching the client."

He doesn't wait for my reply when he strides out of the office, leaving me alone to grapple with this situation. With an exasperated sigh, I pick up my phone and dial Chloe's number. She's always the one I turn to when work becomes unbearable, especially since I got her the job here.

She picks up on the first ring. "What happened?"

I lean back in my chair, feeling the weight of the world suddenly on my shoulders.

"You won't believe the mess I'm in right now. Mr. Williamson just dropped this colossal problem on my desk. Jacobsen & Associates is about to jump ship because of some disaster with their portfolio. And guess who's responsible for this disaster?"

"Who?"

"Jimothy."

Chloe lets out an empathetic groan. "Jimothy again? That guy is a menace. I don't know how he keeps getting away with things around here."

I shake my head, my frustration mounting.

"You and me both. I've had it with his antics. The guy must have glossy pictures on someone here because nothing ever happens to him."

As I sift through the mess on my desk, I sigh into the phone.

"I hope this colossal blunder will be the final straw that leads to Jimothy's long-overdue termination from the company. Maybe, just maybe, it's time for him to face the consequences of his actions once and for all."

She grunts in disbelief. "I doubt it. Nothing ever happens to him. Not even when the Head of Human Resources filed a complaint. You know she left because of him."

"I didn't know that," I murmur, flipping open the client folder. "But right now, I must figure out how to salvage this relationship. I am going to have to work late tonight and all weekend to sort through this mess."

"Taylor, you're overworking yourself." Chloe's voice softens with sympathy. "This isn't healthy. When was the last time you went out and had a little fun?"

I can't remember.

"I don't even know, Chloe. It feels like forever. But I can't afford to drop the ball on this."

There's a brief pause on the line before she speaks again.

"I get it. Just promise me you'll take some time for yourself soon. We can plan a weekend getaway or something. Maybe get laid. Oh, wouldn't that be nice? To find two hot guys to wine and dine us, then drill me into the mattress."

I manage a faint smile. I can't remember the last time I had sex either. At least no one since the ex. That's absolutely something that needs to be rectified once I get past these deadlines.

"Yeah, a wild and carefree weekend is long overdue. I'd like that, but after this and after my quarterly filings." I sigh for the third time as if the exhalation will somehow change my reality. "Anyway, I need to order my dinner since security won't let anyone up after 6 pm."

"Okay, call me if you need me."

I put the receiver down, pull the folder closer, and begin poring over the documents.

Fucking Jimothy.

Read the rest of Paolo and Taylor's story in *Paolo*.
(The Cougars and Cubs Series, Book 1)

When a weekend fling turns into more ...

In the heart of the bustling city, Taylor Woods, a seasoned executive, finds herself engrossed in an impromptu work project at an enchanting bakery, and her life takes an unexpected turn. There, she meets Paolo Cavallaro, a younger man whose magnetic charm draws her in. With a boldness that takes her by surprise, Paolo asks her to dinner that very night. Intrigued by the novelty of being pursued by a younger man, Taylor agrees, leading to a passionate one-night stand that neither can forget.

But when Paolo surprises her with a text inviting her for breakfast the next morning, their chemistry ignites a weekend fling that defies age and expectations. As their whirlwind romance unfolds, they find themselves caught in a corporate scandal that forces them into an unexpected partnership. Together, they set out to unmask the corrupt executives responsible for a possible company's downfall, all while navigating the complexities of their age-gap romance, meet-cute beginnings, and the irresistible pull of desire.

Embark on an exhilarating journey of forbidden romance, corporate scheming, and the unwavering strength of their connection. Follow Taylor and Paolo as their paths unexpectedly converge at a quaint bakery, setting the stage for a romance of undeniable chemistry and steamy encounters.

Can their blossoming love withstand the turmoil of the corporate world, or will the pressures of their demanding lives extinguish the flame of their fateful encounter?

Paolo is the first book in The Cougars and Cubs Series and is a connected standalone. It is a steamy, reverse age-gap, forced proximity, multicultural couple, office romance.

ACKNOWLEDGMENTS

To my beautiful Elle. Thank you for coming up with the name Molli Sitara and sweeping your hands across the ceiling when pronouncing it.

To my handsome Elkan. Thank you for forcing me to the gym to reverse all the neck and back problems I get from hunching over my computer.

To my sweet sister, Tara. Thank you for advising me on Colorado law, criminal defense proceedings, and procedural case law, so it sounds like Hamilton, Rico, and Agent Hunt know what they are talking about.

To my sweet mother, Judith. Thank you for telling me it's too late to quit as an author, as I am too far into my journey to return to corporate America.

To my beta readers. THANK YOU to Sally Williams and Robyne Hunt. The word count on this story was already coming in way too long, and the storyline was off-track. Both of you dived in at the beginning to help me get it back on the rails. You ladies are beautiful, and I'm so lucky to call you my friends.

To my street team. THANK YOU to Bekah, Jessica, Kacie, Kimmy, Robyne, and Sally for joining my street team, brain trust, and overall therapy group. I love your feedback and ideas. You're all so special to me and this series.

To my readers. THANK YOU. Your love for these characters is truly heartwarming and cherished. Crafting a story that captivates and resonates with you all brings me immense joy. You're the reason I write. 🖤

ABOUT THE AUTHOR

After retiring from a thirty-year career in corporate America, GiGi Meier is delighted to be writing romance novels about strong female characters and their complicated, swoon-worthy men.

She loves telling stories and figuring out why her characters do what they do. With heartbreaking angst, panty-dropping lust, and enviable love, her stories linger long after you close the book.

When GiGi is not eating over her laptop, she likes to spend time in the pool with her children, walk her furry babies, and film videos for Instagram and YouTube. Whether attending a book club or hosting a game night, she loves connecting with new people and making friends.

www.gigimeier.com

Books by GiGi Meier:

Standalone Book
Coyote
Sammie and Carlos's forced proximity
cartel, kidnapped, Military hero, dark romance

The Cañon Series
Tomlin
The start of Dani and Tomlin's
slow burn, enemies-to-almost-lovers
Tomlin Takahashi Duet #1
The Cañon Series, Book #1

Takahashi
The conclusion of Dani and Tomlin's
friends-to-lovers, happily ever after
Tomlin Takahashi Duet #2
The Cañon Series, Book #2

Hamilton
Hamilton and Molli's second chance,
small town, police officer romance
The Cañon Series, Book #3

Isla
Isla and Gabe's opposites attract,
age gap, forbidden love romance
The Cañon Series, Book #4

The Cougars and Cubs Series
Paolo
Taylor and Paolo's reverse age gap,
forced proximity, office romance

The Cougars and Cubs Series, Book #1

Sebastian
Sebastian and Chloe's reverse age gap
Opposites attract, Christmas romance
The Cougars and Cubs Series, Book #2

Giovanni
Giovanni and Kacie's reverse age gap
Protector, Alpha male romance
The Cougars and Cubs Series, Book #3

Kadus
Kadus and Bex's reverse age gap
Best friend's brother, rockstar romance
The Cougars and Cubs Series, Book #4

IF YOU ENJOYED THIS BOOK

Thank you for reading *Hamilton,* the third book in the Cañon Series. Stick around for *Isla*, the fourth book in the series.

If you enjoyed it, please consider leaving a review on BookBub, Goodreads, or your favorite retailer to let others know about this second chance, small town, cop romance.

Reviews are greatly appreciated!

They help independent authors, such as myself, get our books in front of more readers.

Check out my website for deleted or bonus scenes not found in the book.

https://www.gigimeier.com/freebies

HOTLINES FOR HELP

Help for Suicide Prevention and Crisis Lifeline

- Call 988
- TTY: Dial 711 then 988.
- Website: https://988lifeline.org/

National Helpline - Substance Abuse and Mental Health Services Administration (SAMHSA):

- Phone: 1-800-662-HELP (1-800-662-4357)
- Website: https://www.samhsa.gov/find-help/ national-helpline

National Council on Alcoholism and Drug Dependence (NCADD) Hotline:

- Phone: 1-800-NCA-CALL (1-800-622-2255)
- Website: https://www.ncadd.org/help-resources/get-help/helpline

National Institute on Drug Abuse (NIDA) Hotline:

- Phone: 1-800-662-HELP (1-800-662-4357)
- Website: https://www.drugabuse.gov/about-nida/
  noras-blog/2020/04/help-available-people-
  struggling-substance-use-disorders

Crisis Text Line:

- Text "HELLO" to 741741
- Website: https://www.crisistextline.org/

Partnership to End Addiction Helpline:

- Phone: 1-855-DRUGFREE (1-855-378-4373)
- Website: https://drugfree.org/article/get-help-
  support/

Alcoholics Anonymous (AA) Hotline:

- Visit their website to find local helpline
  numbers: https://www.aa.org/

Narcotics Anonymous (NA) Helpline:

- Visit their website to find local helpline
  numbers: https://www.na.org/

National Suicide Prevention Lifeline:

- Phone: 1-800-273-TALK (1-800-273-8255
- Website: https://suicidepreventionlifeline.org/

Please remember that these hotlines are here to provide

support and guidance for individuals dealing with substance abuse and related issues. If you or someone you know is in immediate danger or facing a life-threatening situation, please call your local emergency number or go to the nearest emergency room.